Praise for
Fatal Deduction

"Six-letter word for author Gayle Roper: adroit.
Nine-letter word for the plot: intricate.
Six-letter word for the heroine: plucky.
Ten-letter word for the villain: determined.
Eight-letter word for *Fatal Deduction*: riveting.
Advice to the reader: go get it!"

> —DONITA K. PAUL, author of the best-selling
> DragonKeeper series

"In *Fatal Deduction*, Gayle Roper has expanded on her trademark style of honest characterization and intriguing plot twists. She creates characters with real human flaws and shows those characters learning to forgive, giving me hope that this might even happen outside the pages of a novel. An excellent read that I could not put down."

> —HANNAH ALEXANDER, author of *Double Blind*
> and *Hideaway Home*

"A two-word phrase to describe Gayle Roper's latest book? Page-turning! *Fatal Deduction* had me from the opening line, to the clue-dropping crossword puzzles, straight through to the inspiring and breathtaking end."

> —TAMARA LEIGH, author of *Splitting Harriet*
> and *Faking Grace*

"I've been a Gayle Roper fan for many years, and this is her finest book. I was handcuffed to the characters, chained to the suspense and intrigue, and imprisoned in the plot."

—DIANN MILLS, author of *When the Nile Runs Red*
and *Awaken My Heart*

"Gayle Roper unravels a mystery, filled with twists and surprises, in a Philly neighborhood populated by quirky, delightful characters. Libby's spiritual journey is evidence that God can redeem the past, keep regret from consuming us, and teach us to love difficult people. A charming Ben Franklin historian, crossword puzzles, and a peek into the world of antique dealing add elements of fun to this unique mystery."

—SHARON DUNN, author of the Bargain Hunters Mysteries

"*Fatal Deduction* is a poignant and madcap ride, Gayle Roper style. This romantic mystery is a captivating combination of an intricate plot and well-rounded characters facing extreme family issues. Roper crafts the multiple relationship layers with compassionate insight, even for characters you'd like to slap. And she never loses sight of the burning question: who left the body and the crossword puzzle on the doorstep and why?"

—JILL ELIZABETH NELSON, author of the To Catch
a Thief series

FATAL DEDUCTION

CHAMBLIN'S UPTOWN
215 N. Laura St.
Jax, FL
904-674-0868

OTHER NOVELS BY GAYLE ROPER
Allah's Fire

SEASIDE SEASONS SERIES
Spring Rain
Summer Shadows
Autumn Dreams
Winter Winds

AMHEARST MYSTERY SERIES
Caught in the Middle
Caught in the Act
Caught in a Bind
Caught Redhanded

FATAL DEDUCTION

A NOVEL

GAYLE ROPER

MULTNOMAH
BOOKS

FATAL DEDUCTION
PUBLISHED BY MULTNOMAH BOOKS
12265 Oracle Boulevard, Suite 200
Colorado Springs, Colorado 80921
A division of Random House Inc.

All Scripture quotations or paraphrases are taken from the Holy Bible, New International Version®. NIV®. Copyright © 1973, 1978, 1984 by International Bible Society. Used by permission of Zondervan Publishing House. All rights reserved.

The characters and events in this book are fictional, and any resemblance to actual persons or events is coincidental.

ISBN: 978-1-60142-013-8

Copyright © 2008 by Gayle Roper

All rights reserved. No part of this book may be reproduced or transmitted in any form or by any means electronic or mechanical, including photocopying and recording, or by any information storage and retrieval system, without permission in writing from the publisher.

MULTNOMAH is a trademark of Multnomah Books and is registered in the U.S. Patent and Trademark Office. The colophon is a trademark of Multnomah Books.

Library of Congress Cataloging-in-Publication Data
Roper, Gayle G.
    Fatal deduction : a novel / Gayle Roper. — 1st ed.
      p. cm.
    ISBN 978-1-60142-013-8 (alk. paper)
    1. Sisters—Fiction. 2. Twins—Fiction. 3. Family secrets—Fiction. 4. Crossword puzzles—Fiction. 5. Domestic fiction. I. Title.
    PS3568.O68F38 2008
    813'.54—dc22

                        2007048922

Printed in the United States of America
2008—First Edition

10 9 8 7 6 5 4 3 2 1

For Pamela Pike Gordinier,
artist, friend, sister-in-law,
with much love
and great respect

Acknowledgments

Thanks to Lois Matter, eBay queen, for your expert help.

Thanks to the Evening Writers Area, especially Rosene and Georgia, for your advice and encouragement.

Much gratitude to Mark Mynheir and Mark Young for their counsel on police matters. Any errors are mine.

Thanks to friends who shared their personal bipolar stories or those of loved ones. You have my respect and admiration.

And thanks and love to Chuck, who discovered that dinner at nine was better than none at all.

"For I know the plans I have for you," declares the LORD, "plans to prosper you and not to harm you, plans to give you hope and a future. Then you will call upon me and come and pray to me, and I will listen to you. You will seek me and find me when you seek me with all your heart.

JEREMIAH 29:11–13

Prologue

□□□

I OPENED THE FRONT DOOR at 5 a.m. on a July Thursday and stepped into murder.

Not that I recognized it as such right off.

And actually I tripped into murder, catching my foot on the body lying on the front stoop of my late great-aunt Stella's Colonial-era row house in Philadelphia. I went flying, all grace and beauty, landing on my hands and knees in the narrow lane. What was Aunt Stella thinking, making me live where drunks slept off their hangovers on innocent people's doorsteps?

I pushed myself to my feet and checked the extent of the damage to my knees and palms in the light of the lamp beside the front door. There were slight brush burns on the pads of my palms, the kind that sting like crazy but don't actually bleed much, and a tiny trickle of blood rolled slowly down my left leg.

I would have to go back inside and wash up, apply Bactine—did

Aunt Stella have any? I didn't think I'd brought any with me in spite of dragging along everything but the kitchen sink—and put a Band-Aid on my leg. Then I needed a pitcher of cold water to throw on the man to waken him and get him to move. The last thing I wanted was for Chloe to come out and find him. She'd have a thirteen-year-old hissy fit. Then again, she might find him fascinating, local color and all. I could never predict my daughter anymore, and I found it very disconcerting.

I raised a foot to step over the drunk when I noticed three things. No smell of booze and body odor wafted off the man like you'd expect with a street person in summer. A neat white rectangle lay on the dark of his shirt with TORI, my twin's name, written on it.

And the man did not appear to be breathing.

1

☐ ☐ ☐

One day prior

I TURNED INTO THE ALLEY and slammed on the brakes. My van quivered to a stop with the front bumper nose to nose with a row of concrete stanchions. Princess tumbled off the backseat and hit the floor with an indignant doggy *humph!*

I stared in amazement at the narrow lane ahead of me. The alley had proved to be about two car lengths before it narrowed dramatically into the passage ahead, which was too constricted for a small car, let alone my van.

"Wow, Mom," Chloe said with a definite lack of approval. "Those houses are little!"

I stared at the eight attached row homes lining each side of the cobbled lane. They were little, as in narrow. Olde as in authentic Colonial era. And they were probably dark and depressing inside, a

far cry from our suburban New Jersey bungalow on its, by comparison, huge third-of-an-acre lot. And we had to live in the fifth house
on the left for the next six months.

With Tori.

Aunt Stella, what were you thinking?

Chloe opened the passenger door and stepped into the alley. She
stared at the four cement posts just beyond the nose of the van. They
had obviously been placed to prevent anyone from trying to drive
where no car would fit. "How do we get our stuff to the house,
Mom?"

"We carry it, sweetheart." For a smart kid, the girl could ask the
dumbest questions.

"I told you we should have gotten movers." She slid open the
side door and pulled out her duffel and backpack.

Yeah, yeah. And who would have paid the bill? Besides, we weren't
moving furniture, just ourselves. But I wasn't having that discussion
again. "Shut your door, Chlo, before Princess escapes."

With a put-upon sigh, she slammed the slider hard enough to
make the van shudder.

I turned off the ignition, pulled the keys free, and clutched them
in my hand as I climbed out into the heavy, humid air of July first.
I slid the keys into my shorts pocket, feeling like I should glance
around to see if anyone had seen where I'd stashed them. Foolish. No
one was going to rush me, grab the keys, and make off with the van.
It wasn't a matter of crime not happening in broad daylight. It was
more that no self-respecting car thief would be caught dead taking
our dinged and scabrous van. The only positive thing that could be
said for the vehicle was that it ran, most of the time. And it was big
enough to lug all my flea market, estate sale, and auction acquisitions.

"I am so not a city person," I muttered as I walked to the rear of the van and lifted the hatch. "The size alone scares me."

"I'm not scared. I think coming to Philadelphia is cool."

"Yeah, cool." I stared at my daughter, the joy of my life. Thirteen was so scary. And so were the bad guys lurking around every city corner, ready to prey on the girl's innocence.

Maybe if I hadn't dealt with so many bad guys myself, I wouldn't worry as much. But I had, way more than my share, and I didn't want Chloe to face the same horrors.

"Trust in the LORD with all your heart. Trust in the LORD with all your heart. Trust in the LORD with all your heart." The Scripture eased my tension somewhat as I reached for Princess, who sat on the cooler and stared at me while doing her miniature poodle version of Snoopy's vulture. Poor Princess. It's hard to look threatening or reproachful when your topknot has a pink bow in it, courtesy of Chloe.

I snapped on the dog's lead and determined not to think about all the daunting possibilities lying in wait for Chloe and me. No sense in looking for trouble before it came. And it would come. I knew it as certainly as I knew Princess's shrill bark would alienate all the neighbors.

If Tori didn't accomplish that feat first.

"Come on, baby." I set Princess on the ground and eyed the cluster of row homes set so close together that one's right wall was the next's left wall. I desperately missed my yard and my flower garden, and I'd only left home an hour ago. Growing up, I'd always compared our suburban homes on their little plots with Philadelphia's row houses and felt blessed to have a yard and space between houses. On this lane I didn't even have a driveway. Or fresh air. Would six months smelling the city's fumes shorten our lives appreciably?

Not that I had a choice. Aunt Stella had made sure of that.

She wasn't really my aunt but my great-aunt, Pop Keating's sister. She was the one who moved away and sought her fortune and became head buyer for Wanamaker's, retiring just before the giant department store closed its doors. She was also the only one in the family who actually had an estate to leave, but sadly no one to leave it to, as she'd never married. So she'd reached into the bottom of the familial barrel and picked Tori and me.

It was sad, really. We saw her about once a year, and those visits were always laden with tension because Mom and Nan resented her so much. Aunt Stella had money, and they struggled to make ends meet. She could come and go as she pleased, taking exotic vacations in fascinating locales around the world, while they were tied down in Haydn. She had an ordered and genteel life in a lovely, historic house while they lived in a Depression-era home that was slowly falling apart around them.

The resentment had been simmering for a long time. Both Dad and Pop treated Aunt Stella like the Queen of the World whenever she showed up, which only fueled Mom's and Nan's antipathy. She was Pop's only living relative, and as his older sister, she had raised him after their parents died, their father in 1945 in the South Pacific and their mother eight years later of pneumonia when Stella was eighteen and Pop fifteen.

Since Mom and Nan were always and already mad at the men in the family for what they considered Dad and Pop's cheerful and unapologetic disregard, adding Aunt Stella to their hate list didn't take any effort at all.

I shook off the malaise that thoughts of family frequently brought and turned my attention to Chloe, who I was determined wouldn't suffer as I had.

With a sigh at the imposition of carrying her own luggage, she started down the narrow lane, dragging her duffel. Princess pulled on her lead, choking herself in her desire to follow Chloe. I made sure the van was locked, then grabbed the suitcases I'd tugged out, pulled up their handles, and followed, trying not to step on Princess, who zigzagged in front of me like a drunk driver on New Year's Eve.

I studied the block of Olde Philadelphia as I walked toward Aunt Stella's house, the bags bumping and complaining their way over the uneven surface. I should be happy to be living here, being in the antiques and collectibles business as I was, but I guess no one likes having her life rearranged without her permission. At least I didn't. I'm not very adaptable.

This little block of Colonial-era homes was removed from the tourist area, a mere five blocks from Broad Street—or the Avenue of the Arts, as they were calling this section of it now. How had it survived when so many of the old places were gone? And how had Aunt Stella ended up living in what had to be a very expensive home? Being head buyer undoubtedly paid a nice wage, and she'd had only herself to support, but still…

All the brick-fronted homes were impeccably kept, their brass door handles, knockers, lamps, and locks shining in the sun, the paint on the doors and matching shutters gleaming, the window boxes full and flourishing. I stopped at the fifth unit, the one with the glossy black door and shutters, the window boxes stuffed with deep red geraniums, white petunias, and brilliant blue lobelia, with bright green and crimson sweet potato vines trailing to the ground.

Aunt Stella's home. Now Chloe's and my home for six months. And Tori's.

Taking a deep breath, I inserted the key in the front door.

"Are you Libby or Tori?"

Jumping slightly, I turned to find a woman with beautiful white hair and a warm smile standing in the lane in front of the house directly across from ours. Her midnight blue window box, visible over her shoulder, was crammed with bright pink geraniums, miniature snapdragons in light pink and white, and light blue lobelia. English ivy trailed over the edges.

"I'm Libby Keating." I held out my hand. "And this is Chloe."

"I'm Tinksie Mowery." She looked at Chloe curiously. "I didn't realize a child was coming. Stella never mentioned her."

I bit back a smile at the expression on Chloe's face at being called a child. As far as Chloe was concerned, the only thing keeping her from leaving home to manage on her own was lack of a driver's license. And money. At least Aunt Stella hadn't made the mistake of providing that.

"Mrs. Mowery," I said. "It's nice to meet you."

"Oh no, dear. Tinksie."

Oh no, dear was right. How could I ever call a woman older than my grandmother *Tinksie*?

"I know, dear. Terrible name for an old lady, isn't it? Why don't people think about the fact that you're not always going to be a three-year-old when they give you nicknames?"

"A very good question," I agreed.

"My husband's name is James." Tinksie twinkled at the mention of his name. "Everyone calls him that. Not Jim or Jimmy or, heaven forbid, Jamie. James. We both loved Stella." Tinksie blinked rapidly, and I realized that just mentioning Aunt Stella had made her teary.

"I'm happy to meet one of Aunt Stella's friends." I smiled warmly.

Tinksie nodded. "She was my dearest friend. We lived across from each other for, oh my, I don't know how many years. But James will know." She pulled a tissue from the outside pocket of the large bag hanging over her shoulder and brushed it across the end of her nose. "He knows everything."

"Are there any kids in this block?" Chloe asked, either missing or ignoring the tears for more pressing matters.

"Just one, dear. For a few months. Drew Canfield's girl."

"How old is she?"

"I don't know exactly, but she might be about your age." Tinksie tucked her tissue back in her bag's pocket. "James will know."

James was going to be a very interesting person to meet.

"Well, I must go." Tinksie adjusted the pearls at her neck, the huge rock on her ring finger flashing in the sun. "Today is my day at the Kimmel Center. But welcome to the neighborhood." With a cheery wave she walked past the van and turned left.

"Well, she was nice." I wondered what Tinksie did at the Kimmel Center, the city's replacement for the old Academy of Music.

"A *chi-uld.*" Chloe's voice dripped with disgust.

I bit back a smile. Tinksie would have to go a long way to recover from that inadvertent insult.

"Is she gone?" The whisper emanated from the minuscule crack in our now-open front door. "She's so cheery she drives me nuts."

"Tori?" I peered into the shadowed interior.

"Yep, it's me!" The door flew open, and I blinked at the vision before me. Tori's blond hair was pulled into a curly topknot with tendrils falling coquettishly against her nape and over her ears. Her eyes were a vivid blue, the color accented by artfully applied shadow, mascara, and liner. She wore a tight pink camisole with a built-in bra—at least I hoped there was a built-in bra—and a short denim skirt. Her long tanned legs were bare, as were her feet. She looked beautiful. As always.

I thought of my own blond hair scraped back in a haphazard ponytail, any strands breaking free not tendrils but springs of frizz.

My cheap navy T-shirt had side seams so skewed that they ended up in the centers of my stomach and back, and my khaki shorts were more wrinkled than a dozen Tinksies.

I could feel myself begin to shrink. Thirty seconds with Tori and I was back in Wonderland. I didn't need the contents of Alice's little bottle with the Drink Me label to dwindle to nothing. I just needed my sister, my twin, my other half. My nemesis.

"Aunt Tori!" Chloe threw herself at Tori as I stepped inside.

"Hey, kiddo!" Tori hugged her, then held her away, looking amazed. "Good grief! You're as tall as I am." She sighed. "Your mother simply has to bring you to visit me more often. I can't take shocks like finding my niece a grown woman, you know."

Chloe smiled happily. "That's what I keep telling Mom."

Which? That I need to take you to visit more often or that you're a grown woman? Neither option made me happy.

"And you, little lady." Tori bent to pet Princess, who was jumping against her shins, barking for attention. She scooped the little dog in her arms, unhooked her lead, and planted a kiss on her nose. Princess returned the favor with an enthusiastic lick and settled against Tori.

Traitor. I retracted the leash and put it and my purse on a living room chair, carefully tucking the door key in the purse's inner pocket.

Tori, Chloe, and Princess disappeared into the house, talking and laughing.

"Chloe, there's more to carry in!"

But Chloe was struck with selective deafness, an affliction common to teens, its cure unknown to modern science.

I looked at Chloe's duffel, abandoned on the stoop beside the suitcases, and sighed as I dragged the luggage inside.

It was going to be a long six months.

2

□□□

"HI," CAME A YOUNG VOICE behind me.

I turned from pulling more supplies out of the van's side door and saw a girl standing in the lane watching me. She looked about Chloe's age with straight dark hair tucked behind her ears and eyelashes the rest of us would kill for.

"Hi," I answered with a smile.

"Did you have a good trip to Atlantic City?"

"Not me." I tucked a bag of groceries into the crook of my arm. "That would be my sister."

She squinted as she studied me. "Boy, you look alike."

"Identical twins. My name's Libby. She's Tori, but you already know that if you met her."

"Elizabeth and Victoria. Queens."

Quick study, this kid. "That's us. Rulers of all we survey." Not. I had a quicksilver flash of Mom calling us her "little princesses." How old had we been when she stopped that? Five? Six?

The girl laughed. "I'm Jenna, after no one famous."

My smile widened. I liked this girl. "Perhaps you'll be the one to make the name famous." I caught a second bag in my other arm.

She rolled her eyes. "Right. Can I carry a couple of bags for you?" Without waiting for an answer, she grabbed a pair, and we began walking toward the house. "Do you have to live here for six months like your sister?"

"I do."

"Why?"

I wasn't going to tell her about Aunt Stella's hope of healing our family's broken relationships, especially since I was the cause of much of the trouble. "It's what Aunt Stella said in her will or the house gets sold and all her money goes to charities."

Jenna seemed shocked. "All the money? Can she do that?"

"*All* the money. And she can do whatever she wants with her estate."

"So you get nothing if you leave in, like, November?"

"You got it. Or if Tori leaves."

"Weird."

"My thoughts exactly." If Aunt Stella was waiting for me in Glory, and I was afraid the *if* was a rather large one, I planned to ask her which of us she expected to change as a result of this forced intimacy—Tori or me. Of course, if she was waiting for me in Glory, then it was Tori she had hopes for.

"We're here for six months too." Jenna hiked a sliding bag up with a flip of her hip. "Third house over there." She pointed to one with a red door. "No money involved though. Dad's doing one of those house exchange things while he's on a sabbatical from teaching. He's over the moon about getting to stay in a Colonial-era place. He's a Ben Franklin scholar, and he's writing a book."

I studied the row of old homes, most extended trinities like Aunt Stella's. A genuine trinity was a house of three stories with one room on each floor, called a trinity after the Father, the Son, and the Holy Ghost. The old homes on Elfreth's Alley down by Independence Hall in the historic district were trinities. Those on our little lane—or at least Aunt Stella's—were extended in the back to add another room or rooms to each floor. I could see why an Early American historian would love the idea of living in these little, inconvenient places, provided his family wasn't too large.

Personally I yearned for my own little house. I'd only managed to buy it last year, and I wasn't at all blasé about it yet. "How about you? Are you glad to be in Philadelphia too?"

"Ask me in a couple of months, okay? Back home our neighbors have a swimming pool, and I had unlimited access." She grinned. "They also have two hottie sons. Dad says they're too old for me, and they probably are. They're seventeen and eighteen, and I'm thirteen. But a girl can dream, right?"

"And all I've got to offer as a replacement is a daughter." I shook my head in sympathy. "But she's your age and looking for someone besides me to hang out with."

Jenna looked interested.

We reached Aunt Stella's, and I turned the knob on the front door and pushed. Nothing.

"It's locked." I know I sounded surprised.

"Probably always locks. Our front door does."

Ah.

"Then at night you turn all these other locks." She mimed turning a series of locks from top to bottom. "Deadbolts. What kind of a name is that? Sort of creepy, you know?"

"The joys of city living."

"It's not like we don't have locks at home," Jenna went on as I set down one of my grocery bags and patted my pockets, looking for the house key. "But it's one per door, not four like on the inside of our front door here."

I nodded as I pictured myself putting my key back in my purse like a good little girl. I also saw the purse sitting inside on a living room chair. I rang the bell. Somehow the thought of having to get Tori to let me in grated. It was petty of me, but I didn't want to owe her anything, even something as simple as entry into the house.

I needn't have worried. In fact, I should have known better. It wasn't Tori who opened the door. It was Chloe.

"Oh. It's you."

Glad to see you too, kiddo. Who else were you expecting?

"Chloe, this is Jenna." I indicated that Jenna should go inside before me. "She was kind enough to help me carry in some of the bags." Hint, hint.

Chloe brightened perceptibly as she caught sight of the cute dark-haired girl with me. "Here, let me help you." She took one of the grocery sacks from Jenna's arms and led the way to the kitchen, where they set their burdens on the counter.

I picked up my bag and followed them. I left the girls eying each other as I went to the living room for the key. I found it exactly where I'd left it. After tucking it carefully into my pocket, I started for the van and the several bags still inside. I'd brought tons of food and supplies because I didn't know where any grocery stores were in Philadelphia.

I was humming as I approached the van. The song died in my throat when I saw the unhappy old man standing at my bumper, his arms crossed and a frown puckering his brow.

"I'm sorry." I hurried forward. "Am I in your way?"

He glanced from me to the van. "You can't leave it here. What if we need an ambulance or the fire company?"

"They can't get in anyway." I indicated the cement stanchions with a wave of my hand.

"They lift out," the man said. Then lest I think about removing them and driving in the lane, he quickly added, "For emergencies."

"O-kay. Well, I'm just emptying the van. Then I'll park it over in the lot." I pointed to the square of macadam between the set-back lane and the street. I smiled, hoping to make him less frosty.

He stuck out his hand. "You must be one of the nieces. I'm James Mowery. I go with Tinksie."

This dour man was genial Tinksie's husband? Talk about opposites! "So we're across-the-street neighbors." I'm so clever with chitchat.

"We are. I saw you and Tinksie talking when you first arrived. Did she tell you about our Fourth of July block party?"

"No, but it sounds like fun."

"Yeah, fun." He nodded and his bald head reflected enough sunlight to blind me. "I'm the chairman. What can you bring?"

"To eat?"

"Of course to eat."

"I thought maybe you meant a game or something."

He was appalled. "I don't do games. That's my wife. I do food. Every adult has to bring something to eat. That means a husband and wife equal two dishes. We don't want to get caught without enough food." He studied me. "Stella always brought wonderful baked limas she made from scratch."

"I can do that." Now I'd have to find a grocery store around here fast. I had brought no dried beans along. "How many of us will there be?"

"About thirty or so from the lane and some guests. They have to bring food too."

I laughed. I couldn't help it. I could just hear Mr. Mowery saying to his friends, "You're invited to our Fourth of July bash, but only if you bring food. You can't come if you don't. One dish for each of you. Got it?"

"I take it you like to eat, Mr. Mowery."

For a moment he seemed startled at my irreverent comment, and I was afraid I'd been put on James's forget-her list. Then, though he didn't smile, he patted his substantial paunch. "I don't know where you got that idea."

It took only two more trips with Mr. Mowery gallantly carrying a bag or two to get everything into the house. Then I slid the van into the numbered slot that matched the house number. I wondered what you did if you had two cars, then remembered I was in the city. Lots of people living here didn't even have one car. They used public transportation and taxis. You could take a lot of taxis for what a car cost, to say nothing of insurance, upkeep, and parking fees.

But where was Tori's car? Last time I'd seen her, she was driving a flashy red convertible of some kind. There was nothing like that in this little lot, and the van completely filled our slot. No room for sharing.

Lugging my canvas L.L.Bean tote filled with paperbacks and my Sudoku books—I didn't know where any bookstores were either—I let myself into the cool interior of our for-the-time-being home. I found Chloe and Jenna had already hooked up my computer on the kitchen table and were glued to the screen, Chloe's blond head side by side with Jenna's dark one. Tori's *New York Times* crossword puzzle book was pushed to the far corner, one page slightly torn and sticking out, something that would not make my sister happy.

The girls were oblivious to any damage they might have done, intent on what really mattered.

"That is so cool." Jenna pointed to a picture on Chloe's Facebook page.

"Wait until you see this."

Jenna was suitably impressed. "My dad won't let me on Facebook. He heard it wasn't safe anymore. Too mature." Her voice was full of can-you-believe-that?

Chloe glanced at me as if fearful I'd require her to shut down too, now that I'd heard about potential trouble. She asked Jenna, "Is your dad really strict?"

"You wouldn't believe. I know it's because he loves me and all, but it's a pain. I'm not allowed to have an Internet connection on my laptop, only on the PC in the family room. Or the kitchen table in the little house here. I think it's because of my mom." She made a rude little noise.

Chloe heard only the part that interested her. "You have your own laptop? What kind?" She glanced at me again. She'd been on her knees for a laptop for the last couple of years. *Just for my games, Mom! Everyone has one.* "Mom won't get me one."

She was right. In my selfishness, I picked mortgage payments over my kid having a laptop of her own. How cruel.

Tori breezed into the room just in time to hear that last remark. "You don't have a laptop of your own?" she asked Chloe, apparently appalled at this lack.

Chloe shook her head.

"And you won't get her one?" Tori gave me her patented Libby-you're-an-idiot expression. She swung back to Chloe. "Don't you fret, sweetcakes. We'll go buy you one tomorrow."

Chloe's mouth dropped open. So did mine.

"No, you won't, Tori. That's way too much money." I tried to gain control of a situation fast getting away from me. "She's managing fine without."

"Are you?" Tori asked Chloe.

"Definitely not." She sounded like I didn't feed her and death was reaching its bony fingers to grab her.

"Just as I thought. We'll go tomorrow before I leave for work. And we'll pick up a couple of games. Maybe *The Sims*?"

"Cool!" Chloe had stars in her eyes as she hugged her aunt.

I forced a smile. Why couldn't Tori buy her niece a sweater or a CD like a regular aunt? Foolish question. When had Tori ever been "regular"?

"And I think the room on the third floor should be yours, kiddo," Tori said. "It's not too large, and you have to watch the sloping roofline so you don't crack your head every time you get in or out of bed, but it's been fixed up as if it awaited visits from a pretty girl like you."

Chloe flushed with pleasure. Mentally I had to thank Tori for the compliment. Thirteen is a peak age for considering yourself ugly, and my compliments didn't count. They fall into the you-have-to-say-that-because-you're-my-mother category.

"Want to come and help us pick out the laptop, Jenna?" Tori asked. "Since you have one and all?"

"Wow, can I?" Jenna was almost as excited as Chloe.

"If your father says so," I hastened to say, since I doubted Tori'd think to. She'd never waited for parental permission in her younger days, so I doubted she'd think to have Jenna seek it.

Jenna grabbed Chloe by the arm. "Come on. Let's go ask him. I think he's home by now. He's been at the library doing research. Did you know that the first subscription library in America was started by Benjamin Franklin?"

Chloe just stared at her new friend.

"Sorry." Jenna giggled. "It's a curse that comes from living with my father. I know way too much trivia."

"Be back by six for dinner," I called.

But they were gone, and all I knew was the house with the red door. I had no idea what Jenna's last name was.

Trust in the LORD with all your heart. Trust in the LORD with all your heart. Trust in the LORD with all your heart.

I took a deep breath and turned to my sister. "Tori, you can't—"

"Sure I can. It's no big deal."

"I don't mean you can't buy the computer. That was a very nice offer, and Chloe will love you forever. I was going to say you can't do stuff like that without checking with me first."

Tori looked at me as if I were nuts. "Would you have said no?"

"No, but—"

"But you're the mom. Yeah, yeah. I get it."

But she clearly didn't. She couldn't. She didn't have a kid she worried about, prayed about, anguished over. She wasn't the person of last resort for another human being. She was sort of like Aunt Stella, footloose and fancy-free.

"By the way"—she held out a hand and checked her perfect nails for chips—"I won't be sleeping here two nights out of three. I checked with Aunt Stella's lawyers as executors of the estate and explained about my job, and we came to an arrangement. I'll go to Atlantic City tomorrow afternoon, work tomorrow night, spend the night there, work Friday and spend that night, then return for Saturday and Saturday night, then leave again Sunday afternoon. The important thing is that one of us is here every night. I talked with my boss too, and we arranged that I could be here every third day. He wasn't happy, but"—she paused and smiled complacently—"I'm too good to lose."

Tori's job was caring for the high rollers who came to the SeaSide Casino, arranging to fly them in on private jets at SeaSide's expense, putting them up in the best suites, comping their meals, and meeting their every need and desire. Keeping them happy by whatever means necessary was her whole purpose, the idea being that they'd stay and gamble as long as they were happy. By providing this service, she made more money in a month than I did in a year. And she got free room and board at the SeaSide. And had only herself to care for.

"I'm glad you were able to work things out," I said. "I wouldn't want you to lose your job over all this, and I don't think that was what Aunt Stella had in mind either. I'm just glad my work is so adaptable."

I hoped my sister couldn't intuit the wave of overwhelming relief I felt about the intermittent reprieves I'd get when she went to work. That reaction said terrible things about me as a person, but my relief outweighed my guilt in about the same proportions that a Saint Bernard outweighed Princess.

But Tori didn't care what I thought. She had more important things to worry about. She was checking her reflection in the mirror that I suspected was an American Federal-style Hepplewhite mahogany over the Hepplewhite mahogany side table by the front door.

"Don't wait dinner," she called over her shoulder as she pulled the door open. "I have a date."

And I had a tension headache and a counter full of unpacked groceries.

3

☐ ☐ ☐

THE QUIET SETTLED AROUND ME, and immediately I began to relax. Just me and Princess, the little traitor. I could deal with this, at least as soon as I pulled her out of the bag she was climbing in to get to the Hershey's Kisses, her favorite candy. "Chocolate can kill you," I told her as I put the Kisses on a high shelf. She glowered at me.

I grabbed the frozen things from the cooler and stashed them in the freezer before they had a chance to melt. Then I forgot all about the rest of the groceries—they weren't going anywhere, unfortunately—opened the french doors, and stepped into a small Eden right here in Center City, Princess at my heels.

In the far corner, a small waterfall cascaded over faux rocks tumbling into a small pool bordered with ferns swaying in the slight breeze. Princess made straight for the little pool, and next thing I knew she was standing in water up to her chin. I wasn't worried about the dog—poodles were swimmers—but her little claws could pierce a plastic liner. I hurried forward in a slight panic.

A pair of koi huddled together as far from her as they could get. She looked up happily at me and scrabbled toward the side to climb out. I waited to see punctures appear in the lining and widen into Grand Canyons, all the water seeping out and the poor koi lying gasping on the exposed dirt.

No punctures appeared as Princess hauled herself onto dry land. I reached in and touched hard plastic and felt my shoulders ease. We wouldn't wreck Aunt Stella's lovely garden our first day after all. The dog shook, and the spray felt wonderful in the heat.

"If I were small enough," I told her, "I'd climb in with you."

Companionably we explored the rest of the small yard.

I sat in one of the wrought-iron chairs on the flagstone patio and felt more tension drain away. How wonderful it would be to sit here in the gathering dusk and relax, a can of Off! at my side. I was sure mosquitoes plagued Philadelphia just as they did New Jersey. The Delaware River might force man to take account of that boundary between states, but not those little flying bloodsuckers.

As I drank in the color and the peace, I found myself wondering who had planted the zinnias. The impatiens. The geraniums. The vinca. They were all annuals, and Aunt Stella had been too ill in May to have worked in the garden. Maybe there was a gardening service. Wouldn't that be classy?

I could hear Tinksie say, *"James will know. He knows everything."*

Smiling, I went inside and wandered back into the living room. Staring at me from the foot of the stairs were Chloe's and my suitcases. I grabbed one of mine and lugged it up the narrow steps.

If Tori had already given Chloe the only room on the third floor, then I assumed I had a room here on the second floor. I walked the short hall and peered into the master bedroom. The antique Hepplewhite bedstead with its high posts and heart-shaped headboard and the tall cherry Hepplewhite chest I was willing to bet was early eighteenth century were amazing. I ran my fingers over the beautiful finish of the satinwood armoire. The value of the furnishings in this one room was enough to stop my breath.

The walls were covered with a crimson moiré; the white ceiling, woodwork, and antique bed covering and pillows were wonderful foils. Window treatments in red and white toile were repeated in the seat cushion of a balloonback chair and an overstuffed chaise lounge, and the rug was a vintage crimson Oriental.

Everywhere lay clothes carelessly tossed. On the chest sat an amazing array of bottles and vials, a strange combination of creams, perfumes, and cosmetics. I checked for anything that would leave a ring on the chest's top and breathed more easily when I saw a slab of glass protecting the surface.

In the small private bath, towels hung askew or pooled on the floor. More bottles littered every surface, and a brush and curling iron sat on the back of the toilet.

Tori had staked her claim on the master bedroom.

I wandered back into the hall and looked at the two doors opening into rooms toward the back of the house. The first I checked was a bathroom fitted with an amazing clawfoot tub. It would be wonderful for soaking once the weather became cool enough to choose to sit in steaming-hot water.

I went to the last door, obviously my bedroom for the duration. I stopped dead in the doorway, staring in dismay. There was almost room to turn around on the ugly braided rug in the dim room's center. An old, white iron bed that looked like it came from an ancient hospital's going-out-of-business sale rested against one wall with a tipsy bookcase leaning against the wall opposite. An old Singer sat on a card table pushed into a corner. A bureau that was Early Salvation Army sat under the window, blocking part of the light. The rest was blocked by an old, ugly discolored shade. As with most early houses, there was no closet in the room, and there was also no armoire to stand in its stead.

I felt old resentments flair. I loved my sister, but much of the time I didn't like her very much.

Tori, who always took what she wanted, regardless.

Tori, who assumed she deserved the best and me the leftovers.

Tori, who wasn't even going to be here most of the time, yet who took the best room as her due.

Tori, self-proclaimed Queen of her World.

And Libby, bitter anchorite.

I thought immediately of my mother and grandmother. Mom and Nan felt life and their husbands had cheated them, and their pique and acerbity stung all who were close to them.

Oh, Lord, I don't want to be like them! I don't! I want to be honey to You and others, not vinegar.

I knew the Lord heard the panic in my thoughts and understood. He knew of my desperate fight to escape where I'd come from because He walked the road with me.

I left my suitcase beside the bed and went downstairs to retrieve another. This time I took Chloe's and climbed to the third floor to see what terrible accommodations Tori had stuck her with.

The stairs decanted me into a bright, lovely room done in warm yellows, golds, and greens. *Chloe's living inside a large daffodil! She'll love it up here.*

She had a lovely antique bureau and a good reproduction armoire for her clothes, more than enough space even for her overblown wardrobe. And it was so cozy here, with the dormers narrowing the room even as the sunny colors kept it open and airy.

I sat on the edge of the queen-size bed and smiled. I lay back, and the mattress embraced me. Delightful. I shuddered as I imagined what my bed would feel like.

With a sigh I walked down to my room. As I stood in the doorway, I knew that if I had arrived first instead of Tori, I would not have taken the big bedroom. It would have felt selfish. I'd have left it for Tori. And I'd have known the moment I saw the third-floor aerie that it was perfect for Chloe. I'd have ended up with this room anyway.

So what was bothering me so much?

The lack of choice, I realized. I *had* to stay here.

Lord, can You help me see one nice thing about this room?

I wandered over to the Singer. I knew very little about sewing machines, but it looked old enough to be interesting, yet seemed to be in pretty good condition. I stashed it in the hall for the time being. I'd have to do my research, but I bet I could get a good price for it on eBay.

I folded the card table and put it on the bed. Then I put my shoulder to the bureau and pushed it over to the now-empty corner. It slid into the space between the foot of the bed and the wall.

I walked to the window, now fully exposed, and pulled up the utilitarian shade. I gazed down at the yard and felt much better.

The bookcase along the wall opposite the bed called to me, and I went over to browse. I counted fifty Reader's Digest Condensed Books and well over two hundred mystery, suspense, and romance paperbacks. There were also numerous hardbacks on the history of World War II, several quite expensive according to the dust jackets.

The topic was something of a surprise. The paperbacks seemed more like Aunt Stella. Fun, optimistic, happy ending-y. The unpalatable statistics and horrors of war, even the Good War, seemed at odds with the sanguine woman I remembered, however dimly.

I had one of those flashes of understanding that strike every so often. It wasn't just her unfettered life and her handsome salary that made Mom and Nan jealous of her. It was also her positive outlook on life. They lived with such grimness after Dad and Pop were arrested that Stella's ability to laugh and be happy rubbed like coarse sandpaper on tender skin.

I pulled out one of the war books and flipped through it, looking at the photos. I found them fascinating, a record of events long gone. Aunt Stella had unexpected depths, but then, no one was simple. Even the most straightforward person was complex and full of contradictions. Romances and war histories. Priceless antiques in the master bedroom, Reader's Digest Condensed Books in my bedroom.

I wasn't sure I liked the symbolism inherent in that last thought. I was not the cheap version, the abridged version of Tori. If anything, she was the shallow one and I more complex. I was the one who thought about the big questions of the universe. She was the one who went to all the parties. I was the one who yearned for something for my soul. She was the one who longed to be on everyone's Most Popular list. I was the one who turned to God and redeemed my life. She was the one walking that broad road to destruction.

And I'd better guard my thoughts. They were turning ugly.

Chloe came home from Jenna's, and we ate out on the patio, enjoying the slight lessening of the oppressive heat. I'd brought a pedestal fan with me, and I set it in the doorway and blew air-conditioned air out onto us as we ate taco salad and fresh fruit cup. I loved being able to do such foolish things as blow cool air outside, things that Mom never let us do growing up.

"Shut that door, Elizabeth," she'd order. "This is not a barn. All you ever do is let the hot in in the summer and the cold in in the winter."

I adjusted my chair to better feel the cool air from inside. *Mom, I'm letting the cool out this time.*

"Jenna doesn't have a mother," Chloe announced as we neared the end of the meal. "I mean, she has a mother, of course, but her mom left her and her dad. Just up and walked out one day. After she dyed her hair red and green and met some motorcycle guy."

My first thought was to wonder whether she left at Christmas, what with the red and green hair. "Poor Jenna!" And things probably weren't too great for her father either.

Chloe frowned at what was left of her taco salad. "Is it harder not to have a mother or not to have a father?"

My heart tripped, and I swallowed my guilt with my mouthful of fruit cup. I didn't want to let Chloe see my distress at her question. The less she knew and asked about her father, the better. "That's a hard one to answer, isn't it?"

"Yeah. Both are bummers."

"That they are." Life was loaded with bummers.

She studied me for a minute, and I held my breath at what was coming next.

"Or is it harder having your father in jail?"

Since I had no answer, I just shrugged and kept eating. For a while, the only sound in our little Eden, into which our blighted pasts intruded, was the scrape of our forks on the dishes.

"Life isn't fair," my daughter suddenly pronounced. "And that's not fair."

"Life isn't fair," I agreed. "It can be hard and it can hurt."

"It is hard, and it does hurt."

"But God is good."

"Then why's He let all the bad stuff happen?"

I looked at my kid in delight. Considering her gene pool, I often worried that the real issues of life might not seem relevant to her. "Philosophers and theologians have debated the good God/bad stuff conundrum forever, and I certainly don't have the answer. When you figure it out, be sure and let me know. It'll look good on your application to Harvard."

She rolled her eyes at me, and I grinned. I loved that she was thinking about more than clothes and being popular and who her favorite celebrity was, but it often scared me that I might not be able to give her satisfactory answers that turned her toward God. When I was growing up, no one in our house thought about stuff like this but me. When I asked a question like Chloe's, they looked at me half in anger, half in confusion that such questions occurred to me.

"Get a grip, Libby," they'd say. "And who cares?"

So I stopped asking, but I didn't stop wondering. I didn't want Chloe to ever stop asking about whatever she wondered. "What I do know, Chloe, is that we make choices. We choose to do things God's way or turn from His way. We choose to believe He is in control, or we write Him off."

She nodded. "I want a laptop like Jenna's."

I reminded myself that she was thirteen, and I should be glad she had even asked the question, though apparently we weren't securing her admission to an Ivy League school tonight. "Is it a Mac or a PC?"

Chloe looked at me blankly. "I don't know. It's just cute."

Given my limited knowledge of the inner workings of computers, cute was as good a reason as any to buy.

"I have to leave for an estate sale tomorrow morning about five," I said as we finished dishes of chocolate marshmallow swirl ice cream. "You'll be okay with Aunt Tori?"

"Oh, Mom."

"And be sure you say thank you about fifty times at least, okay? A hug and kiss or ten wouldn't be out of line either."

She giggled.

I've always been very careful about how much time Chloe spends with Mom and Nan and Tori. We live in the same small town as Mom and Nan, so we can't avoid them. And I don't want to. I don't want to deny my daughter her family, but I don't want them to overly influence her either. I go with her when she visits, and I try to counter the negativity that lives at their home.

With Tori, the visits are rarer. She's so busy she only comes home at Christmas if we're lucky. I try to take Chlo down the shore for a couple of days each summer, and we visit Tori then. Limited access always meant limited influence.

But now that we were living with her for six months, how would I ever be able to counter bright and shiny Tori who has so much money that she could run out and buy my daughter a laptop without denting her bank account?

"I should be home about the time Tori leaves for Atlantic City, so you won't be alone. If I'm late, just lock the front door and stay inside." I cringed at how much like an overprotective mother I sounded. I shrugged. I was an overprotective mother. So sue me.

Chloe gave me a look. "I can take care of myself, Mother."

Yeah, she was so city savvy. I didn't correct her, just determined to be back by noon.

"Did Aunt Tori tell you that a limo is picking her up?" Chloe's eyes were wide. "The SeaSide is sending one for her. Is that not the coolest thing you ever heard?"

"Very cool." I was impressed in spite of myself. At least the question of why I hadn't seen her car was answered.

We went up to bed around ten, and when I turned off my light, Chloe's was still on, spilling out back. I wasn't bothered. It was summer, sleeping-in time. What did bother me was that Tori didn't come home until I was getting up at four thirty. I heard the thump of the front door.

But what bothered me most was the man I tripped over when I went out the front door a half hour later.

4

□□□

I FROZE, HORRIFIED. Was the man dead or just unconscious? Gritting my teeth, I made myself bend over him and feel for a pulse. I had never done anything so creepy in my life.

You're a cop's kid. You can do this.

And just how many cop's kids find dead men on their doorsteps?

There was no pulse, but the body was still warm. My head began to buzz, and my vision blurred a little. I had to lean against the flower box and swallow several times. Dead bodies on TV were very different from dead bodies at your front door. For one thing, there weren't flies flocking on TV.

Then, just as I felt fairly confident I wasn't going to pass out or throw up, I saw the folded paper resting on his shirt. TORI was written on it in square black letters. Coincidences happened, sure, but I doubted this was one of those times.

So what did the dead man have to do with my twin?

I looked right and left to see if anyone was watching, but I was the only one about in the gray, suddenly eerie dawn. I grabbed the folded paper, hunching my shoulders, as if that would keep anyone from seeing me snitch what was undoubtedly a major clue in the coming investigation. Even if the man had died of a heart attack, which he clearly had not, he had died by himself, and that fact alone demanded a police presence. I did know that much.

I opened the note, braced for I didn't know what. Something ugly. Something threatening. Something perverted. Instead I stared in surprise at a crossword puzzle, the free-form kind you can create with online programs. The tidy little squares sat above a list of clues, across and down. Frowning, with unsteady hands I refolded the paper. Who would be sending crossword fanatic Tori a puzzle, and more to the point, why was it lying on a dead man?

I was just stuffing the paper surreptitiously into my shorts pocket when a tall brown-haired man in jogging shorts and a T-shirt with the sleeves cut off stepped from the house with the red door. It had to be Jenna's father. Drew Canfield. He saw me and nodded.

I just stared at him. I have no doubt that my eyes were wide with shock and fear, and I probably didn't look much better than the poor man at my feet. I felt like a great, red neon arrow was suspended in space right over me, blinking on and off, on and off, pointing to my pocket.

Drew frowned. "Is something wrong?" He walked quickly toward me.

Was something wrong? I had an insane desire to laugh as I tried to look less wild-eyed and unnerved than I felt. How could I answer his question without sounding like a heroine in a badly written melodrama? *Yes, something's wrong. There's a dead man on our doorstep* sounded too weird, no matter how true. *My sister is involved some-how in the death, and I'm scared for her* sounded even worse.

So I said rather stupidly, "I tripped and fell." I pointed to my bleeding leg.

By now he was close enough to see what I'd tripped over. He stilled and stared. "Is he—"

I looked back at the dead man in his gray shirt and black shorts. "He is. No pulse, at least that I could find."

But Drew bent to check anyway. I stuffed my hand in my shorts pockets and felt the paper, heard it crackle as my fingers brushed it. I froze, half expecting him to stand and demand, "What was that strange noise? Are you hiding a clue?"

He did stand, but he said, " 'Man is destined to die once, and after that to face judgment.' "

I stared at him. "What?"

He seemed embarrassed. "Just a Bible verse."

I nodded. I knew that. I just wasn't used to people quoting the Bible quite so freely.

Drew cleared his throat. "Who is he?"

I shook my head. "I never saw him before." My voice sounded thin and shocky.

"Have you called the police? That's what you do when you find someone dead of unknown origins."

"I know. I was just going to when you came out."

He glanced around. "I wonder how he died. I don't see any blood. But he's lying here too neatly to have just keeled over."

He did look neat, now that Drew mentioned it. Legs straight. Arms bent. Hands together. All that was missing was a white lily in his grasp for him to be laid out for viewing. The only mark on his

person, and granted I couldn't see much of him, was a bright red welt
on the back side of his neck. Either he'd met a giant mosquito, or
something I couldn't imagine had bitten him.

I shuddered and remembered every bad thing I'd heard about
the city and random violence. I took a step closer to Drew.

He pulled a cell phone from its clip on his waistband and hit
911. He reported the death—murder?—and very quickly a black-
and-white pulled up to the stanchions at the lane's end. A pair of uniformed cops walked over and studied the body for a minute as if they
doubted Drew's word. One pointed to the mark on the man's neck.
The other bent to examine the area in question, then called for
homicide.

Since Dad and Pop's fall from grace—cops gone bad—I had an
uneasy feeling around the police. Once, Pop had been the chief in
our small town and Dad had been his lieutenant. We were a family
of some standing in our little world. Then came the day the state
troopers took Dad and Pop away amid flashes of cameras from print
news and not-a-hair-out-of-place reporters from TV.

They were guilty of suppressing evidence, demanding protection
money, and selling confiscated drugs and guns, among other things.
Their flagrant disregard for the law they had sworn to uphold was
inescapable, though Mom and Nan acted as if they had been set up.
I was never sure whether their declared faith in their men's innocence
was for Tori and me to help us cope or whether it was a case of if you
say it enough, it becomes true. Or maybe they actually believed
Dad's and Pop's protestations of innocence.

I didn't, and neither did Tori. The evidence was too overwhelming. I handled the whole tragic mess by turning to Eddie Mancini
for comfort. Tori chose to brazen it out, telling everyone who would
listen that she believed in our father's and grandfather's guilt.

"I'm glad they were caught, and I don't want to have anything to do with them."

Even though it was fourteen years ago, I still expected officers I dealt with today to say with an expression of disgust, *"So you're Jack Keating's daughter, Mike Keating's granddaughter. Huh. They sure disgraced the uniform."* And unspoken would be the sentiment, *"Don't expect any help from us."*

When the homicide detectives arrived, there was, of course, no recognition when I gave my name. Jack and Mike were old news. The detectives behaved very professionally as they surveyed the scene and questioned Drew and me.

Tinksie came outside to see what the commotion was all about and was appalled and fascinated by turns. She had James bring me a folding beach chair to sit on, since I wasn't allowed to go inside because it meant stepping over the dead man. The police were unhappy enough that I'd tripped over him and thus disturbed their crime scene.

Tinksie also brought both Drew and me cups of coffee. Mark and Tim, the men who lived next door to Tinksie, brought us some fresh-baked coffeecake.

"What a terrible way to be welcomed to Philadelphia." Tim looked as distressed as if it were his doing.

I indicated the delicious coffeecake. "This is a very gracious way to be welcomed to the lane."

He relaxed and smiled.

Doors continued to open up and down the lane, and the residents all came to see what was happening, many obviously detouring for a look on their way to work. I met three professional couples, a bachelor, a set of elderly sisters, and a glitzy, well-endowed woman of a certain age named Maxi who, Tinksie whispered, used to be "on the stage." Somehow I didn't think she meant legitimate theater.

A cab pulled up to the far end of the lane as the neighbors all faded away except for Tinksie, James, and Maxi. And Drew, who hadn't yet been released by the police either. Tori climbed out of the cab and sashayed down the lane as if she'd just been out for a stroll instead of finally returning from a night on the town.

"What is going on, Libby?" she called before she got close enough to see. "Did you have such a wild party that the cops had to break it up?" She laughed merrily at such an outlandish idea.

Then she saw past the flashing lights and the crime-scene tape to the dead man. She went ashen.

And I knew exactly when the body'd been delivered to our door. Four thirty this morning. It wasn't Tori's returning that I'd heard. It was the man being dumped. He'd been left to die—or already dead—on our stoop with a note for Tori lying on his chest while I'd gone calmly to take a shower in the clawfoot tub.

As I stood to go tell the homicide cop, a Patrick Dempsey look-alike named Holloran, about my time deductions, our front door popped open and Chloe stuck her head out. Princess was in her arms, squirming to get free.

"What's going on, Mom? Why are the cops here?" Then she saw the man lying at her feet and screamed. Few can scream as well as thirteen-year-old girls.

Princess gave a frightened squeak, jumped to the floor, and headed for the kitchen and safety.

I raced for Chloe, but Holloran stepped in my way. "Use the back door."

I stared at him blankly. How did I get to it from here? The houses were attached.

"Right down that little walkway between your house and Maxi's." James who knew everything pointed.

I hadn't even seen the opening, it was so narrow.

"Meet me at the back door and let me in," I told Chloe, who was now torn between sobbing and staring in fascination. "Chloe! Did you hear me?"

She gave a vague wave of her hand. I took off down the narrow walkway, my shoulders almost brushing the walls of the two houses, Tori on my heels. There was a gate in the privacy fence that decanted us into our yard next to the patio. Chloe opened the french doors, and Princess raced out, her bark sharp and shrill. She jumped against my shins, and I picked her up, absently patting her. She didn't know what was going on, but she knew something was wrong.

Chloe raced to me, and I grabbed her in a great hug, squashing Princess. The dog squirmed until she broke free, then gave us a good piece of her mind. Chloe clung for just long enough that I knew she was truly upset.

"My heart's pounding, Mom! I think I'm having a heart attack."

"You'll be okay, honey. You'll be okay." I stroked her night-tousled hair.

"His eyes were all open and staring! At me! I mean, how scary is that!"

I patted her back and made soothing mother sounds. Tori picked up Princess and calmed her, her face almost as white as the dog's.

When Chloe pulled away, she swiped at the tears that ran down her cheeks. "Who is he—was he, Mom?"

I shook my head. "I have no idea."

"How did he get here, at our house?" She took Princess from Tori and cuddled the animal in her arms, a reassuring presence that comforted her without making her seem like a clingy kid.

"I mean, who killed him? Was he shot? Knifed? But there wasn't any blood. Maybe he OD'd? Are we in trouble? Did Aunt Stella know bad guys or something?" As she talked nonstop, we went inside where Tori and I collapsed at the kitchen table.

"Don't know. Don't know. Don't know. Don't know," I mumbled. I felt both numb and jumpy, something I would have said was impossible a mere day prior. My limbs were leaden, but my nerves were twitching under my skin, and I imagined tiny fight-or-flight guys inside me, poking at me with little pointy sticks.

Before I started trembling, I pushed to my feet and filled the tea kettle with cold water. My hands shook as I put the kettle on the stove. I clasped them together and took several deep breaths. All the activity and company outside had delayed my reaction, but the horror and distress now had me swallowing frantically to keep from gagging.

Chloe turned abruptly to Tori, slouched in one of the kitchen chairs. "Aunt Tori, we can still go for my laptop, can't we?"

"Chloe!" I was appalled at her callousness.

"Well, why not? We don't know the man, and we can't do anything to solve the crime."

"That's my girl," Tori said with a look of approval on her still-pale face. "Don't get distracted by nonessentials."

Like dead men.

When the water boiled, I made tea in a lovely blue Wedgwood teapot I found in Aunt Stella's china cabinet. I toasted a couple of English muffins and put them on the table on Wedgwood blue plates rimmed in white raised flowers. I poured Tori and me tea in Wedgwood cups, thinking I'd never had breakfast on such fine china in my life. She and I settled into our chairs as if we were good friends. I looked at the muffins and knew I couldn't eat any.

"One thing you've got to say for Nan." Tori placed her cup back on its saucer. "She taught us how to make a great cuppa."

I shrugged. "English girl come to the U.S. to be a nanny. How could it be otherwise?"

"I like that old picture you have of her and Great-Pop, Mom," Chloe said around a mouthful of muffin. Her appetite clearly wasn't affected by the excitement. "He looks so handsome in his uniform, and she was so pretty."

I knew the picture she meant. He was a rookie, just out of the police academy, and Nan was all of twenty. They had married a month later, Dad already on the way.

There was a very similar picture of Mom and Dad at about the same age, Dad a big bull of a man in his uniform, Mom impossibly slim in her jeans and shirt. Tori and I had shown up a mere five months later.

What had happened to all that fine promise?

"Nan and Pop are still a pretty good-looking pair." Tori spread marmalade on a muffin, but she only managed one bite before pushing her plate away. "I hope I look that good when I'm their age."

"I bet you'll be even prettier," Chloe said. I noticed wryly that she didn't include me in that comment.

Tori shot me a mocking look. "And I didn't know you kept family pictures, Libby. I thought you'd washed your hands of us sinful Keatings."

I shrugged uncomfortably. I loved my family, I truly did, but for me they were as toxic as arsenic. It wasn't because of Dad and Pop being in jail, though that was obviously no picnic. It was the family mind-set, all negativity and criticism, bitterness and resentment. Life had not turned out the way everyone had expected, and they blamed the universe. Certainly it wasn't their fault.

From the day I became a Christian at seventeen, I was often the target of everyone's verbal battery. Not that I had escaped before, but it was as if I had betrayed them when I trusted my life to Christ. The nicer I tried to be, the more critical they became, even Tori. Especially Tori.

"You're too sensitive," she told me once when she'd made me cry. It was like she had a momentary pang of conscience. "You just need to tell us all off. Stand up to us for a change. Sass us for all you're worth."

There were two problems with that advice. One, I had never sassed anyone in my life. I was a peacemaker, not a troublemaker. And two, as a new Christian still feeling my way in matters of faith and practice, I didn't think I was supposed to give as good as I got. There was all that turn-the-other-cheek stuff.

So I kept pictures because pictures were safe. They never mocked you or made fun of your faith or heaped bitter invective on you. They smiled at you and let you make believe your family loved and appreciated you.

Chloe carried her dirty dishes to the sink without being told. I held my breath as she bumped her plate on the edge of the sink, but nothing seemed to chip or break. She smiled at Tori. "I think you sinful Keatings are cool."

"That we are, kiddo. That we are," Tori said with a smirk at me.

Oh, God! I prayed as that all-too-familiar fear washed over me. *Please let Chloe see through them. Please don't let her go down the same path they've followed. Please let her follow Christ! Please!*

"I'm going to take a shower, Aunt Tori." Chloe walked out of the room, all unaware of my alarm at her comment. She paused at the base of the stairs. "Then I'll go get Jenna. We'll be ready whenever you want us."

"Ten," Tori said, amazingly perky after her night out.

I shifted slightly as Chloe raced up the stairs, and the paper in my pocket crackled. I glanced at Tori's *Times* puzzle booklet, now sitting on the counter. Everyone who knew Tori for any length of time knew she was crazy about crosswords. She carried puzzles with her the way ardent readers carried paperbacks.

"Did you know that man on the steps?" I watched Tori closely. She was one of the best liars I'd ever met. "Because he somehow knew you."

Her eyes went wide with innocence, a sure sign she was about to lie.

5

□□□

Tori shook her head, her eyes earnest. "I didn't know him."

"You turned awfully pale when you saw him."

"I'll bet you did too," she shot back. "And cops make me turn pale too."

I reached into my pocket and pulled out the paper. I unfolded the eight-and-a-half-by-eleven sheet until only one fold remained. I held it out for her to see.

Tori, handwritten in block letters.

A flash of something like fear appeared before she could stop it. Even if the paper hadn't been on a dead man, that quick inability to school her features would have told me it was somehow significant, because Tori was a master at controlling herself, her technique perfected when Dad and Pop got into so much trouble.

I opened the paper and laid it on the table. A free-form crossword puzzle with circles around certain spaces stared up at us.

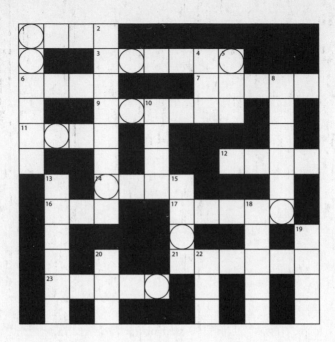

ACROSS

1 competent
3 truth
6 rent
7 strange
9 wild waves or men
11 red stone
12 — one's throat
14 avain home
16 half a laugh
17 escape
21 Dutch kindnesses
23 aware

DOWN

1 from the heart
2 all
4 shirt or time
5 affirmative
8 cause to happen
10 hand and shot
13 intimidation
15 written words
18 … one's heels
19 cruising
20 precious mineral
22 practice theft

Tori glanced at her *Times* booklet, open on its spiral binding to the current project.

"No comparison, is there?" She sneered at the paper on the table.

I read clue one. "Competent." I checked the puzzle. Four letters across. "Able." I wrote it in. "One-down: from the heart." I frowned. There was a reason I did Sudoku instead of crosswords.

Tori reached for the puzzle. "Don't bother, Lib. I'll do it later."

I firmed my hold on the paper. "We'll do it now, Tori. Before Chloe comes down and learns something uncool about her favorite aunt."

"Her only aunt." Tori tried for the paper again.

"Careful." My voice was hard. "You'll tear it."

Tori narrowed her eyes. "I believe this was addressed to me. It's my private concern."

I shook my head. "Not when I find both it and the dead body it's resting on. We're doing it together and now."

"When did you become so stubborn?"

Obviously stubbornness was not a good character trait, at least in me. "About five o'clock this morning." I held tight to the paper. "It's amazing what tripping over a dead man does to you."

"I'm not doing it." Tori flicked a finger over the puzzle.

"Yes, you are. I kept this puzzle from the police, which is probably very illegal and could get me in a lot of trouble. But you're my sister and deserve a chance to explain all this to me."

"There's nothing to explain."

"And even if there was, you wouldn't tell me, right?"

She just looked at me. I clearly did not have a corner on the stubbornness market.

I leaned forward, invading her space. "If you don't cooperate here, I will call Detective Holloran." I kept my voice even, but I hoped she heard the iron intent behind it.

Tori leaned back, and her face would have been funny under other circumstances, her mouth and eyes wide in disbelief. "Are you threatening me?"

I thought for about a second. "Yes, I believe I am."

She glared at me.

"I'm also trying to protect you, so let's get to work here."

It took Tori less than five minutes to do the puzzle, with me looking on. I never eased my grip on the paper the whole time she worked.

I stared at the circled letters when she was finished. "'Areyounext.' Are you next?" I blinked. "That sounds like a threat."

"Don't be foolish." Tori tried to appear unruffled as she lounged back in her chair.

"Tori, this puzzle with your name on it was found on a dead man. Is someone out to kill you too? Is that what this message means?"

I'd spent a good part of my growing-up years waiting for Dad or Pop to get bumped off by some druggie in a raid or at a simple car stop, and my adult years waiting for some inmate to take their resentment of law enforcement out on either or both of them in prison. I'd never thought I would fear the same thing for my sister.

"Get a grip, Libby." She stood.

I grabbed her hand. "Talk to me, Tori."

She pulled her hand free. "My life is none of your business."

"Yes, it is. If your poor choices endanger my daughter or me in any way, it's my business big-time."

The front doorbell rang, and Tori knew reprieve when she heard it. She all but ran to answer it, beating the barking Princess by a hair.

With a sigh I collected our empty plates and cups and took them to the sink where I hand-washed them. No way would I put the Wedgwood in the dishwasher. I went back to the table and studied the puzzle. I could hear Tori's animated voice from the living room over Princess's happy yips.

"Chloe's upstairs, Jenna. Why don't you go get her and tell her whenever she's ready, we'll leave."

I heard the clump of feet rushing toward the third floor accompanied by the *click, click* of little poodle claws. And I heard a deep voice.

"I just wanted to stop and ask how you and your sister are doing."

"We're fine." Tori's voice was bright and cheerful. You'd never know she'd just gotten a death threat or watched the police lug away a dead man.

"I know that body this morning must have given you a jolt."

"It certainly did." Now she was properly solemn. "Thank you for being concerned."

I heard a small laugh from Drew. "Jenna's mad because she slept through all the excitement."

"Have no fear. Chloe will fill her in. I'm surprised the kid's scream when she opened the door didn't waken Jenna and all the rest of Philadelphia."

There was a clatter of feet as Chloe and Jenna rushed downstairs. How they made so much noise in flip-flops was an interesting question, though not one I cared to ponder.

"Look, Dad," Jenna said. "This is Princess. Isn't she cute? Don't you want one?" I imagined her cuddling the dog.

Drew gave a noncommittal laugh and sidestepped the question.

"Well, you girls have a good time shopping. And, Jenna"—his voice took on that reasonable parental tone kids so hate—"you do whatever Chloe's aunt asks."

"Dad," came her embarrassed cry.

And I knew he knew Tori wasn't me.

Interesting, since everyone else tended to confuse us.

6

□ □ □

DREW GRINNED BROADLY as he walked back to his home away from home. Jenna was so easy. And he was undoubtedly a terrible dad to enjoy teasing her like he did, but it was such fun to get a rise out of her.

He hoped she had a good time with Chloe and Tori. He knew spending his sabbatical here was hard on her. She was away from her friends and would miss the first part of the coming school year, an eternity in the shifting cliques and clashes of eighth grade.

And then there were the Conlin boys next door back home, to say nothing of the swimming pool. She swooned over the guys and enjoyed the pool. It used to be the other way around, and he longed for those safe days again.

But it was a different story now that Jenna was no longer the tubby little kid next door. He lived in fear that the Conlin boys would see what she was becoming. If he had his way—and realistically he knew he wouldn't, but a man could dream—there would be no males besides him in her life until she was at least thirty. It still unnerved him every time he looked at her and saw her rapidly developing a figure so like her mother's, a two-edged sword if ever there was one.

He sighed. The curse of every father of daughters was that he remembered all too well when he had been young and teeming with hormones.

It had taken all the courage he possessed to have the purity talk with her, although she seemed to already know everything he told her, a very disquieting realization. He had sweated bullets and she had sat calmly, nodding her head as he stammered his way through the facts of life. He wasn't sure he had yet recovered or ever would. It was probably the one time he'd missed Ruthie in years. His fragile peace of mind on the premarriage sex score came because Jenna willingly wore the purity ring he had gotten her, and she was still young enough to think sex sounded "yucky."

But...

What if she didn't just *look* like her mother? What if she *became* Ruthie?

Even the thought made him grow rigid with tension. No matter how much he prayed, no matter how much he encouraged her toward good things, no matter how much he watched over her, he couldn't put to rest the specter of his wife walking out on them with the words, "The only thing more boring than Jesus is you! I can't stand it any longer! I've got to have room to breathe!"

He guessed he was boring, a college professor who spent hours researching B. Franklin, printer, when he wasn't preparing lectures, delivering them, and meeting with students. He liked order and thought things like loving Jesus and being part of a family, being responsible, and being on time for appointments were positive things.

"You're rigid!" Ruthie used to yell. "Who cares if we don't go to church this week? Are they going to excommunicate us? And if you quote, 'Let us not give up meeting together,' I'll scream!"

Or, "So we're a bit late. What are they going to do? Refuse us dinner? Besides, it's fifteen minutes less I have to listen to the boring conversation about world events and what they mean. Or worse, how history predicted today's woes."

Since he loved such discussions, he never understood her aversion to them. And he wasn't all fusty and dull. He had a motorcycle. And a snowboard. He just thought it prudent to wear a helmet and behave responsibly when using them.

As he unlocked the front door and pushed it open, his phone vibrated against his hip. He grabbed it and flipped it open without checking the number.

"Where in the world are you?"

His heart sank. "Hello to you too, Ruthie." That's what he got for not checking. Of course, if he'd checked, he'd have answered anyway. He always did. Besides, she'd just keep calling until she got him.

"Where are you?"

"Right here at the end of the phone." Drew rubbed the spot between his eyes where a headache was gathering strength, like swirling winds over the sea gaining momentum for a massive storm. Ruthie always gave him a fierce headache.

"Yeah, but you're not at the house."

Drew grimaced. That meant she was. He walked into the surprisingly old-fashioned kitchen and grabbed a bottle of cold water from the fridge. He twisted off the cap and took a drink. "What do you want, Ruthie?"

There was a moment of silence. Then Ruthie said in a strangled voice, "Mick's gone."

Which number boyfriend was he? Drew could never keep the count straight. Butch. Bugs. Rascal. Bubba. Mick. He felt sure he was missing a few. Wasn't there one with a regular name in there somewhere? Bill or Sam or Joe? Tom. That was it. Jenna said she almost liked Tom. He even had a real job as an artificial inseminator of cows. Ruthie liked him at first because it was such a bizarre occupation to her, but with it came schedules and responsibilities. Tom made the mistake of taking them seriously.

When Mick came along, poor Tom hadn't stood a chance. Personally, Drew thought Tom should thank his lucky stars for Mick. Ruthie could make a man lose his sanity and self-respect if he was around her too long, something Drew knew only too well.

"What do you want me to do about Mick's defection?" Drew asked wearily, wondering as always what it was that Ruthie wanted from him. He was pretty certain he'd never figure it out because he was pretty certain Ruthie herself had no idea. Beyond fixing everything, that is.

He had been a new Christian when he first met Ruthie. She had been twenty to his twenty-one, and he was smitten from the beginning. She had been lovely to look at, but more important at the time, she seemed to be the perfect Christian girl—sweet, demure, kind, and spiritually oriented. She took him to meet her family, and he fell in love with them. They were everything his family was not—honest, honorable, and committed to Jesus. Not that his family was any worse than most. It was just that Ruthie's family was well above average.

When Ruthie agreed to marry him, he was sure it was the beginning of happily ever after. He started his graduate work while Ruthie worked as an administrative assistant at an ad agency following her graduation from Bible school. His hours were long, and he spent many evenings at the library, reading and researching. Ruthie grew tired of coming home to an empty house. She started stopping off with co-workers for happy hour. What was originally only cola soon became wine, then beer, then hard liquor. What had been an hour became two hours became most of the evening—once or twice, all night.

"I just spent the night at Bettie's," she'd explained. "I knew you wouldn't be home."

He chose to believe her because the alternative was too terrible to contemplate.

Jenna's birth slowed Ruthie down a little, but not for long. She quickly became desperate for escape from the demands of caring for a baby. She cried and spent long hours sitting in the darkened living room, staring at the television without seeing it.

"My life is over," she'd sob. "I might as well be dead."

"Are you taking your medications?" Drew asked, scared by her unhealthy behavior. He knew about postpartum depression, knew it could get so bad a mother wanted to harm her baby. What if she did something to Jenna when he wasn't around to prevent it?

She ignored him just as she ignored Jenna.

The first time he came home and found Jenna alone, he panicked. Something had happened to Ruthie! No mother would leave her four-month-old baby alone. He called the police, then called them again when she waltzed in around midnight.

"She wasn't going anywhere," Ruthie said, all energy and effervescence. "She was fine in the crib."

Soon he had to hire a baby-sitter to stay with Jenna in the evenings because Ruthie made it clear she wasn't staying home.

It was by accident that he learned that she'd had a man in the house while he was gone. He picked up a T-shirt lying on the floor beside the bed. When he looked at the picture on the front, he knew it was not one he owned. The memory of her look of defiance when he showed her the shirt still made his stomach ache.

He heard that same defiance in her voice today. "I need some money."

His headache ratcheted up several notches. "And what do you expect me to do about it?" But he knew. She may have left, but she came back with the persistence of winter.

"I'm your wife," she said as if that still meant something.

"You aren't my wife, Ruthie. You haven't been for several years." He refrained from saying that even when she had been, she wasn't.

"Just a hundred bucks, Drew." she wheedled. "You'll never miss it. I'll pay you back when I get on my feet."

Now there was a line he could take to the bank. "Get a job, Ruthie." How many times had he spoken those words? As always she ignored them. "Or call your dad."

She made a rude noise. "I do not want lectures about how I've turned my back on God. Besides, you owe me. You've got Jenna."

"Yes, I do."

"What if I fight you for her in court?"

"Threats are not very becoming, Ruthie. And do you honestly think any judge would give Jenna to you?" *And do you think Jenna'd actually go with you?* But he didn't say that out loud. Not only was it cruel. Nothing would be gained by telling her how little her daughter liked and how much she resented her.

"Come on, Drew baby. Where's all that Christian kindness?"

Drew baby. It was hard to believe there had been a time when he loved her calling him that. He shook his head at his stupidity. "Let's just call it tough love."

"So you do still love me! I knew it!"

He had loved her deeply once, or at least the person he believed she was. He thought she hung the moon, and when she agreed to marry him, he was ecstatic. He thought her bouts of melancholy were due to life being in flux, and when she was manic—not that he knew it as such—she was such fun to be with. He didn't know that when he took her home at night, she often didn't sleep, in fact, didn't sleep for days.

For some reason a picture of Libby Keating standing over a dead body flashed through his mind. He knew nothing about her except that she had a polite daughter and a killer of a twin. For all he knew, Libby was responsible for the man being dead, though he really didn't think so. There was something wholesome about her, something good.

And then there was his ex-wife.

"I'm hanging up now, Ruthie."

"Don't you dare! I don't know where you are. You can't keep me from my daughter."

"Good-bye, Ruthie." As he flipped the phone closed, he heard her yell, "I'll find you, I swear, and when I do, you'll be sorry! I prom—"

7

☐☐☐

AFTER DREW LEFT, I WANDERED from the kitchen to wave Chloe, Jenna, and Tori off in a cab for their shopping expedition. I held Princess close because she wanted to go too. She always took it personally when either of us left without her.

"It's okay, baby." I straightened the bow in her topknot. "You can say hi to Madge."

I collapsed in the comfy recliner in the living room, a more modern piece than most of the furniture in Aunt Stella's house. I dialed Madge's number and settled back as I waited for her to answer.

I was sixteen and pregnant the first time I ever talked to Madge Crosson, but she had fascinated me ever since she moved into our neighborhood with her husband and little boys. She lived two doors down from us and across the street. I watched as she went out at least once a week with an empty pickup and came back with a full one. I'd sit on our porch or watch out my bedroom window as she unloaded the most eclectic collection of things: old bedsteads, linens yellowed with age, dolls with knots in their hair and dirt on their clothes, stained-glass windows, ceramic and porcelain pieces of all sizes, and box after box of stuff I couldn't identify from my distant vantage point. Once she brought home an old wooden airplane propeller and a horse from a merry-go-round.

It was late March, unseasonably warm, the day I finally talked with her. I hadn't gone to school for two weeks straight in despair over my life. Dad and Pop had just been sentenced on police corruption charges, and I was trying to figure out how I should respond to this dramatic change in all our lives. Up until the arrest, Tori and I had enjoyed being the kids and grandkids of the two top cops in Haydn. Tori especially was happy to threaten anyone with their authority.

"You ever do that again, and I'll tell my father and grandfather. They'll make sure you never bother us again," was one of her favorite lines.

I rarely said anything, but I was proud that they held such important jobs.

Then one day they were as corrupt as the criminals they were supposed to be arresting. They took bribes. They sold confiscated drugs and guns. They were on the payroll of a small-time mobster.

Confused, upset, and scared, I turned to Eddie Mancini, a handsome young rogue with a silver tongue who became my rock. Then I became pregnant.

I was afraid to tell anyone because of all the chaos of the trial and sentencing. Things were so bad that Nan moved in with us so they could sell her house to raise some money for Dad and Pop's expensive lawyers.

Nan glared at Mom on moving day, like it was a terrible thing that our kitchen was full of our toaster and our dishes and our canned goods. "Just where am I supposed to put my things?"

"I don't know and I don't care." Mom had had a short fuse ever since they led Dad away. Having another woman in her house, in her kitchen, made her sharp tongue even sharper.

"If you hadn't wanted so much stuff," Nan said, flinging a hand to indicate Mom's good dishes and the new wallpaper and curtains, "Mike and Jack wouldn't have gotten into trouble."

"Oh, so it's all my fault?" Mom stood with her hands on her hips, her lips curled in a sneer. "You were married to one and raised the other. If there's any blame, it's yours, not mine."

"Where's that heirloom sterling silver you had?" Nan ignored Mom's too-close-to-the-bone barb.

"Where do you think? Sold for the money to pay the lawyers for your husband and your son."

Nan shot Mom a look that would have scorched another woman, spun, and saw Tori and me trying to sneak upstairs to our bedroom. "Go get my suitcases. Now. Put them in the blue room."

"But Nan," Tori began. She and I each had our own rooms, but Mom had put us together in the blue room to open up a room for Nan. We were given that one because it was the larger.

"But Nan nothing. The blue room!"

I was lugging the last suitcase up the stairs, trying to figure out how Tori and I were going to get all our stuff in the yellow room, when Eddie appeared. I dropped the suitcase right where it was and ran to him.

"We've got to get out of here!" I was a mass of nerves, and all I could think about was how much worse it was going to be when they found out about the baby.

Eddie and I went to a movie, some martial arts thing he thought was wonderful and during which I fell asleep. Then we went to our usual parking spot.

"I've got some important news," I said, uncertain how he'd react but hoping he'd say, "Don't worry, Libby. We'll work it out. Everything will be all right." After all, he had been there for me these past months, his love and affection the only things that got me through.

What I got was anything but sympathy.

"I'm not takin' responsibility for your mess, Lib." Eddie looked at me like I'd crawled out from under some rotten log. "You're a big girl. It's all yours." Then he laughed. "And I don't think I need to worry about anyone coming after me, do I?"

Though I saw him at school, I hadn't spoken with him since that night, and every sighting was a knife in my young heart.

When the burden of my pregnancy became too heavy to bear alone, I finally told Tori. She looked at me with interest, an eyebrow raised. "Eddie Mancini, huh?"

And suddenly she was dating him. A couple of times he even came to the house as if he had no previous history here. I hid in our room and cried the evening away, feigning sleep when Tori finally got home.

Soon everyone at school knew about my predicament, and I was sure they all had a good laugh at my expense. Dumb Libby. Hadn't she ever heard of the pill? Or a condom? Stupid Libby, whose father and grandfather were in jail. Idiot girl.

Well, they were right; I was dumb. Stupid. Add naive and blind and too trusting.

I was trying to get up the nerve to have an abortion. Mom and Nan sat around all day crying when they weren't fighting, the blinds closed and the phones off their hooks. No one knew when and if Dad and Pop would be home again; jail was not a healthy place for cops, corrupt or not. No one knew where the money to live and pay the exorbitant, ongoing legal bills was going to come from. And no one knew what emotional ramifications the shame of everything would have on all of us.

There was no way I could bring a baby into such a mess.

I was sitting on the front porch, thinking about an abortion, when Madge pulled into her drive, her pickup loaded as usual. I watched her lug off a mirror as big as she was, its frame an ornate but ugly brown. Then came several cardboard boxes of what appeared to be crocheted and lacy linens. Even from a distance I could see they were yellowed and, to my eye, worthless. Who wanted old yellow stuff when you could get new, crispy white stuff in almost any store?

I had to wonder about Madge. What in the world made her love broken and ugly stuff?

She and her husband, Bill, had made their garage into a little store with red and white striped awnings over the windows and a red sign with white letters that read Madge's Collectibles and Antiques. I actually went inside a couple of times when I was about twelve and the store was new, just to see how she got her customers to buy the crummy stuff she pulled off her truck. I was astounded to find that nothing in her shop was crummy.

On the day Madge changed my life, I wandered slowly to the curb so I could see what else she had brought home. When she pulled three wooden Coke crates off the truck, I couldn't keep quiet anymore.

"Do people actually buy empty wooden boxes, Mrs. Crosson?" I called across to her. I knew Mom and Nan wouldn't give such things house room. They were both anti-old stuff, one of the few things on which they agreed.

She grinned at me, and I could see a dirt smudge on her cheek.

"Wooden boxes are choice items, Libby, especially vintage Coke ones."

"They are?" To whom? I always thought it was the stuff *in* the boxes that people wanted, and the Cokes once there were long gone.

"People collect them."

"I guess people collect most anything, don't they?" *Stupid people.*

"Would you like to see my workroom?" Madge asked. "I could show you what I do with all these wonderful things."

I tried to look nonchalant, but inside I was both nervous and bubbling. A mystery was about to be solved, but it meant going into the fanatic's house.

"She just thinks she's so holy," Mom said disparagingly of Madge. "All she wants is to convert us. Make us holy rollers."

"Don't get too near her, girls," Nan warned us when we were younger, "or she'll make you pray and read the Bible before she lets you go. She'll drag you into her cult."

Every time Nan said that, I wondered what was so bad about praying, and even as a kid I knew that Madge would never stay in business if she made people read the Bible in order to get out of the store. Since the arrests, Mom's and Nan's attacks on Madge had increased, especially after she stopped at the house with a pan of homemade cinnamon buns and an invitation to go to a women's Bible study.

"Maybe you'll find God can help you through hard times," she'd said with a smile.

They'd taken the food but turned down the invitation with something like horror. Since then I'd heard real meanness and jealousy in Mom's and Nan's catty comments.

"She thinks she's so much better than us."

"She probably asks God to strike us dead and clean up the neighborhood."

"Did you see her? She was laughing at me when she waved!"

She was smiling. That was all. I knew because I was with Mom when Madge waved.

But Madge had a husband who came home every night and who stood on the front porch with his arm around her as they waved good-bye to company. She had a husband who had made their garage into a shop for her and who held her hand when they walked around the block for exercise. She had a husband who played with their little boys and who took them all on vacations down the shore.

Mom and Nan had husbands who had gotten fifteen to twenty.

"Come on over," Madge invited again as I stood on the curb, unaware that I was about to make the most significant decision of my life.

I glanced guiltily toward home but took a step into the street toward Madge. "Sure. I guess."

"You're Libby, right?"

I looked at her animated face and warm smile. "How do you know? Most people can't tell us apart."

"Ah. You are the one who always watches. You're the sweet one."

The sweet one? My stomach rolled. If she only knew.

She took me around back and into their basement by a sliding glass door. Half the large space was filled to the rafters with the junk she brought in her truck every week. The other half was a workshop filled with tools and supplies. A small table stood under the light on a spread of newspapers covered with dark brown stains.

"Look around while I make a phone call," Madge said, and I began wandering about the room. The stuff might be old and useless,

but there was something about it all that made my pulse beat faster—
which was ridiculous. I liked new stuff.

I picked up an old picture of some town and ran my finger over
the satiny wood frame.

"That's a lithograph of Stratford-upon-Avon," Madge said as she
waited for someone to answer her call.

"Like in Shakespeare? In England?"

She nodded.

"It must be really old."

"Not as old as Shakespeare, but old."

"Huh." I wanted to ask if it was worth money, but she held up
a finger and began talking into the phone. I continued looking at her
other pictures—dried flowers arranged in pretty patterns, two other
lithographs, watercolors, and a weird one with the design all in dried
beans—now who would ever want something that ugly?—until I
heard her mention those Coke boxes. Then my ears perked up.

"I've got three of them for you, Sally. Two are in excellent condition; the third is a bit dinged." Madge listened. "Sorry, I'll need at
least—"

And she named a price that surprised me because I'd have paid
maybe a dollar. That much for old and empty wooden boxes? I
looked at the jumble of things in the room. How much money did
this old stuff represent? I was studying the dolls, all carefully arranged
on a shelf, when I saw a funny-looking doll in a box. The figure sort
of looked like Barbie, and she was wearing a black-and-white striped,
strapless bathing suit, but the face was different from any Barbie I
ever saw. And the texture of the hair was different.

"That's a very old Barbie doll." Madge came up behind me.
"Way back in 1962 or 1963. How do you like the pearl earrings with
the bathing suit?"

"That's Barbie? Her bangs are all curly and weird. And she's got a ponytail."

"She's a collector's dream." Madge picked up a plastic bag lying on the shelf. "And here are some uncut vintage Barbie paper dolls."

"I didn't even know there were Barbie paper dolls." I looked at the funny dresses, so like the ones my grandmother wore in old photos.

Madge turned them over and pointed. "See the 'Whitman' printed there? They were licensed to make the Barbie paper dolls back in the sixties and seventies."

"And people want things like this?"

Madge nodded. "People love things like this. See that doll with the porcelain head? She's very old, in very good condition, and some doll collector will grab her up."

I stared at the doll. She was certainly pretty, but I had no compulsion to grab her up.

"There's a world of collectors out there, Libby. It's my happy job to provide for them. Someone will love this baby doll of no specific heritage." She lifted down a doll in a long white nightgown trimmed in delicate lace. "Her moderate price will find her a happy home."

I walked to a table covered with piles of ratty-looking linens. I slid my hand under a discolored piece of needlework. "How about these things? Who wants them?"

"That's a tatted tablecloth, and I think it's about one hundred years old." She gently ran her fingers over it. "Isn't it lovely?"

"So that's tatting." I looked more closely at the intricate workmanship. *Lovely* didn't seem the right word to me. Maybe stained or ripped or just plain old, but what did I know? I thought all dolls came from Toys "R" Us and Santa Claus. "I've read about tatting in books, but I never saw it before."

"It's a dying art, I'm afraid. When's your baby due?"

"August," I said automatically. "I think." Then I heard the question and my answer, and I stared at Madge, appalled. How would a religious fanatic like her respond to my being pregnant and unmarried?

"The dad?" Madge busied herself arranging some cut-glass vases that arced little rainbows onto her hands.

I made my fingers loosen on the tatting before I tore it. "He's gone."

"As in left town?"

I shook my head. "As in left me. I know where he is. I see him at school all the time." When I went. I couldn't make myself say he was now dating my twin.

"Is that why you bagged today and so many other days?"

I looked at the baby doll she still held cradled in her arm. "Yeah." It came out a whisper. There was no way I could explain the anguish of Eddie, the baby, the trial, and the family. All I knew was that I wanted to stay in bed with the quilt pulled over my head for about ten years. Then maybe I'd come out for something to eat. Maybe. Mom and Nan were so caught up in their own misery they'd never miss me.

Mom and Nan hadn't asked me a single question when Tori told them I was expecting, just looked at me with disgust, disbelief, and finally resignation. There wasn't much they could say anyway. They'd both been pregnant when they got married. But at least they got married.

Madge—the neighbor they mocked all the time because she didn't smoke or drink, went to church, and had a neighborhood Bible study she'd actually had the nerve to invite them to—was the only one who ever asked.

"But I'm okay." I tried to grin like I didn't feel absolutely alone in the world. *Change the topic, Lib! Change the topic before the pain kills you!*

I noticed the pin she wore on her collar, and I grabbed on to it. "Did you get that cute pin at an estate sale too?"

She reached up and fingered the little silver replica of a pair of tiny feet. "No. This is a pin that shows the size of a baby's feet at ten weeks after conception."

I felt like someone had shoved me hard in the chest, and I could barely draw a breath. My hand went to my stomach. My baby's feet looked like that? I sort of thought it was just a blob.

"Your baby's feet are larger by now but just as well formed," Madge said as if she knew exactly what I was thinking. "To me it's one of the great God-mysteries, how a baby with a beating heart and a functioning brain and perfectly formed little feet can grow from almost nothing." She took my cold hands in hers. "I know you are in circumstances you don't like, Libby, but you are growing a little person in there. I applaud you for sticking it out, for getting up every day and eating and doing things to care for this child."

I blinked. Was I doing that? I hadn't even been to a doctor.

"Are you interested in a part-time job, by the way?"

When I'd had my life-changing conversation with Madge, I thought she was so old and mature, but she was only about thirty then, my age now. Little by little she'd taught me everything she knew, taking me along to seminars and workshops at her expense, showing me how to strip an abused piece of furniture, training my eye to recognize the fine from the merely good, the true antiques from the collectibles.

But mostly she loved me, showed me a healthy family, and modeled Jesus before me.

I sat in Aunt Stella's living room and wished I was in Madge's shop or workroom or even at the eBay store, mailing one of our online sales to somewhere on the other side of the country or world. It was not an exaggeration to say that I—and Chloe—owed my life to her.

"I didn't get to the Hutchinson estate sale today," I told Madge when she picked up her phone. "I found a dead body instead."

"What?"

I could just picture her, eyes wide with disbelief and curiosity as she danced around the room. Madge was a fidgeter of immense proportion. Bill seemed to find her constant movement amusing, and her boys, ages nineteen, seventeen, and fifteen, took it for granted. Since Bill always looked rested, I took it to mean that she somehow stayed still when she slept.

"I found a dead body," I repeated and gave her a rundown of the morning. I pulled myself out of the recliner as we talked and wandered into the kitchen for a glass of sweet tea.

"That note with Tori's name on it is troubling."

"Tell me about it." As I passed Tori's *Times* puzzle book resting haphazardly on the counter, my elbow caught it, and it tumbled to the floor. A piece of folded paper that I had earlier thought was a torn page fluttered out.

"You've got to give that puzzle to the police, Lib. Tori's got to talk to them."

I sighed. "I know." I bent to pick up the booklet and the piece of paper. As I stood, the paper fell open and a puzzle appeared, circles around specific letters but none of the answers filled in. My breath caught. I flipped the paper and there was Tori's name in all caps, just like the note on the dead man.

A chill raised bumps on my arms. "I just found another one, Madge."

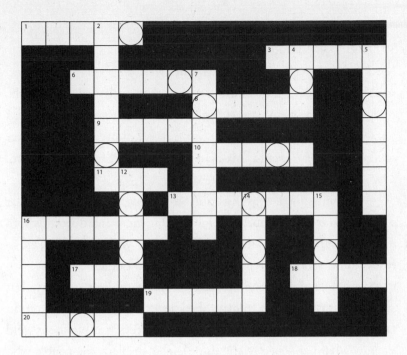

ACROSS

 1 now
 3 small bush
 6 one who owes
 8 solitary
 9 a thousand
 10 one not too smart
 11 squealer
 13 covered, as a wall
 16 precious metal
 17 burglar or pet
 18 to deceive or trick
 19 noted
 20 to take without permission

DOWN

 2 one who gets even
 4 shade or tint
 5 thief
 7 extreme
 12 turn from
 14 finished
 15 two card
 16 locked storage units

"Uh-oh. Is it filled in?"

"No. I've got to go."

I heard her yell, "Call me!" as I hit Off. I grabbed my purse and scrabbled around until I found a pencil, then collapsed at the table, the puzzle spread before me. Clue one-across was *now*. Five letters. I wrote *today*. Two-down was *one who gets even*. I didn't think the answer was *mean person*. I went to six-across, which cut through two-down. *One who owes*. Six letters. I wrote *debtor*.

My hand stilled. Was Tori a debtor, or was it just a word that supplied an *o* to the embedded message? If she was a debtor, whom did she owe? Certainly not a bank like me with my mortgage—banks didn't send threatening puzzles or dead bodies.

Gambling debts? She worked in the gambling industry, but surely she was too smart to play. She knew the house always won. In fact, I didn't think the SeaSide let its employees gamble there. And she saw what happened to the disordered gamblers, the people who got caught in the addiction. She saw the ruined lives and broken homes of those for whom the bet was all.

Still, even knowing the pitfalls well, I feared she had tumbled down the abyss of empty promises and vain speculations. The question was: how deep was the water in her pit? The threats buried in the puzzles, to say nothing of the dead man on the front steps, seemed to indicate she was in well over her head. How long could she successfully tread water?

If she owed money, who did she owe it to? Casinos didn't send threatening puzzles any more than banks. What kind of a lender would be ruthless enough to send a dead man as a message?

Oh, Lord, did You bring me here to save Tori?

I just wondered if I could bear the emotional cost.

8

□□□

WHEN I FINISHED solving the puzzle, I stared in distress at the message. YOU ARE OVERDUE.

Library books could be overdue.

So could taxes and your time of the month.

Reports at work could be overdue, and trains and planes.

I doubted any of these things were Tori's problem.

Loans could also be overdue.

My stomach cramped. Had Tori borrowed unwisely? It certainly made sense. *I want it. I need it. I'm buying it.* That was Tori, no matter how expensive the item and how empty her bank account.

If she borrowed unwisely, it also meant she'd run her legitimate credit avenues to the max. It had to.

And no one left dead bodies lying around unless big money was involved. The sweet tea sloshed uncomfortably in my teeming stomach.

Had Tori really been foolish enough to go to a loan shark?

Even thinking of her with such a connection seemed absurd. I would have thought that she'd have learned from the example of Dad and Pop that wrong choices eventually caught up with you. However, knowing Tori, she no doubt thought she could charm her way out of her payments if she couldn't make them or if she wanted to use her salary in some other manner, like betting more or buying my daughter a laptop. Since life generally went as Tori scripted, Dad and Pop excepted, she assumed she could write this scenario too. If half of what I saw on TV was accurate, she was being unbelievably naive. Loan sharks weren't used to taking "no" or "wait" for an answer. They expected what was due them when it was due them, exorbitant interest rate and all.

I looked around Aunt Stella's living room, all rose and beige with a gorgeous crimson, beige, and black patterned rug. Her formal dining area was more Hepplewhite, the shield-back chairs mahogany with needlepoint seats. We were living in a museum filled with priceless antiques.

No wonder Tori was willing to stay here with me for six months. She needed the money from Aunt Stella's estate more than I did, *much* more than I did. All she had to do was hold the shark off for six months and everything would be fine, assuming no one got tired of waiting and made her the next body on the front stoop.

I got up, restless from all these black thoughts. I wandered to the living room corner cupboard with its scrolled pediment and studied the books resting inside on little stands. I blinked, then blinked again, goose bumps popping up on my arms as I realized what I was looking at. I opened the door and carefully lifted out the nearest, a cloth copy of *Lady Windermere's Fan* by Oscar Wilde. I carefully opened the cover and confirmed that it was a first edition, 1893. A slip of paper lying inside the cover read, "One of only five hundred copies, sale value—$2,800.00."

The next book was *The Great Gatsby* by F. Scott Fitzgerald. I opened it carefully and read on the paper lying inside: "First edition, first printing, original dark green cloth, $1,500.00." There was also a volume of William Wordsworth's poems, a first edition with its note reading, "Contains the extra stanza in 'Ode to Duty' omitted after this printing. 500 printed. $6,000.00."

I thought of the collectibles and the occasional good antiques Madge and I moved. They were nothing compared to these rare books. I held a treasure in my hand, and I reverently put Wordsworth back in the cabinet.

The next book was a Thomas Wolfe, *Look Homeward, Angel*, whose slip read, "in a first state book jacket, first edition, first printing, and signed by the author. $16,500.00."

My heart gave a queer jump. These four books represented more than $26,000.

Then I picked up the next to the last book and almost hyperventilated. *Frankenstein* by Mary Shelley, printed in 1833 in two volumes. The second volume sat quietly on its stand in the cupboard. The combined value of the two was $36,000.

I lay volume one back in place and gently closed the glass door. $62,800. I looked again at the furniture, the costly objets d'art sitting casually on the end tables and coffee table, the original art on the walls. Where had the money for all these things come from? And if Aunt Stella had all this money and hadn't kicked in to help with Dad's and Pop's massive legal fees, no wonder Mom and Nan resented her so much.

I thought about the little notes in each book. Someone had had the volumes appraised since Aunt Stella's death. No doubt everything else had been valued and recorded too. For the first time I wondered who the executor of the estate was. Someone besides or in coordination with her lawyer? A bank, maybe? Some close friend I had never met?

I hadn't wanted to live here before I knew that this place was a veritable museum, my room being the exception. Now I was terrified. The responsibility was too much, especially with a thirteen-year-old used to a home that was definitely lived in. Suddenly I was glad for my bedroom with its iron hospital bed, where I didn't have to worry about damaging anything. I could put my feet up, stuff my clothes in the unimpressive bureau, and knock the books on the floor, and it didn't matter. I couldn't hurt a thing. Reader's Digest Condensed Books never died. They didn't even fade away.

And once again I wondered where all the money came from for all the wonderful things. Granted, Aunt Stella had a good job and a nice income, but this house represented an extraordinary income.

"James will know. James knows everything."

I was going to have to talk with James.

But my twin was my problem du jour, and I needed to concentrate on how to extricate her from the pit into which she'd fallen, assuming she'd let me help. Life had taught me that she didn't value my suggestions very highly, and more so—less so?—since I'd become a Christian. It was like when I said, "I believe, Jesus," she said, "Stay away, dummy."

What would happen when Tori realized the wealth sitting right here in the living room? Not that she could legally touch anything before the end of December. But if she was threatened enough, scared enough, would she take things anyway? She could rationalize that they would soon be hers. She was just taking possession a bit early.

YOU ARE OVERDUE would be a powerful incentive to me to take advantage of every means available to find money. And if the note wasn't enough, there was the body.

And that was another thing. What did the body have to do with the loan shark? Had he been another client? But a loan shark would never kill someone who owed him money. Hurt maybe, but not kill. It was the one action guaranteed to prevent collecting.

Was that why Tori wasn't more afraid? She knew he wouldn't kill her? I went to the kitchen and looked at the puzzle still lying on the table. Words started pulsing like red flares: *debtor*—Tori? *avenger*— the shark? *scam*—what Tori was trying? What about *burglar* and *steal*? Did they refer to Tori somehow, or were they just words?

I looked at the ARE YOU NEXT puzzle.

Threat. Guns. Rob. Slit. As in throat? I glanced back at the clues. That was what twelve-across indicated. Then there were nice words like *gem* and *ruby* and *treats*. And strange ones like *eerie* and *incite*.

I didn't understand everything, but I understood one glaring fact: My twin was in trouble. Therefore so was I.

Lord, here I am, right in the middle of everything I've tried to stay away from and keep Chloe away from! Help!

I slid both puzzles into the *Times* book for lack of another place to keep them. Tori and I would talk tonight whether she wanted to or not.

No, we wouldn't. She was going back to Atlantic City this afternoon, and I was willing to bet she'd see to it that she and I were not alone before she left.

Well, I didn't think waiting until she came home on the Fourth would hurt anything. If she was gone, the danger should be gone too. But on the Fourth we were definitely talking. I knew Tori saw me as weak, but she hadn't accounted for the fact that mama bears do most anything to protect their cubs, even confront twin sisters who historically have come out on top in every fight we'd ever had.

Feeling strangely at loose ends, I sat at my computer and logged onto eBay. Work was just what I needed to put Tori and her situation from my mind. I quickly checked the items Madge and I had listed. One, a lovely and unusual white Wedgwood pitcher with gold grapes and vines all over its surface, had caught the eye of three collectors, and they were bidding against one another with all the fervor of three enemy generals campaigning in battle for the same spoils. A seller's dream scenario.

Bidding with equal enthusiasm but smaller purses were a pair of collectors who wanted the twenty-five pairs of fifties-era cat's-eye sunglasses we had listed. To my surprise, the hobbyhorse with the real-hair mane and tail that Madge had found at a flea market and refurbished was far outstripping what we expected to get on it. In contrast, the pieces of cut crystal hadn't caught anyone's eye yet.

I heard the front door lock turning and got up from the table. I arrived in the living room just as Chloe burst into the room, Jenna on her heels.

"I got it, Mom!" Chloe swung a black backpack off her shoulder and unzipped it. She pulled out a sleek little laptop and ran a hand lovingly over it. "Isn't it beautiful?"

Tori entered the room more sedately. She looked at me and smiled. Sharks looked friendlier when they bared their incisors.

My blood chilled as I recognized the old I-won-this-round smirk tilting her lips. For the first time I understood she was competing with me once again, and Chloe, not Eddie Mancini, was the prize this time. The realization made me dizzy with dread.

I forced myself to *ooh* and *aah* enough to make Chloe happy while Tori went upstairs. I heard the shower run, and when she came back down an hour later, her hair was a perfect halo of shining golden curls and her makeup was flawless.

"You look so pretty, Aunt Tori. I love your hair."

Tori lightly touched her carefully highlighted hair with the satisfied air of a woman who knows she looks better than anyone in the room. Not that she had much competition. "You and your mom have hair just like mine."

"Yeah, right." Chloe looked from Tori to me. "Not."

"Well," Tori said lazily, "maybe I should rephrase. You could have hair just like mine."

For how much? I was certain I couldn't afford either the time or the money. That mortgage again.

There was a knock on the door. Tori opened it, and there stood a uniformed chauffeur. Chloe's eyes grew large, as did Jenna's.

"Ready, Miss Keating?"

"Ready, Carl." She gave a little wave in our direction and left, Carl trailing behind.

Chloe and Jenna rushed to the door. I followed, curiosity and my Chloe-panic warring inside, and watched my sister saunter out to the street where the limo waited. Carl opened the back door for her, and she stepped gracefully inside.

"Wow!" Chloe's voice was reverent.

"I never knew anyone who had a limo pick them up before," Jenna breathed.

I had to admit I was impressed too. Obviously Tori's employer thought very highly of her, and obviously she had perks that I'd never see in a million years. All those hated inferiority feelings flooded back, and for a terrifying moment I was sixteen again.

Tori sat back in the cushions of the limo, a glass of pinot grigio in her hand. Carl was good about having her preferences waiting for her. On the seat were three of her favorite magazines, and in the little dish in the limo bar were cashews, lightly salted, just as she liked.

Too bad Carl wasn't the man she had to deal with. Carl had a crush on her, not that he'd ever act on it, and he'd be a pushover, forgiving any offense, any debt.

Luke Henley was an entirely different matter. Even thinking of him made her heart beat faster. She was used to being the one in charge of an affair, but she might have met her match in Luke.

She picked up *InStyle* and flipped through the pages. Features, photos, and articles that would normally have held her attention couldn't compete with the vision of the dead man lying on her front step.

Poor Mick. She'd known he worked for Luke long before she met Luke. Mick was one of the contacts she used when any client of hers at the casino needed quick cash. He wasn't the sharpest knife in the drawer, but he had been nice. What had he done to incur someone's wrath? Luke's wrath?

The idea made her go cold, the kind of cold that all the fur coats in the world couldn't take away. She was well aware that Luke skated happily on the wrong side of the law, but there was a huge difference between loan sharking and murder. The thought of him killing peo-

ple scared her. It scared her enough that she knew she wouldn't mention Mick to him. If she didn't know, she could make believe everything was all right, that Luke was the man she thought he was.

Still, poor Mick.

And poor Ruthie What's-her-name. Not that she was any great
shakes, but she seemed to care for Mick. Did she even know he was
dead? Probably not. How would the cops know to notify her, assuming they were able to identify him so far from his home turf?

That puzzle found on him bothered her the most. There had
been no guarantee that she or Lib would find the body. What if it
had been Tinksie or the effete Tim or Mark? Or the bombshell
Maxi? They wouldn't have hidden the paper. They'd have given it to
the cops, and all kinds of offal would have rained down on her.

*"How do you know the dead man? What connection is he to you?
Where does he work? Who does he work for?"*

No, it couldn't have been Luke who'd left that puzzle, because he
knew that if trouble fell on her, it would fall on him. Their associa-
tion was hardly a secret. They'd been an item for almost a year.

So where had Luke been last night when he stood her up? Her
anger at him burned white hot when she thought of waiting for him
for hours at the hotel. He'd made her feel like a fool, a simpering
woman waiting for her man. Too much like Mom and Nan, and she
wasn't going there for anyone, not even Luke.

Tori was still furious when she emerged from the limo in Atlantic
City, when she climbed the steps to Luke's office on the second floor
of a shoddy-looking building that sold popcorn and fudge down on
the boardwalk level. When she stalked in, raring for a fight, he rose
from his black leather ergonomically correct executive's chair behind
his massive desk, smiling his welcome. "Blondie! You're back."

"And where were you last night?" She squinted at him in the glare of the huge window that gave a magnificent view of the Atlantic Ocean, today a shiny gray blue reflecting the late-afternoon sun.

Luke moved around his desk toward her. His eyes were steel blue beneath his newly barbered, spiked brown hair. He was dressed as usual in tasseled loafers with no socks, tan gabardine dress slacks, and a navy silk long-sleeved shirt with the sleeves rolled up his forearms. Personally Tori always thought he looked more Vegas or Hollywood than Atlantic City. Still, the man was gorgeous. Beautiful.

Not that anyone would call him soft, either physically or professionally. He radiated strength and power, and she liked going toe to toe with a man strong enough to give as good as he got.

He held out a hand to her. "Come here."

"Where were you, Luke?"

"Missing you, babe." He grabbed her hand and started pulling.

"Don't you dare!" She put her hand on his chest and pushed. "I want an answer."

He just smiled lazily and continued to reel her in. When he lowered his head, she turned hers so he found only her cheek.

He looked down at her, still smiling, his arms holding her tight against him, her hands trapped between them. "You're the only person I know who can get away with challenging me, Blondie. Just shows how much I love you, doesn't it?"

"Ha! You keep putting pressure on me to pay up!" The puzzles flashed through her mind in spite of her previous conclusions. No one else knew the things the puzzles knew about her. "If you loved me, you'd forgive the debt!"

This time when he kissed her, he connected. For about five seconds she held herself rigid. Then she melted against him as she always did. He eased his hold, and she raised her arms to encircle his neck. Her anger transmuted into a rush of a very different passion.

When they came up for air, he led her to the cozy nook that had another huge window overlooking the ocean and held several comfortable chairs, a sofa, and a well-stocked wet bar. This elegant sitting room, where favored business associates were greeted and entertained, was the other half of the second-floor throne room from which he ruled his little kingdom—this half above a run-down boardwalk store that sold what Luke always called "cheapy tourist junk that no one in their right mind would sell, let alone buy." The store did a brisk business all summer, much to Luke's perverse delight.

The third floor of the building was Luke's private living area, and Tori was one of very few ever invited there.

He poured her a glass of wine and himself two fingers of Jack Daniel's. When his free hand circled her waist, she leaned into him.

"What's your work schedule for tonight, Blondie? The usual?" He kissed her ear, making her shiver.

"I'm finished an hour after the floor closes."

"I'll see you then."

She looked up at him. "I'm still mad, you know."

"Over last night or the money?"

"Yes."

"I know." He tossed back his drink and released her. "Remember, business is business and sex is sex. Separate."

She was hurt more than she ought to be—after all, this was Luke—and she turned quickly for the door before he saw how distressed she was. She had never let him see her cry, certain he'd see it as a sign of weakness, and she wasn't about to start today. She yelped when he slapped her on her bottom.

"See you." His voice was rich with sensual promise.

She nodded, not looking back. As she clattered down the narrow stairs to boardwalk level, she fought tears. She'd read how guys compartmentalized but women didn't. For sure she didn't. Couldn't. When she loved someone, it spilled over into every aspect of her life.

She loved Luke with everything in her.

He said he loved her, but she questioned his definition of love. It was more that he sort of, maybe, kind of cared for her. He certainly liked her in bed. But she owed him one hundred thousand dollars, and he wasn't about to forgive her debt. *"Business is business and sex is sex."*

But if you loved someone…

She put on her dark glasses to shield her eyes from the sun and to hide their unseemly sheen. There was nothing she could do to change him.

Once the limo disappeared, carrying Tori off to the SeaSide, I saw with great relief that Chloe and Jenna seemed to forget Tori. They played with their laptops, with the new games Tori had bought, and wrote endless messages they posted on Facebook for their absent friends.

I puttered around the house for the rest of the week, leaving only to go to another estate sale at an old farm in southern Chester County horse country very early Saturday, the morning of the Fourth. The site of the sale was a small gentleman's farm that had somehow survived amid the large surrounding spreads that trained Olympic-quality horses. The old gentleman who had died was an only child of an only child and had never married. At least that's what the sales ad said, and it was a clarion call that no family had pillaged the contents of the house.

I walked around the many items on display and was amazed at the quality of some things sitting on tables cheek by jowl with the cheapest and shoddiest I'd seen in a long time. All around me were other buyers and dealers also looking for bargains, flea-market aficionados open to whatever caught their eye, and Amishmen who sought good deals on the farm equipment scattered for inspection across what had probably been a horse paddock. The sale was an intriguing mix of a tag sale with lots of smaller items marked with price stickers, especially boxes of miscellany, and an auction for larger pieces and the farm equipment. In our area, sales are usually one or the other.

I found a box of doll furniture tucked in a corner of the dining room beside the beautiful curly maple sideboard. The sideboard didn't interest me because Madge and I dealt in what are called smalls. We stuck with them with rare exceptions because they were easy to handle and easy to package if we sold them online.

The doll furniture was in great condition, and I turned it over to check for a mark. Strombecker. Yes! Strombecker used to make furniture for the Ginny doll as well as boy toys like airplane and train kits made of wood. I rooted through the box and found a crib, an armoire, a rocking chair, a cradle, a bureau, and an end table. I opened the door of the armoire and found it stuffed with doll clothes. I pulled them out and found the Vogue label sewn in the pieces. I used to think that meant *Vogue* magazine or maybe Vogue patterns, but it meant an early twentieth-century doll shop in Massachusetts called Ye Olde Vogue Doll Shoppe. The shop owner created the Ginny doll, still made today, and Strombecker made furniture to fit the eight-inch doll. I took the box to checkout and put it in the van. I went back and bought some cut glass and a set of Fostoria goblets that we should be able to move either in the shop or online. I also found two watercolors that I loved and might actually keep for myself, and a mantel clock that was a steal at fifty dollars.

I had been milling around the tables out in the yard when I stepped into the cool of the emptied barn to escape the heat and brilliance of the sun. I leaned against a support and took a drink from the water bottle I carried in my fanny pack. As my eyes adjusted to the dim interior, I saw the corner of a box jutting out of a manger, a white angle rising unnaturally from a light cover of hay, a straight line where none should be. I went to investigate and discovered a shoebox, women's size eight.

Curious, I pulled the box out and lifted the lid. A cache of vintage jewelry winked up at me.

Yowzah!

I slammed the lid back in place, looking around to see if anyone was watching. I wondered briefly how it had gotten into the manger instead of on the tables either in the yard or in the house, but only for a minute. In the chaos of getting things placed for sale, someone had obviously set this box down and forgotten it.

Hugging the box, I hurried back to the checkout lady and paid the princely sum of twenty-five dollars, the price she decided would be right for an untagged box.

"Your lucky day, ducks." She waved me on to get to the next person eager to pay for their treasure, never taking time to check the contents.

I could feel the return on this investment feeding us for the next month.

"I got some wonderful jewelry," I told Madge, cell pressed to my ear as I sat in the parking lot at a Dunkin' Donuts, drinking a Coke and eating a chocolate glazed doughnut. I had my seat pushed back, the bag with the second and third doughnuts on the passenger seat, the Coke in the cup holder, and the shoebox in my lap. As I pawed through the contents, I told her about discovering it in the barn. I hadn't taken the time for any serious study at the sale, just grabbed the box and run, knowing vintage jewelry was always a good risk.

"Here's a wonderful iridescent rhinestone pin with matching clip earrings. Very fifties. All the stones are intact. And a pretty gold circle pin, same era, with a ribbon of faux pearls tied on it. Oh, what a lovely little cameo on a gold chain. I'd say it was considerably older than the other two. Maybe the twenties or thirties. Might have some real value. Oh, and there's a lovely opal brooch with one large opal in the center and"—I counted quickly—"two circles totaling twenty smaller opals circling it, all set in gold."

I flipped the brooch and found a stamp for fourteen-karat gold. "Madge, I don't think this is some cheap piece. We'll need Sam Pierce to give us an appraisal before we market it." Sam appraised all our jewelry at his store in the mall at Haydn because he was always honest with us. "Oh my! You should see this funny little dog pin with big blue glass eyes and a long slender tail set with glass chips. Very fifties."

I laughed as I put it back and pulled out another brooch similar in design to the opal, only instead of opals encircling a central gem, the seventeen stones were cubic zirconium. I held the pin toward the window and watched the sun touch the stones and paint rainbows in them.

I sat up straight. "Madge." My voice was barely a whisper.

"What? What's wrong?"

"Nothing. I think it's a matter of what's right." I could barely talk. I looked around the parking lot, but no other folks were foolish enough to be sitting in the sun with their cars running so they had some air conditioning while they ate their food. They were munching as they drove off the lot to wherever. Still, I lowered the pin lest any unseen lurkers see it. "I think I've got a diamond pin here. Real diamonds, seventeen of them." I flipped it and found the stamp. "Fourteen-karat gold."

I heard a little choking sound in my ear. "Oh, Libby, you can't be serious."

I nodded, as if she could see me. "I know the eye can't tell the difference between diamonds and CZ, but my gut tells me we may have something way more valuable than vintage here. I'm probably wrong and will be terribly disappointed, but I'm coming home and taking them to Sam."

"Right now?"

"Right now."

"I'll call him and tell him you're coming. And I'll meet you there." Madge hung up.

I put the pin carefully in the box and put the car in drive. An hour later I met Madge outside Sam Pierce's jewelry store.

"Did you forget that today is the Fourth?" Madge asked. "The store was closed."

"What?" I'd driven all this way for nothing?

"But I got Sam's curiosity piqued, and he agreed to come in for a brief consultation."

Sam, jeweler's loupe at the ready, was waiting for us at the back door.

"You just got me. Marly and I leave this afternoon for a month down the shore." He took the shoebox and disappeared into the back of his store. Madge and I waited in agony while he gave the pieces a quick once-over. To help pass the time, I told her about Aunt Stella's house and the rare books and the Hepplewhite.

"Interesting, but we can talk about them later. I want to hear about the body on the doorstep."

I told her what little I knew and described the puzzles, reciting all the words with potential criminal meanings. She had just started to lecture me again about going to Detective Holloran when Sam Pierce came out of his back room and gestured to us.

We followed him into his office, where he offered us seats across from his desk. "Where did you get these pieces?" He gestured to the jewelry sitting on a piece of black velvet he'd laid across the desk. The stones winked at us in the overhead light.

"An estate sale near Kennett Square, Pennsylvania."

"Well." He stared at the pieces, frowning, and I knew I'd gotten us excited over nothing and pulled him needlessly away from his family. The pieces were the usual collection of good costume jewelry and would bring us a nice profit, but nothing like I'd started to dream.

Then he smiled broadly. "You have lucked out, ladies. There are some very, very fine pieces in this mix as well as some dime-store stuff."

"Like the little dog." I reached out and picked up the little pin. "But you gotta love the big blue eyes."

"That you do," Sam said. "They're marquise-cut sapphires."

I stared at the little pin.

"And the chips are diamonds. It should sell for $2,700 to $3,000."

My mouth fell open, as did Madge's. The dog was cute, but I'd never pay $3,000 for him. But someone out there would, and that was what mattered. "And this one?" With a shaking hand I held up what I thought was a diamond brooch.

"I found a similar one for $3,250 at a very reputable online site." Sam sat back and folded his hands over his stomach. "How much did you pay for it?"

"The entire shoebox cost me $25." I laughed and Madge laughed along.

"Twenty-five dollars." Sam grinned. "Someone, as they say, was robbed, and it wasn't you. I'd suggest you leave them in the safe here until you decide how you want to dispose of them, but I set the timer yesterday when I left, and it won't open again until next week when the store opens. I've got a young woman who works here who could probably override the commands, but I have no idea if she's even home today. You'll have to keep them with you." He looked apologetic.

"Don't worry about it," I said, though I did wish for the security of his safe. "We just appreciate that you were willing to come in."

"I'll come back from the shore one day next week and give them the time I need for a thorough evaluation," he assured us. "I'll let you know which day. You can leave them in the safe then if you want."

We wrapped everything carefully, placing each piece in its own little cotton-lined white box. Madge and I were putting the boxes carefully in the shoebox when Sam's cell rang. He answered, then rolled his eyes.

"Coming home right now, Marly!" He was on his feet before he hung up. "I'm late. I've got to go."

He was herding us out the door when Madge's cell rang.

"That was Bill," she explained after her brief conversation. "I'm late for a cookout and swim party at the Winstons' place. We leave from there for a week in Massachusetts at my in-laws' summer place. I've got to run!" She gave me a quick hug and left, Sam on her heels.

By default, I ended up driving back to Aunt Stella's with a small fortune in jewels in the van with me. I almost raced from my parking spot to the house. If the local thieves only knew what I had!

I unlocked the front door as quickly as I could, my eyes darting up and down the lane for thieves lurking behind window boxes. I slammed the door behind me and twisted all the locks. I know. Paranoid.

As I turned from the door, my nose wrinkled, not at my personality foibles but at the smell.

"What's going on in here? It smells like a beauty parlor!"

"Mom!" Chloe called from the kitchen. "I'm getting highlighted!"

I gulped. The only person I could think of that Chloe knew here was Jenna, and the thought of the girls coloring each other's hair was unnerving. It wouldn't be the end of the world if Chloe's hair turned bright orange or green or something, but it would be the end of Chloe's world. The weeping, wailing, and gnashing of teeth would continue for weeks until it grew out.

I set my shoebox on the dining room table and peeked hesitantly into the kitchen. Chloe sat at the table wearing enough foil to transmit to Mars, and Tori sat on the counter watching a stranger brush smelly, foamy stuff on a strip of Jenna's beautiful dark hair, then wrap it carefully in more foil.

"Tori! What's going on? And tell me you checked with Jenna's dad." *Please.*

"Hey, Libby." Tori waved negligently, ignoring the Jenna's dad issue. My heart sank. "This is Mindy. She's a friend of a friend."

"Hi." Mindy glanced at me. "I went to beauty school with Tori's friend Val."

"Val does my hair," Tori explained.

I had to admit that Mindy knew what she was doing—which didn't make doing Chloe's and Jenna's hair without checking okay.

Mindy nodded. "Val called me this morning because she knew I lived here in Philly. She told me I had a gig making three ladies beautiful." She grinned at me. "I guess you're lady number three."

9

□□□

THE LANE'S FOURTH OF JULY block party was well under way when, newly highlighted and coiffed, I took my baked beans out to set on the tables James had lined up along the walk in front of his house and Mark and Tim's.

James eyed my dish as I set it on the red, white, and blue covering. "They don't look like Stella's beans."

"That's because they're Libby's," I said. "Not the brand, but mine. I've got to say, James," I added hurriedly to distract him from the fact that being Libby's meant, at least in this case, that they came out of a can, "this is a very impressive spread."

And it was, a curious melding of traditional area dishes and ethnic contributions. Garden salad, caesar salad, potato and macaroni salads, three-bean salad, pickled eggs and deviled eggs, cole slaw, creamed cabbage, falafel balls, couscous, a platter filled with hoagie makings, and a squeeze bottle filled with oil to moisten the Italian rolls, sliced and waiting. On the other side of the rolls was a hot dish holding razor-thin slices of roast beef in gravy and beyond it another hot dish filled with sausage and green peppers. Then began the table filled with homemade desserts—pies, cakes, cookies—and finished off with two boxes of Tastykakes, one Butterscotch Krimpets, the other chocolate cupcakes. They were Tori's contribution, which she rushed out to buy when she realized I wasn't making a second dish for her. Chloe brought a giant bag of potato chips and a dish of brownies. She brought the chips because she and Jenna had eaten half the brownies as they beautified themselves earlier in the day.

"I can't take just this," she'd cried as she looked in dismay at the half-empty platter she'd arranged the brownies on.

"Is there another box of mix? Make more." I pulled the baked beans out of the oven.

"There isn't time!"

"Then put them on a smaller plate," I suggested. "It'll look like more."

She grabbed a luncheon plate.

"Not the Wedgwood!"

She gave me a look. "Easy, Mom." She put the Wedgwood back in the cupboard.

"There are paper plates over there." I pointed to a cabinet.

"Paper?" Her voice dripped disdain.

Three days and already she was disparaging paper plates? "Paper," I said firmly.

She complied. "Still too little." She brightened. "I know!" She grabbed a bag of vinegar-and-salt chips.

So we sallied forth, food in hand, hair gilded and curled. As soon as Chloe put her food down, she ran to find Jenna. I didn't blame her. The lane was crawling with adults she'd never seen before. I was a bit overwhelmed myself.

I took a plate and began helping myself to the glorious bounty. I wanted some of everything, so I took little dibs and dabs, filling my plate to the point I feared its collapse.

As I turned away from the feast, I saw Drew Canfield emerge from his home, dish in hand, Jenna and Chloe on his heels. In his shorts and polo shirt, he looked rugged and very unscholarly. I smiled. He didn't look very much like a cook either, and I couldn't help wondering what he'd made. Jenna carried a nine-by-thirteen cake pan.

"You're drooling, Elizabeth."

I spun at Tori's mocking words.

"Though he is certainly handsome. A hunk."

I shrugged. Never would I admit to my sister that I felt some sort of connection with him after our early morning experience with murder. "I'm not drooling, and the world is full of handsome men."

"True, true." She looked at me with that disdainful smile that made me squirm every time I saw it. It always preceded a barb.

"But sadly none of them are yours." She shook her head in mock sorrow. "That's what comes of trying to pretend you're a virgin all these years."

I tried not to flinch. The last thing I wanted was to let Tori see how her taunts hurt. "Don't, Tori. Let's just enjoy the night without any pettiness, okay?"

"Why, honey, I wouldn't want to hurt you for the world, bless your heart."

Like I didn't know "bless your heart" was a euphemism for "don't believe a word I've just said."

She sauntered away, hips swaying, to talk with Tim and Mark.

She was gorgeous in red cropped pants, her toenails, visible in her stiletto sandals, a matching red. Her white tight tee was cropped so that the gem in her bellybutton—a real diamond or a cubic zirconium? And wouldn't the loan shark like to know?—winked when it caught the setting sun.

I had on navy slacks and a red tee neatly tucked in, a white belt, and white flat sandals, my nod to the patriotic nature of our party.

Bling and bland. That was the Keating twins. Well, at least my hair looked good tonight. Funny, I hadn't thought it looked bad until Tori showed up all highlighted and lovely. I sighed and went to get something to drink from the coolers filled with ice and beverages.

I straightened with a Coke in my hand and found myself face to face with Drew. I gestured toward the coolers. "Quite a selection."

He glanced at the coolers but made no move to get a beverage.

I smiled. If he didn't want something to drink, maybe he had sought me out. Now there was a lovely thought. And where was Tori when you wanted her to notice something? "I want to thank you for being so helpful the other morning."

He gave a little nod but didn't smile back.

I plowed on. "It was very nice of you to check on us that afternoon too. My sister appreciated your concern."

"Speaking of your sister—"

My smile tightened to a wince.

"Jenna tells me she arranged for the hair job."

Uh-oh. His tone of voice made it clear he wasn't happy with the "hair job."

At that moment the girls came rushing over.

"Mark and Tim have invited us to come up on their roof to watch the fireworks." Chloe was so excited she vibrated.

"Philadelphia has big, huge, awesome fireworks because this is where it all started," Jenna bubbled. "Tim says."

I glanced at Mark and Tim, sitting in a pair of padded lounge chairs in front of their house. Tori sat on the foot of Mark's chair, talking animatedly with them. The men each held a plate and were making their way through an impressive mound of food, nodding at Tori's remarks, pausing in their eating every so often to comment. Mark saw me watching and waved a fork at me. Tori turned, saw Drew beside me, and raised an eyebrow. I made believe I didn't see it, though I was smugly glad she saw him beside me.

"You're invited too, Mom." Chloe, no dummy, picked up on my cautious reaction to the invitation from two men I didn't know. I was sure Tim and Mark were gay and therefore not interested in Chloe in that sense, but still, I didn't know them. And this was the city, home of mayhem and murder, one of which I'd already encountered.

"And you too, Dad." Jenna bent for a soda, and the blond streak that began at the hairline over her left eye and flowed across and down to flip at her chin fell forward over her cheek. She straightened with a bounce, a bottle of root beer in her hand. "They have a clear sightline, and we should bring our own chairs if we want. I don't think we have chairs, at least not here, but who cares? Everybody comes. Isn't that cool?"

"Definitely cool," I agreed. "A real treat!"

Drew grunted something that could have meant anything, but Jenna seemed happy with his response.

With a wave the girls raced off to the food table, where they each grabbed a pack of Butterscotch Krimpets. The prepackaged generation, passing up all the great homemade goodies for assembly-line sweets, though there was no question that such goodies didn't get any better than Tastykakes. Chloe's blond hair gleamed in the lights shining up and down the street. The highlighting and the new cut made her look about five years older, a fact that dragged at my heart. I didn't want her to grow up too fast. I wanted her to enjoy being young with a relatively uncomplicated life.

Drew's eyes followed his daughter. "Did either of you ever think of asking me what I thought about dying a thirteen-year-old's hair?"

I glanced over at Tori. I longed to say, "Yell at my sister," but I didn't. "I'm sorry."

"Yeah, well…"

"Don't let it happen again" hung unspoken in the air.

"I think it looks cute," I said with what I hoped was a charming smile that would defuse the moment.

He looked at me like I'd lost my mind. "She was cute before. Cuter."

"Drew, it's only hair." Through my years of mothering I'd learned the value of picking your wars. A bit of dye wasn't worth a war when real issues like sexual purity and dressing decently and telling the truth needed to be addressed.

"My daughter's hair."

"It'll grow out. And I wasn't home when she had it done."

As soon as that lame-sounding excuse left my mouth, I could have kicked myself. It was true, but it sounded as if I was defending myself—which I guess I was.

"And if you'd been there?"

"I think I'd have remembered to call."

He made that grunting sound again. " 'The absent are never without fault, nor the present without excuse.' "

I paused with my fork halfway to my mouth and stared at him.

He flushed. "Sorry. Ben Franklin. I do that all the time according to Jenna. Quote him, I mean."

I nodded. I thought the quote absolved me of responsibility for Jenna's hair though I wasn't one hundred percent certain. "I'll mention to Tori about checking with you first if something else comes up."

"She's planning to do something else?" He sounded appalled. "What? Pierce Jenna's navel?"

I thought of Tori's abdominal ornament. Even as the thought of Chloe with such a piercing made my blood run cold—she was just too young—I couldn't help grinning at Drew's expression. "I don't think Tori has other plans, but a navel ring wouldn't be the end of the world."

"No?" He rubbed his eyes. "You must think I'm going overboard here, but I worry about her growing up too fast."

"Don't worry. I understand completely. Being solely responsible for a kid, especially a girl kid, must be very scary for a man. It's sure scary for me."

He looked at me in surprise. "Jenna told you about her mom?"

"No, she told Chloe, who told me."

"'Keep your eyes wide open before marriage, half shut afterwards.' B. Franklin, printer." He sighed. "Not that the advice did me any good." He turned and walked toward the food table, stopping to speak with Tim and Mark on the way, undoubtedly checking the validity of the fireworks invitation.

As I watched him go, I wondered at the woman who painted her hair red and green and rode off on the back of a motorcycle with some guy. Drew was not a man to be easily left.

I blinked. Now why did I think that? I knew he had a caring if somewhat overreacting heart as far as Jenna was concerned. That made him worthy if slightly stuffy. And he was good-looking and had a keen mind. At least I assumed he had a keen mind. I tried to think of some example where I'd witnessed his mental agility. After all, he was a college professor and a Ben Franklin scholar. All professors and scholars were keen, right?

Tinksie wandered up, and we talked about living on this lane, steeped in Olde Philadelphia and situated in the middle of modern Philadelphia.

"I imagine everyone is as avid a collector of antiques as Aunt Stella was," I said. "How could you put modern pieces in these homes?"

"Maxi, our 'star' of stage and screen, manages." Her tone was dry, and I laughed. She was right; Maxi and antiques didn't go together.

Tinksie glanced at Stella's house. "Stella's collection is one of the best. She and Andrew loved going antiquing. They traveled up and down the East Coast searching for just the right pieces."

"Andrew?" Aunt Stella had a boyfriend I'd never heard of?

"Stella's significant other." Tinksie got a faraway look in her eyes. "They were together for the better part of forty years."

"Forty years? And they never married?" I'd bet anything that Mom and Nan didn't know about Andrew. If they had, I'd have known. It would have been a family tidbit thoroughly chewed over, especially the not-married part. Oh, the spleen that could have been vented.

"They couldn't marry. Andrew was already married," Tinksie said with calm acceptance. "Daughter of his law firm's senior partner. He couldn't divorce her, and she wouldn't divorce him."

Was I, the unwed mother of a thirteen-year-old, the only person who thought such a situation was ridiculous? "Aunt Stella didn't mind?"

"Uh-uh. I think she liked it that way. She had her freedom, her job, and she had Andrew several nights a week. He showered her with most of the lovely things you see in her place. In fact, he bought her the house."

I blinked. *Yowzah!*

"He loved buying her things. It was so sweet."

"I wonder what his wife thought of the situation." I always identified with the injured party. After all, I had a history as such a person.

"Who knows?" Tinksie said as if it didn't matter. "Stella was happy, and she was my friend, and that's what counted to James and me."

Not *right vs. wrong* but *happy vs. unhappy.*

"We were so sad for Andrew when she died." Tinksie sighed. "Poor man. He was here day and night at the end. James invited him tonight, but he couldn't face coming without Stella." She sniffed as she looked up and down the street. "He was right. It isn't the same without her."

With a sad little wave, she wandered off to talk to someone else, and I pondered the new information about my aunt and wondered what Andrew's last name was.

I noticed Tim and Mark stand and fold their chairs. They gave a wave, and people began to follow them down the narrow opening between their house and Tinksie's. Chloe and Jenna danced up.

"Come on, Mom." Chloe grabbed my hand and began pulling me. I glanced at my watch. Nine o'clock. Dusk was falling, and soon it would be full dark. I let her lead me down the alley, lit by a lamppost at the far end. We stepped out in the men's backyard, a lovely garden fragrant with roses.

"They're Mark's hobby," Tim said as he saw me bend to sniff

one. "He has a green thumb, but I'm not allowed to touch even one little bud. I am the kiss of death to anything flowering. When Stella and Andrew had us to dinner, I wasn't allowed to even breathe on her plants." He grinned, obviously not distressed at all. "I'm a computer geek. As I always tell Mark, I'm useful."

I was laughing as we climbed the steps to the men's flat roof. I was surprised to discover a lawn up there with a patio and multiple container gardens. The girls were enchanted.

"But what if we all fall through?" Chloe whispered. "This is an awful lot of weight up here."

Tinksie leaned in. "They've had special supports put in to bear the weight. Not very consistent with the era of the house, but it sure is lovely on a summer evening when the heat hangs in the close confines of our yards."

"Hey, Dad!" Jenna waved violently. "Over here."

Drew made his way to us, excusing himself from Maxi, who watched him go with hungry eyes. Maxi was no dummy.

"You've got an admirer." I couldn't help teasing him.

He rolled his eyes.

"You don't want to get mixed up with her, Dad. She's not suitable stepmother material."

"Jenna, I don't think one conversation of five minutes' duration is reason enough to become worried. Besides, she's not my type."

"Yeah," Jenna said. "She's too old. Besides, she's the type that would send me away to boarding school."

"You've been watching *The Sound of Music* again," Drew said.

"Nope. *The Parent Trap*. Lindsay Lohan when she was little and cute."

"Love that movie," I said. "Only it's Dennis Quaid I like. Great smile."

"Huh," Drew said.

"Hey, there's Aunt Tori." Chloe waved at Tori, who had just stepped onto the roof. "She's got some guy with her."

I took one look at the man at her side and felt all the blood leave my face.

10

□□□

DREW LOOKED AT LIBBY with astonishment as she spun, turning her back to her sister and the man with her. He studied the man, because certainly Tori wasn't the one Libby was giving the old cut direct. The question was, why did she want to ignore—avoid?—him.

"Do you think that's her boyfriend?" Chloe watched her aunt and the man with her walk toward them.

Jenna frowned. "Nah. She's too pretty for somebody like him."

That was true, Drew thought. Tori was a knockout, if you liked the over-the-top type. The man was average in height and stature and had lots of black, carefully moussed ringlets around his head, one falling strategically over his left eye. The better for some woman to brush it back for him, no doubt.

Tori waved to the girls and started toward them, the man following right along as they wove their way through the crowd awaiting the fireworks.

"Are they coming?" Libby asked, her voice strangely constricted. "Did he see me?"

"Given the girls' waving like semaphores, I don't think he could possibly miss you."

"That's what I was afraid of." She shook her head. "I can't believe it. Eddie Mancini. Here."

Drew stared down at her. Her shoulders were hunched, and she was gazing at the bottom of the placket on his polo. "Are you okay?"

"No." She put a hand to her forehead. "No."

"An old boyfriend?" Drew looked at Eddie again. He definitely had his eyes fixed on Libby. So did Tori.

"Worse."

Suddenly the sky was alight with spectacular bursts of color. Red chrysanthemums blossomed, blue novas exploded, and white starbursts erupted into a shower of iridescent sparks that rained down to burn themselves out in the night.

Chloe and Jenna forgot all about Tori and Eddie. They stared at the sky with rapt delight, the rainbow colors washing across their faces.

Drew ignored the fireworks. "Worse?" Then it clicked. "Chloe's father?"

"Shh!" Libby gave a quick, panicky look at Chloe, saw her gazing skyward, and went back to staring at his placket. "He's the last person in the world I want to see, and Tori knows it. I can't believe she'd do this to me!"

Neither could Drew. " 'Tricks and treachery are the practice of fools that don't have brains enough to be honest.' "

Libby gulped what sounded like a strangled laugh. "Don't let Tori hear you call her a fool even in a Ben quote."

"I am not that foolish." He watched Tori and Eddie thread their way ever closer. He wished he knew some way to protect Libby from—what? a devious sister? an unwanted visitor? unhappy memories? "I take it you don't see him often?"

"I haven't seen him for years. More to the point, Chloe's never seen him."

Yikes! "You've never told her about him." It was a statement.

She shook her head. "I know. Colossal error. Madge always tells me that. 'She needs to know, Libby, and from you.'"

Drew didn't know who Madge was, but her advice sounded right to him.

"But I was trying to protect her." Libby glanced up at him with eyes that pleaded for him to understand. "He's a total sleaze! Who wants to know her father is that kind of a jerk?"

"Hey, Libby, look who I found," Tori called, all surprised astonishment as she and Eddie drew near, only to get waylaid by Tinksie and James. James probably wanted proof of food brought before he let Eddie stay.

"He works at the SeaSide Casino like Tori." Libby shoved at her shiny curls with shaking fingers. "She sees him frequently."

"So if he works and presumably lives in Atlantic City, what's he doing on our lane in Philadelphia?"

She didn't answer, just looked at Drew, her face shadowed in the poor light. A great white incandescence lit the sky, which clearly illuminated the pain and fear in her eyes. It smote him in the heart. He took her hand in his. It was cold and trembling. "You can do this, Libby. If you can face a dead man, you can face this guy."

She gave a wry half smile. "The dead man didn't threaten my baby."

Drew smiled back. "Mama bear on duty."

She growled, a very unscary bear, and he laughed, then sobered. "You're going to have to turn around, you know."

"I know." She sighed and glanced over her shoulder at the advancing pair. "I can't believe I used to think he was my hero. How could I have been so dumb?"

"You were what? Sixteen? Don't be so hard on yourself." *I was twenty-two,* he thought, *and I still made a royal mess of things.*

Drew studied the approaching man in the blue and green wash of light. Though he was slim, he had a slight paunch and a swagger that told quite clearly what he thought of himself. " 'A man wrapped up in himself makes a very small bundle.' "

Libby slapped her hand over her mouth. "You are terrible."

Maybe, but he'd made her relax a bit. Her shoulders weren't hunched as much, and the panic had receded. "Not me. Ben."

"How does Jenna stand it?"

"Not well. You're sure Tori knows who he is?" He wanted to be certain about the purposefulness of the woman's actions.

"Oh yes. She knows."

There was a story to be told here, and he wanted to hear it, though this wasn't the moment. "Can you trust her to keep quiet? About Chloe, I mean."

"I don't know. She's got something up her sleeve, or she wouldn't have brought him this evening."

"He's he—"

"Libby!"

Before Drew got the warning out, Eddie snaked his arms around Libby's waist and lifted her off her feet. Her back to his chest, he swung her in a circle. Drew frowned as he saw Libby's horrified face and Tori's satisfied smile.

"Put me down, Eddie." Libby's voice was low but firm. "Now. Before you make a bigger fool of yourself."

Instead he leaned around and kissed her cheek. Libby flinched.

All Drew's protective instincts sprang into action. He liked Libby, and he didn't like Eddie. He reached out and rubbed the wetness of the kiss away with the back of his hand. Libby looked at him with such gratitude that he felt his chest size expand about four sizes. Then he reached for her and gently pulled her out of Eddie's arms.

He turned her so she faced Eddie and Tori, and though he dropped his hands to his sides, he stood very close to her, offering her whatever of his strength she needed. For a brief moment she actually allowed herself to lean on him, but she straightened quickly. It was just enough to let him know she knew what he was doing and, he thought, appreciated it.

He stuck out his hand. "Drew Canfield." After he shook Eddie's hand, he turned to Libby's twin. "Tori." The nod he gave her may have looked polite, but the chill in his voice made Tori blink. Good. No one had the right to upset another as she had her very own twin.

There was a brief moment of quiet in the sky, and Chloe turned to Libby. "Wow, Mom, aren't these great?" She grabbed Libby around the neck and squeezed. "Thanks for coming to Philadelphia!"

Libby hugged her daughter—Eddie's daughter—and nodded. "They are absolutely spectacular and you're welcome." Then, arm around Chloe, she turned all her attention to the sky and the brilliant, beautiful pyrotechnics, ignoring Eddie completely.

Drew had to admire her stiff spine. He moved and stood behind her, again offering his support if she felt the need of it. He turned his eyes skyward, but all his attention was on Tori and Eddie just off to his left.

"I thought you said she'd be glad to see me," a disgruntled Eddie said in a whisper that was as audible as a shout. Why did people think whispers didn't carry?

Tori was staring at her sister's back, her expression stony. "I've never known her to be so rude. You know her. She's everybody's patsy."

"Who's her watchdog?" Eddie shot Drew a hard look.

"Just some guy who lives on the block. That's his kid hanging out with Chloe."

Just some guy? Drew liked that. He continued to strain his ears and eyes as he listened and watched Eddie watch Libby and Chloe.

"The kid's cute," Eddie said.

"She is," Tori agreed.

"Sort of looks like me, don' cha think?"

Drew rolled his eyes. The black-haired minihood thought that blond pixie looked like him? It was the worst case of wishful thinking he'd ever encountered, and he knew all about wishful thinking from personal experience.

"Maybe I should introduce myself." Eddie took a step forward. Drew braced himself, ready to step between Eddie and Chloe if need be.

Tori grabbed Eddie's arm. "What? Say, 'Hi, kid, I'm your dad'?" She looked at him like he was crazy.

"Why not? I am."

"I didn't bring you here to scare Chloe but to see Lib."

Eddie gave her a sardonic glance. "Upset Lib, you mean. I don't know why, but I know you, Tori. I know how you think, and you never do anything without it benefiting yourself." Then he turned back to watching Chloe. "And you really think I'd scare the kid? I'm her old man."

"You're a stranger, you idiot."

"Yeah, well, maybe it's time to change that."

"It was time to do something like that thirteen years ago."

"Right. Like I'da done that. I was a punk back then."

"Your loss."

Eddie stared at Tori speculatively. A look of amazement washed across his face. "You're trying to win the kid away from Lib."

"Go home, Eddie." Tori sounded hard and angry.

He held up his hand as he dipped his head. "Sure. I know when I'm not wanted. But first I got something for you. When I said I was coming to see you, I was told to deliver this." He reached in his pocket, drew out a piece of paper, and held it out to her. Printed on it in black caps so big that Drew could read it was the name TORI.

Tori pulled her hand back as if the paper could burn. "I don't want it."

Eddie grabbed her hand and slapped it in her palm, closing her fingers over it. "I gotta be able to say I delivered it."

He turned, walked to the stairs, and disappeared from view. Tori stood staring at the paper. Then with a gagging noise and a shaking of her hand like she was ridding herself of something foul, she flung the paper to the ground. As diamonds, rubies, emeralds, and sapphires exploded across the black velvet sky, Tori ran down the steps and into the night.

What could possibly cause her such revulsion? Curious, Drew picked up the paper she'd dropped and opened it. He stared in surprise at a crossword puzzle.

▢▢▢

When the final shimmer of incandescence burned itself out and the sky fell black and still, I wasn't certain I dared move. What if Eddie was still here? The thought of having to face him, talk with him, introduce him to Chloe, even if only as Eddie Mancini, old friend, was making me practically hyperventilate.

"He's gone," a deep voice said quietly in my ear.

The relief was so great my knees went weak. *Thank You, Lord.*

"That was so super!" Chloe squealed.

"Now the fireworks at home will seem rinky, Dad," Jenna said.

"Cozy," Drew corrected. "Think cozy."

Jenna snorted.

"I want some dessert," Chloe announced as if her life depended on it. "I must have some dessert."

"Come on, then," Jenna said. "We've got to beat all these old guys down there if we're going to get the best stuff."

"Don't forget to thank Tim and Mark," I called as they took off running for the stairs, cutting in front of one of the professional couples whose name I couldn't recall. Thankfully the couple had the grace to smile at the fleeing girls.

Drew stared after them with a bemused smile. "Old guys? Now that hurts." Then he looked at me. "Are you all right?"

I gave a shrug. "I'll survive." I ran a hand over my hair, feeling suddenly awkward. It was embarrassing to remember how upset I'd been, and all because I'd kept my secret all these years. I felt my cheeks flame and was glad for the darkness. I found myself staring at the placket on his polo shirt once again rather than look at him. "Thanks for your moral support. It meant a lot."

This was the second time Drew had come to my rescue. A dead man and a dead romance. I didn't even want to think about how he must see me, a weak woman without the internal fortitude to speak the truth to her daughter. Or a keeper of secrets, causing her own predicament.

It was past time that I acknowledged that when a secret is known to others, especially untrustworthy others, it's not a secret. It's information, and it was a certainty that this knowledge would be passed on whether I wanted it to be or not. It was up to me to see that the information was shared properly and soon.

My stomach cramped at the very idea.

"By the way, your sister dropped this." Drew held out a piece of paper.

I saw the TORI and my breath hitched. I took the sheet and opened it. A puzzle stared up at me.

Betrayed as I felt over her bringing Eddie here, I was still scared for her. She might not be nice or kind much of the time, and I might not always like her, but she was my twin, and I always loved her.

"Where did she get this?" I spoke more to myself than Drew, but he answered.

"Eddie gave it to her."

Eddie. How was he involved in all this? Did he have anything to do with the dead guy on our step? Eddie might not be my favorite person, but his being involved in a murder strained my imagination. Still, he had brought this puzzle. Had he brought the others?

I nodded my thanks to Drew and folded the puzzle, slipping it in my slacks pocket. Déjà vu. "I have to find Tori."

My face must have shown my distress because Drew studied me much too closely.

"She acted like the paper was something dirty she'd stepped in. You're distressed about it too." He frowned and waited, not quite asking what was going on but clearly wanting to know.

I shook my head. I wasn't about to tell him that my sister was in hock for some unknown amount of money and had someone making threats on her life. It was bad enough he knew about Eddie. I

ACROSS

1 good looking
5 made rigid
8 not old
12 precious metal
13 a slip
15 oyster indigestion
17 evergreen or funeral
18 marks or pledges
20 pancakes or fabrics
21 quick

DOWN

2 severe anger
3 three
4 patellae
6 determination
7 require
9 betting term
10 takes hold of
11 taken out on an enemy
14 rises above
16 gives for a time
19 narrow opening

gave him the best smile I could manage, which I imagine was pretty sick. Then I set out to find my sister.

I didn't find her. She'd disappeared for the night, whether with Eddie or someone else, I didn't know. Instead I sat by myself at the little kitchen table and sweated over the puzzle, finally solving it. The embedded message read, "payuporelse." PAY UP OR ELSE.

Or else what? She was next? That threat still made no sense. Dead clients do not repay you.

Words embedded in the puzzle leaped off the page at me. *Rage, demand, loans, contract. Trey, odds,* and *slot* were gambling words. Of course pretty words like *gold* and *pearls* were in the puzzle too. But *wreaths* could refer to funeral wreaths as well as Christmas ones, and black *crepes* were what you draped funeral things with. *Kneecaps* jumped out, and my hand automatically went to my patella, whole and bullet-free.

I shuddered in the comfortable air conditioning of Aunt Stella's lovely house. Chloe and I were knee deep in Tori's mess!

□ □ □

Chloe flopped back on her bed in her daffodil room. "Is this not the coolest place in the world?"

Jenna sat in the yellow squishy chair under the window and surveyed the room. "I know. My room's all shades of pink. It's sort of like living in the Barbie aisle at Toys "R" Us, but it's still really pretty. I've got this hot purple room at home. Dad says it gives him a headache just looking at it, and I say the better to keep him out." She grinned.

Hot purple? Chloe thought daffodil was better. More bedroom-y, as in letting you sleep. When she got home, she was going to repaint her room just like this one. "Did you ever live where they had a party like this and the whole street came and everyone went up on the roof for fireworks?"

"We live in a pretty small town. A college town in the middle of nowhere. We definitely don't have fireworks like the ones tonight, but we have college things and town things. Today there was a parade and all."

"Haydn has a parade too. It's pretty hokey," Chloe said.

"So's ours. The high school band marches, at least the kids not on vacation, and the mayor and the Little League teams and the girls' soccer teams and stuff."

"We've got all these little kids riding decorated bikes, running into each other. And there are a bunch of these Shriner guys who drive around in little cars and stuff, and one of the Philadelphia string bands, but they don't look anywhere as neat as they do in their costumes on New Year's Day."

"Did you ever go to a Mummers Parade?"

Chloe shook her head. "Maybe we can stay until January first and go this year."

"January first. Next year." Jenna laughed. "Do you march in Haydn's parade?"

"I used to when I played soccer."

"Me too. I've marched for as long as I can remember. I still do because I still play. Dad marches too because he's our coach. When you pass someone you know, they all clap and cheer for you and you wave. It's fun. One time my mom's parents came, and they whistled and cheered. It was so embarrassing and so fun."

"I wonder where we'll live when we grow up," Chloe said. "A big city or a small town?"

"Well, one thing. We never had a body show up on our doorstep back home. Bad guys live more in the cities, I think."

Chloe thought of her grandfather and great-grandfather. "I think there are some in small towns too. Maybe there are more in cities because there are just more people in cities. Population concentration."

They fell silent as they contemplated this for several seconds. Then Chloe grabbed Princess and rolled over, pinning the dog beneath her, though she was careful to keep all weight off the little animal. Princess went satisfyingly nuts, barking like an off-key soprano stuck on one note. Chloe rolled onto her back and opened her arms. Instead of fleeing, Princess stood on her chest and washed her face thoroughly. After she dried her face on the bedspread, Chloe looked at Jenna.

"Did you see that guy my Aunt Tori brought?"

"Ugh." Jenna made a face. "That Eddie guy."

"Icky Eddie. I think Aunt Tori and my mom knew him back in high school."

"All kinds of people go to high school."

Chloe thought about some of the weird guys she knew. How much weirder would they be by high school? Now there was a scary thought.

"I like your mom."

Chloe looked at Jenna in surprise. "Thanks. I like your dad."

"Wouldn't it be neat—"

"Do you think they—"

And the girls laughed. Like that would ever happen.

11

□□□

I WAS BLEARY-EYED SUNDAY MORNING, having spent a restless night tossing in my surprisingly comfortable iron bed, getting up to stare down at the quiet of the garden, even going down there to sit for a half hour, alone, scared, and weepy.

Half the time I was worried about Tori and totally without any kind of idea on how to help her, assuming she'd take my help if offered. The rest of the time, I thought about the mess I'd made of my own life. I had no room to be too upset with Tori.

I was such a fraud. People thought I was this great Christian, standing for Jesus in the face of my family's opposition and mockery. They thought I had turned my life around and pulled it from the toilet where I had lived pre-Christ.

Ha!

Five minutes with Eddie and all my deceit and weaknesses became much too apparent, at least to me. At the core, I was still me. What a fake!

"You've got to tell her, Lib," Madge had been saying for years. "She needs to hear it from you before someone else tells her. And mark my words, someone will."

She was right; I knew it. Secrets known by others were not secrets. But how did you tell your lovely and beloved daughter that her father was a stinking rat who deserted our sinking ship?

When I mentioned that to Madge, she'd hooted derisively. "You think she didn't figure out Eddie's nature when she was about five? Get real, Lib."

But it was so embarrassing to acknowledge what a fool I'd been. I'd been so needy that I'd believed Eddie's assertions of love and fallen into his arms. Jumped into his arms. But it wasn't only my shame that kept me silent. In all honesty I could also say I wanted to protect Chloe from her father and his ability to be purposefully cruel.

One day, when I was about five months pregnant, I had been standing by my school locker, blocked from view by its open door, when Eddie and two of his cronies came down the hall. I heard his voice and wished I could crawl into the locker so I didn't have to see him or he me. I'd never sparkled like Tori, and now in the overly big clothes I was wearing to minimize my pregnancy and hopefully get through the school year without the school authorities finding out, I was an even greater embarrassment to myself than usual.

"I'm short of cash for the weekend," he said. "I sure miss Chief Keating at times like this."

"Did he ever know about the drugs?" That was not-so-bright-but-oh-so-loyal Rick Woods.

Drugs? Eddie was doing illegal drugs? My hand went to my stomach. What effect would that have on the baby?

"Where do you think I got 'em?" Eddie asked. "You think I'd risk my neck gettin' involved with the hopheads out there?"

"The chief supplied you?"

"Him and the lieutenant, but only to sell. The deal was that if they ever found out I was keeping any product for myself, I was toast."

Relief made me lightheaded. My baby didn't have a druggie for a father. I grabbed the edge of the locker for balance, resting my forehead against the cool metal door.

"Toast? As in dead?" Rick sounded incredulous.

"Who knows? I never pushed it. It was a sweet deal, easy money while it lasted."

Their voices were so close I knew they were almost on me.

"Aren't you afraid one of 'em'll rat you out for a lighter sentence?"

"They know I know too much."

"What do you know?" Rick asked eagerly.

"I know they were selling to the drug ring in the Camden projects. Those are nasty people, let me tell you, and they've got lots of contacts inside the Jersey prison system. It'll be hard enough for the Keatings to stay alive in prison, them being cops and all, but if they name names, they won't have a chance, especially the chief, the old man. And then there's the fact that I could tell the world that I had both twins. Trust me, they don't want the world to know that sordid little fact."

"So you're out of business."

"Let's just say I'm exploring other possibilities."

Rick laughed. "You are the man, Eddie. You are the man!"

"You had both of them?" That was Jim Sarnoff, true to his one-track mind. He thought himself a modern-day Casanova, but he lacked any of the charm and charisma of the legendary ladies' man. He made my stomach curdle with his "accidental" brushing against the girls, his groping hands touching anywhere they could. "Which one was best?"

There was a silence. With my neck prickling, I could feel them right behind me. Even as I told myself not to turn, I was unable to help myself. Rick and Jim had their backs to me, so only Eddie saw me. His eyes locked with mine.

He smirked. "Which one do you think?"

"Tori," Jim said right away. "She's got fire." He wasn't quite drooling, but close.

"Poor little Libby." Rick shook his head. What was so awful was that his pity was genuine. Dumb Rick pitied me!

"Yeah," Eddie agreed, his smirk deepening. "A distant second. *Very* distant."

Even today that spear of agony hurt, which I knew was absolutely ridiculous, but there it was. Fortunately I rarely had occasion to think of that scene. Still, Eddie's deliberate nastiness had always made me extremely leery about letting Chloe know anything about him. What if he turned that ruthless cruelty loose on her?

And here I was living with the one person besides Madge who could bring both Chloe and me great pain. And given last night, apparently she planned to, though I had no idea why. Try as I would, I could see nothing for her to gain by bringing Eddie around.

Though as I thought of the puzzle Eddie'd delivered, maybe I had it backwards. Maybe Eddie had sought Tori out, which was not a comforting thought.

I finally managed to fall asleep around five. I dragged myself out of bed at nine and went down for some tea. When the best thing about the day so far was that Tori appeared to be sleeping in and I didn't have to deal with her, I once again felt like a bogus Christian. I certainly wasn't loving my sister as Scripture said I should.

Chloe came to breakfast full of limitless curiosity.

"Aunt Tori says you guys knew Eddie back in high school." She shook cinnamon and sugar onto her toast.

"We did." I forced myself to take an unhurried sip of tea. What else had Tori told her?

"She said you both dated him."

"We did."

"Mom! He's slimy."

I grinned at her unexpected comment. I was just shallow enough and unspiritual enough to love her insight. "Let's just say it was at a time when I wasn't very perceptive."

"Why'd you break up with him?"

I made a little puff of self-disparagement. "I didn't. He broke up with me."

She looked at me in surprise. "Really?"

I nodded. "For Aunt Tori."

She laughed.

I gave her the eyebrow. "And what's so funny? It broke my heart."

"It's sort of like a TV soap. Over-the-top family drama and deceit. Sister against sister, the eternal triangle, all that stuff."

If she only knew. "Yeah, well, it's almost time to leave for church. Ready?" I had to get her moving before she asked how old I'd been when I went with Eddie and then did some math. I stood and collected our dirty dishes.

"Just gotta brush my teeth." She rushed from the kitchen, only to come rushing back. She leaned in and kissed me on the cheek. "He didn't know quality when he had it." And she raced away again.

I had tears in my eyes as I brushed my own teeth.

The soothing calm of the sanctuary at the historic Tenth Presbyterian Church was balm to my frayed emotions. It was a spiritual adventure to be in the place where the renowned James Montgomery Boice had preached for years before cancer took him prematurely. Even today, several years after his death, his raspy bass could be heard preaching on the local airwaves every Sunday morning.

Oh, Lord, forgive me for resenting Tori so. Help me find where the boundaries should be. And help me tell Chloe.

By the time the final chords of the music died and it was time to go into the world again, I felt much calmer. I turned and came face to face with Jenna and Drew.

"Hey," Drew said.

"What are you doing here?" I demanded.

He just looked at me with a slow, slightly mocking but totally nonoffensive smile. "Going to church?"

I put a hand up, acknowledging what a stupid question I had asked. I decided I'd chalk it up to the sleepless night.

"Bad night?" The man saw way too much.

I shrugged and gave a pathetic little smile. "I'll be fine." Maybe some day a million years from now. Of course, by then I'd be in heaven, and I would be fine. Something to look forward to. I wondered uselessly if you could ask stupid questions in heaven or if I'd be spared that embarrassment—if you even got embarrassed in heaven.

"Guess what?" Jenna bubbled as we went down the front steps to the sidewalk. "We're going to a Phillies game tonight. More fireworks. Want to come? We've got extra tickets."

I glanced at Drew. Did this invitation mean Chloe, or did it mean both of us?

He nodded. "A friend at Penn has season tickets, but he's away this weekend. He gave them to me. We've got four, and we were thinking it was a shame to waste two."

Both of us. How very—nice. Understatement. I couldn't remember the last time I'd gone anywhere with a single man on an almost date, if you can count going somewhere with two thirteen-year-old chaperons even an almost date.

"Oh, I don't know." I tried my best to look uncertain. "Chloe was so tired when she got up this morning. I'm not sure she can manage another late night."

Chloe looked at me, horrified. Jenna looked distressed. Drew grinned. How did he know I was kidding?

"Gotcha!" I pointed a finger at Chloe.

She and Jenna looked at each other and rolled their eyes.

"The game starts at seven thirty," Drew said. "I'll find out the best way to get to the stadium. I don't even know where it is."

"It's down by the river in the sports complex where the old Veterans Stadium was, but I couldn't tell you how to actually get there." We exchanged cell phone numbers as we walked back home.

"Look! McDonald's!" Chloe pointed at the fast-food place sandwiched between two stores. "Chicken McNuggets!"

You'd have thought it was the pot of gold at the end of the rainbow. I realized I didn't have to worry about Aunt Stella's Wedgwood completely turning her head, though someday I would have to take the child to a classier eatery just so she got comfortable smiling at a server and leaving a tip. And eating something besides Chicken McNuggets.

Drew looked equally delighted. "Big Mac with cheese." He pulled the door open, and we all stepped inside. Once we collected our food, we sat at a table for four. I had a momentary fantasy about how much we looked like a real family as Jenna talked about the hunky guys next door back home and Drew did his best not to shudder.

When we left, the girls walked ahead, and I had a chance to thank Drew for his rescue the previous night. "I don't think I've ever had a white knight ride to my rescue before."

"I don't think I've ever been called a white knight before."

"No?"

"Never." He was emphatic. "Usually I'm called dull and pedantic."

I laughed. If ever there was a man who was not dull and pedantic, it was him.

"You shouldn't take your students' comments to heart. They wouldn't know a knight if they saw one."

"Oddly, my students seem to like me. My classes always fill quickly."

I did not find that odd at all. "Jenna calls you pedantic? That's not a word typically used by thirteen-year-olds."

"That's the truth. Nor by many college freshmen. But Jenna's never said that. She and I do pretty well together."

And I understood. The missing wife with the red and green hair. "Ah. Amazing how it hurts, isn't it?"

He gave a tight little smile.

"Even when it's untrue. Even when it was said years ago."

He looked at me, and we acknowledged the shared experience of being run through by those we had loved. We walked the next block in companionable silence.

We made the final turn for home in time to see Tori's limo pull away. Tension that I hadn't even been aware I was carrying left, loosening my shoulder and neck muscles. I sighed mentally. I didn't have to confront her about the puzzle just yet. Instead I had two restful days, including an exciting evening with Drew. And Jenna.

☐☐☐

Drew was smiling as they turned into the lane. Not only had he been blessed by the service and delighted to see Libby—and Chloe—sitting two rows in front of Jenna and him, but the walk home had given Libby and him a chance to talk, really talk. He was still surprised that he'd told her about "dull and pedantic," and it was probably pretty sad that the thing they shared was pain, but having someone understand was such a relief.

And he'd get to spend time with her—them—tonight.

She looked so fresh and pretty in her yellow top and blue and yellow swirly skirt. Her blond hair was pulled back in a ponytail with a yellow flower sitting on it, all jaunty and feminine. Little wisps of hair had worked their way loose to curl around her face and neck, and he kept wondering what those curls felt like. Would they wrap around his finger like Jenna's baby hand had? Would they be silky or coarse or somewhere in between? And what business was it of his?

Still, he couldn't remember the last time he'd felt so at ease with a woman. Usually he felt either guilty or hunted when anyone single spent time with him. The guilty feelings were ridiculous, he knew. His marriage had been dissolved over ten years ago. Ruthie had long ago killed any affection he'd ever had for her. All he felt now was sorrow, pity, and a vague sense that if he'd been more of a man, he could have prevented her from leaving, which he knew wasn't true, but guilt was funny that way.

The hunted feeling came when a woman got that predatory look, one eye on him and the other on *Modern Bride*. Granted, he was as lonely as the next guy, but he wasn't anyone's answer to the husband hunt. Once burned, forever smart, or so he liked to think.

Or as Ben would say, "Experience is a dear teacher, but fools will learn at no other." And he'd learned.

But Libby was different from all the others. Restful. She'd had a hard time of things too, and look at how she'd turned out. Warm, charming, and brave, committed to the Lord.

He opened his mouth to tell Libby that he'd call about the time he would stop for her when he saw someone rise from his front step.

"Where have you been?" The strident voice rang through the lane. "I've been waiting here forever!"

Ruthie had found him. He sighed mentally and tried to dredge up the emotional stamina to deal with her. And Jenna.

His daughter stood frozen. "Mom?" He couldn't tell if she was more upset, surprised, or delighted. She didn't see Ruthie much, and every time she did, it was an adventure into the unknown.

Ruthie rushed at him, ignoring Jenna. She threw herself into his arms and began sobbing. "He's dead, Drew. Mick's dead. He was murdered!"

Drew closed his eyes. All he wanted was an orderly life, a place for everything and everything in its place. Instead he had Ruthie and all her melodrama. Like Mick had really been murdered. He'd probably gotten tired of being called whatever was his equivalent of "dull and pedantic" and taken off. If he was wise, he wasn't coming back.

For want of a better idea, Drew patted Ruthie's back. "I'm sorry, Ruthie."

"Who's Mick?" Chloe whispered to Jenna, who watched her mother with a look of resignation and sorrow that seemed to say, *"Ignored again."*

"Her boyfriend. Number 554."

Chloe blinked. "Oh."

The hurt and bitterness in Jenna's voice broke his heart.

Drew looked at Libby over Ruthie's head and was surprised by the sympathy he saw there. He'd expected distaste at the very least. Ruthie looked like a wild woman. Her bleached hair hung over her shoulders like straw. There were dark circles under her eyes, and her too-tanned skin was lined from hard drinking and smoking as well as the elements. She was much too thin, her cami drooping on her, her legs mere twigs hanging out of her shorts.

"Don't worry about tonight," Libby said. "Take care of her. She needs you."

He glanced from lovely, kind Libby to Ruthie who couldn't even say hello to her own daughter. "No."

Libby looked confused.

"I mean, no, don't forget about tonight. We have a date."

Ruthie had gone still and wasn't wailing to the skies anymore. She pulled back and stared over her shoulder at Libby, her expression hard. "What are you doing here?"

"She's Dad's girlfriend," Jenna blurted. "They're getting married next month."

"Jenna!" Drew was horrified.

"I know it's supposed to be a secret and all," Jenna continued, her eyes full of tears. "But I had to tell."

Chloe saw the panicked look on Jenna's face. "Yeah, and we're going to be bridesmaids. We've got these great dresses."

"Pink," said Jenna.

"Blue," said Chloe.

They looked at each other, then scrambled to clarify their lie.

"Mine's like a rose pink," Jenna said. "And hers—"

"Yeah, hers is rose pink, and mine's royal blue. They let us pick our favorite colors."

Drew knew that Jenna's lie grew out of a world of hurt caused by Ruthie's indifference. He couldn't jump on the girl in front of everyone. *But what do I do, Lord?*

He dared a glance at Libby, who stood frozen, blue eyes wide. Then she gave a slight shake and stepped forward with her hand extended to Ruthie.

"I'm Libby Keating. I'm so sorry for your loss, Ruth."

For a minute Ruthie seemed confused. "Libby?" Then her face collapsed and two tears rolled down her cheeks. "Mick!" She did look bereaved, and Drew, idiot that he was, felt bad for her.

"Why don't you take her home, Drew?" Libby stepped close and laid her hand on his arm. "Let her lie down."

He nodded. What else could he do?

Libby moved to Jenna, who looked shocky. She probably couldn't believe what she'd said. Drew's heart broke for her. Ruthie still hadn't said a word, not even hello, to her.

Libby put her arm around Jenna's shoulders. "Why don't you come home with us, honey? Let your mom rest. Then maybe you can talk with her."

Jenna nodded gratefully, and Drew thought he'd never be able to repay the debt of kindness Libby had just given his child.

"Go on, girls." Libby shooed Jenna and Chloe toward her house. They took off running. Then she turned back to Drew. "I'll see you this evening, sweetheart." She said the last with a smirk and a smile, though how she actually managed both at the same time was a mystery.

He grinned at her. "Right, love." And arm about Ruthie's waist, he led his ex away. When they reached the house, he took her to the spare room so she could rest.

No way was he letting her near his bedroom ever again.

□□□

I found Chloe and Jenna in Chloe's room, huddled on the bed, Princess sitting beside them with a worried expression on her face. Jenna had been crying, and Chloe had an arm around her shoulder. Both faces reflected fear, uncertainty, and defiance. The only things missing were a Solidarity poster and raised fists.

I leaned against the doorjamb, wondering where to begin, wishing I had just a bit of Solomon's legendary wisdom. Ruthie was a much bigger issue than the spontaneous lie about Drew and me.

"You doing okay, Jenna?" I asked.

In answer, her face crumbled and she began sobbing.

Princess whined, unhappy at the loud weeping.

"Mom!" Chloe glared at me. "Sheesh!"

Okay, stupid question. I walked to the bed, sat on the edge, and put a hand on Jenna's heaving shoulder. Princess immediately climbed onto my lap, leaning against me for comfort, her eyes on Jenna.

"I'm so sorry you were hurt, Jenna honey." I bit back the automatic *"But I'm sure it'll be all right"* that seemed a natural follow-up to the *"I'm sorry."* It wouldn't be all right. I thought of a pastor friend who'd said that he disapproved of divorce not just for scriptural reasons but because of the sociological upheavals resulting from split families.

"And it's always the kids who suffer most," he'd said.

Proof of his assertion drooped with misery on Chloe's bed.

I opened my mouth to say some inane thing like, "Well, we love you, Jenna," when she burst out, "I hate her!" The vehemence of her declaration was undercut considerably by the pain in her wobbly voice and the tears streaming down her face.

"Shh, honey. That's your hurt feelings talking. You don't hate her."

Chloe rolled her eyes. Stupid parent comment number two.

Jenna sniffed and wiped at her tears. "I wish I did. It'd be easier." And fresh moisture slid down her cheeks.

This was exactly the kind of pain I was trying to save Chloe by not telling her about Eddie. He would hurt her like this, I knew it, maybe even worse, with his indifference and false charm and sharp tongue.

I sighed and ran a hand over the quaking Princess. "I know about moms who aren't there for you, Jenna. And I know it hurts like nothing else."

Jenna looked at me skeptically.

"She knows what she's talking about," Chloe said. "Mom-Mom and Great-Nan—that's my great-grandmother—are very self-absorbed."

That was a nice way of putting it.

"They love me," she continued, "but they sort of ignore Mom."

Jenna frowned. "But moms are supposed to love you."

"They are," I agreed. "But some never seem to get that message."

We were silent for a minute, thinking about that sad fact. Princess climbed off my lap and made her way to Jenna, putting a small paw on her leg in an offer of sympathy. Jenna pulled the dog in for a hug, burying her face in the fluffy topknot, knocking the pink bow more askew.

"Well, at least you know who your mother is," Chloe said. "I have no idea who my father is."

Though I knew her comment wasn't aimed at me but intended as a comfort to Jenna, I felt as if I'd been punched in the chest.

"I mean, I could meet him and never even realize it. Now that's megaweird."

Jenna looked at Chloe with something like pity. "That is weird."

"Yeah," Chloe said. "So you're a step ahead. You know."

"A lot of good it does me." Jenna sounded bitter. "What kind of a mom doesn't even say hello when her kid is standing right next to her?"

I pushed Jenna's hair back from her damp face. "A very blind mom not to realize what a wonderful, beautiful, intelligent young woman you are."

Chloe gave me a small smile, and I realized I had finally said the right thing. *Thank You, Lord!*

I leaned over and kissed first Chloe on the cheek, then Jenna. I stood, thinking I'd better leave on a high note.

"Chlo, take Jenna to the bathroom so she can wash her face. Then come on down and we'll have some chocolate marshmallow ice cream in the backyard."

We could talk at a later time about my impending marriage to a man I'd met three days ago.

12

□□□

THE GIRLS CAME DOWNSTAIRS late in the afternoon. I was checking things on eBay, pleased that the pair of buyers who wanted the sunglasses were still duking it out, especially since I had another twenty-five pairs I would post in a couple of weeks. I had to wonder, though, why anyone besides a seller like me wanted twenty-five pairs of cat's-eye sunglasses. Maybe these people were sellers too with stores where they would sell the glasses one pair at a time for a nice profit.

I was vaguely aware of the girls pulling Oreos from the cupboard and sweetened iced tea from the fridge. I exited eBay. "Pour me a glass, will you, Chloe?"

The glass she handed me was blown so thin it was a wonder it didn't break when I held it, dumping tea all over me and the floor.

Chloe pulled at least a half dozen Oreos from the pack. She held them out to Jenna, who took only two. Nice to see a non-grabby kid. Jenna's eyes were still puffy, but she looked more under control than she had a couple of hours ago. The cookies ought to give her a good jolt of sugar, making her feel even better.

"Jenna's going to spend the night with me, Mom. Okay?" Chloe twisted the top off the sandwich cookie and began licking the filling.

I wasn't surprised that Jenna didn't want to go home, what with Ruthie in residence, but I had no idea how Drew felt about her continuing absence.

"If her father says it's okay." I smiled at Jenna, then stiffened. Pinned to her knit top over her right shoulder was a stylized dog with diamond chips for its tail and marquise-cut sapphires for its eyes.

"Jenna! Where did you get that pin?"

I must have barked because she jumped and put her hand over it. She looked at me uncertainly. "Chloe gave it to me."

"Chloe?" By now I was on my feet, hands on hips. I was appalled that the girls had gone into my room and picked through the shoebox of jewelry.

Chloe looked at me, clearly not understanding my anger. "Easy, Mom. Aunt Tori gave it to me."

It was like a slap across the face. "Aunt Tori?"

Chloe nodded. "Did you know she keeps her jewelry in a shoebox? I mean, how weird is that?"

I raced up the stairs and into my bedroom, Princess hard on my heels, barking in excitement since running through the house was not my normal style. I'd left the precious box on my bureau, but it was no longer there. I thought back to when I'd changed into cropped pants after church, but I couldn't remember whether the box had been here or not.

I ran to Tori's room, aware of Chloe and Jenna watching me from the top of the stairs with uncertain expressions. There on my sister's unmade bed sat my box, its many little boxes strewn about the bed linens.

Anger bubbled up. How could she! And what did she take besides the dog pin?

I stalked to the bed and began opening each box, lifting the little pieces of cotton batting protecting the pins and brooches. Princess jumped up and studied each box with me, ears pricked. There were two empty boxes. The dog Jenna was wearing belonged in one. I thought through the inventory and realized Tori'd taken the pin with the large diamond in the center and two circles of chips surrounding it. Thirty-two hundred dollars, give or take a few bucks.

My twin sister had stolen from me.

I sank onto the bed, feeling betrayed once again and surprised at how much it hurt. You'd think I'd have grown armor plating after so many years and so many offenses. So what if she thought the pin was costume jewelry and didn't realize its value? This wasn't like a teenage girl taking her sister's favorite sweater. This was one adult purposely going into another adult's room and searching for something to filch. I glanced around this room at all Tori's wonderful, expensive things, knowing these were only the things she had here. What wonders were still back at her suite at the SeaSide? Why take from me when she had all this and more?

"What's the matter, Mom?" Chloe asked from the doorway. She and Jenna were staring at me, unsure what was wrong but knowing I was truly upset.

I took a deep breath, trying to think how to explain without making Tori sound as wicked as she was. Princess lay pressed against my leg, looking at me with concerned eyes. I petted her absently, glad for her comfort.

"This jewelry is mine, not Tori's."

"Yours?" Chloe walked into the room, Jenna on her tail. "How come I never saw it before?"

"Because I got it yesterday at the estate sale."

As I spoke, Jenna reached up and took off the little dog. She held it out to me. "We didn't know."

I managed a small smile for her. "I know. I'm not upset at you, either of you." Of course I'd be happy to strangle Tori. "I'd let you keep the little thing except it's got a value of about three thousand dollars."

Both girls blinked and stared at the dog in astonishment.

"Those are marquise-cut sapphires," I explained. "And those are real diamonds."

"Really?" Chloe was fascinated now that she knew I wasn't upset with her or Jenna. "Can we see the rest of the stuff?"

We spent an absorbing hour studying the jewelry and trying to come up with the best descriptions of the pieces for when Madge and I sold them with Sam Pierce's help. One positive thing Tori's theft accomplished was taking Jenna's mind off Ruthie for a while. When Drew came for us, she was pretty nearly her usual, perky self.

We arrived at Citizens Bank Park and found our way to our seats about midway up the stands. Chloe's reaction to being at the Phillies game was the same one I'd had the first time I attended a game.

"They're so small!" She pointed to the little men out on the field. Courtesy of games on television, she was used to the men looking large as they filled the screen. She was also used to the cameras following the ball. When the first batter hit a long fly and it disappeared against the backdrop of people sitting opposite us, she jumped to her feet. "Where did it go?"

She and Jenna became bored halfway through the third inning. Drew bought us all hot dogs and sodas, and both girls seemed content for another inning. Drew, in the meantime, proved to be an ardent, knowledgeable, and very noisy fan. He encouraged the players on both teams by name, applauded for all the good plays, but saved his really raucous cheers for the Phillies.

When he jumped to his feet to call his appreciation for a double play, Jenna whispered to Chloe, "He is so embarrassing." Now I understood why the girl had made certain she was the first into our row of seats with Chloe following, then me, then Drew.

"Is it just baseball he's so nuts about?" I asked. After all, a "fiancée" should know things like this about her man, right?

"Any sport, but especially baseball and football. He yells at the TV all during Eagles games. 'You should have caught that, you idiot!' 'Throw the ball! Throw the ball!' 'Your running game is in the toilet!' 'I could have made a better play call! Ben could have made a better play call!' That's his real insult, calling up a man who lived before football was even invented."

Drew leaned across me to eye Jenna. "Mocking your old man isn't very nice. Remember, he holds the family purse."

Jenna grinned at him. "Like I'm worried."

He grinned back.

We made it to the fifth inning with the Phillies ahead by three before Chloe announced, "I have to go to the bathroom. Come on, Jenna." She stood and held out a hand to me. "Can I have ten bucks?"

"It costs ten bucks to use the ladies room?" I reached for my purse. "Wow. Maybe you'd better wait until we get home." I slapped a ten into her hand.

"Me too." Jenna held out her hand to Drew, who filled it.

"Stay together," I admonished as they clambered over me.

"And don't talk to any strange people of the male persuasion," Drew growled. "In fact, don't talk to anybody."

They paused at the end of the row just long enough to shoot us that my-parent-the-dork eye roll. Then they were off, giggling as they went.

Drew watched them go, missing a terrific catch by the right fielder, who jumped way up the wall and prevented a double, maybe even a triple.

"Sometimes being a single parent is absolutely terrifying." He tore his eyes from the girls and turned back to the game.

I forgot the game as I looked at him. "It terrifies me every single day. Every moment."

He nodded and gave a halfhearted clap for the runner stealing second. "I start to think maybe we're doing okay, she and I. We'll make it through to her adulthood after all. Then something happens and boom! I say she can't go someplace or with some boy she likes and it's like she becomes someone else."

I smiled in sympathy. "Been there, lived that."

"The worst is when Ruthie calls or, disaster of all disasters, shows up. That really sends Jenna into a tailspin. As if she wasn't volatile enough being thirteen."

"You've got Ruthie. I've got Eddie."

I waited for him to tell me I had to tell Chloe about Eddie, but he surprised me.

"I wonder if it isn't easier for Chloe, not knowing, than it is for Jenna with Ruthie. Being ignorant versus being ignored."

"Yeah, Chloe and I were talking about that just the other night." And about having a father and grandfather in jail, but I didn't think now was the time to pass on that bit of information. I sighed. "I don't want to tell her."

He shot me a look. " 'Three can keep a secret if two are dead.' "

"I take it that piece of wisdom is from Ben?"

He grinned sheepishly. "It just pops out. Will he be around more?"

"Eddie? I hope not!" I was appalled at the very thought.

"Okay." He seemed to relax, though why he'd be tense I didn't know. "I thought maybe that was why she needed to know."

I shook my head. "It's that not knowing eats at her. When she was little, I could dodge the questions, but it's becoming harder and harder. I'm afraid she'll start resenting me and creating wonderful fantasies around him. Madge—that's my best friend and business partner—keeps telling me I have to tell her."

Drew waved at a vendor for a container of terrible ballpark popcorn. Somehow hot dogs tasted wonderful at a ball game, but the popcorn was just plain lousy, all soggy and flat. He offered me some, and I declined. He took a large handful and chewed with obvious enjoyment. "Can't Chloe just check her birth certificate for her father's name?"

"She's threatened that. I'll tell you the same thing I told her. When he left us without one scintilla of concern for our future, when he took up with my twin sister, I decided I would not name him. He didn't deserve to be listed as her parent. I might have been scared to death about the future, but he wasn't having any part of her. Ever."

We fell silent as the organ blasted "Take Me Out to the Ball Game" for the seventh-inning stretch. Then I turned to him. If we could talk about my embarrassing past, we could talk about his.

"What was Ruthie like when you first met her?" I knew she had to be different than she was now. Drew wouldn't be attracted to the crass, wild woman I'd met earlier.

He grinned. "Curious about me, huh?"

Yes, very, but I sure wasn't going to say so. "Curious about Ruthie."

He eyed me for a minute, then got that faraway look that means you're seeing into the past. "She was very pretty in a wholesome, innocent way."

Huh. *Wholesome* and *innocent* and Ruthie certainly didn't go together now. But then I'd guessed she was different, so why was I surprised?

"I was a new Christian, and she seemed the epitome of all that the Christian life stood for. She was going to Bible school and came from this wonderful family. I *loved* her family. Still do."

He fell silent and I thought for a moment that he wouldn't say any more, and I knew I couldn't ask anything more, at least not now.

"I still don't understand it all." He had genuine pain in his eyes. "I know some of it's my fault, but I know it's not all my fault. I spent long hours in the library when I was in graduate school, and Ruthie resented being alone. I should have been smart enough to pick up on that, but it never occurred to me. My father traveled a lot on business, and my mother seemed to have no trouble being alone. And she could be alone for a week at a time. I at least came home every night, though it might be ten o'clock or midnight."

"Not everyone can handle being alone." I thought of my mother and Nan. "Didn't she tell you how much it bothered her?"

"She finally did, and I invited her to spend the evenings in the library with me." He gave a rueful smile. "I thought I was being husbandly, but I learned that not everyone likes spending hours in libraries."

"And it's one of your favorite things, right? It's like that with me and estate sales and garage sales. I love them!"

He looked at me and shuddered. "People's trash."

"One man's trash is another's treasure." I told him about the sunglasses.

"People are actually in a bidding war over sunglasses no one wears anymore?"

"Wonderful, isn't it?"

He took a moment to boo when one of the home team struck out. Philadelphia fans are the world's greatest booers and very proud of their reputation.

"Our living room rug at home is one I picked up in front of someone's house on bulk trash day."

"You're kidding, right?"

"I had it cleaned, and it's lovely."

"At least a library—"

I don't know what he planned to say, but I cut in with "—is full of old books. Used books. It's one huge used-book warehouse." I grinned at his nonplussed look, then steered the conversation back to Ruthie. "It seems to me that when Ruthie married a historian, surely she understood that libraries go with the territory, just like trash picking goes with me."

"You'd think. But that wasn't the real problem, just something she could articulate. Ruthie's bipolar, and that was the major confounding issue."

Uh-oh. Hard, hard issue coming up here, almost as hard on the families as it is on the one who suffers.

"When she was still under her parents' roof, they were very good about making certain she took her meds, and as long as she did, she was fine. Also the illness hadn't gripped her as it did in her twenties.

"I knew she had to take stuff every day, but I assumed that, like most people, she disciplined herself to take it. Her father warned me, but I didn't understand the sufferer's tendency to think it wasn't needed, the penchant for stopping regardless of all the advice from doctors and counselors. I'd never been around someone who needed supervision like that."

"You can't make an adult take medicine if she decides not to. Her failure wasn't your fault, Drew."

He leaned forward, his arms resting on his knees, his hands dangling. It was amazing how alone we seemed in the middle of thousands of screaming people.

"It was and it wasn't," he said. "Through the years I've stopped blaming myself for everything like I used to. I've learned that Jesus is the great Guilt Bearer, and I've given my marriage failures to Him. And I know that Ruthie must accept blame too—not that she does. She's very intelligent. She knew she was vulnerable. She knew health was in that little bottle. She knew she shouldn't listen to her compulsions but to her caregivers."

"But it only takes a couple of days listening to your feelings and not taking your meds, and your mind is confused too."

He nodded bleakly. "The daunting thing is that bipolar issues are permanent. It's not like she's going to be cured."

"But bipolar people can learn to live productive lives."

"They can, but it takes all the discipline of being a recovering alcoholic and then some."

We were silent for several minutes during which he halfheartedly cheered. I watched his sad face and felt guilty.

"I'm sorry. I've ruined your game."

He gave a sad smile. "Believe it or not, it's good to talk about this, especially with Ruthie back at the house. Gives me perspective when I get confused."

Lord, I could use some perspective on Eddie.

"When we were first married and she was feeling good, she'd wait up for me and make these absolutely wonderful dinners at midnight." He obviously wanted me to understand. "I felt like the luckiest man alive. Then the depressions would hit, and she started drinking to deal with them, to dull the pain. I still struggle with why she would self-medicate with alcohol instead of her prescription. But that's logic speaking, and for her, logic is the least of her considerations."

I thought of how depressed I'd been when Dad and Pop went to jail and how logic had had nothing to do with my turning to Eddie for relief and comfort.

"Drew." I leaned toward him. "If it's going to be too distressing for you to have Ruthie at your place, she can stay with me tonight. Tori's room's available."

He looked at me, and I was struck by how handsome he was with his strong jaw, dark brow, and wonderful brown eyes the color of Princess's adored Kisses. Then there was his strength of character, accepting his responsibility for the demise of his marriage and for poor Ruthie even now, and I wished much too fiercely that I really were his fiancée.

Suddenly he smiled, a devastating smile that made my heart leap. "Thank you."

"For what?"

He sat back and slid an arm across the back of my seat. "I can't remember the last time anyone was concerned about me."

I sat back and made believe that his arm was really around me.

Chloe studied her new best friend's sad face. Jenna had done well through the ball game and all the way home. Chloe suspected it was because she didn't want her dad to feel any worse than he already did. But now in the dark privacy of Chloe's bedroom, her real heart poured out.

"It's so embarrassing." Jenna pushed at her pillow until she was comfortable. "And scary."

And painful, Chloe thought, though Jenna didn't say that. "I get embarrassing, but why scary? Do you think she'll hurt you?"

"What if I turn out the same way?" There was a little sob in Jenna's voice, a catch that swallowed some of her words. "What if I grow up to be like my mother?"

"Why would you?" No one would choose to be like that.

"It's an illness. You can't prevent all illnesses. And there's no vaccine."

"True, but that doesn't mean you'll get it either."

"I sure have a better chance than you."

Chloe shuddered at the idea that sweet Jenna could end up like Ruthie. "It's genetic?"

Jenna nodded. "My dad doesn't know it, but I've researched bipolar disorder online. If you've got a parent with the disease, you've got a twenty-five percent chance of getting it."

Yikes. "But that means a seventy-five percent chance of not."

Jenna gave a little smile. Chloe heard it when her friend spoke. "That's true."

Chloe thought for a moment. "It's sort of like my mom being a glass-half-empty kind of person if she's not careful. Part of it's because she was born that way. Part of it's because of my grandmother. She'd make anyone turn half empty."

"Your Aunt Tori doesn't seem half empty."

Chloe nodded. "Because she doesn't have the born-that-way part, she doesn't pay attention to Mom-Mom's depressing take on life. She's too selfish. If she doesn't like something, she ignores it. Mom takes it to heart and blames herself."

"She didn't seem selfish when she bought you the computer."

Chloe heard the slight reprimand, but it didn't faze her. She knew what she was talking about. "Believe me, she's got a reason for that too. I know she does. She has a reason for everything. I just haven't figured it out yet."

"Maybe she's trying to buy your love. I've got a friend whose father hardly ever sees her. He lives with his second family in Texas, and he always buys her lots of stuff when he does see her. He's trying to buy her affection."

Chloe thought about the laptop and the hair stuff. Jenna might be right. "What Aunt Tori doesn't understand is that both Mom and I already love her just because she's Aunt Tori."

"That's like my mom. She doesn't understand that I want to love her just because she's my mom. I know she's sick and can't help lots of what she does, but I still want to love her." Jenna's sigh was deep and hurt Chloe's stomach. "She just won't let me."

When Tori left the SeaSide at 3 a.m., she was exhausted. These long holiday weekends were murder! And there was still tomorrow to get through. With any luck, it wouldn't be a repeat of today. Well, it couldn't be. Miles Denbigh was on his way home to the little lady who was in for the shock of her comfy, pampered life.

Miles loved gambling, and he'd been coming to the SeaSide for

years. As the owner of a huge construction company with projects
and housing developments in thirty of the fifty states, he had ample
resources to gamble. He was one of her favorite customers—usually.

She'd arranged for the SeaSide jet to pick him up in Hartford,
Connecticut, on Friday evening for the long Fourth weekend, gratis
of course. Why he insisted on coming to Atlantic City when he had
Foxwoods, one of the biggest casinos in the country, in his backyard,
Tori never figured out. But she and her bosses were happy enough to
help him drop a nice portion of his considerable fortune here.

When he arrived Friday, she saw him to his suite and comped
all his meals. The bar in the living room of the suite was stocked
with all his favorite beverages, and the refrigerator was full of hors
d'oeuvres. While the bellman took his bag into the bedroom and
Miles threw his jacket over a chair, Tori prepared his Manhattan with
a thin slice of orange.

He took the glass and sipped. "Perfect! You're amazing."

She smiled her thanks, thinking about the notebooks she had
full of the preferences of the SeaSide's major clients. "Do you want
to decompress here alone, or do you want me to arrange dinner for
you? The Boardwalk Lounge has a great new singer."

"Eat with me?"

"I'd love to." And she didn't mind eating with Miles. He was a
nice man who still believed in being faithful to his wife, who rarely
came with him; she didn't like the shore because the ocean breezes
made her hair frizz. At least with Miles there were no groping hands
to discourage without angering the client. At ten she left him at the
blackjack table, excited as a kid on Christmas morning.

"Tori." He caught her arm. He pressed a bill into her hand.
Before she could say thanks, his attention was back at the game.

When she'd left to return to Philadelphia on the Fourth around ten in the morning, he'd just come down to the lobby, all bonhomie and brio, ready for breakfast and a day of gaming.

When she came back to Atlantic City yesterday, Sunday, he'd had a disastrous night, betting big and losing big. When she approached him about six to make dinner plans, he was dug in, determined to recoup his losses.

She took his arm. "Come on, Miles. I need a drink and a dashing man to share it with."

Not that he looked dashing anymore. He looked desperate. She frowned, all too aware that determined gamblers often mortgaged their homes and businesses to the hilt for the cash they needed for big stakes play. She'd never thought Miles such a player before, but looking at his desperate face, she recognized that very real possibility.

Tori took Miles's arm and gently pulled.

But Miles refused to move. He continued to bet huge sums, his pile of chips and markers disappearing at an alarming rate. He was driven by the fever, and Tori understood. She'd experienced it herself. *My next roll—or card or turn of the wheel—will win it all back for me.*

But nothing won it back for him. It was 10 p.m. when Carl drove Tori and Miles to the Greyhound depot where she bought Miles a ticket for Hartford via Philadelphia and New York.

"It's gone," he kept saying. "It's all gone. How will I ever pay Robert back?"

Tori tensed. "Robert who?"

"Robert Big Eagle."

Tori shook her head. Robert Big Eagle was a shark of the lowest sort. He was also brutal in demanding his money. Of course his real name was no more Big Eagle than Tori's was. It just made him sound like one of the Indian tribe that owned Foxwoods.

"Have you been going to Foxwoods as much as you've been coming to the SeaSide?"

Miles nodded.

"Betting as heavily there?"

He nodded again.

Idiot. But she didn't say it.

As she walked down the darkened boardwalk to Luke's, she thought it would be nice if she called Miles's wife to meet him tomorrow when the bus rolled in. After all, they had much to discuss now that he'd gambled away not only his business and his portfolio but his house and his kids' education fund. And he had Robert Big Eagle to contend with too.

Tori yawned as she climbed to the third floor and Luke's sumptuous apartment. She pushed her hair back over her shoulder and winced as a lock caught on the brooch she'd borrowed from Libby. Who would have thought Libby'd have such great jewelry? When she started exploring her sister's room, it was strictly for entertainment value, a chance to laugh at how cheap her clothes were, how hopelessly old-fashioned she was.

And then she'd found the shoebox.

She brushed her fingers over the pretty pin. The gold setting was fourteen karat, the *14k* stamped on the back. Maybe there was some value to the stones too. She'd give the thing to Luke as her next payment. She'd given him other jewelry—necklaces, pins, earrings that she'd acquired from clients in the past.

Tonight old Mr. Krasnicki had given her a very nice tip for introducing him to the fifth dancer from the right in the revue in the Pink

Shell Lounge. And there was the tip Miles had given her the other night. Luke didn't need to know about these bits of change. She would keep them for her Chloe campaign.

She was in a very good mood when she fell into bed beside Luke.

13
□□□

THE DOORBELL PLAYED the "Westminster Chimes" at nine o'clock Monday morning. As I walked to the door, I thought how nice it would be if that lovely sound wakened the girls instead of my having to do it. While Jenna might be polite when I made them get up so we could go to Sam Pierce's, Chloe would have no such inhibitions. Morning was most definitely not her strong time.

I looked through the peephole in the front door and saw Drew standing on the stoop. I pulled the door open with a smile.

"Good morning." I waved him inside. "How about a cup of coffee?"

"Sounds good." He followed me into the kitchen. He glanced around. "Nice. You should see the one we've got. Very fifties, and not in the retro sense. It's just old. The rest of the place is great, but the kitchen—bad. I figure they never ate in."

I surveyed Aunt Stella's compact and wonderful kitchen. "It is pretty great, isn't it?"

Drew took a chair at the kitchen table as I pulled the coffee maker forward on the counter.

"I came to check on Jenna. How's she doing this morning?"

"I haven't seen either girl yet today. I was about to go wake them when you arrived." I measured the coffee, filled the well with water, and turned on the machine. "Toast?"

Before he could answer, Chloe and Jenna stumbled into the kitchen. They wore shorts, knit tops, and sleepy faces.

Drew stood immediately and pulled Jenna into a hug. "How are you doing, sweetheart?"

She shrugged. "Okay, I guess. Is she still here?"

Drew nodded. "I can't just kick her out on the street."

Jenna made a face, though she didn't contradict him. "I'll come home when she leaves."

Drew looked so sad my heart broke for him. "Jenna, it's your house, not Ruthie's."

"Yeah, well, try and tell her that."

"Can't you just make her leave, Mr. Canfield?" Chloe asked. "I mean, you're not married anymore or anything."

I caught my daughter's eye and shook my head. This situation was one Drew and Jenna and Ruthie had to resolve, not Chloe or me.

Drew, bless him, didn't seem to take Chloe's comment as butting in. "I will tell her to go, but someone she cared for was just killed. Right now she's in mourning."

Jenna snorted. "Until the next guy comes along."

Drew winced. "Jenna, she's still your mother, even if she is difficult."

"Difficult doesn't begin to cover it, Dad."

Jenna tried to act like she didn't care, but her hurt and yearning were stamped on her face. I knew how Mom's indifference had hurt me through the years, but I couldn't begin to imagine Jenna's hurt.

"She doesn't like me." The girl's voice broke. "And I don't much like her." The last was said with defiance.

It was time to redirect the conversation. It was clearly going nowhere good, and Drew wouldn't want to air his family problems in front of us. "Sit down, girls, and tell me what you want for breakfast." I was Mary Poppins, all good cheer and a spoonful of sugar.

"Toast or English muffins," Jenna said. "And orange juice if you have any."

"Me too." Chloe looked through the sliding door. "Can we eat outside?"

"Sure. Why not?" I poured the coffee into two mugs for Drew and me. When the toast popped, I buttered it. Chloe opened the slider, and we all followed Princess into the backyard, where we took seats around the table on the patio. Princess raced to the back of the yard for her daily bath in the koi pool. When she started to scrabble out, I sent a disgruntled Chloe to save the edges of the pond.

"One of these days she's going to step on one of those fish," she grumbled as she resumed her seat. "And you're going to lose all your inheritance."

"I don't think the kois' lives are a condition of the will." I put my empty coffee mug on the table and wished all I had to do today was sit here and enjoy the lovely garden. "I have to take that jewelry to Pierce's today. Do you girls want to come with me? Chloe, you can show Jenna where you live."

Chloe lost a bit of her morning grouch. "Want to come, Jenna?"

"Sure."

"We'll leave as soon as you're finished eating." I turned to Drew. "Is it all right if Jenna comes with us today?"

Jenna turned to her father. "Please, Dad."

He nodded. "Sure. I don't see any reason why not."

"All right!" Chloe abandoned her dirty dishes and raced up to her aerie, Jenna on her heels.

Drew watched them go. "Thanks, Libby. She needs something to distract her until I can figure out what to do with Ruthie."

Ruthie. "Look, I know it's none of my business, but can't you say something to her about the way she treats Jenna? She's breaking the kid's heart."

"Don't you think I have?" He put his hand to his forehead and rubbed like a massive headache was brewing and it wasn't something that aspirin or ibuprofen would touch. He sighed. "She's a master at ignoring what she doesn't want to hear, and I don't feel right just putting her things on the front step and locking the door."

"She was your wife. You feel responsible for her, for caring for her." I couldn't help wondering if, even after all the trouble she'd been, he still loved her. The thought made me sad.

"I feel lots of things for Ruthie, and I guess responsible is one of them. So is anger. And distress and sorrow and frustration. I even feel this weird sort of love, like you would for someone way less fortunate. The woman is, after all, ill." He was silent for a moment. "Sometimes I even feel hate."

I stared at Drew, shocked. Not that his emotions surprised me; they seemed what anyone facing such a hard and unsolvable situation would feel. It was the fact that he actually spoke his feelings out loud that amazed me. So very un-guylike, at least in my limited experience.

He shook his head as if surprised himself. "I'm sorry. I never say things like that."

"Well, it was probably good for you, and as your fiancée for a day, the least I can do is listen."

He gave a quick smile in recognition of my attempt to lighten the mood, but he wasn't finished unburdening himself yet.

"She actually asked me to move Jenna's things out of that wonderful third-floor room so she could have it, like she was planning to move in long term. I lost my temper on that one. 'Are you nuts? You don't live here. She does!'" He ran a hand through his hair. "She just looked at me and cried, then went back into the little bedroom on the second floor and shut the door."

"She's trying to make you feel guilty."

"She's succeeding. And I was planning on working at home today." He shuddered.

Poor guy. Talk about a rock and a hard place. "Want to come to New Jersey with Chloe and Jenna and me?" I knew it wasn't much, but it was all I had to offer.

His face lit up like a kid given a new Webkinz. "Can I? You have no idea what a reprieve that would be."

I rinsed the dishes and stacked them in the dishwasher. The girls clamored downstairs, Chloe with the shoebox under her arm.

"Dad, you should see the beautiful pins and stuff in this box." Jenna pulled the lid off the box and picked out the little box with the dog in it. "I got to wear this one." She held it out for Drew to see. "It's worth three thousand dollars."

Drew looked skeptical.

"Tell him, Ms. Keating," Jenna said.

"It is and she did," I confirmed as the girls showed him more of the jewelry. "I got the pieces at an estate sale Saturday morning. Surprisingly valuable stuff. We're taking it to the jeweler Madge and I use, and he's going to keep it in his safe for us until we sell it."

It was a good thing Drew was impressed with the jewelry, because my van had the opposite effect. He took one look and said, "Uh, why don't I drive?" He pointed to a nifty red Honda CR-V.

I was content to let him drive. Maneuvering in the city made me nervous. Everyone but me seemed to know where they were going, and they believed in getting there as quickly as they could by squeezing through spaces barely big enough for a baby stroller. And there were the issues of one-way streets and signs too small to read until you were on top of them and then it was too late to get in the appropriate lane or make the correct turn. I followed him happily to his car.

"Let me pay for the gas and bridge tolls," I said.

"Forget it. You're saving me from a day of agony." He pushed the unlock button on the car key, and the doors clicked and the lights flashed. The girls climbed in the backseat, and I took the passenger seat.

Drew had just thrown the car into reverse when there was a loud thump against the side of the car, followed by several more. My first thought was that we'd hit something, but we hadn't moved. Then Ruthie's angry face appeared beside Drew.

"You knew!" she screamed at him. "You knew! And you didn't say a thing!"

Drew lowered the window. "Ruthie, what's wrong?"

"You knew! You were there!"

"Where?"

Then she saw me. "And you!" She pointed at me.

I drew back against the passenger door. "Me what?"

"He was killed at your house! I bet you're the one who killed him!" She was so distressed she could hardly get the words out.

Drew put it together before I did. "The man on Libby's doorstep was Mick?"

"What?" I squeaked. This was taking coincidence too far.

"And now I know why you seem so familiar." Ruthie's look was full of venom. "You hang around with Mick's guy, Luke, in Atlantic City." She turned to Drew. "Did you know that your good little Christian fiancée works for a casino and has a boyfriend on the side?" Spite curdled the words.

"Not Libby," Drew said with amazing calm. "That's her sister, Tori."

"Right." Clearly Ruthie didn't believe him. "What is she, an identical twin or something?"

"She is."

His quiet, steady answer merely slowed Ruthie, and only for a couple of seconds. In that tiny break, I glanced into the backseat. Chloe and Jenna sat transfixed, staring at Ruthie. Jenna had tears coursing down her cheeks.

"Well, twin or not, she's probably a murderer!"

I sputtered in angry disbelief. It was bad enough being the daughter of a crooked cop. I wasn't going to be called a murderer too. "I had nothing to do with his death! I just found him. And I never saw him before in my life."

Ruthie grabbed the car door with both hands and leaned in, forcing Drew to pull back. "That's what you say," she spit out. "But I bet the cops know better."

Drew put a hand over Ruthie's. "Stop it." Again his voice was steady and calm. "You mustn't make unfounded accusations like that."

She pulled away from him like he'd burned her. "I should have known you'd side with her. No one ever sides with me." Just like that the anger was gone and she began to weep.

By now Jenna was sobbing, her hand over her mouth, as if she was trying to hold the pain in. Chloe had her arm around Jenna's shaking shoulders.

"We have to go, Ruthie." Drew reached into his pocket and pulled out his house key. He handed it to her. "Go back to the house and sleep. You'll feel better if you do. We'll talk more when I get back."

Hot fury replaced the tears. "That's right! Run away! You're a coward! And make her get rid of that blond streak. It looks stupid."

Without a word Drew raised the window. Ruthie held on until the last second when it was let go or get her fingers pinched. Fixing his eyes on the rearview mirror, Drew backed out of his parking space. His lips were pressed together, and the nerve in his jaw was jumping.

My heart wept for him. He had had to deal with Ruthie's uncertain and sometimes bizarre behavior for years. How did he do it? How did he keep his temper?

And poor Ruthie. Much as she made me angry, she also made me sad. She didn't seem to realize that her belligerence and her demands would force him to choose between her and Jenna. He couldn't care for both as long as Ruthie behaved as she did.

He'd choose his child over his wife, I knew, but he'd try and placate Ruthie too. Couldn't be done, and the sooner he let Jenna know she was his priority, the better.

Her weeping was the only sound in the car. I reached back and put what I hoped was a comforting hand on her knee. She didn't acknowledge me, but she didn't pull away, so I left it there. I wished I felt free to do the same thing for Drew. He could use some comforting too.

It wasn't until we had crossed the Walt Whitman Bridge into New Jersey that Drew pulled into a strip mall on the Black Horse Pike and parked. Without a word he climbed out of the car, opened the back door, and pulled Jenna into his arms.

"Shh, baby," he murmured as he rocked her. "Shh. It'll be all right."

Chloe and I looked at each other, and she was crying too, not that I blamed her. I saw in her face that she knew Drew's comforting *"It'll be all right"* wasn't going to be that easy and maybe not ever be true.

"What's wrong with me, Daddy?" Jenna buried her face in his chest. "Why doesn't she like me?"

My heart broke as I heard her questions and saw Drew's face contort with pain.

"There's nothing wrong with you, sweetheart." He rested his cheek on the crown of her head. "Not one thing. You are a wonder. You're beautiful and intelligent and all that's hopeful. You're the marvelous girl God made you to be, and I love you so much it hurts." He choked on emotion and had to clear his throat to continue. "You are the best thing in my life."

"But she hates my blond streak!"

"Your blond streak is beautiful." His eyes met mine over Jenna's head, and he gave a slight, rueful, and very sad smile.

They stood together for several moments while Chloe and I

waited in the car, both of us wallowing in silent tears. I don't know about Chloe, but I kept praying over and over, *Oh, Lord, help that wonderful child realize how precious she is to her father and to You.*

When Jenna and Drew finally got back in the car, we drove in silence, the only words my directions. Jenna rested her head against the headrest, her eyes closed. Chloe stared out her side window. Drew drove, his eyes straight ahead, his expression stoic.

I wanted to make it better for all of them, and it hurt because I knew I couldn't.

We pulled into the parking lot of the mall that housed Pierce's Jewelry. Drew parked and I pulled out my wallet, handing Chloe a twenty.

"Why don't you take Jenna over to the Magical Garden and get whatever you want to eat or drink?" I pointed to the restaurant at the opposite end of the mall.

Chloe took the money, tapped Jenna on the arm, and the girls walked away. I looked at Drew.

"You okay?"

He shrugged. "I'll live. I just hate the hurt to Jenna." He blinked rapidly lest he fall victim to that emotional outlet most hated by males, tears.

"Papa bear on duty."

He caught the reference and nodded. "The thing I hate is that this problem won't go away. Ruthie will always be there, upsetting Jenna, turning to me for help whenever she feels like it. There are all lengths of cycles for bipolar people from two to three years to two to three days. Ruthie's cycles are short and seem to be getting shorter."

"We had a lady who lived down the street from us when I was growing up," I said. "Mrs. Garborg was bipolar back when they called it manic depression. She'd go off the rails about every three years, leave home, fly to Florida, and buy a souvenir shop, always a souvenir shop. She'd run up all kinds of debt. Then the mania would wear off, and she'd come home, contrite, depressed, and oh so sorry. She'd take her medicine for a couple of years, feel so well she believed she didn't need it anymore, and soon she was off to Florida again. Not that I realized what was going on as a kid. I just knew Mrs. Garborg disappeared every so often."

"Poor Mr. Garborg," Drew said with feeling.

"Slippery Mr. Garborg," I corrected. "He put all their money in an account in his name, and the third time she left, so did he. When she came home, he wasn't there. He'd filed for divorce and taken off with his girlfriend. What a scandal! Mom and Nan couldn't talk of anything else for months."

"What happened to her?"

"As I understand it, she became a street person in Philadelphia. Mom saw her once when she and Dad went to a play, a matinée. They were leaving the theater, and there was Mrs. Garborg, wearing a dirty skirt and sweater and terribly aged, all her belongings in the grocery store cart beside her. She was sitting on the steps of a building they passed on their way to the parking garage. She was changing her underpants, oblivious to the stream of people walking past her."

He blinked. "What did your parents do?"

"Nothing. They were so shocked they just kept on walking."

He swallowed. "I don't want anything like that to happen to Ruthie."

"Of course you don't."

He gave me a sad look. "It's a good thing you aren't my real fiancée. You'd be saddled with her for the rest of your life too, if you married me."

I merely smiled, though I thought that Ruthie might be a small price to pay for a man like Drew.

"You're a very nice person, Drew Canfield." I patted his arm. "The Lord must be very pleased with your caring heart."

He snorted. "My hypocritical heart. You have no idea how much I resent feeling responsible for her."

"But you're still kind."

"It doesn't feel kind; it feels like I have no choice. It's what the Lord's asking of me, and I have to do it whether I want to or not."

"Then you aren't a hypocrite at all. You're an obedient servant of the Lord."

He frowned, uncertain, like that was a new thought. He pondered it for a moment, then actually smiled. "Thank you."

Oh my, but he had a wonderful smile.

"Now let's take care of your shoebox. No more Ruthie." He spread his arms like he was erasing her. "I'm Ruthie'd out."

I clutched the box tightly as I led the way to the store door. I took hold of the handle and pulled. Nothing happened. I pulled again. Still nothing. I looked inside and realized there were no lights on at the same moment Drew said, "Uh-oh."

"What?"

He pointed to the sign in the window: Closed Mondays in July and August.

I frowned at the sign. Why hadn't Sam said something? I held a small fortune in my hands, and I'd have to keep it for another night in the big, bad city.

Drew and I were walking back to his car when the girls came running across the lot. Both were giggling. There was only one cause for that kind of noise: boys.

I held out my hand for any change from my twenty, and Chloe slapped a ten in my palm.

"What did you have?" I asked.

"We each got a Coke and a doughnut. Chocolate glazed."

"And that cost ten dollars?"

Chloe grinned. "I knew you wouldn't want to be bothered with all the small change."

"Right. And what were their names?"

"Whose names?" Chloe looked innocently at Jenna, who looked innocently back.

"You keep forgetting that I was thirteen once, and I know a guy giggle when I hear one."

Chloe and Jenna giggled.

"Aha! See?"

The girls glanced toward the Magical Garden just as two young guys in jeans and tees emerged, one carrying a ladder, the other a toolbox. They climbed into a truck that read Smollens Electrical on the side panels. Even to my jaundiced thirty-year-old eyes, they were cute, if a bit young.

The girls went scarlet at the sight of them, turned their backs, and fell to giggling all over again.

Drew eyed the guys with disfavor. "And I thought the kids next door were too old."

Ignoring her father, Jenna pointed to the shoebox. "Haven't you been to the store yet?"

"It's not open."

"What?" Chloe raced over and pulled on the door as if Drew and I had been too weak to handle its weight. She cupped her hands over her eyes and peered into the darkened store.

"You're right." She walked back to us. "It's closed."

I resisted the urge to look at Drew and roll my eyes.

"So what are you going to do with the jewelry?" she asked.

"Hold on to it real tight."

She grinned. "At least Aunt Tori won't be back until tomorrow. You won't have to sleep with it tonight."

Tori reached for her cell, glancing at the number as she flipped the lid. Luke. How unusual. Luke didn't call people on the phone. He summoned them to his presence.

"Tori, where did you get that pin you gave me?" he asked without wasting time on a greeting.

She blinked. "Is something wrong?" When she'd given him the pin this morning, he'd been all smiles at her payment on her debt.

"I knew you'd come through, doll face." He'd kissed her until her knees were weak.

"Then no more puzzles, okay?" she'd asked when she recovered her breath. She really couldn't take the nerve-racking things anymore. The one Eddie had given her Saturday night had made her feel sick to her stomach, and she'd had to leave before she disgraced herself in one of Tim and Mark's flowerpots. She hadn't even had time to enjoy Libby's distress.

Luke had looked at her sort of strangely when she mentioned the puzzles, then shrugged. "Sure, no more of 'em if you don't want. I thought you enjoyed stuff like that."

"Not those."

Now he asked again, "Just tell me where you got the pin."

"I got it from my sister. Why?"

"It's hot merchandise," he said.

"What?" If there were two things she could never in this world imagine together, they were Libby and hot merchandise. "You're kidding."

"You didn't know?"

"Believe me, I didn't know. After all, we're talking St. Libby of Haydn here."

"I had Clem take the piece to be appraised, and he comes hurrying back with the news that the pin's on the stolen jewelry Web sites."

Tori went cold all over. "I didn't get you in trouble with the law, did I?"

"Nah. You can thank your lucky stars that Clem went to Manny Gottlieb. Him and me have done lots of business in the past with the goods you've used for payments. And other things, of course," he added. "Don't worry. Manny gave me a good price."

Weak with relief, Tori asked, "What'd you get?" It was, after all, her debt that she was whittling away at. She hoped it was at least a thousand dollars.

"Eight hundred fifty dollars. Not too bad for a hot piece."

But hardly enough to make a dent in her debt, especially with the interest Luke charged. She should never have gone to him for help when she found herself so deeply in hock. Of course, then she never would have met him, and she could no longer imagine life without him.

"Does your sister have more?"

Tori thought of the shoebox full of little boxes. "She does."

"Get the rest, Blondie, and I won't charge any interest for the next month. You'll be a double winner. Debt paid down a bunch, and no more interest added."

Tori hesitated. That meant stealing from Libby. It was one thing to take a single pin. It was sort of like borrowing without intent to return. But to really steal? To take it all? From her twin?

But then Libby had stolen the goods to begin with. It'd serve her right if someone stole them from her. And then it was Luke who was asking. Libby or Luke? Now there was a hard choice.

"How can I turn down a deal like that?"

"You are a woman after my own heart, doll face." His voice was husky and warm and sent shivers up her spine. "See you after closing."

"Absolutely." She flipped her slim phone shut and slid it into the V-neck of her white Marilyn Monroe ripoff, the one in the pictures with the pleated skirt being blown up. She moved her head in a circle in an attempt to relieve the tension in her neck.

Steal from Libby. And, of course, not get caught. That was the challenge. As she walked to meet her next client, she tried to come up with a plan to get away with getting away with the goods.

When she caught a glimpse of Eddie Mancini in his guard's uniform standing by one of the exits, she grinned. She wasn't the offspring of Jack and Mike Keating for nothing.

14

□□□

WHEN THEY PULLED UP in front of a white bungalow with a door and shutters of green, Drew studied it with interest. Anything that had to do with Libby Keating interested him, much as Libby herself fascinated him. This house was one more clue as to who she was, this intriguing combination of strength and wishful thinking.

He liked the strength. She had, after all, made a life for herself and Chloe in spite of long odds. As a single parent himself, he knew how unending the pressure was, how demanding it was to provide even a basic life for another dependent being. And he'd had an education to pave the way to a good job. And he hadn't had Tori.

Yet for all Lib's depth of character, she couldn't bring herself to hurt Chloe with the truth about her origins, hoping against hope that she could hold that information secret. It was akin to Ben trying to keep his wife from knowing about his illegitimate son. Not possible. As Philadelphia in that day was way too small, so Libby's world was much too crowded with people who knew. There was Tori, and that was complication enough, but her parents also must know. And Eddie, who now knew where she was and what a prize she had become, to say nothing of what a cutie Chloe was.

Slimy little moussed-up joker. Drew pictured Eddie strutting across the roof Saturday night with the sole purpose of upsetting Libby. *I know Jesus died for him too, Father, but I don't trust him any more than I trust Tori.*

Drew climbed out of the car and followed Libby up the walk.

"It's not much." Libby pulled out her keys and unlocked the door. "Only two bedrooms. But it's ours." A quiet pride radiated from her.

The door opened directly into the living room, and even though Libby'd been gone less than a week, the house had that shut-up smell to it, all musty and closed.

"Since it's an old house, it has no central air." Libby flipped on a window unit in the living room and went through to the kitchen where she repeated the action. "That was one of the reasons the price was something I could manage."

Drew looked around the kitchen at Formica counters of faux wood and cupboards painted a crisp white. The walls were papered in a blue and yellow plaid, strong and optimistic, just like Libby.

"Want a Coke, Mr. Canfield?" Chloe reached in the refrigerator and pulled out four cans.

Drew took it gratefully and trailed Lib back into the living room as the girls disappeared down the short hall to the bedrooms.

The house had just begun to cool when there was a knock at the front door. Libby checked through the peephole and got an expression of surprise. "It's my mother and grandmother." She opened the door, and the two older women came in, frowning.

Drew thought that if the older one would stop frowning, she would be an attractive woman with her short, curly light brown hair and large brown eyes. And the younger one, also frowning, was very pretty with blond hair and blue eyes. It was easy to see where Libby and Tori got their good looks.

"What are you doing here?" Libby's mother demanded as she all but glared at her daughter. "Aren't you supposed to be in Philadelphia?"

"Hi, Mom." Libby hugged the woman who gave a minimal hug in return. "It's good to see you. And you too, Nan." Libby hugged her grandmother.

But the older woman wasn't paying attention to Libby. She was staring at Drew, her scowl making crevices that rivaled the moon's craters in depth. He tried not to blink as he nodded to her, offering what he hoped was a charming smile.

"Who's he?" she demanded.

"Mom, Nan, I'd like you to meet my neighbor, Drew Canfield. He's a Ben Franklin scholar and is in the city doing research. Drew, this is my mother, Mimi, and my grandmother, Cynthia." She pronounced *Cynthia* in the British fashion, Chin-see-ah.

"That your car out front?" Cynthia asked. Her frown had eased, but she still looked very skeptical about him.

He nodded, again with the charming smile.

"We saw it on the way to the store, and we were worried," Mimi said. "We thought maybe someone had broken in."

Cynthia shook her head. "The world is full of thieves and crooks. You can't be too careful these days."

"Rest assured that I'm neither a thief nor a crook," Drew assured her. "I think Libby has better taste than to hang around with such people."

Suddenly there was a charged beat of dead air that took Drew by
surprise. He thought back over what he'd said, looking for something that might have given offense. He could find nothing.

Libby, Cynthia, and Mimi all began talking at the same time.

"Chloe's in the bedroom with Drew's daughter, Jenna," Libby
said.

"Did Chloe come with you?" Cynthia asked.

"So you've been in Philadelphia less than a week, and you've
already picked up a man?" Mimi looked Drew up and down.

He tried not to squirm.

"Mom!" Libby flushed, embarrassed.

Chloe walked into the room just in time to overhear Mimi's
comment. She went to Mimi and Cynthia and gave them a dutiful
granddaughterly kiss. Then she glanced at Libby with a light in her
eye that made Drew brace himself.

"He's not just a man, Mom-Mom. He's her fiancé."

"Chloe!" Libby looked horrified.

"What?" Mimi and Cynthia yelped together.

Chloe grinned at Drew. "Right, Mr. Canfield?"

Jenna had walked into the room on Chloe's heels. "We're bridesmaids. I'm wearing rose pink and Chloe's wearing royal blue."

Drew gave Chloe and Jenna the evil eye, but they merely smiled
sweetly back.

"It's a joke, Mom," Libby hastened to assure. "A joke."

Mimi's and Cynthia's facial expressions, Drew noticed, were a
cross between alarmed and unconvinced.

"Right, Drew?" Libby demanded.

He nodded. "Right."

"What's the matter?" Cynthia asked. "She isn't good enough for
you?"

"Nan!" Libby went scarlet all over again.

"She's wonderful," Drew said, and he meant it, "but we've known each other less than a week."

"There's always love at first sight." Cynthia smiled, the first lightening of her expression since she'd come in. "It was love at first sight for Mike and me."

Mimi gave a disparaging laugh, and Cynthia turned on her. "It was!"

Chloe threw her arms around Cynthia. "It's a wonderful story, Great-Nan." She turned her attention to Mimi, hugging her. "Right, Mom-Mom?"

Mimi hugged Chloe back with more enthusiasm than she'd hugged her daughter, and the tension defused, at least temporarily. Drew suspected that the two women took potshots and probably howitzer shots at each other frequently.

"This is my friend, Jenna." Chloe pulled Jenna forward. "Mr. Canfield is her father."

Mimi smiled at Jenna, ignored Drew, and turned to Libby. "We were going to call you later today. We have some very good news."

"Indeed we do," Cynthia said, her eyes bright. "Mike and Jack are coming home."

"What?" Libby was clearly surprised.

"Really?" Chloe cried.

"Who are Mike and Jack?" Jenna asked, but no one answered. She looked at Drew who shrugged. He had no idea who they were either.

"They'll be released tomorrow."

"Tomorrow?" Libby squeaked. "And you just found out?"

Released? From where? The hospital?

"We've known for a week," Mimi said.

"And you're just telling us?"

At Libby's expression of dismay, Mimi said quickly, "We didn't want to get you excited in case things didn't work out after all."

Libby nodded. "Have you told Tori?"

Cynthia nodded. "Friday, I think it was. Mimi called her."

Drew saw distress flash across Libby's face before she smiled again. He felt angry on her behalf. Her mother had called Tori but not Libby. That meant Tori had also known all weekend and not told Libby. Drew felt Libby's hurt, and so apparently did Chloe. She slid close to her mother, slipped her hand in Libby's, and squeezed.

"Anyway," Cynthia continued, "we pick them up tomorrow morning, and we're having a welcome home party tomorrow night. Tori's free then."

Another twist of the knife. No one had yet thought to ask Libby if she was free. Did they realize that they treated her as an after-thought and just not care at the hurt they caused, or was the subtle cruelty unconscious?

"Jack and Mike are my father and grandfather," Libby explained to Drew and Jenna. "They've been—" She stopped as if she wasn't sure what to say.

"They've been in jail." Cynthia's eyes narrowed, challenging him to react improperly. "They were falsely accused. They were set up. Their incarceration is a travesty of justice."

Libby's carefully neutral expression made him wonder, but all he did was nod. "That must have been a terribly difficult thing to deal with."

"Fourteen years." Mimi wiped at a tear. "But at last, parole!"

"The word has already spread around town," Cynthia said. "So many people are coming to celebrate with us, and of course we want the whole family to be here to welcome them."

Libby nodded. "Of course you do. Chloe and I'll be there. We wouldn't miss it!"

Mimi eyed Drew. "You can come with her if you want. And your daughter. Chloe will need a friend."

Drew grinned. He'd never been to a party for a couple of ex-cons before, just professors ready to kill each other over tenure. "Thank you. We'd love to come."

Tori walked down the aisle between the quarter slots. All around her were men and women, many of them seniors, pushing the buttons and watching the images rotate, hoping for their machine to act against the odds and start flashing and ringing, indicating a win. The SeaSide was a cashless casino, and Tori missed the cascades of coins that used to flow from a winning slot, clanging into the tray and at times overflowing onto the floor. Cashless meant ease of management and less theft, but some of the aural magic was definitely gone.

She finally found her quarry, a woman in her early thirties with very black hair, a freckled face that screamed that she had been born a redhead, and a very pregnant belly.

"Suzy! There you are!"

Suzy Merchant looked up but only for the smallest second. "Hi, Tori." Her eyes went immediately back to her machine. The images rotated and settled into a mixed collection. "Bleh!" Suzy muttered as she pushed the button again.

Her belly jumped. Tori actually saw the taut cloth covering her tummy move. Suzy's free hand came up absently and massaged the small foot or elbow that had stuck her.

"Your husband sent me to find you. He's worried about you."

Suzy made a face. "Ron's paranoid. You'd think no one's ever had a baby before."

Ron and Suzy Merchant were among Tori's favorite clients because they were such characters. Ron and his father owned a large garbage and refuse business. Rumor had it that they had obtained their large fleet of trucks through somewhat murky circumstances.

"This other trash guy was driving north on I-95 one evening," Luke had told her, "and he looks into the southbound lanes just in time to see two of his big trucks going south. Thing is, he didn't think there was any reason for them to be going anywhere at that time of day. So he calls his office, but nobody's there. He calls the police, but what can they do when you say, 'I think I saw my trucks'?"

"I take it he did have two stolen trucks and they were never recovered?"

Luke nodded. "By the time he got home, checked his lot, and found two trucks missing, they had disappeared from the face of the earth."

Whether Ron and his father actually owned a fleet of stolen vehicles wasn't Tori's affair. The facts that they were making money hand over fist—interesting in this day of strict EPA regulations— and that they loved gambling made them her concern.

"Ron thinks you should go up and take a nap," Tori told Suzy, who made another *bleh* sound.

The whirl of a red light and the shrill ring of a clarion made them both spin to watch an old lady stand rapt with joy as she watched her slot machine indicate she'd won a hundred dollars.

Suzy made another *bleh*, pulled her credit card from the slot in the top of her machine, and rose, still rubbing her stomach. She suddenly looked tired.

"Come on." Tori took her arm. "Upstairs for a nap."

As they walked past the old lady whose payout had everyone around her pushing their buttons faster than ever, Suzy said, "Congratulations."

The old lady looked at them with a dazed smile. "First time I ever gambled. I thought it was hard. Boy, was I wrong."

Tori and Suzy walked toward the elevators. Suzy glanced back over her shoulder toward the lady. "She'll lose it all before she's done. Wanna bet?"

"Just so that's all she loses." Miles climbing aboard that Greyhound flashed through Tori's mind. "You being careful?"

Suzy shot her a look. "I am not a loser."

"I didn't mean to imply you were. I've just had too much experience with the overreachers."

Suddenly Suzy looked sad. "Me too."

Tori waited, but Suzy didn't say more. She just fell into a grim and brooding silence.

The elevator door slid open and Tori held out a hand in a you-go-first motion. "In you go."

They rode in silence and walked down the hall with Suzy's depression casting a funereal pall about them. In a weird way, Tori found the bleak mood encouraging. It proved there was more to the woman than the frivolous gambler Tori had previously seen. It also made her feel slightly better about the future of the coming baby.

Tori used her master key card to open the door to Suzy and Ron's suite. "Want something to drink before you lie down?"

"Why? I'll just have to get up in five minutes to go to the bathroom." A ghost of Suzy's normally sassy smile tugged at her lips.

While Suzy flopped on the bed, Tori pulled the drapes over the big window to shut out the brilliant summer sun.

"Thanks," Suzy mumbled as she tried to find a comfortable

position. "You might want to consider things carefully before you ever decide to get pregnant."

Laughing softly, Tori pulled the bedroom door closed behind her. Sarcastic Suzy was back.

Tori walked to the center of the room and studied the chaos that Suzy seemed to generate wherever she went. Tori smiled.

There on the coffee table were the diamond earrings Suzy had worn the first night she and Ron arrived, three nights ago. When worn, a large diamond rested against the earlobe and five others dangled on fine gold chains. Suzy'd had them on with a pair of black maternity slacks and a black sleeveless empire waist silk top. They looked terrific as they caught the light every time Suzy moved her head.

Tori slid them into her cleavage. Suzy would never even notice they were gone.

15

□□□

"HAVE MR. CANFIELD DRIVE past where you grew up and past the store, Mom," Chloe said as we walked to the car to leave Haydn. "I want to show Jenna."

Drew complied, and soon we were driving down Carlisle Road. Memories, many painful, some wonderful, surged. I pointed out the store, really Madge's garage, with its striped awning, and then across the street, Mom and Dad's house. It was slightly ramshackle with its porch needing painting and the lawn semibald. I studied it sadly.

"It used to be a showplace, the grass thick and green, manicured lovingly by my father. The azaleas were the fullest in town, and the garden was alive with blooms from April through October. I think he worked off the tension of his job by working outside."

"What did he do?" Drew asked.

"He was a cop."

He frowned and I could feel his questions. "A crooked cop who gets out of jail tomorrow," I said. "Don't you love the red and white awnings at the shop?"

Drew swallowed all his questions and studied the awnings. "Wonderful. Attractive. Especially to women, who I assume are your main clients."

I fell silent as we drove back to Philadelphia, worrying about my father and grandfather as well as Drew's opinion of us now that he knew a bit more of our history.

I had worried for years about when Dad and Pop got out of jail. What would they do with themselves when they were again free men? Obviously they could no longer be involved in law enforcement. With their criminal records they couldn't even get a private investigator's license. My darkest fear was that they would become involved in more shady doings for lack of training in anything else. Well, maybe it wasn't my darkest fear. That was reserved for telling Chloe about Eddie. But it was a close second.

If ever I felt a mix of emotions, it was at this moment. I was really glad that Dad and Pop would be getting out of that horrible place, and I rejoiced with Mom and Nan that they would have their husbands back. They were already more ebullient and upbeat than I'd seen them in years.

Of course, once they had to live with their husbands again, things might well change. Certainly the men had been altered by their incarceration, and the husbands returning were not the men who left.

Still, if I had my druthers, I would have preferred that Drew not know about my family's unhappy circumstances yet. I liked Drew, probably more than I should. He seemed to like me. However, there was a big difference between wanting to get to know a woman with just an untrustworthy sister and a woman whose whole family was sailing on the other side of the law. Some information was better kept quiet until a friendship was more secure, when the woman's charms and positive attributes could overcome her family drawbacks.

I sighed. Who was I kidding? Nice Christian men liked nice Christian families. I did not have this to offer Drew or any man.

Anyway, it no longer mattered. The cat was out of the bag and stalking the blossoming friendship between Drew and me like a tabby lying in wait for a cardinal. I shoved that happy thought aside. There were plenty of real problems to be concerned about. I'd handle the disappearance of Drew from my life if and when it happened.

I glanced in the backseat. The girls had fallen asleep, no doubt a result of spending half the night talking.

"They were guilty," I quietly told Drew as we drove up the Black Horse Pike toward the Walt Whitman Bridge. He might as well know the worst. "Selling confiscated drugs. Selling confiscated guns. A couple of the guns they allowed back in circulation were actually used in cop killings." I shuddered. "I've always thought that was the reason for the long sentence and the lack of an earlier parole."

"How did they manage all this? Didn't any of the cops who worked with them report them? Or did one and that's how they got caught?"

I frowned, surprised at his overt interest. Most people had the sense to avoid the topic. "It doesn't matter. They did it, okay?"

"Yeah, but how? They didn't actually go out on the streets and sell the drugs themselves, did they? I mean, talk about risky! And they didn't stand on street corners until someone came along, then flip open their raincoats to show all the guns stashed in pockets sewn into the coat."

"Very funny." My voice could have chilled sub-Saharan Africa. I knew he was only being curious. He was, after all, a researcher, and researchers asked questions. But I'd lived all the pain of their activities and all the anger at them for being so consummately stupid as to think they could avoid detection. Add to that the ignominy of their trial and incarceration.

Drew glanced at me and began back-pedaling. "I'm sorry. I forget that, for you, this isn't just a fascinating story."

Somehow his step back with its intrinsic understanding of how much it had all hurt allowed me to open up, something I rarely did. "The guns they sold to a couple of gun shops in Philly, neither known for keeping good sales records or for requiring firearm registrations. The drugs they got kids to sell for them." I thought of the conversation I'd overheard all those years ago. "Eddie was one of them."

Drew blinked. "Eddie? And he never got caught."

I didn't say anything, just shook my head. What was there to say? We rode in silence as we swept through Runnemede, Bellmawr, and Mount Ephraim.

"So how did you escape all that corrupt influence?" he asked as we paused at the light in Audubon. The Walt Whitman Bridge was just ahead.

"Well, I didn't know about it until the arrest. None of us did." I paused. "At least I don't think Mom and Nan knew." That possibility had never occurred to me before. "I know Tori was as shocked as I was. I drew inward and turned to Eddie. Tori got furious and screamed her outrage to the world."

"But in spite of it all, you came through with your integrity intact."

I smiled and told him about Madge and all she meant to me. "She not only gave me a job, led me to Jesus, and saved Chloe's life. She also encouraged me when I got down, baby-sat Chloe when I needed her, and showed me how Christian love works. She also got me back in school and on to college. I only have a couple of more classes to take, and I'll have my bachelor's."

Drew backed off the gas as he came up behind a Winnebago pulling a bright yellow compact behind it. "Believe it or not, Ruthie's father was to me all those things Madge was to you. Del took me under his wing and taught me all he knew. My father was a nice enough man, but all things Christian were anathema to him. He also liked skating close to the legal edge. He did a lot of electrical work for people on the side, but he never declared the income. Stuff like that. The day a cashier gave him too much change was a day worth celebrating. So Del's absolutes were hard to comprehend at first. I still remember when he called me on copying music illegally. I'd never thought about breaking copyright law before. But as I learned more and more about God's Word, I appreciated Del more and more. I think the greatest hurt of my divorce was losing Del."

"He cut you out of his life?" I was surprised, since he sounded like such a wonderful guy.

Drew checked over his shoulder to be sure no car was in his blind spot and moved out to pass the Winnebago that was weaving a bit too much for comfort, especially with the narrow lanes of the bridge fast approaching. "No, he didn't. Ruthie was the one who had a fit because I wanted to stay close to him and Peg. She made it so uncomfortable for them, swearing at them, berating them, that I stepped back to spare them. We still talk, especially by e-mail, and we meet occasionally for dinner, and of course they love seeing Jenna, but Ruthie goes ballistic whenever she finds out." He smiled sadly. "It's just easier not to push that button. She has so many others that you can't avoid pushing."

We took the bridge, turned onto 95N, got off at the historical district, and drove on past. I realized my shoulders were tense about what we'd find when we came to our lane. I breathed a relieved sigh when no one, dead or alive, was waiting for anyone on the steps. The girls woke up when the car stopped moving.

"I think I'll stay with Chloe," Jenna announced, chin raised.

"Sorry, sweets," Drew said. "Not tonight. You need to come home."

"Dad, please!"

Drew just shook his head.

With a long-suffering sigh, Jenna accepted defeat, which led me to believe she had expected Drew's answer. "I'm going to go to my room and live there until she leaves."

He threw his arm around her shoulders. "We'll be okay, Jen. You'll see."

The two of them walked to their house and disappeared inside. I unlocked our door, and we walked into Aunt Stella's. I was emotionally exhausted.

And tomorrow with its welcome home party would be much worse.

□□□

Tori's cell phone vibrated. She smiled apologetically at her client as she glanced at the number. It was her boss.

"Excuse me a minute, Ron. It's Anders."

Ron nodded. "I just wanted to thank you again for taking care of Suzy." With a wave he disappeared into the throngs heading onto the floor. Ron loved his poker.

"What's up, Anders?" Tori caught glimpses of the boardwalk and the ocean when the darkened-glass automatic front doors opened.

She noted with approval that more people were entering than leaving, many with red faces from a day on the beach without enough SPF. She never went out without at least 30 on her face. She glanced at her arm, evaluating her tan. She was losing valuable beach time with all the traveling back and forth to Aunt Stella's. Pretty soon she'd be as pale as the old ladies at the nickel slots.

"It's Suzy," Anders said. "She's calling for you. She's—"

Suzy! Tori's hand went to her chest even though the earrings were no longer there but safely hidden in her room. Suzy'd missed them! Tori's vision grayed at the edges as she fought panic. Then Anders' words sank in. "She's where?"

"She's on the floor, literally, in an aisle in the quarter slots area not too far from the back door. Can you tell me why a woman with money like hers plays the quarter slots?"

"Who cares?" Tori caught her reflection and admired both the huge, relieved smile—Suzy hadn't found her out—and her slinky image. If Marilyn were alive, she'd be jealous. "Be happy, Anders. She began with the nickel ones. What's she doing on the floor?"

"She's having her baby."

"In the casino?" Tori's voice squeaked in surprise.

"In the casino. One of the players took time from her machine to call 911, so the EMTs should be here soon, but in the meantime, get over there!"

Perspiration broke out all over her body. "I don't know anything about having babies!"

"I don't care. She wants you."

Phone still to her ear, Tori ran across the floor, dodging customers intent on finding their area of play and servers with drinks on trays as they did their part to keep everyone lubricated and betting.

"Where's Ron?" Anders asked. "Do you have any idea? Though she didn't ask for him. Just you."

Tori spied a cluster of people all staring down at the floor and guessed that was where Suzy lay. Her stomach did a slow roll as she elbowed her way through. She swallowed back her fear. When this was over, she and Anders were going to have a talk about her job requirements. No more babies!

Sure enough, there was Suzy, her flowing gauzy dress hiked up to her waist, her knees bent, her hands grasping her stomach, and fluid and blood pooling beneath her. Instead of her *bleh* noises, she was making breathy little gasps.

For the second time in five minutes, Tori thought she might faint.

"And don't you dare pass out!" Anders yelled in her ear.

"What? You can see me?" She knew cameras were everywhere.

"No, but I know you."

"Ron's playing poker!" She flipped the phone shut, stuffed it in her cleavage, and looked down at Suzy.

"Hey, girl, what are you doing here? I left you resting in bed just a couple of hours ago."

"Boring," Suzy managed between pants. "More fun down here. At least it was. Besides—*ohhh,* that hurt!—I'm not due for another month."

"Like babies pay attention to schedules," one of the onlookers muttered. "They come when they want."

And this one wanted. Suzy let out a great groan, and Tori had to bite back one of her own.

"Anybody got a beach towel?" she yelled. The least she could do was mop up the mess.

To her surprise, two people grabbed towels from bags and shoved them at her. They smelled of suntan lotion and beach, but it was not the time to be picky. She knelt and slid one under Suzy's legs and rump to make things a bit more comfortable and to mop up some of the stickiness. The other she draped over Suzy's knees. Suzy may have lost all her modesty at the moment, but Tori hadn't.

Suzy grabbed Tori's hand, gave a shriek, and squeezed so hard Tori had to fight not to shriek right along with her.

"I thought labor pains came on gradually," Tori said. "Didn't you have any warning?"

"Sure, but I thought they were those phony things. Besides, I was on a roll. I won ten dollars, and I could feel a hundred was just a minute or two away. That's twenty-five hundred free turns. Yeeow!"

"Twenty to one it's a girl," said a guy watching from the end of the aisle.

"You're on," said a lady in bright pink shorts.

"Take the bet, Tori," Suzy whispered. "It's a sure thing."

"Which way?"

"Either."

Tori frowned.

Sweat soaked Suzy's face and dress. "One of each."

"Where is she?" Ron's frantic voice floated through the gathering crowd. "Where is she?"

"Over here, Ron," Tori called, ready to stand and give him her place.

"Don't you come near me, Ron Merchant," Suzy hissed. "Ooow! This is all your fault!"

Ron ignored her and fell to his knees across from Tori. He grabbed Suzy's free hand. "Breathe, baby. Come on. Breathe. Just like they taught you in class."

"It's coming! I can see its head!" a woman yelled. The beach towel apparently wasn't doing what Tori had hoped.

"A nurse? A doctor?" Tori yelled frantically.

No one responded. Where were the EMTs?

"She or he's coming," Suzy managed through gritted teeth. "Tori!"

Not knowing what else to do, Tori moved between Suzy's legs, and sure enough, a little head was visible.

"Here!" Someone pushed several beach towels into her hand. "They're new. I just got them."

Tori rested them on her lap and put out her hands. The little head was followed by shoulders and a body, all slimy and bloody. Tori held it in her shaking hands. "It's a boy. Ron, open one of the towels!"

"Joseph," Suzy ordered. She might be weary and soaked in sweat, but she was still Sassy Suzy. "Joseph Ronald."

Ron held out a towel. "After her late brother," he explained. "He'd love the irony of his namesake being born in a casino, considering how he loved gambling." He rubbed a finger over his son's cheek. "Hey, Joey."

Just as Tori wrapped the tiny boy in the towel with a garish sunflower superimposed over royal blue waves, two EMTs pushed through the crowd. In a daze, Tori offered Joey to them. One took the baby and cleared the air passages and cut the cord. The other wheeled a gurney into place to move Suzy to the waiting ambulance.

She let out a great yell. "She's coming!"

"Another?" the EMT said in surprise.

"Another," Ron confirmed as he leaned over Suzy. "Come on, baby. You can do it."

The EMT shoved Joey back into Tori's arms and dropped to help deliver the second baby.

A few minutes later, Tori walked beside Ron as they followed the gurney and Suzy down the aisle toward the back entrance. She still held Joey in her arms; Ron, the baby girl in his. Suzy seemed remarkably unmoved about having the twins but extraordinarily displeased about leaving the casino.

"Take me back! I was on a roll. Just let me have a couple more tries. And my credit card's in the slot!"

"Shut up, Suze," Ron said. "You can play later. I'll go get the card."

As he spoke, a light began to flash behind them and a bell made that up-and-down clarion call that Tori always thought sounded like cop cars in Europe.

Suzy turned the air blue. "That was my money! I know it!"

"Be thankful the bug hasn't bitten you like that, Tori," Ron said as he turned to go retrieve Suzy's credit card from the machine. "It isn't a pretty thing."

□□□

Tuesday morning dawned overcast and muggy. I sat in the back garden and frowned at a noise that sounded like a lawn mower drifting over the fence from Maxi's. I hadn't given much thought to caring for this little Eden I so enjoyed. I looked at the grass. It hadn't grown tall so much as shaggy in the week we'd been here. When we arrived, it was like every blade had been measured to length. Now, some dared to be a quarter inch to a half inch off level, disrupting the symmetry like a Rockette who kicked too high.

So what was I to do about the problem? Bring my lawn mower

from home? I hadn't seen anything here I could use. There was no little shed for keeping gardening tools and supplies and a mower. Of course there was so little grass that an old-fashioned push mower would be ample to keep up with the trimming. Still, there was no push mower anywhere around either.

I'd have to ask James what Aunt Stella did about lawn care. James knew everything.

As I thought that, the side gate in our fence opened, and a Latino guy in shorts and a tee that read "Lopez Lawn Care" walked in pushing a power mower. Behind him was a second man in an identical shirt, wearing gloves and carrying a large green trash bag.

They stopped when they saw me and smiled, each sporting a gold incisor that flashed in the sun. I smiled back and decided it wouldn't do to ask to see green cards. I gestured toward the lawn with a nod and went inside. In less time than I could have imagined, they were gone, the grass was again all one length, and a couple of geranium heads that were getting a bit ratty had disappeared.

Newest question to ask James: Who paid these guys? In fact, who paid any of the bills here? Water? Gas? Electric? Cooling? I assumed the estate, but what if I was wrong? Were Tori and I going to get stuck with these costs for the next six months? The lawyers could tell me, but I hesitated to call them because they were always on the clock. I didn't want the estate billed several hundred dollars for something James might be able to tell me for free. Since he knew Aunt Stella's significant other, maybe he knew about the money too. It'd certainly be easy enough to find out.

But first I made a phone call I'd been wanting to make for several days.

"Homicide, Detective Holloran," the handsome policeman boomed in my ear.

"Hello, Detective. This is Elizabeth Keating. I was wondering if you could tell me how the man I found on my doorstep died. It's been eating at me for days now, the not knowing."

He was silent for a moment. Didn't other crime victims call for information? Was it not the done thing? Did his silence mean unhappiness? Surprise?

"You know I can't discuss an open case with you, Ms. Keating," he finally said, his voice carefully neutral.

I sighed. I'd been afraid of this answer. "I understand. I'm not asking about the investigation itself. I just would like to know how the poor man died. Surely you can tell me that much."

There was a heavy sigh, and I knew the last thing this man wanted was to waste time talking to me. Then I heard the click of computer keys, a hopeful sign. Or he'd decided to play Spider Solitaire until he got rid of me.

"Okay. It says here that Mick Brewer died of heart failure."

"What? He had a heart attack and laid himself neatly on my step to die?" With TORI on his chest?

"He didn't die on your step. He was carried there."

"That's ridiculous. It makes no sense."

"I agree. But here's the interesting thing, Ms. Keating. He had two small burn marks on his body, one on his neck—"

"I saw that!"

"—and one on his back. They are consistent with marks from a Taser. The coroner says that the electrical shock of the gun was what triggered the heart attack. Your friend apparently had a bad heart, and *zap*! That's all there is, folks. And I gotta go."

As soon as his phone clicked off, I went to my computer and signed on to HowStuffWorks.com for a quick lesson in electronic weapons. I learned that a Taser shoots two electrodes up to fifteen or so feet. These electrodes are attached by wires to the gun, and when the electrodes hit a person, the body completes an electrical circuit with the weapon. High voltage, low amperage current flows and disrupts the body's natural electrical system. Muscles and nerves are overstimulated. They contract randomly, causing temporary incapacitation. While Tasers and stun guns, their close-quarters cousins, are nonlethal, the jolt is very painful. In a person with a prior health issue, the strong stab of current may be enough to cause a heart attack.

It all sounded very *Star Wars/Star Trek* to me, but I remembered seeing cops bring down violent suspects on the various reality cop shows as I clicked through the channels. I never lingered on those shows for long. They were too "guy" for my taste, and they brought Dad and Pop too much to mind.

Poor Mick. Whoever had shot him hadn't meant to kill him. It was just his bad luck to have had a preexisting cardiac condition.

While I was online, I checked our eBay auctions and smiled in satisfaction. I closed them out and grinned widely at the thought of Dave at our local Mail N More when I gave him the hobbyhorse to package for me.

I wandered up to Chloe's room to waken her and tell her I was going to Tinksie's and to get ready for the trip back to New Jersey.

"Do I have to go back with you?" she moaned. "I can stay here alone."

"We're going to the party today, remember? First we'll drop off the shoebox. Then you can help me package some eBay items for mailing."

"The hobbyhorse?"

"Did well after things got going."

"And someone actually bought all those sunglasses?"

"And at a very nice price. Then we'll go help Mom-Mom and Great-Nan get ready for the big welcome home party."

"Why don't I just come with Jenna and Mr. Canfield?"

"I want to give them the chance not to come." I still felt bad about the way Drew had been more or less forced into accepting Mom and Nan's invitation.

Chloe looked surprised. "Why wouldn't they come?"

"Why would they?"

"Oh." She thumped her pillow until it was more comfortable beneath her head. "When you put it that way…" She studied me a moment. "Does it make you nervous to think of them coming home?"

My smile was more rueful than humorous as I tried to ease the tension drawing my neck and shoulder muscles tight. No need to ask who *them* was. "It does."

"Me too. I've never known them anywhere but in the visiting room at prison."

I looked at her uncertain face. "You'll get used to them being around."

"Will they still be nice?"

"What do you mean?"

"Well, the guards were always standing around and all."

"Oh, honey." I sat on the edge of the bed and pushed her tousled hair back. "They were never mean men. Foolish. Selfish. Prideful. Certainly all those and more, but never mean." I kissed her cheek. "It'll be fine."

"I don't have to go over there more than usual, do I?"

I studied Chloe. She'd never shown reluctance to visit with my family before. "I thought you liked the 'sinful Keatings.'"

"Yeah, but not every day. I can only take so much gloom and doom."

I nodded. I understood all too well. "Things might not be as negative there now, but we'll keep the frequency of visits much as they are. The only difference is that when we go over, we'll see your grandfather and great-grandfather as well as your grandmother and great-grandmother."

"We need to keep those boundaries, Mom."

I looked at my daughter with astonishment. She was absolutely right. We needed boundaries. On the one hand, we needed to keep connected to the family because families should care for each other, even dysfunctional ones like ours. Then too we wanted them to find the Lord. But set against these truths was the counterbalance that they could pull Chloe and me down emotionally and spiritually with their constant criticism and sniping.

"How did you get so smart so young?"

"I've got you for a mom." She grinned with a gleam in her eye. "But don't let that go to your head. It's early in the morning, and my defenses are down."

I laughed as I stood. "Up you get, cookie. I've got to go see Tinksie for a few minutes. Well, James really. Be ready to go when I get back, okay?"

I left her heading for the shower and went across to Tinksie's. When I rang the bell, she opened the door, as bright and alert as an elderly chipmunk.

"Come in, come in, my dear." She studied me a minute. "Libby, right?"

"Very good! Not many people can do that."

She shrugged like it was nothing at all. "It is a bit harder since you had your hair brightened."

"So how do you do it?" I knew my face was a bit more rounded and my brow a bit heavier, but the differences were too subtle for most people.

Tinksie looked a bit embarrassed.

"It's not because I walk around with spinach caught in my teeth or something equally gross, is it?" I teased.

She laughed. "Not at all. It's just you are so friendly and genuine. Your sister, on the other hand, has an air about her, like the world doesn't deserve her divine presence. Very off-putting, if you ask me." She put a hand to her mouth. "That wasn't a very nice thing to say about your sister."

It didn't seem very loyal to tell her I agreed, so I kept quiet on the subject, patting her hand to show I took no offense. "Is James home?"

"He's in the backyard with Andrew."

I blinked. "Aunt Stella's Andrew?"

Tinksie nodded. "Come meet him. You'll like him."

Andrew Melchior was a handsome man—slim, white haired, and goateed, sort of an aged Captain Jack Sparrow without the dreadlocks. It didn't take me long to see why Aunt Stella loved him. He oozed charm and seemed genuinely delighted to meet me.

"I always regretted I never was able to meet Stella's nieces. She loved you two so much."

I flushed with embarrassment when I thought of how little thought I'd given Aunt Stella through the years. I hoped Andrew took my red cheeks as pleasure.

"So how's it going?" he asked.

I thought of Drew and Jenna, the stolen pin, and the dead man. The good, the bad, and the ugly. "All in all, we're managing."

"I'm glad. Stella was a bit nervous about putting the two of you together."

Then why in the world did she do it? "Fortunately Tori spends a lot of time at work." I slapped my hand across my mouth much as Tinksie had done just a few minutes ago. "That sounded terrible. I'm sorry."

Andrew waved the comment aside. "Let me just say that if things get too bad, come see me."

"Come see you?"

"I can't tell you why. I probably shouldn't even tell you to come see me, but please do."

Mystified and intrigued, I nodded. "Thank you. Now I have questions I wanted to ask James."

At the sound of his name, James sat up straighter, a springer spaniel going on point.

I grinned at him. "After all, Tinksie says you know everything."

James gave his slow smile to his wife, who grinned back. "I've spent our whole marriage teaching her that. She's a very apt pupil."

Tinksie made a face at him.

I thought about the level of comfort between these two older people who had lived together for so many, many years. They still liked each other. Different as they were, they had somehow crafted a solid marriage.

How did you do that? How did you end up like them instead of like Drew and Ruthie? Or like Mom and Dad? How did you manage to love each other for fifty years and more? How did you manage to be yourself, which Tinksie most definitely was, while you also served the needs of another? Madge and Bill had managed it too, though not for nearly as long.

At home, even before the troubles, there had frequently been tension, days of not speaking after virulent arguments. I sometimes wondered if the marriage would have lasted if Dad had not been forced to spend so many years away. In his absence he had acquired an aura of wonder in Mom's mind.

I expected that his return and daily presence would dispel that quickly enough. The demise of the marriage could still be in the offing.

I looked at James sitting comfortably in his padded lawn chair. "Can you tell me who is paying the costs at the house? Is it the estate, or are we going to get several unexpected bills?"

James glanced at Andrew, who answered. "Let me assure you that the estate will carry all the costs for the duration of your stay."

"That's a relief!" Now all I had to deal with was my sister, my parents, and my feelings for Drew.

And an unhappy Jenna who sat at the kitchen table with Chloe when I returned to the house.

□□□

Drew wanted nothing more than to grab his trusty Lands' End briefcase, flee the house, and hide in the stacks at the Penn Library. Or the historical society. He remembered with longing the anticipation he'd felt at the approaching six-month sabbatical. He'd thought this time would be so relaxing and invigorating.

Instead he was slumped in the kitchen chair across from the weeping Ruthie. What had he ever done to deserve all this emotional chaos?

"Nobody loves me," she sobbed. "Nobody. I could die tomorrow and no one would even care." Tears streamed down her face and dripped off her chin onto her dirty cami. Her hair was uncombed and had reached the point of desperately needing a shampoo. She rubbed her fists into her eyes like a child, and Drew noticed that her nails were bitten to the quick.

"You've had any number of people love you, Ruthie. Your parents. Me. Your boyfriends." Though Drew doubted there had been much real affection in those short-lived relationships. Just lust and chemistry.

"Jenna doesn't love me." She sniffed and swiped an arm under her nose.

Stifling a feeling of disgust at the glistening streak on her forearm, Drew reached for the napkin holder and pushed it toward her. She took a napkin and blew her nose. Then she held the dirtied thing out to him. Feeling revulsion and certain he was the shallowest man alive, he forced himself to take it. He couldn't drop it in the wastebasket fast enough.

"She doesn't love me," Ruthie sobbed. "She thinks I'm a lousy mother."

He couldn't say, "You're pretty much right on both counts." Jenna wanted to love Ruthie and be loved in return. All kids wanted to be loved by their mothers, but all kids weren't that fortunate. Most kids perhaps, but not all. Not his Jenna. And that made for raging conflict in her aching heart.

Oh, God, help Jenna turn to You to fill that void! And please help me here. I want to speak truth to Ruthie, but I don't want to inflict unnecessary hurt.

"She rarely sees you, Ruthie."

"And whose fault is that?" She glared at him through her tears. "You keep her with you all the time."

Drew had learned long ago that rationality wasn't Ruthie's strong suit. Her illness skewed her thinking, and she thought she was saying truth when no one else saw it that way. At least that was the situation some of the time. Other times he was convinced she was cunning and devious, three steps ahead of him, manipulating him to get her way. Since he was by nature a straightforward man, he had trouble following her thought processes when she was being wily. He had learned long ago that the best policy was to keep silent. Still, the urge to defend himself was astonishingly strong in spite of all the years and all the fruitless arguments.

"You're here with Jenna now, Ruthie. You just need to sit and talk with her."

She leaped to her feet. "I don't *need* to do anything! You do. You need to give her back to me. I'm her mother!"

That was when he heard the front door quietly close. Jenna had left the building. She'd undoubtedly heard the wailing and escaped.

Unfortunately Ruthie heard the soft *whoosh* too, though how she did through the noise of her yelling and sniffling was a mystery. She collapsed into her chair and started weeping again. "She's running away from me. She doesn't want to talk with me."

Before he'd taken another breath, her tears dried up as if an internal firestorm was sucking all the moisture out of her.

"And it's your fault!" She jumped up, face hard with fury, and raced to the front door. "I'll get her back here, and we'll talk. She'll talk whether she wants to or not! She can't run from me!"

Drew leaped from his seat and charged after Ruthie. He grabbed her around the waist just as she was about to pull open the door. No way would he allow this madwoman to chase after Jenna. The girl was hurting badly enough as it was.

As quickly as she'd reached boiling point, Ruthie collapsed. Her legs gave out, and she'd have landed on the floor if Drew hadn't been holding her.

"I want to die," she mumbled. "Just let me die. I'm all alone. Nobody loves me. Just let me die."

Drew picked her up with an arm under her legs and another

across her back. Her head lolled against his chest. He was astonished and dismayed at how weightless she felt. He climbed the steps and put her down on the bed in the extra bedroom. He noticed for the first time that she had no bag with her, no backpack or duffel. All she had were the clothes she came in. No wonder she looked and smelled as she did.

"Sleep for a while, Ruthie. Then we'll talk again."

She ignored him, turning from him and rolling into a ball. "I should just die."

How many times had he heard her say this? How many times had he panicked and tried to talk her out of her despair, holding her, rocking her, assuring her of his love and of God's? How many times had he taken her to professionals—doctors, counselors, pastors, anyone who might be able to help? How many times had he felt on the edge of despair himself because of his inability to help her?

And, God forgive him, how many times had he wondered if her death wouldn't be the easiest way for all of them, Ruthie especially?

□□□

Just like yesterday morning, I opened the front door to Drew. He looked weary and a bit embarrassed.

"Is Jenna here?"

I gestured him in. "She's in the kitchen with Chloe."

He took a deep breath. "Well, that's one worry dealt with."

"She's not a very happy girl." I knew I was stating the obvious, but I was concerned that he wasn't sending Ruthie packing. I sighed. That probably made me a hardhearted shrew.

He rubbed his forehead, uncomfortable. "I have a very weird request. Could I borrow some of your clothes for Ruthie?"

"What?"

"She has nothing with her. Nothing."

I looked into his sad eyes, and the words I wanted to lecture him with died. "Wait a minute. I'll be right back."

I ran upstairs and grabbed some underwear, a tee, and a pair of elastic-waist shorts, the last because the woman was skin and bones. I knew my regular things wouldn't stay up on her. I ran back downstairs, stuffed the clothes into a plastic bag, and handed it to Drew.

"Thanks." He turned to leave, then turned back. He moved ever so close to me. "You are a very nice person, Libby Keating." And he kissed me, just a light brush of his lips on mine.

I flushed with pleasure even as the air suddenly snapped with electricity. "So are you. I don't think I know any other man who would go to all this trouble for someone like Ruthie."

He ran the back of his knuckles over my cheek and smiled sadly. "It's not like I have much of a choice."

I wrapped my arms around him for a comforting hug. He hugged me back and kissed the top of my head.

"I'm so glad you're here, Lib. So glad."

I leaned back and looked up at him. "Me too."

He started to lower his head and I closed my eyes, anticipating another kiss, when I heard a pair of "Yikes!"

Staring at us from the kitchen door were two wide-eyed girls.

I cleared my throat, as embarrassed as if I'd been caught trying to crash James's Fourth of July party without food. It was a tossup whether it was Drew or I who moved back first and faster.

After a little moment of "now what" silence, during which my mind stayed utterly blank, Jenna said, "I'm going to stay here today, Dad."

He nodded. "I think that would be good."

The girls disappeared upstairs to Chloe's room. When their footsteps died away, I turned to Drew.

"You have to tell her to go, Drew."

He stared at the ceiling. "She wants to die."

"Does that mean she'll actually do something dangerous, or is she just talking, looking for sympathy?"

"Who knows? Certainly not me."

"But you've still got to tell her to go."

"I know." He sounded so frustrated, torn in two.

"I know you want to help Ruthie, but Jenna deserves to have her home back."

"I know." His voice was clipped, and I should have realized that his frustration with the situation was turning into anger at my pushing.

"Send her to her parents. Better yet, maybe they'd come and get her. Let Del struggle with her for a while."

His jaw hardened.

"Or send her back to wherever she lived with Mick."

"How about I send her away when you tell Chloe about her father?" Now the sparks flying weren't passion but annoyance.

I drew back and immediately became defensive. "It's not the same!"

"Isn't it?"

"I'm trying to protect Chloe. You're hurting Jenna."

He stuck his index finger under my nose. "Lack of action is lack of action, Libby, whether it's yours or mine." He turned on his heel and let himself out of the house, the plastic bag of clothes for Ruthie hanging incongruously from his clenched fist.

I stood there stunned, trying to figure out how we had gone from kissing each other to hurting each other in just minutes. Apparently he didn't know how to do the Tinksie/James or Madge/Bill thing any better than I did.

I was caught completely off guard when an agitated Chloe came running down stairs with an upset Jenna behind her.

"Mom, the shoebox is gone!"

16

▫▫▫

"WE'RE NOT GOING TO CALL the police," I said after I ran upstairs and checked to be certain Chloe hadn't missed the shoebox. Of course she hadn't. It was definitely gone from the top of my bureau.

"But, Mom, you've got to call them." Chloe stared at me, confused. "That's what you do when there's a robbery."

"I-I need to talk to Aunt Tori first."

Chloe stared at me for a moment, and I could see her distress when she understood the ramifications of my comment. This was her clever, beautiful, exciting Aunt Tori I was casting in the role of major thief. "Do you really think she took the stuff?"

"I don't know." I rubbed my hand over my unhappy, teeming stomach.

I realized with a deep pang that I did think Tori was guilty based on prior history and present opportunity. I reminded myself that it was only right to give her the benefit of the doubt. Innocent until proven guilty and all that. And she had been in Atlantic City—or was supposed to be.

"I know I threw the deadbolts when I went to bed last night," I told the girls, "and they were still in place this morning because I had to open them when I went to visit Tinksie and James."

"That means someone came in through a window or the back door." Chloe made a face and glanced over her shoulder as if she expected to see the thief behind her.

I nodded. *Or used Tori's keys,* but I didn't say it.

"And he was in here while we were asleep!" She shook her hands like she was trying to flick off something unwholesome stuck to them. "Oh, that gives me the creeps!"

"Tell me."

I checked all possible portals of access for scratches or gouges left by a burglar's tools, even the windows to Chloe's aerie. I'd seen *To Catch a Thief* enough times to know that sometimes burglars came down from the roof, though I doubted if many of them looked like John Robie/Cary Grant. My heart sank when I found no sign of forced entry.

"I have a question, Ms. Keating. How did anyone know the jewelry was here? And why would someone only take that shoebox? I don't know much about valuable stuff, but this house seems to be loaded with stuff worth taking."

"You're asking questions that need answers, Jenna. I intend to ask them of Tori when we see her this afternoon at my parents."

Oh, Lord, what do I do if she's guilty?

A little black cloud wanted to park over my head, blocking the Light. It was taking shape, sending out thunderbolts of doubt and confusion. What did I owe my sister, especially if she was guilty? What did I owe family? What did I owe God?

Could my heart stand the conflict?

No matter how I looked at things, it all came back to the question of who besides my sister had access and knowledge. She'd already taken one pin. There was a terrifying logic in the thought that she'd taken the rest. But why? I'd not told her of their worth.

"Uh, Mom."

I looked at Chloe, caught by the uncertainty in her voice. *Oh please, Lord, not another problem. I'm not sure I can handle any more than my disagreement with Drew and my fears over Tori.*

"Jenna wants to go with us to Mom-Mom's. And I want her to come too. Then I won't be the only kid."

"My mom's in bad shape this morning." Jenna's eyes filled with tears. "I don't want to be near her."

I could almost see the black cloud hanging over Jenna's head. If Drew had a hard time figuring out what to do about Ruthie, how was a thirteen-year-old supposed to figure it all out?

"We'd be happy to take her," I said stiffly to Drew on the phone a couple of minutes later. "You needn't worry about her." I rested my head against the cool enamel of the refrigerator and mourned. The first man I'd even looked at since Eddie, and I'd killed the romance before it even began by pushing my way into an issue that I hadn't earned the right to discuss.

"Aren't you getting tired of her at your house?" he asked, equally stiff.

"Not at all. We're glad to be her refuge." I heard myself and wanted to bite my tongue, but it was too late.

"Huh." He hadn't missed the little barb. "Are you saying you don't want me to come this evening?"

I blinked, surprised he'd still want to. "No, I'm not saying that at all. I'm just saying she'll be fine with us."

□□□

After his little contretemps with Libby, Drew was not in any mood to face Ruthie. He walked several blocks to calm himself, the change of clothes for Ruthie dangling from his hand in its plastic bag.

"I'm trying to protect Chloe. You're hurting Jenna."

He ran his fingers through his hair in frustration. All he wanted was an ordered and orderly life. He never chose the chaos of Ruthie and Jenna and even Libby, who made his stomach twist with her too-cool, precise, and incisive evaluation.

I just want peace and quiet, Lord. Is that asking too much? I don't want to be stretched and twisted and forced into some mold not of my choosing.

No sympathetic voice from heaven answered with a soothing, *"I understand, Drew. I agree you deserve uninterrupted tranquility. Let Me fix things for you so there are no worries, no tensions, no stress. After all, you're My favorite person in the whole world, and I'll see to it that you and you alone have no problems."*

Okay, Lord, so I'm a selfish idiot. Some days being a mere human is hard, but I know it's not a valid excuse for my anger, resentment, and pride. Forgive me.

A Ben quote popped into his mind: *"God helps those who help themselves."* Hard on its heels was one from Scripture: *"Whatever you do, whether in word or deed, do it all in the name of the Lord Jesus, giving thanks to God the Father through him."*

So Your message to me is do something. Do something, but make it something that honors You.

He thought hard as he retraced his steps to the house. Ruthie was waiting, her earlier desire to die apparently on hold.

"If you give me some money, I'll leave," she told him as she trailed him to the kitchen, where he started the coffee maker.

"What does 'some money' entail?" There was no way he was giving her money. It'd go to alcohol or worse.

She studied him for a minute as if evaluating her options. She indicated the house with a flick of her hand. "You must be paying significant rent to live here. That means you can't be hurting."

"I'm here on a house exchange," he said patiently. "Didn't you meet the people living in Colby Creek?"

"Oh. Well, you can still give me some money."

"What I want to give you is this." He held out the plastic bag.

She opened it and saw the contents. "What's this? Used clothes?"

"Clean clothes. Go take a shower, Ruthie."

She let the bag fall to the floor, folded her arms across her chest, and stared defiantly at him.

He made believe he hadn't seen the challenge. "When you're finished, we can talk about what I can give you."

She studied him as he got a mug from the cupboard. When he paid no attention to her, she eventually picked up the bag and went upstairs to the bathroom. When he heard the pipes creak as the shower started, he breathed a sigh of relief. With a quick prayer, he picked up the phone.

He'd barely hung up when it rang again. It was Libby, voice formal and chilly, asking if Jenna could drive with them to Haydn. "We're glad to be her refuge."

Ouch.

Drew hung up the old-fashioned kitchen wall phone, calling himself all kinds of fool because he still planned to drive to Haydn. Did he think she'd appreciate his presence, his support? Too bad he

hadn't brought his winter parka with him. He might need it if there
was no thaw in her manner.

He turned and found Ruthie watching him with a mocking
smile. She had showered and put on the clothes Libby lent her. She
still looked too thin, but at least she no longer appeared ill. And she
no longer smelled, or at least she didn't smell bad. The scent of soap
and shampoo competed with the aroma of coffee.

"Trouble with the little fiancée?"

First things first, he thought. "She's not really my fiancée. That
was Jenna's little joke."

"Strange joke."

"She's thirteen." Drew moved to the stove and poured himself a
cup of coffee. "Want one?"

Ruthie shook her head. "I'll take an orange juice."

Wow. Something healthful. He pulled the Tropicana No Pulp
(because Jenna couldn't stand pulp) from the fridge and poured a
glassful. Ruthie took it with a murmured thanks.

Unfortunately the surcease would be only temporary. As soon as
he gave her his message, she'd be off the walls again. He rubbed at
the ache once again thundering through his head. But it was as Ben
said: "Even peace may be purchased at too high a price." The price
of peace with Ruthie, at least for the moment, was Jenna, and it was
incontrovertibly too high.

"I called Del while you were showering, Ruthie."

"What?" She was on her feet, fury sparking from her eyes, orange
juice forgotten.

"He and Peg will be here Thursday."

"You had no right."

He took a sip of coffee. "I have a right to ask anyone I want to
my house, and if I want to ask your parents, I will."

She had no answer to that. "I don't want to see them."

"You don't have a choice. In fact, they're going to take you home with them."

Her eyes went wide and wild. "I'm not going! You can't make me."

He wasn't going to touch the "you can't make me" part because he wasn't sure he could make her. What was he to do? Carry her out kicking and screaming? That'd really be good for Jenna. "You are going. You have no choice. It is not debatable."

She collapsed in her chair. Her face crumpled. "You'd kick your own wife out?"

"Ruthie, you are not my wife. You haven't been for years and by your own choice. I think it's time you stopped dragging that argument out. It will not work. But you are Del and Peg's daughter, and they love you and want you to come home with them."

"I don't want to go. They'll beat me up with God."

"They won't, and we both know it. They are kind, gracious, and loving people. You have put them through hell, but they are still there for you."

"But you aren't?"

"No, I'm not. You have forced me to choose between you and Jenna."

"You can have us both," she cried.

He shook his head. "I'm still the same dull and pedantic man you disliked before. Colby Creek is still the same college town filled with the same academic types."

"But I like being with you." Desperation tinged her voice.

"You like having a temporary roof over your head."

"I'll be good, Drew. I will! I won't drink. I won't smoke. I won't shoot up. I won't sleep around. I promise."

Shoot up? He wasn't all that surprised. It explained why she was just skin and bones. "For how long, Ruthie? But that's not the point. You're making Jenna feel unwelcome in her own home."

"She makes me feel guilty." She stared at the floor as she made this confession. Tears ran down her cheeks. "I don't like feeling guilty. It makes me too sad. It makes my world too black."

Drew looked at her. In less than five minutes she'd been furious, desperate, and awash in self-pity. "Ruthie, have you ever thought about joining a bipolar support group? Or getting involved in church again?"

"Hello, my name is Ruth and I'm bipolar? Not in this lifetime."

"Then what about church?"

She turned sly. "I could go with you."

Why did he try? "No, but you could go with your parents."

She held up her arms, palms facing out. "No. You or not at all."

Another quote from Scripture flashed through his mind. *"Fathers, do not exasperate your children."*

"I'm making the choice for Jenna, Ruthie. She has no one but me. You have Del and Peg. You'll go with them, and she stays with me. That's the way it's going to be."

"But I don't like it that way."

"I'm sorry about that, but it changes nothing." Drew noticed his headache lessening. Just showed what making decisions could do for your health. "Your dad and I have decided to buy you a one-bedroom condo about a mile from their place."

"I don't want a condo in my hometown!"

He ignored her protest. "This way you will always have a place to live, but you don't have to live with your parents. You may leave there whenever you want, but you will always have someplace to come back to if things get rough."

Her anger reappeared. "You just want to make that blond bimbo your real fiancée."

The thought of protesting Ruthie's description of Libby flashed through his mind, but he stifled it. Rabbit trail. "I can think of worse things."

"Like me living here."

He did not contradict her.

She stormed out of the room, and when he left for Haydn later in the afternoon, he still hadn't seen her again.

When we arrived at my parents', the front door was open, letting in the heat. That in itself indicated that today was a special day. The girls and I climbed out of the van and walked to the house carrying our various offerings. Chloe and Jenna had made chocolate chip cookies and managed not to eat all the dough before baking. I carried a bowl of freshly cut fruit, the palette of melons and citrus, grapes and berries glorious to the eye. I gave a quick knock for courtesy's sake and stepped inside.

I saw my father almost at once. He had always been a big man, and he'd spent a lot of his incarceration pumping iron. At fifty-two he looked strong and healthy, though pale. A few days working in his bedraggled garden would bring his color back.

He saw me at the same time I saw him and opened his arms. "Libby!" He grabbed me in a bear hug, and Jenna grabbed the fruit bowl to keep it from being dumped on the rug.

Dad stepped back and grinned at me. "I was afraid you wouldn't come celebrate your old man's release. Religion does strange things to people sometimes, and Mimi's told me that you get more religious all the time."

I bit back a comment and said, "It's wonderful to see you, Dad." And it was. My eyes filled with tears, and I prayed fiercely that he would keep his nose clean. And that he would find Jesus.

"And there's my Chloe!" He grabbed her and gave her a bear hug too. I grabbed the chocolate chips. "I tell you, I'm too young to have a beautiful, grown-up granddaughter like you."

Chloe blushed, pleased at the compliment. "This is my new friend, Jenna, Granddad."

Jenna appeared a bit uncertain, like she wasn't sure how to greet an ex-con, but Dad put her at ease with a pat on the shoulder. "I'm glad you came with Chloe, Jenna. The poor kid needs someone her own age instead of all us old guys."

"Well, Libby, you made it." Mom came to stand beside Dad. "I wasn't sure you'd bother."

I sighed inwardly and forced a smile. I never meant to make Mom unhappy, and quite truthfully I wasn't certain how I did it, but somehow it always happened, even before I became a believer, just more strongly after. "Of course I'd come. This is a very big day."

She ignored my assurance. "Well, your sister beat you. She arrived in a limo."

I'd arrived in my flaking van.

"She looks beautiful, very stylish."

I was wearing khaki slacks and a white polo.

"She's in the kitchen helping out with the final touches on the food platters."

I was standing in the living room talking.

I forced another smile. "I'll just take these things out and see how I can help." I held out the fruit and the cookies, both of which I'd somehow ended up holding. She ignored them and so brushed aside the hours we'd spent making them.

Remember, Libby, you did this for Jesus, not for your mother.

Still, my black cloud released a little drizzle.

"Hey, Jack! Welcome home!" The next-door neighbors came in the front door, Mrs. Edgar with a tray of brownies in hand.

"Pete and Laura!" Mom said, all smiling and welcoming. "Thanks for coming over. And, Laura, what wonderful-looking brownies! How thoughtful of you."

As Mom and Dad turned their attention to the Edgars, Chloe sidled up to me.

"How are you going to talk to Aunt Tori about the jewelry with all these people here, Mom?" she whispered. She was worried, and I knew exactly how she felt.

I shrugged as Dad dragged the Edgars over to greet me. While we tried to establish how long it'd been since we'd last seen each other, Dad turned to Chloe and Jenna.

"Why don't you girls sit in the rockers on the front porch and say hi to everybody who shows up?" For a moment he looked uncertain. "That's assuming anyone bothers to come."

"Of course people will come," Mom said quickly. "You have lots of friends, Jack, and you know it."

"Had," Dad said. "Back then. We'll see about today."

There was a small silence. Then Dad grabbed the cookies from my hand. "Here, girls. Take these for sustenance."

"The girls made those for your party, Dad," I said as Chloe took the bag of cookies with a smile.

"Yeah?" He beamed at them and they beamed back. "That was so nice of you! Make sure you get a glass of iced tea or lemonade or Coke or something to wash them down."

The girls grabbed a soda from the cooler in the dining room and ran to the porch.

"Hey, Jack, you get to watch the Phillies much in there?" Mr. Edgar asked. "Not that you missed much if you didn't."

I left Mom and Dad and the Edgars and went to the kitchen with my unacknowledged bowl of fruit. I found Nan and Tori leaning against the counters. Tori had a fistful of plastic wrap that she had pulled from platters of lunch meat and cheese purchased at the supermarket, her "helping out with the final touches." The platters themselves sat ready to go out onto the dining room table.

When the two of them saw me, all conversation stopped. Of course I immediately assumed they had been talking about me. A few more drops fell on my head.

Nan gave me a tight smile. "Glad you came, Libby."

"What's with everyone thinking I wouldn't come?" I set the fruit on the counter with a bit more force than appropriate. "I wouldn't miss Dad and Pop's homecoming for anything."

"You don't visit much," Nan said.

I bit back the facts that Tori visited less than I and that in all the time I'd owned my house, Mom and Nan had only come over once before yesterday, and that was at Christmas for about fifteen minutes. They'd barely had time to eat a couple of Christmas cookies before they made their escape. I decided they thought that I, like Madge, would probably force them to read the Bible before they left. The fact that I had a Bible on an end table open to Luke 2 and the Christmas story probably confirmed their irrational and erroneous fear.

Nan pushed away from the counter. "Mike's in the backyard, taking inventory on how things have fallen to pieces while he's been gone. I think I'll go join him."

And it was Tori and me, alone in our mother's kitchen. Mom

was right; she did look gorgeous. Her black linen shorts were topped with a sapphire knit, its scooped neck revealing a generous amount of cleavage. Her black slides had a strip of twisted sapphire leather studded with mirrors that glittered when she moved. She wore her hair in one of those artless-looking dos that take forever to arrange, and her makeup was perfection. Dangling from her ears was what appeared to be a small fortune in diamonds, creating iridescent rainbows where the sun struck them.

She grinned at me, looking as fresh and innocent as dawn. "You won't believe what happened to me last night."

Did that mean she wasn't sneaking through our house stealing my jewelry?

"I helped deliver a baby! I was just telling Nan about it."

I started to laugh. I couldn't help it. The image of Tori delivering a baby was more than I could take in. After all, work was involved, and so was mess. She avoided both with a determination that matched Princess's resolve to get to the Hershey's Kisses.

"The wife of this client of mine had her baby on the casino floor, right between two rows of quarter slots."

"On the casino floor? Like literally on the floor?"

"Yep, and I was the midwife." Tori laughed. "You should've seen me, Lib, on my knees in my Marilyn Monroe dress, catching this baby as it popped out." She held out her hands to demonstrate. "Then out came the second baby, but the EMTs had arrived by then."

"Twins. Two girls?"

"A boy and a girl. They named the girl—that's the one EMTs caught—Victoria, because I helped with the delivery."

"After you! Now that is something very special."

Tori grinned, and I saw a real person in that pleasure, not the creation she had made herself to be. And I was filled with relief. If she was delivering babies on the casino floor, she wasn't sneaking around in our darkened house snitching shoeboxes.

"Where's Chloe?" Tori asked.

"Dad assigned her and Jenna to welcome patrol on the front porch."

Tori's eyes lit up. "Jenna, huh? Does that mean that her daddy's here too? Mom said she invited him."

"Drew's not here." I struggled to keep my face and voice neutral. The last thing I wanted her to know was that Drew and I had had words and that I ached more than was appropriate over it.

Tori studied me for a moment, and I wondered what she saw. Then she pushed away from the counter. "I've got something for Chlo."

"Oh no, Tori. I don't want you buying any more things for her. Nothing. You've done more than enough already."

She waved her hand, as if she were swatting my words away as she would a bothersome mosquito. "I've already bought it."

"So return it. You know as well as I that you shouldn't be spending money on things for Chloe. Don't you owe a bunch to some not-very-nice man who keeps making threats?"

She glanced at me quickly, then gave a negligent shrug. "It's nothing. It's taken care of."

"You paid off your debt? All of it?" *With the contents of my shoebox?* All my ugly suspicions rushed back. "What about the puzzles?"

"They're nothing, Libby. Just forget it, all of it."

"Nothing? I read those puzzles, Tori. I even did the one you dropped on the Fourth. PAY UP OR ELSE."

She grinned at me. "How many hours did it take?"

"This is not funny. PAY UP OR ELSE. Or else what? Are they going to kill you too?"

Tori gave a strange little laugh. "You're overreacting to a bad joke."

"A dead man is a bad joke? Give me a break! I know you're deeply in debt, and I-I don't want to trip over you some morning."

"You're crazy, Libby."

"No, I'm not. I'm scared. For you. I'll help you any way I can."

She frowned. "Listen hard, Lib. I do not need your help. I do not want your help. There is no threat. None. I've taken care of it." She spun on her heel and strode into the living room.

I followed her, more worried than ever.

"Hey, Chloe!" Tori called. "Come in here, sweetie. I've got something for you."

Chloe appeared in the front doorway. "For me?" Her eyes were eager.

Tori nodded as she reached into the corner behind the sofa and pulled out a bulging garbage bag, the big green kind that people put leaves in. She thrust it at Chloe as everyone gathered to watch.

"Whoa!" Chloe took it with a large smile. "My own garbage bag. Gee, thanks, Aunt Tori." She glanced at me, and I smiled. I could see her relax. Whatever her present, she might as well enjoy it.

There was a curly ribbon bow tying the bag shut, and Mom had to get a pair of scissors to cut it loose. The bag fell away revealing a green microsuede pillow, the kind that looks like the top half of an overstuffed chair.

"Cool." Chloe nodded her appreciation as she hugged it to her chest, its arms wrapping around her sides in an inanimate hug. "It'll go great in my daffodil room."

"Very cool," Jenna echoed. "Look, Chloe! It's got speakers in each arm and a sound jack."

Chloe pulled the pillow away to see where Jenna pointed. Her smile was glorious. "Thanks, Aunt Tori!" Chloe dropped the pillow on the sofa and threw herself into Tori's arms.

Tori smiled smugly at me over Chloe's shoulder, and the little dark cloud over my head grew blacker, the raindrops denser. I felt very ugly as I told myself I should be grateful instead of suspicious, but there it was, the nasty truth about Libby Keating. She expected ulterior motives.

"Wait! That's not all." Tori pulled a small package from her purse. She held it out to Chloe.

Chloe ripped the paper away and held the gift high for everyone to see. "An iPod! I've been wanting one forever!"

That was news to me, but even if I'd known, there was that pesky mortgage.

Tori pulled a rectangle from her hiding place by the sofa and held it out.

"More?" Chloe tore it open, and there was a docking station for the iPod.

"And here." Tori handed over an envelope.

Jenna peered over Chloe's shoulder. "ITune cards! Fifty dollars' worth!"

"You can download to your heart's content, kiddo." Tori was all sweet smiles. With a wink at Dad, she added, "And legally too."

I forced myself to smile along with them, but I felt anything but glad. What I felt was threatened and wary and distressed. When a knock sounded on the door, I was only too happy to play hostess. When I saw Drew standing there looking much too handsome in cutoff cargoes, sandals, and a deep brown polo that was a perfect match for his hair, my eyes teared. "You came!"

He frowned. "Of course, though I usually don't make people cry when I show up."

The tears overflowed. "I'm just so glad to see you." Someone on my team. Even if he was still miffed at me, he had come.

He took me by the elbow and pulled me onto the porch. "What's wrong, Libby?"

I wanted to tell him, but my throat was too clogged with gratitude at his appearance to get words out. "Walk?" I managed.

Without a word, he turned and stepped off the porch beside me, his hand still warm on my elbow. We walked two blocks while I struggled to get my emotions under control.

"I feel so stupid," I muttered, my eyes fixed on the sidewalk. "The last thing you need is another woman getting weepy on you."

He stopped and put a finger under my chin, forcing me to look at him. "We both know you aren't stupid. Opinionated, perhaps." And he smiled slightly.

I managed a watery smile in return. "I'm sorry about that."

He nodded, his eyes warm. "Me too."

And just like that, things were fine between us. I gave a mental blink. Was that how it worked? You apologized and let the anger go? Was that what the Bible meant when it said, "Do not let the sun go down while you are still angry"?

"So since you're not stupid nor given to being overly weepy, whatever's bothering you is real. So tell me."

I did. I told him about Tori's gifts to Chloe and my fear that she was trying to woo my daughter away.

"I know it's paranoid; I know it." I sniffed. "But Tori could hurt her so badly. She could teach her to be like the rest of the family. She could turn her from the Lord. She could turn her from me." And I started crying again. "I'm sorry," I blubbered, though I wasn't certain what I was sorry for this time.

He pulled me close, just holding me. I wrapped my arms around his middle and rested my cheek in the hollow below his shoulder. I couldn't remember the last time someone had held me like this, and it felt so good. I wanted to stay leaning on his strength forever, so I straightened away. When I swiped at my teary face, Drew pulled a handkerchief from his pocket and handed it to me.

"Thanks." I mopped my cheeks and blew my nose. So feminine and attractive, to go with my red eyes. I was about to shove the handkerchief into my slacks pocket when he held out his hand.

"You don't want this back."

He wiggled his fingers in a give-it-here gesture. Slightly embarrassed, I returned the handkerchief, and he slid it back in his pocket.

"Feeling better?"

I nodded. "But there's more."

He reached for my hand and started walking again. "So tell me the rest."

This time I told him about the missing jewelry and the puzzles. "And then there's the body. Mick."

"What makes you think he has anything to do with Tori?"

I confessed how I'd found one of the puzzles on Mick's body.

"And I thought my life was complicated," he said as we stopped at the walk to Mom and Dad's. We'd made a large square, arriving back where we'd started. He'd held my hand the whole way, and he gave it a little squeeze. "Don't worry. We'll figure something out."

Those six words untied the knots in my stomach, and ribbons

of hope unfurled in their place. My little black cloud faded away, and the Light was once more visible. God had sent me a lifeline.

Drew and I had just stepped onto my parents' porch when Tori's limo pulled to the curb. The driver gave a single beep.

Tori appeared in the doorway and gave a wave. "Be right there." She turned to Drew. "Hey, handsome."

"Hi, Tori. Nice to see you."

"But nicer to see Lib?" She stared pointedly at our clasped hands. I immediately tried to pull away, but Drew tightened his grip. In some indefinable and slightly scary way, I felt he was making a statement, but I was unsure what he meant. Was it merely *"Don't pick on Libby; it's not nice?"* Or was it more personal? I was afraid to speculate. Too much hope could swamp me.

Tori pushed the screen door open, and Drew and I stepped into the crowded living room. Mom saw us immediately. She turned to Dad, spoke to him, and led the way to where we stood with Tori. Again I tried to pull my hand free, and again Drew held tight.

"Well, Drew, I'm so glad you came," Mom said with more enthusiasm than she'd shown me. "When Libby showed up with just the girls, I thought you were going to let us down."

"I'd never let Libby down like that," Drew said quietly.

My breath hitched in my throat.

"Dad," Tori said, "this is Drew Canfield, Jenna's father. Drew, my father, Jack Keating."

Drew had to drop my hand to shake Dad's. "Nice to meet you, Jack. This has got to be a good day for you." When he released Dad, he casually laid his hand across my shoulders.

"You've got that right. Home with all my girls." He smiled at Mimi, Tori, and me, and I realized he was truly glad to see all of us.

"Hey, Dad!" Jenna wore a smile as she crossed the room, and I could feel Drew's great delight that his girl was so happy. "You should see all the stuff Chloe got from Aunt Tori!"

"Does that mean it's what you want too?" He smiled so she knew he was teasing.

"Of course. Oh my gosh! Look out there! It's a limo."

"Pretty, isn't it?" Tori asked as we all studied the sleek black auto. My van, parked in front of it, seemed especially disreputable.

"You should see the inside," Tori went on. "There's a bar with all kinds of drinks and snacks. There's a fresh flower in a vase every day. And the seats—well, you just sink into them."

"What's it doing here?" Dad asked.

"It takes Tori back and forth to work," Mom said with pride.

"Sweet," Chloe said.

"Very sweet," Jenna agreed.

"Impressive," Dad said.

"Want to ride home with me in it?" Tori asked the girls. "There's plenty of room."

I tensed, and Drew gave my shoulder a light squeeze. *Don't over-react.* I did my best to relax, to see no threat, just a loving aunt offering a good time to her niece.

"Oh boy, do we!" Chloe's face glowed.

Jenna just stared at the limo and nodded, a huge smile creasing her face. "Has it got a sunroof?"

"So we can stand and wave as we drive past!" Chloe's eyes glowed. "Mom, you can take my pillow and stuff, right?"

"Sure. I've never ridden in a limousine, so you'll have to tell me all about it."

"It's much cooler than the van."

Talk about stating the obvious. "That wouldn't be hard."

A car pulled up behind the limo, and we watched a slight man with a developing paunch and lots of moussed dark curls climb out. All my bright ribbons of hope tied themselves in the familiar knots of fear. I took an involuntary step backward, coming up against Drew. He leaned down and whispered for me alone, "It'll be all right."

I tried to believe him but couldn't. *Oh, Lord, help!*

"Look who's here, Jack." Mom threw the screen open and held her arms wide. "Eddie, how wonderful to see you!" She hugged him as if he were a long-lost son.

"Eddie." Dad slapped him on the back several times, rocking him on his heels. "Good to see you, man."

"You too, big guy. Tori. Lib. And—I'm sorry. I forget your name."

Right, I thought. Eddie never forgot anything.

"Drew Canfield."

"Oh yeah." He took in Drew's hand on my shoulder. "Still hanging on Lib, eh? Used to do that myself, you know."

"Well, what do you think of this young lady, Eddie?" Dad smiled at Chloe.

I reached for my daughter and pulled her to me. Drew had been right. Madge had been right. I had been wrong. And it was too late. I knew it as surely as I knew my daughter was about to be deeply hurt.

Chloe came willingly to my side, aware of emotional currents rushing through the room like the Niagara River toward the falls, but not understanding them.

"So, Chloe, what do you think of your old man?" He draped his arm around Eddie's shoulders.

I heard my father's voice through a haze of panic. "Dad, no!"

"What?" Chloe was confused. Over Eddie's shoulder Tori smirked.

Dad glanced at me, then Chloe, and frowned. "Your old man. Eddie here. Your father."

Chloe looked as if she had been struck. She stared at Eddie in horror. "You?"

Oh, Lord, what do I do? What do I say?

"It's true, cookie." Eddie was beaming from ear to ear.

Chloe spun to me, her face green. "Mom, tell me it isn't so. Tell me he is not my father." Her eyes begged, and never had I wanted to lie as much as I wanted to at that moment.

"Come on, Chloe." I tried to pull her toward the door. "It's time to go."

My stomach was churning out enough acid to eat through one of the supports on the Walt Whitman Bridge we had driven over to get here.

She pulled away in revulsion. "He can't be. He can't be!" And she raced out of the house. She took the steps in one bound.

"Hey," Eddie said. "What's that all about?"

For once in his life my father looked chagrined. "I'm sorry! I didn't know she didn't know."

I wanted to be furious at him. I wanted to rail at him, to blame him, to tell him it was all his fault that Chloe was crying. He was a terrible person to make his granddaughter so distressed.

But it wasn't his fault. It was mine. I had let fear keep me from doing what was right. Just another proof that my mother was correct about me. No worth. No smarts. Just someone who always got it wrong.

"Let me talk to her." Eddie started to follow Chloe.

"No!" I grabbed his arm.

"Why not? I've got as much right to talk to her as you do. She's my kid too."

"You've got no rights," I hissed. "You abdicated them more than thirteen years ago." I spun and went after Chloe, but he was right on my heels. She'd reached the front sidewalk and in her rush, probably with her vision blurred with tears, stepped on an uneven section. She went down much as I had when I tripped over Mick.

"Chloe!" I ran toward her.

She heard me coming and pulled herself up. Blood ran down her right leg from a nasty gash. She ignored it and threw herself into the limo. I crouched in the doorway as she huddled in the far corner of the backseat, arms wrapped around her middle.

"Chloe," I began.

She gave me her back.

I climbed in and sat beside her. "Oh, honey, I'm so sorry. I never meant for you to find out this way."

She turned her head slightly, just enough to look at me. I don't think she was even aware of the blood running down her leg. Her eyes were red rimmed and tear filled, accusing me and rightly so. "Him, Mom? *Him?*" Disgust, pain, disbelief, and deep sorrow washed across her face. She made a gagging sound.

"I was sixteen, honey. That's all I can say in my defense."

She stared at me. "Sixteen? I'm thirteen, and I know he's a sleaze."

Jenna appeared in the door of the car, Bactine and Band-Aids in hand. "Your Aunt Tori sent these." Chloe began to cry. She held out her arms to Jenna, and her new best friend climbed over me, held her close, and comforted her. I sat, uncertain. Leaving didn't feel right, but then neither did staying.

Chloe finally looked at me. "Good-bye, Mother."

The ice in her voice froze my heart. I turned, so full of pain I could barely move. A hand reached in to me, and through the blur of tears I saw Drew. I put my hand in his and let him pull me from the car.

17

□□□

CHLOE SAT SILENT AND STONY-FACED as Carl drove them home. Eddie Mancini was her father. Her father! It made her skin crawl just thinking about being related to him. And if she let herself think about what he and her mother—her mother!—must have done, she wanted to throw up all over Aunt Tori's excellent limo.

She glanced at the red stain on the pale gray leather seat. Her blood. There was more on the carpet, but at least it was a deeper gray. Maybe the stain wouldn't be as visible.

She hadn't even realized she'd cut herself until Jenna started mopping her up. Now she had a very sore knee that throbbed in time with her breaking heart.

In one way she didn't know why she was so surprised that the creep Eddie was her father. She'd known for a long time that there was something wrong with whoever he was. Otherwise Mom would have told her about him. Mom was blurt-it-out honest about everything else, sort of like she was afraid God would get mad at her if she even shaded a story, and she didn't want God mad at her. In contrast she was silent as midnight about her paternal unit.

Chloe almost choked when she remembered how she and Jenna had joked about "paternal units." She almost cried with longing when she thought of Jenna's dad. Now there was a man you'd be proud to call your father. He was tall and handsome, and he didn't strut around like he thought he was something special. He was intelligent, a college professor, but most important, he was nice. He loved Jenna. He loved God.

Jenna was mad at him about being so nice to her mom, but Chloe thought it just showed how under-the-skin wonderful he was. It made him seem stronger, and she understood why Ruthie came running to him when things were hard, even if Jenna didn't. She'd feel safe running to him too.

But Eddie Mancini? *Eeyew!*

"Chloe?" Jenna touched her shoulder.

Poor Jenna. She had to deal with Ruthie. Now there was a sad lady. And poor her. She had to deal with Icky Eddie.

"You okay?" Jenna whispered.

Chloe looked at her friend's concerned face and thought that the nicest thing God had done for her in a long time was to have Jenna "just happen" to be living in Philadelphia on her street while she was there.

Jenna studied her with worried eyes, waiting for an answer. Was she okay? Chloe shrugged. In the background Aunt Tori rattled on about her job and how glamorous things were in the casino and how she got to meet famous performers and really rich guys. Yeah, well, if things were so great and everybody was so rich, why was she stealing stuff from Mom?

"Carl," Aunt Tori called to the guy driving. "Did you get what we talked about earlier?"

Carl nodded. "I did. It's up here on the seat beside me."

"Pass it on back, please."

Carl reached to his side, then lifted a plastic shopping bag over the seat. "Had me a great time at Circuit City."

Aunt Tori grabbed the bag and ignored Carl. "I was going to save this for later, Chlo, but I think you need it now, after the evening you've had. I'm so sorry your mother sprang Eddie on you like that."

With a huge smile she set the shopping bag on Chloe's lap.

"Thanks, Aunt Tori," she managed, though the last thing she wanted was to act happy over some present. There was only so much love a person could buy, especially the person who had first brought Icky Eddie into her life. Aunt Tori might think she didn't know that she'd been the one to bring Eddie on the Fourth, but she did. She also saw how it had upset her mother. Not that she'd understood at the time, but she did now.

She glanced from the present to Aunt Tori. Something was not quite right there. Chloe'd seen the way Mom-Mom and Great-Nan gave Mom a hard time, but she hadn't realized Aunt Tori was like that too, not until they'd lived together in Philadelphia. Aunt Tori was fun, and she was beautiful and exciting, but she was also—Chloe searched for the right word—*flawed*. Aunt Tori was flawed.

"Go on," Aunt Tori urged. "Open it."

Chloe pushed the bag away and saw a box that took her breath.

"Chloe!" Jenna squealed. "It's a Wii! With two Wiimotes and lots of games!"

Then again, maybe you could buy a lot of love with the right gift even if you were flawed.

⬜⬜⬜

Drew studied Libby's family as Tori's limo pulled away. They made his family seem like the Cleavers.

Mimi eyed Libby like she was something unpleasant she had stepped in.

Cynthia shook her head back and forth like she wasn't surprised that Libby would ruin this special day.

Jack looked taken aback, and Drew suspected he hadn't expected anything like the reaction he'd gotten from Chloe or Libby. In his years away, he had lost track of the fact that Chloe had been kept innocent of the identity of her father.

Mike—whom Drew hadn't officially met—seemed bewildered, like he didn't have any idea what was going on, which he probably didn't.

Eddie was pale and sweaty, even his moussed curls drooping, though he tried to appear cocky and insulted that neither Chloe nor Libby had welcomed him as part of their little family.

And Tori had been secretly delighted, a small smile playing on her lips as she climbed into the limo after the girls.

He turned to Libby, who was clearly devastated, and it tore at his heart. That she had lived with this subtle abuse and lack of support as a little girl, as a young teen, and as a too-young mom filled him with sorrow. That she had become such a wonderful woman in spite of it all blew him away.

Jack approached her, his hand outstretched. "I'm so sorry, Lib."

Libby placed her hand in her father's. Her shoulders were slumped, and her distress was palpable, at least to Drew, but still she said, "It's okay, Dad. It's my fault. I should have told her the truth years ago. I'm just sorry I ruined your homecoming."

Mimi moved to stand beside her husband. "Well, it's the kind of thing I've come to expect from you."

Libby flinched, and Jack looked at Mimi in surprise. Drew scowled. Maybe Jenna was lucky to be ignored after all.

Mimi glared at the negative reactions her comment brought. "I just meant that Lib has become too righteous to talk about her wild younger days. You all know that's true."

Wild younger days? How about abandoned younger days. He was pleased when Libby actually defended herself.

"You're wrong, Mom. I've talked a lot with Chloe about my mistakes when I was younger." Her voice was barely shaking, and Drew felt inordinately proud of her. "I've told her I was wrong, and I've warned her against making the same bad choices."

Anger flared in Eddie, displacing his pasty look with a red flush. "So I'm just a mistake, am I?" He stood with his hands on his hips, glaring at Libby.

"Of course you were, Eddie," Libby said. "I should have been strong enough to handle all the pressure of"—she hesitated—"*things* myself."

"*Things?*" Cynthia snapped at Libby's heels like an angry terrier. "So it's all Mike and Jack's fault?"

Libby closed her eyes, and Drew suspected she was casting an urgent prayer heavenward. She took a deep breath, opened her eyes, and looked at Cynthia.

"I neither said nor meant that, Nan. My sin was my sin."

"Wait a minute here," Eddie complained.

"Libby." Drew felt compelled to defend her in front of these people who should be her main support, not her accusers. "Don't be so hard on yourself. You were sixteen. Your family was in turmoil. You didn't have anyone supporting you."

Mimi skewered Drew with a baleful look. "So Libby's failures are our fault after all."

About ninety percent, Drew wanted to yell, but he didn't. One of Ben's pithy sayings crossed his mind: *"Any fool can criticize, condemn, and complain, and most fools do."* He bit back the urge to quote it, lest he become another of this crowd whom Ben would consider fools. Instead he concentrated on projecting telepathic support to the hurting woman standing beside him with such grace. Didn't these people see she was hemorrhaging emotionally over her daughter's distress and her contribution to that pain? Where was their triage of touch? Their sutures of sympathy? Their gauze wrappings of love?

"Well, it would have been nice if someone had told me how things stood," Jack said.

Drew could see him beginning to get angry that he had been the one to cause all the commotion. He was a man looking to reassign responsibility. Was that how he handled the knowledge that guns he resold killed others, killed cops?

"Come on, Lib." Drew took her by the elbow before she became her father's scapegoat. He had to get her away from these people. "Let me drive you home."

She looked at him with a dazed expression. "I've got my van."

"We'll come back for it tomorrow."

She studied him for a minute as if she were trying to assimilate his comments. She was definitely hanging on by a thread.

"You don't want to drive alone tonight."

"I don't want to drive alone tonight." She took a deep breath and nodded. "You're right. I don't."

They started toward Drew's CR-V.

"Wait, Libby." Eddie ran up to them. "In all the fuss, I forgot to give this to Tori. It's really why I came. And to see Jack and Mike, a'course."

"A'course." Drew let his sarcasm show. Eddie shot him a venomous look.

"About Chloe, Eddie," Libby whispered, all her fears for her daughter written on her pale face.

Eddie frowned and waved a hand dismissively. "I gotta admit the kid's cute and all, but I don't want a kid any more than she wants me."

Libby pressed her hand to her heart and let out a great sigh. She squeezed her eyes shut, as if she was trying to push back tears. "Thank you, Eddie."

Eddie shrugged, as if giving up a marvelous kid like Chloe was no big deal. "Yeah, yeah. I'm a saint." He thrust a folded piece of paper into Libby's hand. "Just give this to Tori." He turned away and started back to the front door.

Libby stared at the paper. "Oh, God."

Drew recognized it as a prayer even if Eddie didn't, and he understood. He recognized the size of the sheet and the black block lettering: TORI. Another puzzle.

Libby called after Eddie, "Where did you get this?"

When he didn't respond, she ran after him, grabbing him by the arm. He turned with a frown.

"Where did you get this?"

He shook his head as Drew moved up beside them.

"You've got to tell me. Who gave you this to deliver? Who? Who's threatening my sister?"

Again Eddie shook his head, unwilling or unable to meet her eyes, something that struck Drew as hinky, given Eddie's brash nature.

"Tell her, Eddie. It's the least you can do for her."

Eddie glared at Drew, then glanced at Libby, taking in the fine tremors that shook her, causing the paper to flutter in her hand. "The least I can do for her is *not* tell her."

"Come on, Eddie." Jack held the screen door open for the rest of the family to enter the house. "We need to talk about old times, and I need to catch up on what you been doing lately."

"Be right there," Eddie called.

Libby looked from Eddie to her father and back to Eddie in horror. "Don't you dare pull my father back into the cesspool, Eddie. I don't know what you've been up to, and I don't want to know, but I know it's not good." She held out the puzzle as proof.

He grinned cockily at her. "Big stuff coming my way, Lib. Jack'll find it all fascinating."

"Please let him alone, Eddie. Please! It's been one of my worst nightmares for years that Dad'll fall back into what he was because that's what he knows."

"Hey, Jack's a big boy. He can take care of himself."

"Think what it would do to your daughter if her grandfather got into trouble with the law again," Libby pleaded. "I know what it did to me."

"Hey! Don't bring the kid into it! I told you. It's like she's not mine. And you survived just fine." And he rooster-strutted up the walk and into the house.

" 'He who falls in love with himself will have no rivals,' " Drew quoted.

Libby stood a moment, staring bleakly at her parents' home, Tori's puzzle dangling from her limp hand.

"Come on, Lib. Time to go." Drew took her elbow and led her toward his car. He opened the passenger door and helped her in.

Then he knelt beside her, the elevation of the curb making him level with her. He reached out and pushed a fallen curl off her forehead. It was neither as soft as Jenna's hair nor as coarse as his own. It was Libby's alone. "You going to be okay?"

She gave him a wan smile. "Maybe someday."

He leaned forward and kissed her cheek. "Someday's good. We can work with someday."

She put a hand on his jaw. "Thank you."

He stared into her hazel eyes and his heart swelled. "An appreciative woman. What a concept." She'd probably never understand how much her generous spirit meant to him, and he wasn't sure he'd ever be able to convey the depths of his attraction to her. Was it love? It was much too soon to bat words like that around. Would it become love? Who knew? Certainly not him.

"Did you see him lose it when Chloe cut herself?"

He blinked. So much for deep philosophical musings. But what could he expect considering the night she'd had? "Eddie?"

Libby nodded. "He never could stand blood."

"A wimp as well as a weasel?"

"A wimpy weasel." She gave a slight smile. "Once I gave myself a paper cut, nothing bad, but a bead of blood welled up. I thought Eddie was going to fall over. He turned all pale and sweaty. He hasn't grown out of it. Must be embarrassing."

"Anything that embarrasses Eddie sounds good to me."

He shut her carefully in the hot CR-V, walked around, and climbed in. While he turned the motor over and adjusted the much-needed air conditioning, Libby opened the puzzle.

"Help me do it?" she asked. "I'm not real good with crosswords. Sudoku is more my style. Tori's the one who loves crosswords."

"Which someone obviously knows. What's one-across?"

ACROSS

1 not righthanded
5 third part of a suit
6 wrong
8 messy places
11 they aren't smart
12 one who attacks
13 hits, runs, and…
15 straight from the horse's mouth
17 what you owe
18 trouble-making disposition
20 like Mick
21 rim, border
22 arrested
23 take by force

DOWN

2 beneath the roof
3 mm mm good
4 ring carbons
7 crying in fright
9 beating
10 they live in 8 across
14 what was paid for Red Chief
16 there are nine
17 takes life
19 lost balance, swayed

"One-across is *not right-handed.* Five letters. I know that. *Lefty.*" She wrote it in. "And it's not even a scary word."

"Two-across?" Drew asked.

"No two-across. The next across is five. *Third part of a suit.*"

"Are we talking suit as in what a man wears, or are we talking suit as in cards? After all, Tori works in the gambling industry."

"I don't know." Libby sounded frustrated. "See? That's why I do Sudoku. It always uses numbers one to nine."

"Well, something must intersect five-across." Assuming the creator was at all logical.

"Yes. Two-down, *beneath the roof,* five letters, and three-down, *mm mm good,* five letters. They both attach to *lefty.*"

Drew smiled. "I bet you two, *beneath the roof,* attaches to the *e* in *lefty* and is *eaves. Mm mm good* attaches to the *t* and is *tasty.*"

"How do you know that?"

"I don't. It's an educated guess. Does it work?"

She wrote the words in, then said triumphantly, "The third part of a suit is *vests.*"

"*Third part* is singular and *vests* is plural? Someone's not playing quite fair."

She made a sound that was a cross between a snort and a laugh, and it was music to his ears. "Come on now, Drew. I don't think fair is a big consideration for someone who leaves dead bodies and threatening puzzles."

They worked through the rest of the puzzle as they sped toward Philadelphia. By the time they reached the bridge, Libby had to turn on the interior light to see well enough to figure out the embedded message.

Drew pulled up to the toll booth. If he kept going to New Jersey like this, he was going to have to invest in E-ZPass so he could just drive through without having to wait in the lines. He glanced over at Libby. "What's it say?"

"LAST WARNING."

"Huh."

She stared at him in frustration. "That's it? My sister's life is threatened again and all you can say is *huh*? We've got words like *amiss, moneys, murders, dead,* and *busted* as well as *diamonds*—did you see the earrings she was wearing tonight?—and *last warning,* and all you can say is *huh*?"

He was delighted to hear her grumpiness because it meant she had come out of her daze. "Don't forget *raider, swine,* and *thrashing.*"

"Oh, you sure know how to make a girl feel better about things."

He grinned at her as they crested the top of the bridge and the Philadelphia skyline came into view. She glared at him, trying to hold on to her grouch, but she couldn't manage it. She leaned back on the headrest with a slight smile.

When she fell quiet, he did too, letting her nap, think, worry, or pray as she needed.

After a few minutes she said in a wondering voice, "How could I have been so stupid?"

"Don't be so hard on yourself, Lib. If there's one thing I've learned about you, it's that you have a tendency to beat yourself up."

"But I was wrong!"

"Yeah, and you got caught. 'You may delay but time will not.' But we're all wrong at times."

"Not with so much at stake." Her voice was a bit wobbly again.

"Chloe's a smart kid, and she knows you love her. She'll figure it out. Just give her time."

"But how will she ever trust me again?"

He reached over and patted her hands, which were clutched together in her lap. "She knows there wasn't malice in your silence, but protection. She'll forgive you."

"Oh, God, I hope so! Please!" The prayer was laced with equal parts fear and desperate hope.

"Libby, have you ever thought that maybe you're overreacting a bit here?"

"What?" Her surprised outrage made his ears ring.

"Easy there. Let me finish. Your mistake wasn't an offense against God and mankind. It was a mistake in judgment. People all make mistakes."

She glared at him. "So you've said. And that simplistic reasoning makes it okay?"

"Of course not, but it makes it human. It makes you human."

"So I'm human and Chloe suffers. Great. Now I definitely feel better."

"I bet you think you're a failure as a mother right about now, don't you?"

"I am." He heard the anguish in her voice.

"No, you're not. You have loved her and cared for her for years. She knows that, and she loves you."

"And I ruined it all."

He decided to be a bit brutal to knock her out of her self-pity, which, though understandable, was unacceptable. "Get over it, Keating."

She narrowed her eyes at him. "Easy for you to say, buster. Your daughter's talking to you."

"Barely, but another topic. Just listen to me here without being defensive. I'm not accusing you."

Libby sighed and stared at her hands. "Go ahead."

"I totally messed up in my marriage." He pulled into his parking spot and turned off the engine but made no move to get out of the car. Neither did Libby. The darkness shrouded them, cocooning them in a private world. He reached for her hand and laced their fingers.

"Yeah, but a lot of that was Ruthie's fault." Libby turned in the seat to face him. "None of this is Chloe's. It's mine." She slugged herself in the chest to bring home the self-identification.

Talk about stubborn. Drew rubbed the back of his neck. "What I'm about to tell you is one of the main reasons I survived the guilt after Ruthie left." *Lord, help me say this right.*

She looked at him with a passive curiosity.

"What you're feeling right now is useless regret. Regret is what we feel when we make a mistake or have an accident or embarrass ourselves or commit a crime and get caught or when our conscience pricks. We feel it over things we wish we could change, big things and little things. Regret either eats you up little by little, like being nibbled to death by ducks, or it helps you not make the same mistake again."

He could feel her polite passivity changing to active interest.

"It comes down to being nibbled to nothing or learning from it. You get to choose which."

They sat quietly in the hot car while she thought and he prayed. Finally she turned to him.

"She calls him 'Icky Eddie.'"

Drew gave a hoot of laughter at the unexpected comment. She was flexible steel to the core whether she realized it or not.

"So how do you undo regret?"

"Often you can't undo it. Whatever caused it may be permanent. My divorce is permanent. I'm still dull and pedantic. Ruthie's still ill. But I'm not getting nibbled to death. I've learned to give my regret to the Lord, to remember that Jesus is the great Burden Bearer."

She nodded. "He is. I know He is. He has been for all the other heavy loads I've had to carry. I know He will be with this too. It just hurts a lot right now."

"You wouldn't be normal if it didn't. But if you learn from it…" He opened his door and got out.

She climbed out her side and walked into the lane at his side. He took her hand again as they approached the front door of Aunt Stella's. With a little *tsking* sound, Libby reached out and dead-headed a couple of spent geraniums. She stood a moment, staring at the brown flowers.

"Life's like a flower box, isn't it?" She looked at him. "The brilliant blooms of joy and the past-their-prime moments of pain. You can't have one without the other."

He glanced at his house then and saw Ruthie's silhouette in the window of his bedroom, staring down at them. *His* bedroom. " 'Yet man is born to trouble as surely as sparks fly upward,' Job says. But the apostle Peter says, 'Cast all your anxiety on him because he cares for you.' "

Some days his casting abilities were required so often that he felt sure he'd be a prize winner in any heavenly bass fishing competition going.

18

□□□

DREW FOLLOWED ME INSIDE, where we immediately heard the girls shouting and laughing.

"They sound like they're in Tori's room." I didn't want to go up and check because I was unsure of how Chloe would react when she saw me, but I had to at least say hello even if they didn't want to talk to me. There would be no days of tense silence in my home.

The girls were in front of the large television hidden in the satin-wood armoire. They were whipping their arms all over the place as on-screen little animated figures raced around a tennis court. Tori sat cross-legged on the bed laughing with them.

"Look, Mom!" Chloe yelled as she whipped an arm and just missed clipping Jenna in the ear. "Aunt Tori gave me a Wii!"

I was delighted to see her happy, but I was gripped by the fiercest wave of jealousy I'd ever felt, just what I needed to end a perfect day. I was certain the tears I was furiously blinking back were as vivid a green as the Irish countryside. I'd messed up big-time this evening, and Tori had, as usual, found a way to shine.

I felt a comforting hand on my shoulder and a gentle squeeze. Drew had followed me upstairs and was standing right behind me. The poor man would probably never darken our door again after tonight. If regret did teach you not to make the same mistake again, he'd undoubtedly learned not to have anything to do with emotional women.

"That looks like lots of fun, Chlo," I managed. She was so busy trying to beat Jenna that she didn't even hear my words, much less their forced and false enthusiasm. "And great gift, Tori. Hard to beat." Impossible to beat.

Tori smiled that complacent smile that drove me crazy.

God, I am so terrible! I'd rather see my kid unhappy than made happy by my sister. Forgive me!

"Got anything to drink?" Drew asked quietly in my ear.

I nodded and fled to the kitchen, grateful for the excuse to escape the site of another defeat. I pulled open the refrigerator door and stood staring at the contents without seeing a thing.

After a couple of minutes I became aware of Drew moving his hand repeatedly up my arm from my wrist to my elbow in little painless pinches.

"What are you doing?" I asked as I brushed his hand away.

"Nibbling."

I shut my eyes and shook my head. He was driving me nuts with his desire to stop me from wallowing in my melancholy. Next thing I knew, he'd be quoting, "Rejoice in the Lord always. I will say it again: Rejoice!"

He'd almost had me in the car with his little talk on regret, but

Tori's smug smile and Chloe's joy over something I could never afford to give her threw me right back into my black funk. If I wanted to be sad and hate myself and see all the possible negative ramifications of my errors, who was he to stop me? I had a right to be unhappy. I had reason. If I wanted my theme song to be, "Nobody likes me; everybody hates me. I think I'll go eat worms," I was entitled.

But deep down I knew he was right. I did have to choose. Nibbled to death by ducks. Or do as Saint Paul said: learn to be content whatever the circumstances. I groaned silently. Drew even had the Bible on his side.

"Have you got anything to eat?" He peered over my shoulder. "I never did get any food at your parents'."

I reached for the mayo and an onion. Tuna salad sandwiches would be good for a hot evening. "Poor Drew, caught up in all our family dramas."

He shrugged. "You've been caught in mine, so it's only fair."

I grabbed a can of tuna from the shelf and quickly mixed the salad. "Whole wheat or oatmeal bread? Toasted or not?"

"I really don't care. Just having someone make me a sandwich feels too wonderful to be particular."

I laughed at his open enjoyment and slipped four slices of oatmeal bread in Aunt Stella's toaster. When they popped, I buttered them, then added the tuna mix, tomato slices, and some lettuce. "Let's sit out back."

We carried our paper plates to the table on the little patio. "What would you like to drink?"

"Coke?"

I went inside and returned with a couple of cans and a basket of chips to find Tori sitting in my seat, eating my sandwich. With a sigh I handed her my Coke and went back to make another sandwich and get another drink.

While I worked, I tried to decide how I'd approach Tori about the diamond brooch she'd taken and about the new LAST WARNING puzzle. I felt terrible about parading more family dysfunction in front of Drew, but if I didn't catch Tori while she was here, I might not have another chance. After all, the missing pin and the missing shoebox didn't affect only my finances. Madge would suffer by their loss too.

And wrong was wrong whether we suffered or not.

I grabbed all four puzzles, and with them and my dinner I went back to the patio. I sat and took three bites to fortify myself before I held the most recent puzzle out to Tori.

"Eddie asked me to give this to you."

She looked at her name printed on it. She actually pushed back in her chair as if it was a serpent about to bite. "He said no more," she whispered.

"Who said no more? Eddie?"

She wrapped her arms around herself as if she were suddenly cold. "Luke."

"Who's Luke?"

"A—a friend."

Some friend. "Is he the one you owe the money?"

"What makes you think I owe money?"

"I'll admit it's hard to believe the way you're spending on stuff for Chloe, but we've got these." I picked up the puzzles. "YOU ARE OVERDUE and PAY UP OR ELSE. So I'll ask again: is Luke the one you owe money?"

She nodded as she made little sweat circles on the table with her soda can.

"And is he a loan shark?"

She glanced at me, then back at the circles. "He's a legitimate businessman. He has a string of four paycheck loan shops here in Philadelphia with numbers five and six about to open."

"The kind where you ask for a short-term loan against your next pay?" Drew asked, his voice hard. "The kind that charge exorbitant interest?"

"They don't charge interest," Tori said defensively. "They ask fees for processing and lending. There's nothing illegal in that."

"No, there's not, at least in Pennsylvania where there is no limit placed on the fees charged."

I was unfamiliar with shops like this and looked at Drew for more explanation.

"I know all about them because Ruthie went to them when she first left. We had a joint account, so she borrowed against my pay two weeks in the offing. She went to several of these shops and wrote checks for the amount she wanted plus the 'fees.'"

I could hear the quotes around the word *fees*.

"None of the shops lend large sums. They don't have to. The loan is short term. Three to five hundred dollars is typical, though some shops let you borrow as much as fifteen hundred. Ruthie took the highest loan available at each shop, postdated all the checks she wrote for when my pay was due. On that date she was supposed to either bring in cash and redeem the checks or let them get cashed. Guess which option she chose? Suddenly I found myself owing over fifty thousand dollars, a good portion of that 'fees.'"

He took a swallow of his soda. "The whole scheme is great for getting repeat customers. You have to borrow to get through to the next payday. You get your check, and now you have to pay back all the loan, plus fees, and still have enough to live on until another paycheck. Oops. If you couldn't make it on your full pay, certainly you can't make it on your diminished pay. You have to borrow again to meet your obligations. And again and again and again. And all the while the exorbitant fees mount. They can add up to well over four hundred percent APR! Who can ever pay that back? It's just a good thing that the huge online paycheck loan industry wasn't nearly as developed back then as it is today. I'd have been bankrupt."

"You don't have to make it sound so terrible," Tori complained.

He looked at her like she had missed something in his story. "I lost fifty thousand dollars. It was terrible."

"I mean the business itself. Not everyone has wild wives running around writing multiple checks."

Drew held up a hand. "You're right. There can be times of emergency that a loan is needed, and for some reason a licensed lending agency, like a bank or credit union, won't help you. But it's a system that's just asking for abuse unless there are state laws limiting interest and fees."

"Does this Luke have shops in New Jersey?" I asked. It seemed to me that such places would be a pot-of-gold-at-the-end-of-the-rainbow type of facility for the disordered gambler and a source of unlimited income for the owner.

Tori hesitated. "Not exactly."

"So he is a loan shark!" How terrible is it when you feel triumphant that your sister is involved with a loan shark just because she makes you crazy? "Is that how you met him? You got yourself in debt and needed bailing out? Or wanted quick cash to gamble more?"

Tori studied her perfectly manicured, probably false fingernails. "I haven't gambled for several months. Luke won't let me."

I stared at her, momentarily speechless. She was actually letting someone tell her what to do—or in this case, what not to do? This Luke must be some man. "Does he threaten you about that too?"

Tori's eyes went back to the puzzles, and she looked a bit lost. "But he said no more."

I studied her face, half in light spilling from the kitchen, half in night shadows. "He's more than a friend, isn't he?"

"I-I thought." Her voice wobbled a bit.

I tried to imagine a romantic relationship with a man to whom I owed a large sum of money, especially one who was threatening me, and failed.

"I don't understand why he sends them," Tori said, still transfixed by the sheets of paper. "He knows I'll pay. It might take longer than he wants, but he knows I'm not going anywhere."

"Are you certain he's the one who sent them?" It seemed logical that if she didn't know why he sent them, maybe he didn't.

"What?" Clearly this was a new idea.

"Are you sure Luke sent you the threats?"

She sat back and frowned in thought. The lost Tori was gone, replaced by the Tori I knew, the one who didn't let anyone push her around. "No, I'm not. I just assumed it since he's who I owe. But who?"

"Does he have any business enemies?" Drew asked.

"He does." Her face turned animated. "There's this one guy trying to muscle in on his business in Atlantic City, maybe the loan shops too, for all I know."

"Who?"

She shook her head. "I don't know. I've just heard bits and pieces of conversation Luke had on the phone or with one of his people."

Luke had "people." Interesting. "Does Eddie work for this other guy?" I asked.

"Eddie works for SeaSide."

Drew leaned forward in his chair, resting his elbows on the table. "He may, but you're on to something here, Libby. If this unknown other guy sent the puzzles and if Eddie delivered them, then he must moonlight for the other guy."

Tori looked shaken. "But I asked him—" She stopped.

"You asked him what?"

"Nothing," she said too quickly.

I knew. "You asked him to take the shoebox." So it was Eddie sneaking around in the house. I couldn't decide if that made me feel better—at least I knew him—or worse—it was Icky Eddie, maybe watching me while I slept.

Tori tried to stare me down, but I didn't blink. I was too offended and she too much in the wrong for me to back down.

When she realized that for once I wasn't going to be intimidated, she stood, all innocence. "Thanks for the sandwich, Lib."

"Sit." Out of the corner of my eye, I saw Princess collapse onto her haunches. Absently I picked up a chip and held it down to her.

"I beg your pardon?" Tori was all insulted dignity.

"Sit, Tori. I mean it. We have to talk about this."

"There's nothing to talk about."

"Then I'll have to call the cops."

"Like that threat scares me. You're not going to report stolen goods stolen."

I'm sure my mouth was hanging open. "What are you talking about?"

"That shoebox was full of stolen jewelry." She looked at my shocked face. "Don't bother to pretend, Lib. I'm onto your game. You pretend you're the perfect little Christian and use it as a cover for fencing stolen stuff. I always knew your act was too good to be true. I bet your God-is-my-friend Madge is in on it too." Her scorn could have stripped off my skin.

I thought back to the estate sale where I'd bought the jewelry. "It was in the barn in an old manger. I just assumed it had gotten there by accident in the rush to prepare for the sale." I gave a hollow laugh. "And here I thought I was so clever and had made such a wonderful find."

"You want me to believe you didn't know the stuff was stolen?"

"Of course I didn't know!"

"Of course she didn't know!" Drew's denial was louder and more impassioned than mine.

I looked at him in surprise and grinned. He grinned back.

Tori took another step toward the door.

"I said sit!"

To my amazement, she did. While I was enjoying the unusual but delightful feeling of power, Drew said, "So you asked Eddie to take the whole box after you somehow learned that the brooch you stole from your own sister was stolen?"

She had the decency to look chagrined at his cutting tone. "I only borrowed the pin."

"Then you have it with you to give back?"

She shifted uncomfortably. "Well, no."

"That means, by any measure, that you stole it."

Tori was once again studying her nails too intently to answer.

"And you gave it to Luke to help pay your debt." Drew could consider a career as a prosecuting attorney if he ever tired of Ben.

Still no response.

"Did he ask you to take the rest of the jewelry? Or did you think of it on your own?"

Those fingernails were absolutely fascinating.

"Did you steal those earrings to help pay Luke too?" I pointed to the diamonds dangling on their thin chains of gold.

She jumped as if I'd poked her with a sharp stick.

I stared at her in amazement and consternation. "Tori! What is wrong with you? Do you want to keep up the Keating family tradition of incarceration?"

"She just left them lying on the coffee table." Tori's voice wasn't quite a whine.

"And someone being sloppy is a viable excuse for taking their belongings?"

She still wouldn't meet my eyes.

"What I want to know," Drew said, "is how Mick figures into all this."

This time it was Drew who used the sharp stick, though I don't think he knew he held such a weapon or that it was sharp until Tori jumped. "Mick?"

"You know," I said. "The dead guy. He was tasered and had a heart attack."

"A heart attack? Mick?" Her voice was disbelieving. "But he was a huge guy, very fit."

"Apparently he had a preexisting heart condition."

"He never mentioned it."

She knew him well enough that he'd tell her something like that? "Maybe he didn't even know."

"How did you find this out?"

"I called Detective Holloran."

She seemed impressed. "But how do you know Mick?" she asked both Drew and me.

"He's Ruthie's boyfriend," Drew said.

"I know Ruthie," Tori said. "Skinny, whacked-out blonde, right? I never understood what Mick saw in her. But how do you know her?"

"She's my ex-wife."

Tori fell back in her chair, poleaxed. "You are kidding."

His sad smile said, *I wish.*

My brain synapses were firing so fast I could hardly keep up with them. "Okay, so Mick—whom Tori knows but forgets to mention to me or the police—is found dead on our doorstep. On his chest is one of four threatening puzzles. Two other puzzles are hand-delivered by our good friend Eddie. How did you get the fourth, by the way, or should I say the first?"

"The first was shoved under my suite door at the SeaSide."

"Right. Probably by Eddie."

She shrugged. "Maybe."

"Probably. So we've got four puzzles, Eddie alive, and Mick dead. Eddie works at the SeaSide but has a second job with this unknown party who is trying to squeeze Luke out of his lucrative business as a loan shark in Atlantic City and maybe as a legal loan shark in Philadelphia. Big question: is Eddie merely a messenger boy, or did he have something to do with Mick's death?"

"You mean is Eddie a hit man?" Drew asked.

Tori hooted at the thought.

I nodded. "Can I pick them or what?"

But he knew as well as I that my bluster was a cover for the fear of what all this would do to Chloe and how deeply involved I would find my twin.

☐☐☐

The sliding glass door opened, and not a moment too soon for Tori. This intense Libby was a creature she had never dealt with. She'd been so busy on her Chloe Quest that she hadn't noticed Lib was no longer the easily-pushed-around sister she grew up with. Somewhere in the past few years she had become a woman of substance.

Tori frowned as she pondered briefly why she needed to best Libby. All her life she'd felt she had to one-up her twin. It was like a compulsion, her form of OCD.

Was it because Libby was four minutes older? Because she seemed so smart? Because she was like one of those Weebles, the old toy people, the ones that had round bottoms? You could knock them over a thousand times, but they never stayed down. They popped back up, as caring and loving as ever. Well, the Weebles weren't caring and loving after a good punch, but Lib was. It was so frustrating!

And not worth thinking about right now. Tori pushed it from her mind. There was enough real stuff to be upset about.

Chloe stepped out with a phone in her hand. "You got a call, Aunt Tori. It came in just as we finished a game." She held out the phone. "I thought it might be important."

Tori took the cell, held it to the light streaming from the kitchen, and checked the number of the last call. Luke! For the second time in two days!

"I've got to take this." She rose and hurried toward the house.

Behind her Chloe asked, "Are there sandwiches for Jenna and me?"

Tori paused and glanced over her shoulder. After all the tears and angst of earlier, all Chloe was talking about was food? How disappointing! Where was the snippiness, the disrespect, the "I hate you, Mom!"? Well, maybe expecting the kid to blurt that out was a bit much, but the attitude should be there. It'd certainly be there if her mother ever kept a secret like that from her.

Libby smiled at Chloe. "I made extra tuna salad. It's in the fridge. Help yourselves."

Chloe nodded and spun to come back into the kitchen, and Tori was forced to move too. She stepped into the dining room, where she lingered a couple of minutes to hear what the girls said to each other, a truer picture of Chloe's feelings than anything else.

At first the only noise was the refrigerator opening and things being put on the counter. Tori peeked back into the room.

"You doing okay, Chloe?" Jenna watched Chloe pile tuna onto slices of whole wheat bread.

Chloe shrugged. "It still hurts, and I wish she had told me so I could have been prepared. But I know she was trying to protect me. It was the surprise of the whole thing that got to me."

Tori frowned. The kid sounded like her mother, all understanding and bouncing back with a smile, a second-generation goody two-shoes. How sad was that?

Jenna opened cupboards until she found the cookies. She pulled out a bag of Double Stuf Oreos. "You've got to remember to keep your mom as she is today separate from the girl who was sixteen. They're like two different people."

Tori blinked. When had kids gotten so smart? Where was the me-first, I'm-worth-it mentality? If her Chloe Quest were to succeed, she would have to work a lot harder than she'd thought.

Jenna put several Oreos on a paper plate, closed the bag, and shoved it back into the cupboard. "I have to remember that my mom was a pretty girl who loved Jesus when Dad met her and married her. The bad part of her bipolar disorder didn't kick in until later. I have to tell myself that all the time, or I'd think Dad was nuts for marrying her. Then that makes my thinking about him get all screwed up."

Chloe grabbed a sharp knife and cut the sandwiches in half. "Mom's told me lots of times not to follow her example. But you know something? I want to be like her when I grow up. I really do. She's pretty and nice and works hard. She even bought us a house all by herself. And her faith is deep and true." Chloe handed Jenna a sandwich. She made a face. "But still, Icky Eddie!"

The girls looked at each other and chorused, "Eeyew!" They went out onto the patio to sit with their parents.

Tori walked slowly up to her room. She knew she was selfish and demanding and what some might consider shallow. She knew she was beautiful and had deserved being prom queen and Most Popular. She knew she liked things her way and didn't adapt easily when she was thwarted. She knew she was good at using and manipulating people, at least everyone but Luke, and she was proud of it. She was worth every single one of the accolades and perks that came her way.

She knew she had always been the dominant twin, even if she was the younger.

But while she was busy being vivacious and charming, leaving a trail of broken hearts and accumulating a closet of to-die-for clothes, Libby had been busy too. She'd grown a backbone and inner fortitude. She'd raised a daughter who loved and respected her, which was more than Tori could say for how she felt toward their mother, and she was forced to wonder, if only for a moment, how much Lib's faith had helped her become this impressive woman.

And what in the world did she do with this new woman? It didn't take many smarts to understand that she could try and bribe Chloe from now till doomsday, and she might not succeed in luring her away from all that circumspect living. If finding out about Eddie didn't do it, would anything?

Life had certainly become disorienting.

Libby wasn't malleable Libby.

Eddie wasn't biddable Eddie.

Mick was dead and Ruthie was Drew's ex.

Drew seemed enamored with quiet, mousy Libby. No. Maybe quiet, at least in comparison to her own outgoing nature, but not mousy.

And Luke had called twice in two days.

She shook herself. Too much analyzing was bad for the complexion. She pushed Luke's number in speed dial and listened to the phone ring. She closed the bedroom door behind her as Luke barked, "Tori, where are you? Why aren't you here?"

"I'm at my Aunt Stella's. You know the every-third-night deal. "

"Well, I don't like it." He sounded miffed, and Tori was delighted. He missed her.

"Are you coming up to the apartment tonight?" she asked.

"Probably not. Why don't you just forget that house and come back here where you belong?"

"You of all people should know that I need Aunt Stella's money."

"Yeah, well, we can work something out there."

"Like forgiving my debt?"

He snorted. "Right."

Tori glanced at the old furniture surrounding her. Old stuff didn't appeal to her, but she knew that some people paid big money for things she wouldn't give house room. Look at what Libby did for a living. She'd actually made enough to buy a house in Haydn, though why she'd want to live so near the parents was another thing Tori couldn't understand.

"Luke, I think this house is loaded with antiques worth a lot of money. If I leave, I lose all that lovely green stuff that would come from their sale."

Luke was silent for a minute. If there was one thing he appreciated, it was that lovely green stuff.

"I'll be with you most nights. Two out of three."

"Okay, we'll talk about these nights away another time. I've got other reasons that I called."

She heard the steel in his comment and was immediately concerned. "What's wrong?"

"I just heard Mick Brewer is dead."

"You didn't know?" Relief washed over her, making her light-headed. She'd been right to trust him. He hadn't ordered the hit on Mick.

"How would I know? When he didn't show up for work, I thought he and that sick blonde had gone away for a few days. Mick was not the most reliable of my guys." He paused a moment. "And guess what else I heard."

"What, Luke?"

"I heard they found him on your Aunt Stella's stoop. Make that your stoop." The ice in his voice made her shiver. "A fact you happened to forget to tell me."

"I-I thought you knew." She lay on the bed because she was

afraid her legs wouldn't hold her. Her relief had fled, and anxiety chewed at her. Luke's anger was legendary, and though she'd never experienced it before, she feared tonight would be the first time. "You know everything."

"How would I know here in AC about a body turning up in Philly? Unless I put it there, of course."

Tori tried to think of something to say. *That's what I was afraid of* didn't seem prudent. "That's funny, Luke. Like you'd do something like that." She gave a strained laugh.

"Tori!" His roar rivaled a jet revving for takeoff. "Did you think I'd actually kill a man?"

"Of course not, Luke," she lied.

"You did, didn't you?"

She could imagine him striding back and forth in his office, the tassels on his loafers flopping up and down with the vigor of his steps. She screwed up her face, knowing denial was impossible. She tried to explain. "You didn't show up at the apartment that night. I called you, and you never answered your phone. And I knew you were mad at Mick for being careless with his bodyguarding. All I could think was how he let that irrational woman get near you and how mad it made you."

That woman, weeping and screaming about how Luke had ruined her family and sent them into bankruptcy, had actually been able to grab Luke's shirt before Mick pulled her away. If she'd had a weapon, Luke could have been killed right there on the boardwalk, right in front of Tori.

"I don't know who you are," Luke had said to her in a haughty voice, "but I'm not the one who gambled away what he had no right to gamble. I merely lent your husband money to pay his debts. Now he owes me, and I expect payment. Oh, and I suggest Gamblers Anonymous for your husband."

Luke stalked off, leaving the woman weeping, Tori and Mick scampering behind. After the three of them climbed the steps and entered his office, Luke turned on Mick.

"If you value your life and livelihood, don't you ever fail me like that again. Do you understand me?"

Mick blanched and nodded. "Yes, Luke."

Luke dismissed him with a wave of his hand and mumbled comments about incompetent bodyguards and demented clients.

Two days later, as she and Luke walked toward his apartment, the same hysterical woman got past Mick again, this time actually punching at Luke as he held her away with a grip on her shoulders.

He glared over her head at Mick, who was frantically if belatedly trying to pull her away. "You're fired. I never want to see you again."

As she and Luke climbed the stairs to his private aerie, he muttered, "If it's not the Joe Bennettons of the world, it's crazy ladies. It's a good thing I love my work."

"Who's Joe Bennetton? Did he come after you too?" Tori asked, her heart still pounding in reaction to the woman's assault. *And how did you love doing something that made people attack you?*

"A crazy man, even nuttier than the woman. And no, he didn't come after me." He opened the door, turned, and pulled her close. "But I don't want to talk about them when I've got you in my arms."

She forgot all about the crazies, at least for the moment.

Three days later, as Luke and Tori had walked from his building to the SeaSide, the madwoman rushed at him from behind. Mick, trailing Luke in hopes of getting up nerve to speak with him and plead for his job, tackled her, knocking her to the boardwalk, grabbing at her wrist and twisting it violently enough that the bone snapped. Her scream covered the clatter of the knife she'd been holding as it fell to the boards.

While Tori was certain she'd have a heart attack on the spot, Luke had looked calmly at Mick. "Well done. Keep up the good work. Good bodyguards are hard to find."

So Mick had once again become one of Luke's people, but when he'd turned up dead, Tori had worried that he'd somehow let Luke down another time, and the limits of Luke's patience had been reached.

Tori told him her fears now, for once not knowing how to spin things to her own advantage. "I'm sorry, Luke. Please don't be angry with me."

In the ensuing silence, Tori lay on the bed with her hand pressed to her rampaging heart. What would she do if she lost him? "Are you still there?" she asked after several long moments. "Are you still talking to me?"

"I'm thinking about it."

Tori felt she could breathe again. He didn't sound angry anymore. In fact, he sounded almost as if he were laughing at her. "It was only for the shortest of moments I wondered. Then I decided to trust you."

"It's a good thing because there'll be other nights when unexpected business keeps me from you. Not that I'll like it, but money is money. Just don't go thinking every body that shows up those nights is my doing, okay?"

She laughed, sort of a gurgly, wheezy sound. "Okay. And I don't think you sent the puzzles either."

There was another little silence. "You mentioned puzzles yesterday. What puzzles?"

"See? I knew you didn't send them."

"What puzzles, Tori?"

"Somebody's sending me threatening puzzles. Four of them. One was lying on top of Mick. My sister found it. Eddie Mancini gave me two, and the fourth, actually the first, was pushed under my door at the SeaSide."

"How do they threaten you?" His voice was icy again, but it didn't bother her now. The anger beneath the ice wasn't directed at her.

"They've got messages in them made from circled letters. The one on Mick said ARE YOU NEXT."

"And you thought I'd send something like that to you? That I'd scare you or hurt you?"

"I didn't think you'd hurt me, Luke, but I did think maybe you were trying to scare me." Some of her spunk returned. "After all, you do scare people when they don't pay. And they had words in them that showed somebody knows I've brought you"—she hesitated—"stuff."

"Yeah, I been thinking about that. It's time you stopped with the stuff, Blondie. Somebody's gonna get wise."

"I only take from high rollers who have so much they'll never miss what I take."

"So far nobody's put two and two together, but somebody will, and soon. How'm I gonna deal if you're put away for five to ten? I don't even like this third-night business."

Even as her spirit soared at the confirmation that he wasn't dropping her, that he seemed to really care for her, Tori reached up and felt an earring, the diamonds cool beneath her touch. It was hard, thinking about stopping with the stuff. She got a high when she secreted a piece and walked out of some high roller's suite as if she were as pure as an angel. Of course, now that she thought of it, Lucifer was supposed to have been an angel, wasn't he? Doubtless St. Libby could tell her.

"We don't need the stuff," Luke continued. "The shops are going great, and with two more, we'll be more than fine."

"You giving up 'helping' needy gamblers?"

He laughed. "I think I'll keep on helping the needy. Makes me feel good, you know?"

She laughed with him. Why had she ever felt afraid of him, even for a minute? This was her Luke. She loved him and he loved her. Probably. Maybe. "What about the shoebox of stuff? Should I just give it back to my sister so she can sell it?" Assuming she ever got it from Eddie.

"Still give it to me, and when you do, I'm taking it to the cops."

"What?" Tori was glad she was lying down because she'd surely have fainted on that one if she weren't. "You hate the cops."

"Let's just say they're not my favorite people, though I do have a soft spot for cops' beautiful daughters. But I got someone breathing down my neck here, and I could use a bit of good feelings with the local constabulary."

"Luke, who's after you? I mean, are they after you like they were after Mick? I couldn't bear that, you know. If somebody killed you, I mean. Or are they after the Atlantic City business? The paycheck shops? What's going on?"

"I wish I knew, sweetheart. But don't you worry that beautiful head of yours about it. I can take care of what's mine—and that includes you."

Now she felt angry with him. "I am not some little girl to pat on the head."

"Tell me about it," he said, and she could practically see his leer. She also understood that he wasn't going to tell her anything.

She hung up on him.

19

□□□

I WASN'T QUITE CERTAIN how it happened, but when I left the house at 5:30 a.m. on Wednesday, Drew was with me, though we'd decided to leave the girls to care for themselves.

"We're trusting you," Drew told them the previous night just before they ran up to Chloe's room for bed. Tori had disappeared for her phone call and not rejoined us, no surprise there.

"But you are not to leave the lane," I instructed the girls. I noticed my index finger waving as I gave the order. So did Chloe.

"Yes, Mother," she said with great forbearance.

"Yes, Father," Jenna said with an equally long-suffering spirit.

"Smart mouths," Drew called after them as they tore up the stairs, and we heard them giggle.

"Hear that laughter?" he said to me. "Chloe's going to be all right. You too."

I looked at him with gratitude. I wanted to throw myself in his arms and show him how much I prized his comfort, support, and even his little lectures, but I restrained myself. Instead I gave him a pretty little speech about how much I appreciated his being there for me last evening and being willing to drive me back to Haydn to get my van, a trip we'd decided to put off until Thursday because of an appointment I had Wednesday with Jean, a friend who organized houses and often had thrown-away treasure for me.

He pulled on one of my curls. "Always glad to help out."

"Wear old stuff you don't mind getting dirty," I called softly after him as he went reluctantly home where Ruthie awaited. "This can be messy."

He paused, turned, and studied me. Then he strode back and pulled me into his arms for a wowzer of a kiss. "I think that's how a man's supposed to leave his fiancée."

With that kiss still humming through me, I was actually happy to get up Wednesday morning. A day with Drew. Just Drew. I grinned my way through some strawberry and banana yogurt and a piece of pumpernickel toast and was waiting with coffee in portable cups when he emerged from his house.

"I've got to see this to believe it," he said of my picking.

"Remember," I told him, "there are two rules to collectibles, desirability and rarity. An item is desirable depending on its condition and its aesthetics, both subjective. Rarity is more easily determined. The item must be uncommon, like those first editions of Aunt Stella's I showed you, or it must be unreproducible. That's why limited editions are sought after. There will never be any more. Take a Lawton doll. Only so many of any given doll are made, two hundred fifty or five hundred, as opposed to a Barbie, of which there are millions. The Lawtons are collectors' items. Barbies are kids' toys."

He nodded as if he got it.

We headed for the Main Line, that posh area west of Philadelphia where captains of industry built their gracious and very lovely homes decades ago along the main line of the Pennsylvania Railroad.

As we went, if we passed a community that had trash on the curb, we'd detour to inspect the goods awaiting pickup. When people were redecorating or clearing a house for a move or because of a death, all kinds of wonderful goods ended up on the curb.

In Villanova I found three pictures leaning against a large plastic garbage bag. When I stopped to check them, I found one picture to be quite pretty if you were into florals, which a lot of people are. Its frame was as ugly as they came, but the other two had remarkably handsome frames though the pictures were dreadful. Drew stashed all three in the CR-V for me. Two doors down I liberated a rocking chair with its cane seat unraveling. I knew a man who did excellent caning, and the restored chair would sell quickly in the store. As Drew pushed the chair into the SUV, I decided it was very nice to have someone along to do the lifting and carrying.

In Wayne I found a cardboard box awaiting pickup, filled with old *Life* magazines from the forties and early fifties.

"They're worth forty or fifty dollars apiece," I said as we drove away with the box stashed next to the rocker.

Drew glanced back and did some quick calculations. "That means there's over a thousand dollars in that box."

We continued west of Paoli and passed the Church Farm School and an old sewing factory that was going out of business, a huge green Dumpster in their lot with lumber sticking out the top. My picker's hormones surged.

We zipped into the lot, and I climbed from the CR-V. I knew I needed to get inside that Dumpster.

"Give me a boost, Drew?" I laced my fingers and held my hands as someone might if they were giving an equestrienne a leg up onto a horse.

"You're kidding."

"Absolutely not. There's bound to be wonderful stuff in there." I reached up and took hold of the top edge of the Dumpster, which was well over my head, and tried to walk up its side. My sneakers slid, obeying gravity rather than my wishes.

"Here." With a resigned sigh Drew held out laced fingers, and I stepped into his hand. He straightened and tossed me. I'm sure he meant to toss me gently, but since I had nothing like a saddle to hold on to, I went flying. I ended up in the middle of a pile of large wooden spools, which gave under me and kept me from breaking something. A piece of shelving poked me uncomfortably in the side.

"Libby? Are you all right?" Drew sounded worried. I thought about groaning but decided that wouldn't be very nice.

"I'm fine." I climbed to my feet on the unstable spools and knew they were a great find. "I'm going to pass stuff out." I handed some of the spools to Drew before I noticed the bundle tables. They were the size of end tables and had V-shaped surfaces so that bundles of fabric could be put on them and not slide off onto the floor. I passed several tables out to Drew.

"Who wants tables you can't set anything on?" he called to me, obviously looking at the V.

"Turn one over." If he did, he'd see that the bottom was flat, an excellent support for a lamp and decorator items. Somewhere there were seamstresses who would love the idea of having a couple such tables beside their sofas or beds.

When I found boxes of buttons, I was delighted. "Buttons?" Drew asked when I passed the boxes to him.

"Hot, hot items."

"One man's treasure," he muttered.

There was thread in a rainbow of colors that I passed out and rolls of the long, clear-plastic sticky tags reading Small or Medium, Large or Extra Large, the kind that got stuck on the front of shirts. I didn't pass them out. I also didn't take the manufacturer's labels.

The last thing I passed out to Drew was a wall cabinet with four open shelves, probably used for storing thread. It was about five feet long and would slide into the back of the CR-V nicely. Madge and I just might keep it for ourselves.

I slogged through the Dumpster again to see if there was anything else I wanted. Then I threw my leg over the side and twisted to pull my other leg out. As I tottered there, Drew reached up and grasped me by the waist. He lifted me away from the Dumpster and lowered me to the ground. I was excited over all my acquisitions, and I gazed at him over my shoulder with a big smile. He stared at me solemnly.

"You do this type of thing regularly." He made it a statement.

My smile dimmed a bit as I nodded. He looked so serious.

He turned me to face him. "You are crazy, Libby Keating." And he kissed me.

Chloe grabbed the front doorknob to answer the bell. She was still in her pj's.

"Did you check through the peephole?" Jenna asked. "I don't want it to be my mom."

"It's Mrs. Mowery," Chloe assured her as she opened the door.

"Hello, Chloe," Mrs. Mowery said cheerfully. "Is your mother here?"

"I'm sorry; she isn't. She's working." Chloe decided not to tell Mrs. Mowery, who looked very nice in a pretty navy pantsuit that made her hair an interesting shade of pale blue, that her mother was picking. It was one of the aspects of her mother's job that she tried to ignore. The kids at school seemed to find it a hoot that her mom raided trash.

"Ah, I'm sorry. I was going to ask her if she wanted to go to the Kimmel Center with me. Wednesday's my day. I could give her a tour."

"What's the Kimmel Center?" Jenna asked.

"It's Philadelphia's concert hall. It's big and new and has theaters of different sizes and a rooftop dining room, and would you girls like to come with me instead? I could give you the tour." Mrs. Mowery looked very eager. "You can't be too young to become interested in the arts."

Chloe glanced at Jenna, who gave a slight nod. They'd just been discussing what in the world they were going to do all day.

"We'd love to come," Chloe said.

Mrs. Mowery clapped her hands. "Wonderful! I'll stop for you at noon."

Chloe had breakfast while Jenna showered and vice versa. By this time Aunt Tori was up, wandering around in a short silky nightie and a short matching robe.

"How does she manage to look elegant right out of bed?" Jenna whispered.

Aunt Tori heard. "It's hard work, kids, let me tell you. Better yet, let me show you. I doubt Drew's got many beauty tips to give you, Jenna, and poor Chloe. Heaven only knows Libby's not any great shakes."

Chloe frowned, not liking Aunt Tori to cut on her mom, but the idea of being Tori-fied was irresistible.

Tori took Chloe first and sat her on the toilet in the big bathroom. With blow-dryer and curling wand she performed some magic that made Chloe's hair look wonderful. Then she worked on Jenna, giving her straight hair a distinct curve that cradled her chin and looked way cool.

Then Aunt Tori brought them into her incredibly messy bedroom and pulled out her makeup. If Chloe'd been impressed by what Aunt Tori did with their hair, she was blown away by the sleight of hand she worked on their faces. When she was finished, both Chloe and Jenna stared at themselves in amazement. What was most astonishing was that you really couldn't see the makeup even though you knew it was there.

"Subtlety, girls," Aunt Tori said. "A heavy hand is death."

"I think this is what we'll look like when we're grown up," Chloe said in a whisper as Aunt Tori, a satisfied smile tugging her lips, disappeared into her bathroom to shower.

The doorbell rang.

"Mrs. Mowery's here, Aunt Tori," Chloe yelled through the bathroom door. "We'll see you later."

"I'll probably be gone by the time you get back. Have fun!"

Chloe ran downstairs with Jenna on her heels. Today wasn't so boring after all.

When Drew pulled into his parking spot in the little lot by the lane, it was late afternoon, and I was feeling the buzz I always get when I have a good day picking. Add to that the fact that Jean had offered me treasures, the *pièce de résistance* being a large collection of O gauge Lionel trains at least fifty or sixty years old. Drew started to drool the moment he saw them.

"Thanks, Drew. You made today fun." I leaned across the space between his seat and mine and kissed him on his cheek. I immediately turned red at my forward behavior. I never kissed men. I thought of the kiss last night and the one by the Dumpster. Well, rarely.

Drew smiled his wonderful smile that just about curled my toes. "Always glad to help a pretty lady." He glanced into the back of the van. "Where are you going to store this stuff? If your house is like ours, there isn't any extra room."

"I think I'll take the magazines inside—I want to read them—but leave the rest in the car if it's all right. If we're going to Haydn tomorrow, I can leave it there. Madge's basement is our storage facility."

He looked out the window toward his house. "One more night with Ruthie around." He wiped at the sweat on his forehead as the car rapidly heated now that the air conditioning was off and the July sun was beating down.

"I think what you and Del are doing for her is wonderful."

His smile was rueful. "I don't think she agrees."

"Drew, you can't change her. You can't make her well. You're doing more than anyone would expect."

"I know, I know. But the sad fact is that it just feels like a sop to my conscience."

I reached over and began giving painless pinches to his arm. "Nibbled to death by ducks."

He grabbed my hand and held it. "You listened too well."

I smiled. "You're just a good teacher."

As he grinned, he gave another curl a gentle pull, and my foolish heart immediately began beating triple time. Before I drooled all over him, I climbed out of the CR-V just as a panel van stopped behind us. The driver rolled down his window.

"Can you help me? I'm lost. I'm looking for 1595 Myrtle Street."

"I'm sorry," I said as I pulled the rear door of the car open. I turned to him and smiled to show I wasn't city-surly. "I just moved here, and I don't even know if there is a Myrtle Street in Philadelphia, let alone where it might be. Maybe my friend knows, though I doubt it."

I started to turn to Drew when he gave a terrifying scream of pain.

"Drew!" I managed to take two steps toward him and the man who caught him as he fell before terrible pain shot through my body. I heard myself screaming as if from a distance as I collapsed, then knew only darkness.

20
□□□

CHLOE AND JENNA HEADED HOME with Mrs. Mowery at their side. She had given them a very interesting tour, and now Chloe wanted to hear the Philadelphia Orchestra perform or see a play at the Kimmel Center. Maybe she and Mom could go at least once before they left Philadelphia. The tickets seemed very expensive to her, but what did she know? She was used to movie rental prices.

"Jenna." They were only a block from their little lane. "Isn't that your dad's CR-V pulling in now? I wonder if Mom had any luck."

"You girls can walk faster than I can," Mrs. Mowery said. "If you want to hurry on, go right ahead."

"Oh no, Mrs. Mowery." Chloe smiled. "She'll just make me carry lots of things inside if I get there too soon." She watched as her mom climbed from the car and a white panel van backed up into the lot beside Mom. The driver rolled down the window and started talking with her. The back of the van opened, and a man in a red shirt with "Phillies" across the front climbed out and walked between the cars to Jenna's dad.

"I hope he's not asking for directions," Chloe said. "Mom's a lost cause here in the city."

"My father too," Jenna said.

A man's deep scream reverberated over the noise of traffic, and as Chloe watched, Mr. Canfield gave a shudder and collapsed. One minute he was standing between the CR-V and the car next to it. The next he disappeared from sight, and he'd gone down screaming!

"Oh no! That man shot my father!" Jenna started to run. "Dad!"

Chloe raced after her, so busy watching Mr. Canfield—well, not really Mr. Canfield; he had fallen to the ground between the parked cars—that she would have missed her mother falling if she hadn't given a great cry of pain too. Chloe saw her arch her back, shudder, and fall. "Mom!"

Chloe tried to run faster, but it felt like she was running in slow motion. The van driver climbed out, picked up Mom, and tossed her into the back of the van. He hurried to the red-shirt man, who was dragging Mr. Canfield. He grabbed Mr. Canfield's legs. The two of them tossed him into the van.

"Dad!" Jenna's cry was full of fear.

The red shirt climbed in the back, and the driver slammed the door shut. He climbed into the driver's seat and peeled out of the alley, the one-way street forcing them to drive right past Chloe and Jenna, who stared open-mouthed.

"Stop! Stop! Mom!" Chloe screamed.

As the van sped away, several things happened at once. Tori's limo pulled up to the curb, and Tori came running out of the lane, looking exceedingly grumpy. Mr. Mowery and his friend came out to the street, searching for Mrs. Mowery, who was trotting along after Chloe and Jenna at a fairly good shuffle.

"Aunt Tori!" Chloe pointed after the van. "They shot Mom and Mr. Canfield, then kidnapped them!" She could barely get the words out around the fear clogging her throat. Her mom who hadn't wanted to live in the dangerous city. Her mom who took care of her and loved her. Her mom who might even now be dead. The whole world tilted, and she felt about to slide off.

Before Aunt Tori could respond, Mrs. Mowery wheezed, "They did. I saw the driver's gun. He shot right from the driver's seat through the open window. They put both Libby and Drew in that van!" She pointed to the van, caught in traffic at a red light two blocks away. As they watched, the red-shirt man climbed from the back, slammed the door, and raced to climb in the passenger seat before the light changed.

Mr. Mowery and his friend studied the CR-V and the ground around it. "No blood," Mr. Mowery said.

"None at all," his friend agreed.

"But I saw a gun," Mrs. Mowery insisted.

Carl chose that moment to step out of the limo, preparing to open Tori's door for her.

"Can you follow that van?" Chloe demanded of him. "They took my mom!"

"And my dad!" Jenna had tears running down her cheeks.

The light turned green, and traffic finally began to move.

"They're getting away!" Chloe sobbed.

Mr. Mowery opened the back door of the limo. "Everybody in." He made shooing motions with his hand, and everyone climbed in.

Chloe sank into the lush upholstery, but she couldn't stay seated. She was too nervous and too scared. She knee-walked forward until she was right behind the driver's seat so she could see better. She gripped the back of the seat.

"Hurry! We'll lose them!" she screamed.

Carl threw himself behind the wheel and pulled away from the curb to the bleat of a horn from the car he cut off. He sped down the street, rocking Chloe back on her haunches. If she hadn't been holding the seat, she'd have gone sprawling. She held on tightly as he took the corner at the light just as oncoming traffic began moving again. They blared at him, but he ignored them.

"Do you see it?" Chloe shouted in his ear so loudly he jumped.

"Easy, kid." He rubbed the side of his head.

"Well, do you see it?" she repeated, more quietly this time. *Oh, Lord, please let him see it!*

"There!" Carl pointed. "Pulling onto Vine." He hit the gas and made the same turn at a good clip. Chloe felt the pull of centrifugal force as she tumbled sideways into Aunt Tori. She pulled herself back to her knees.

Mrs. Mowery, seated next to Aunt Tori, grabbed her arm. "Sit down and buckle in, Chloe. It won't do your mother any good if you get hurt."

She pushed Chloe toward a place beside Jenna on the wrap-around seat. Jenna pulled her down next to her.

"Nine-one-one! 911! We've got to call 911." Chloe grabbed for her phone.

"Already done," Mrs. Mowery said with a pat on Chloe's hand. Then she switched her attention to the responder on the other end of her call. "A kidnapping. Two people. White panel van. Just turned south on Vine. We are following in a black limousine." She listened a minute, then looked at everyone. "License number?"

"It was one of those Pennsylvania plates that have the old two-masted brigantines, the one that's all beige and white so you can't read the numbers." Chloe felt pleased she could offer that much, though it wasn't much.

Mrs. Mowery relayed the information as they streaked past the Round House, the headquarters of the Philadelphia police, and around the circle. "He's heading for the Ben Franklin Bridge."

"Why would someone kidnap your parents?" Mr. Mowery studied Chloe and Jenna.

Chloe shook her head. She probably looked as dazed and scared as Jenna did. She grabbed Jenna's hand and held on. "I don't know."

"Me neither." Jenna pulled out her shirttail and blotted her tears.

The van swung onto the bridge, crested its arch, and began its descent into New Jersey.

"Don't get too close," Mr. Mowery cautioned. "We don't want them to know we're behind them."

"Gotcha." Carl eased back a bit, letting three cars come between him and the van. "Too bad there aren't tollbooths heading south anymore. Then he'd have to stop."

Chloe leaned forward. The car was so long it made her feel she was very, very far from her mom. She was glad to have Mr. and Mrs. Mowery and their friend along. They might be old, but she felt as if she and Jenna weren't alone.

The van turned off the bridge and plunged into a maze of narrow streets that hadn't been laid out with limousines in mind. Carl had to slow for corners that were too sharp and cars that were parked too close to intersections.

Mrs. Mowery cocked her head at Aunt Tori like a bright little chirping sparrow. "Does this have something to do with you, dear?" She waited for an answer with the unflinching stare of a raptor.

Aunt Tori shifted in her seat. "Why ever would you think that?"

"Maybe a case of mistaken identity? Maybe something to do with that terrible man you brought on the Fourth?"

"Without food," Mr. Mowery added.

Aunt Tori didn't answer.

I heard a groan from far away, and it took me a while to realize it was me.

I tried to move, but my body wouldn't cooperate. I flashed on Drew's terrible scream and fall. *Dear God, have I been shot too?*

As my mind cleared a bit more, I knew the answer to my prayer. I hadn't been shot. I felt limp and disoriented, but there was no site of pain like I'd expect with a bullet. It was more like my whole body feeling heavy, scrambled, unresponsive.

"Libby. Libby, can you hear me?"

But I had been shot. I remembered the pricks on my back and leg. Then the horrendous though short-lived pain. A shock weapon of some kind? A Taser or stun gun?

"Libby." The whisper was insistent and close.

"Drew?" Relief flooded through me. He was here and he was talking to me. "Are you all right?"

I wasn't. I was lying on my side with my arms pulled behind me. They were restrained somehow. I tried moving my legs, but they were bound too. I looked around as much as I could and realized I was lying in the back of a panel truck, trussed like a Christmas goose.

"I'm lying right beside you," he said softly.

I heard movement and felt the floor vibrate. Our captors? I gasped, tensed, and looked toward the front of the van. I felt more vulnerable than I ever imagined because I couldn't do anything to protect myself.

"Easy. It's just me," Drew said on a thread of sound. He came up behind me until his body fit against mine, my back to his chest, my bent knees cupping his bent knees.

I turned my head toward him as much as I could. "Are you sure you're all right?"

"I'm fine." I felt his breath against my neck.

"When you screamed…" I bit my lower lip. "I don't think I've ever been so scared, except maybe now."

"We got tasered, I think. I can't imagine what else it could be."

I let my head fall back to the floor and felt him place his forehead against the back of my head. Being curled against him somehow made me feel safer, which was ridiculous since we were both completely at the mercy of our captors.

I could hear the tires singing on the road. "Where are they taking us?" It was a rhetorical question because I knew Drew had no more idea than I.

I heard a sliding noise, like a window shushing on a track.

"They're awake." A deep voice came from somewhere beyond my head.

"Check them." I recognized the voice of the man who had asked me directions to Myrtle Street. Who was he? And where were we being taken?

I held my breath, waiting to see what happened. What if "check them" meant zap us again? *Oh, Lord, please, no!*

"We'd rather not shoot you again," the man called. "And we'd rather not gag you. But we'll slap a piece of duct tape on you so fast you won't know what hit you if either of you makes any noise at all. Understand?"

When we didn't respond, he repeated in a grim voice, "Understand?"

"Yes," I whispered.

"Yes," Drew said.

With a grunt of approval he slapped the window shut, leaving us in our darkness.

"How are your arms?" Drew asked.

"They hurt. At least the shoulders do. This is such an unnatural position."

"Tell me about it. Are your arms long enough that you can scrunch your bottom and then your legs through your bound hands?"

"I don't know, but it's worth a try." Anything was better than yielding to the fear and helplessness that nibbled at the edges of my mind. I kept thinking that maybe ducks weren't going to be the end of me, but terror.

He rolled away from me, and I felt very alone without the physical contact.

"Are you still here?" I asked.

There was a rueful little laugh. "Now where would I go?"

"Right." I turned onto my stomach and stuck my rear in the air. My hands lay in the small of my back. I pulled my knees up as close to my chest as I could get them. I bowed my back like an angry cat and pushed until I thought my shoulders would pop from their sockets. It occurred to me that if the driver and his henchman looked back, they could see us trying to get free.

But *trying* was the operative word. I could not get my arms to stretch as I wanted. I took a long, sobbing breath as I felt despair rearing its head.

The vehicle swerved abruptly to the right, sending me tumbling from my three-point stance of head and knees. I slammed against the side of the van and couldn't prevent yelping in pain.

The window slapped open.

"They okay, Bud?" asked the driver as the van slowed and stopped.

"You okay?" the second man called. Bud?

"Fine," I managed. "Just rolled a bit when the van swerved."

"Fine here too," Drew said.

"Well, hang on. We're turning again." He didn't close the window this time, though his voice became muted as he turned to face front.

We made several turns, and I imagined city streets as I struggled to sit up. Finally I was able to lean my back against the side of the truck, a more secure position but a very uncomfortable one with my hands behind me. I rested my forehead on my knees and tried to block the pain in my shoulders.

"How are you doing?" I whispered.

"Not so good," Drew whispered from the other side of the van. I looked up and saw him leaning against that side much as I was doing on my side.

"Hey, there's a limo behind us," the driver said. "See it in the side mirror?"

"You think it's following us?"

"Why else would a limo be in this part of town?"

Carl? The idea exploded like a bright star in my blackness.

Chloe bit her nails as the van sped off the bridge and Carl followed, zigzagging through the narrow streets of inner-city Camden. All the gory things she'd seen on *CSI* played through her mind, making her feel sick. What if one or more of them was happening to her mother?

Or *24.* She'd seen what guys did to you when they tortured you for information. What happened if you were tortured and you didn't have anything you could tell when it got really bad?

Oh, Lord, take care of Mom. Keep her safe and I'll never give her any grief ever again. I promise!

The van screeched to a stop at the red light. Carl hit the brakes and stopped a half block back.

"Quick," Mr. Mowery ordered. "Put your blinkers on, like you plan to stay here." He poked Chloe. "And you. Stand up in the sunroof and wave at the house, like you know the people."

"What?" Chloe was too surprised to move.

"And you." Mr. Mowery's friend pointed at Jenna. "You too. Hurry! When they look back, they'll see you. You'll look innocent."

"We're on—" Mrs. Mowery said into her phone, still talking to 911 as she squinted down the street, trying to read the street sign. "What street is that, Carl? Dispatch needs to know."

As Chloe stood and thrust herself through the open sunroof, she heard the rumble of Carl's voice as he read off the street name and the treble of Mrs. Mowery's as she relayed the information.

Please send help! Please!

She blinked as she and Jenna found themselves the object of intense interest to a pair of gigantic Great Danes, one fawn, one brindle. They sat on their haunches in the weedy front yard of what had once been a row home. All its neighbors had been demolished, and it now sat alone like a skinny, destitute old lady, its flaking paint like mottled skin and its dirty windows like blank eyes, the weeds and brambles pressing in on her like the valley of the shadow. All her across-the-street neighbors were boarded up and wore Condemned signs.

Chloe shivered. Who would ever choose to live here? Or didn't the people have a choice because there was nowhere else to go?

"They're bigger than their house," Jenna whispered as she waved at the animals.

"Hi, guys," Chloe called, feeling like an idiot.

The dogs immediately stood and began to bark, pausing every so often to insert deep throaty growls. They approached the limo with an intense interest that made Chloe glad she was inside and they out. One raised up on its hind legs and ended up almost nose to nose with her. She gave a yelp and leaned as far from the animal and its hot breath as she could. This monster would eat Princess for lunch and want more.

She felt a tug on her shorts and glanced down for a second. She was afraid to ignore the dog any longer for fear it'd get her.

"You can come down now. The van turned," Mrs. Mowery said.

Chloe dropped to her seat with relief, Jenna beside her.

Carl swore. "Move, you stupid mutts!"

Chloe stared out the front window and there sat the two Danes, long forelegs almost touching the front bumper.

Carl blew the horn and swore some more. The dogs showed their teeth.

Mr. Melchior—Mr. Mowery's friend had introduced himself to Aunt Tori as they crossed the bridge—opened his door and stuck a foot out. One of the Danes immediately stood and walked to the side of the limo, growling as it came. Mr. Melchior quickly pulled his foot in.

A man wearing a muscle shirt stretched taut over his bulging belly appeared in the door of the house, beer can in hand. He pushed open the door and strode out. "What you scarin' my dogs for?"

Chloe popped up through the sunroof again. "We're not scaring them. They're scaring us."

"Right. They look so scary." He gestured to his pets with his beer can.

The dog still in front of the car was now lying down, tongue lolling. The other, the brindle, sat beside Mr. Melchior's door, staring in at him. A piece of drool hung from its mouth.

"Could you call them?" Chloe asked. "We need to get going."

"Whatcha doin' here anyway? This is hardly limo territory."

"We just pulled over for a minute. Now we need to leave." Chloe felt desperate. Mom was getting farther and farther away while this dumb man quibbled about why they were on a public road. "Please call them."

"Baby," the man called, and the brindle staring at Mr. Melchior turned her massive head. "Come here, girl."

Baby stood and immediately ambled across the weedy yard to her master. He opened the screen door, and Baby lumbered up the steps and inside, where she turned and stared out at them.

"Now the other one," Chloe called. "Please!" Even with her messed-up emotions, she knew the man had called Baby first because Baby wasn't keeping them here. It was the monster still lying right in front of the limo who was the problem.

"Snooks," the man called.

The Dane lumbered to his feet, ears pricked.

"The nice people want to go, Snooks. What do you think?"

Snooks sat.

"No! Oh please, mister!" Chloe tried not to cry. "Go, Snooks!" She pointed to the man.

Mr. Mowery thrust a limo door open and stepped out. Chloe gasped when she saw he had a gun in his hand.

"Who shall I shoot first?" Mr. Mowery asked as if he were questioning whether it was going to rain tomorrow or not. "Snooks or his master?"

"Both," she heard Mrs. Mowery call.

"Snooks, come here!" The man opened his door and stepped

quickly inside, all the while eying Mr. Mowery. Snooks took his time, but he got to his feet and stepped into the sad-looking yard.

"Thank you." Mr. Mowery saluted the man with the gun. He climbed back in the limo.

Carl hit the gas, and Chloe slid down onto the seat.

"You've got a gun!" She stared at Mr. Mowery. Bald old guys didn't carry guns! James Bond carried a gun. Maybe Harrison Ford. Definitely Bruce Willis, who came from New Jersey, not too far from where they were. Of course, no place in New Jersey was too far from any other place in New Jersey.

But Mr. Mowery with a gun?

"It's mine." Mrs. Mowery held out her hand for it. Mr. Mowery passed it to her, grip first. She put it in her purse. "Crime, you know." She patted her purse. "My arsenal."

How many other little old ladies had she been underestimating? Did Great-Nan have a gun? That was a scary thought, given her grumpy disposition.

"Where are the cops?" Jenna seemed upset as she stared out the back window.

"We're turning left at the light," Mrs. Mowery told the dispatcher. She listened for a minute. "Well, tell them to hurry. No sirens. No lights. And yes, I'll keep the phone line open."

She looked at everyone. "Big hostage situation at a bank over on Admiral Wilson Boulevard. Everyone's busy. They'll get someone here ASAP."

Heart pounding, Chloe searched the road ahead.

The white panel van had disappeared.

21

□□□

I FELT THE VAN SLOW to a stop and idle. A red light?

"The limo pulled over back there," the driver said. "Its blinkers are on. Some kids are standing and waving at the house."

"Who in this neighborhood can afford a limo?"

"Who cares?"

My bright star of hope faded and died. No one was coming after us. No one even knew we were missing. When the girls got hungry for dinner, they might start to wonder where we were, but that was it. Tori was undoubtedly long gone, back to Atlantic City and the SeaSide, and it was a certainty that Ruthie wouldn't do anything. Drew and I were on our own.

The van swung left, and I braced myself against its side. When it straightened, I crawled across the van to Drew and sat beside him, my shoulder against his.

"What if we don't get away?" I said, careful not to look at him as I spoke this terrible thought. "What if we become one of those statistics, the 'disappeared without a trace' kind? What if Chloe has to go live with Mom and Nan—or worse yet, Tori—and Jenna has to go live with Ruthie?"

"Not very good thoughts," he agreed.

"Terrible thoughts! Awful thoughts!"

I could feel him staring down at me. "Are you always so cheery?" But his voice was tender rather than critical.

"I'm a pessimist, if you must know." I said it as if I were confessing to being an ax murderer.

"I'd say that, given your family and your life circumstances, you are one amazing and accomplished woman."

I felt myself go hot and become self-conscious. I tried for levity. "That's because I've been trying to impress you."

"Have you now?"

I looked up, hearing laughter in his voice. "Is it working?" I sounded breathless.

In answer he leaned down and kissed me, a sweet, gentle kiss of such promise that my eyes teared.

He rested his forehead against mine. "If we don't get out of this mess, aside from my fears for Jenna, I will most regret not having had time to get to know you."

The van turned once again, and I heard gravel under the wheels. We slowed, stopped, and this time the motor died. We had reached our destination, whatever it was.

Panic gripped me, and my pulse began to pound. I looked at Drew and saw the same anxiety mirrored in his eyes.

"What do we do?" I whispered.

"We wait and see what happens next."

"Aren't you scared?" He'd better be scared! I didn't want to be worried alone.

"I'm definitely scared. I have no experience with situations like this. I'm an academic, not a Special Forces guy. We do battle over publication and tenure, hardly life and death except in the career sense. Yeah, I'm definitely scared."

Somehow that admission eased my own panic. I think it was because he spoke in a firm voice. Scared but not overwhelmed. I could manage that too. *Couldn't I, Lord?*

The kidnappers climbed out of the van, and their feet scrunched in the gravel as they walked to the back of the vehicle. The latch was freed and the doors swung open.

One of the men reached in, grabbed my arm, and pulled me none-too-gently out.

I had a hard time standing with my ankles bound, and with a snort of disgust, the one called Bud bent and sliced through the duct tape around my ankles with a knife that was a lot like the one my father used to filet fish. Then he cut the tape that bound Drew's feet.

"Where are we?" I asked.

"You don't need to know."

While the driver pulled the tape from my legs, I glanced around. We were in a parking lot of a large cinder-block building, clearly an old warehouse. It might once have been painted beige, but it was now a tired, dirty gray. All the windows on the first level were boarded shut, and those on the second level were black with grime. In the front wall of the building was a large roll-up garage door next to a much-dinged, steel, conventionally sized green door.

Bud stood, making a ball of the tape he'd pulled from Drew. He pointed to the green door. "Inside."

I looked with yearning at the street mere feet away, but no one was there, no one to call to, no one to scream my head off to. In fact, I wondered if the buildings I could see were even occupied. They were decrepit, signs faded to near nothing, windows blank, black rectangles.

But I didn't want to go inside the gray building. Inside was danger and less likelihood of rescue. Inside was the unknown. I prepared to dig in my heels, to tell them I wasn't going, when the driver aimed his Taser at me, intent all too evident.

I glanced at Drew. His eyes were fixed on the gun aimed at me. He'd do whatever they asked rather than get me shot. I appreciated the thought immensely, but I'd rather he rushed the guy. Of course, then he might get shot, and I wouldn't want that.

"Don't they only fire once?" I nodded at the gun, trying to sound like a strong person, not one with knees turned to mush at the thought of either Drew or me being zapped again.

"New cartridge." He smirked at me. "Inside."

We entered a large, open garage area, gloomy because of the covered windows. Overhead fluorescent lights cast a pale illumination, creating shadows and making us all a sallow yellow. Three trucks were parked in service bays, all large trash trucks bearing different logos on their sides.

They're going to kill us!

They had to. They were letting us see too many identifying things, including their faces.

"Just do as you're told, and no one gets hurt," Bud said.

I glanced at Drew, and he looked as skeptical as I felt.

An inner door opened, and a woman walked in. She stopped short when she saw us. Rather, when she saw Drew.

"Who's he? What's he doing here?" she demanded.

"He was with her, boss. We couldn't bring her without him," Bud explained.

"You didn't hurt them?" She grinned. "That's my job."

"Nah. We took good care of them."

Sure, if you call tasering someone and then tying her up *taking care*.

The woman walked up to me with a brilliant smile. I blinked. She was happy to see me? I couldn't say the same under the consequences.

"Hey, Tori! How's my heroine?" She held up a hand for a high-five and saw my taped wrists. "Oops."

Tori! I should have known. I opened my mouth to tell her I wasn't Tori when it crossed my mind that it might be better to pretend I was.

"Hey," I said. "How you doing?" You can't go wrong with a question that generic.

"I'm doing pretty good. So's Vickie. She and Joey are sleeping in the office." She gestured back toward the door she'd come through.

"Wonderful," I said, though I hadn't the vaguest idea who Vickie and Joey were.

The green door opened for a second time, and in walked Eddie Mancini holding a gun and escorting a man wearing a handsome navy silk shirt, gray dress slacks, and black tasseled loafers on sockless feet.

"So nice of you to join us, Luke," said the woman. "Tori's come just to see you."

Luke. Tori's loan shark. Good-looking guy, if you liked them Hollywood. As I studied him, he studied me. With a quirk of his lips, he gave a little nod of recognition, or maybe lack of recognition was more accurate.

Eddie wasn't so discreet. "You idiots! You've brought the wrong woman!"

Tori sat absolutely still in the limo. She had no doubt that Tinksie was right: she was somehow responsible for all that was happening. Well, not the farce with the Great Danes, but everything else. For the life of her, though, she couldn't figure out how. Or why.

One thing she was sure of. The men thought they had her, not her sister. Nothing else made sense. No one would want to grab pure-as-the-driven-snow Libby.

Tori clenched her jaw. It was so frustrating having her for a sister. No matter what you did, she did it better. No matter how nice you were, she was nicer. No matter how popular you were, people liked her more. You just couldn't measure up no matter how hard you tried. So you stopped trying to measure up and started trying to one-up her. At that Tori was champ. Look at all her success with winning Chloe over. She paused. Maybe that was a bad example.

Tori knew beyond doubt that Libby loved her. She knew she worried about her. And she knew Libby prayed for her, something that felt very strange, sort of eerie and sci-fi-ish.

Perfect Libby. Now that Tori'd had time to think about things, she couldn't believe she'd thought for a moment that Libby had taken the jewelry.

She gave an inward sigh. She guessed she loved Libby in spite of Lib driving her crazy, because how could you not love your twin? She certainly didn't want anything terrible to happen to her. Or Drew.

As for Drew being taken, she felt sure he'd been grabbed because he'd been there. No hidden reasons. No dark motives. Just a guy in the wrong place at the wrong time. He was who he said he was, a college professor with a thing for Ben Franklin.

No, clearly she had been the intended victim. The question was, whose? Everything that had happened recently seemed to point to Luke or at least to his involvement. Mick. The puzzles. Her debt. The jewelry. But would he order her kidnapped? Shot with a Taser?

When she thought of him turning on her like that, she felt like throwing up. She swallowed convulsively and made a momentous choice. Even if Luke had turned on her, she wasn't turning on him. She might find out she was foolish, blinded by love, but she would believe in him, at least until she knew what was going on. Then she'd decide whether to forgive him, hit him upside the head with a very stout stick, or turn him in to the cops. Her stomach settled a bit.

She surveyed her companions. Kids, old people, and Neanderthal Carl. No one in their right mind would chase bad guys with such a crew. So where were the cops? Sure, it had only been fifteen or twenty minutes since they'd piled into the limo, but shouldn't someone be here by now?

If she were a Christian like Libby, this was when she'd be praying, "God, help me!"

Tinksie sat beside her, her head bobbing a bit with some minor palsy, her wrinkled brow furrowed deeply in her concentration on relaying details of the chase. The woman carried a gun! If you couldn't trust little old ladies to be little old ladies, what was the world coming to?

And James, who seemed to be very comfortable holding it, used it to threaten people when he wasn't issuing orders to Carl. James was a take-charge person. Look at his ordering everyone to bring food on the Fourth. She just wasn't sure she wanted to trust her life to a little bald guy who seemed to think he was Jack Bauer. Or to be more age appropriate, Patton.

The friend of James's had turned to her as they sped across the Ben Franklin Bridge and introduced himself as if he were an old-world courtier, not an old guy in the middle of chasing kidnappers

"I know you must be Victoria," he said with a charming smile. "I've met your lovely sister, and now I am delighted to finally meet you. I'm Andrew Melchior." He held out his hand, giving her no choice but to bend forward, hunched over like Quasimodo, to shake it. "I was a good friend of your aunt's."

"Her significant other." Tinksie beamed at Andrew. "Stella loved him most dearly."

Andrew blinked rapidly a few times and nodded. "The feeling was mutual."

So the beauty of the bedroom Tori was using wasn't an old maid's attempt to ease her loneliness as she had thought. Rather it was a love nest for Aunt Stella and the white-haired and goateed man now talking chase strategy with Carl. Could life get any more surprising?

She wondered whether she and Luke would get white haired together—if Luke wasn't responsible for kidnapping Libby and thus headed to prison for untold years. Not that she ever planned to let herself get white hair, of course. But would they grow old together? Would he still be interested in her when she had wrinkles like Tinksie? Would she be interested in him when he got bald like James or developed saggy skin and knobby legs like Andrew?

The thought of them ending up that way made her shudder. Laser lipo and cosmetic surgery were invented for people like her and Luke.

But the main question persisted without answer: Had he arranged the kidnapping? Had the money or the jewelry become more important to him than she was?

She took a deep breath and counted slowly to ten, trying to stave off an anxiety attack.

"I'll find them! Don't you worry!" Carl was channeling James Bond, tailing the kidnappers as if he did it every day. "They can't be too far ahead of us."

Chloe and Jenna clung to each other, eyes on the empty road.

"There!" Tinksie pointed out the side window. "In that lot! I see the van."

Carl hit the brakes and yanked the wheel. They all slid as far as their belts would allow as he went into a terrifying turn, the big car slewing into the parking lot with only a minor scrape against the chain-link fence surrounding the place. There were no signs to indicate what the large gray building with the boarded-up windows was.

They all climbed out and stood staring at the building, all except Chloe, who ran to the road and looked for any sign of the police.

"They'll be here any minute, dear," Tinksie said, her phone still glued to her ear.

"We need to reconnoiter," James announced.

"Right," Carl agreed and ran to the front door.

"Don't!" James called, and Carl froze with his hand on the knob.

"I had something a bit more discreet in mind," James said. "We need to see who's here before we barge in."

Barge in? Not in this life, Tori thought as she walked around the side of the building. There she saw a window whose board had come loose. It hung by one nail on its left side, and its weight and gravity had caused it to rotate ninety degrees. She sidled up to it, her back pressed against the wall. She peered in through the grime and saw a large garage bay with three huge trucks parked in it.

Standing by one of the trucks were Libby and Drew, hands bound. Near them were two men, one with a futuristic-looking gun in his hand. As she watched, a woman appeared.

Tori's breath caught in her throat, and she blinked in stunned recognition. Then Eddie Mancini appeared. About him she not surprised. And he was with Luke. As she watched, Luke gave a brief nod to Libby, obviously knowing she wasn't Tori.

Eddie started screaming so loudly she could hear him out here. "You idiots! You've brought the wrong woman!"

Tori swore softly. She hated it when her conscience acted up.

She walked back around the corner, looking for her companions, ready to tell them she was going in. Alone. She found them huddled beside the limo, Tinksie talking into the phone.

She shrugged mentally. What they didn't know wouldn't hurt them. She grabbed the knob on the green door and pulled.

22

☐☐☐

I WATCHED EDDIE, who was practically dancing in frustration.

"That's not Tori!" he screamed.

"Sure it is," the van driver said. "Blond, hazel eyes, real pretty. We got a picture." He dragged a photo out of his chest pocket.

The woman walked over to me, her purple gauze big shirt billowing as she moved, and stared. I stared back, trying to be Tori-brazen.

"Ask Luke, Suzy!" Eddie pointed with his gun to Tori's boyfriend. "He'll tell you."

Suzy, who appeared in charge of this mistaken-identity abduction, turned to Luke.

"It's not Tori," he said quietly.

Suzy studied me some more, a look of dawning awareness moving across her face. She took several steps back as if I had a bad case of bubonic plague. "He's right! It's not! Tori's more vivid!"

Funny how even as I feared for my life, I could take offense. I really was tired of being the bland twin.

"She never told me she had a twin!" Suzy went on. "She delivered one of mine, and she never told me she was one!" Obviously this whole situation had become Tori's fault. Fat lot of good that did Drew and me.

Luke slipped his hands in his pants pockets, the picture of casual, and looked at the infuriated Suzy. "Kidnapping is a federal crime, you know. It's bad enough that you grabbed me, but you compounded the situation by bringing Libby and"—he stopped and indicated Drew—"across state lines."

Suzy smirked. "I wouldn't let a minor thing like kidnapping distress you, Henley."

Minor thing? My heart constricted. There weren't too many crimes considered worse.

Luke continued as if he hadn't heard her. "You thought Tori would be your bargaining chip for whatever it is you hope to get from me. I've tried to think what I've got that you might want, what it is that could possibly be worth the risks you've taken. Or perhaps it's something I've done?"

"Does the name Joe Bennetton ring any bells?" Suzy asked, her eyes cold, her voice hard.

"Joe Bennetton?" Luke flicked a nonexistent piece of lint off the sleeve of his shirt. "The guy who killed himself rather than honor his debts?"

Suzy seemed ready to explode, her face red, her eyes wild. "Joe Bennetton was my brother! And you murdered him!"

Luke looked mildly interested in the news. I, on the other hand, was fascinated, distracted only by a vague sawing noise behind me. I glanced over my shoulder and saw Drew running his bound hands back and forth, back and forth over a sharp piece of metal where an area of the rear fender on one of the refuse trucks had rusted through.

"Turn around," he hissed, his eyes firmly fixed on Suzy and Luke. "Be interested in what's going on. Don't attract any attention our way."

I swung back thinking, *dull and pedantic*? No way. How about *intelligent and creative*!

Luke's voice was lazy as he asked Suzy, "Am I the one who forced Joe to gamble? Am I the one who told him to keep at it until he lost everything he owned? Am I the one who told him to go to a loan shark and enter into a debt he never planned on repaying? Am I the one who put the rope around his neck and knocked the chair out from under him? I think not."

" 'When in doubt, don't,' " Drew muttered. "B. Franklin, printer."

He was the one who said that? I'd heard it lots of times in church when warned about bad behaviors, but I hadn't known the origin. How would a confirmed deist feel about his adage being co-opted by the church?

Suzy was vibrating with rage. "You're the one who kept pressuring him, the one who sent men to scare him, the one who demanded he pay up or else!"

"When you take money from someone like me, you are desperate. I can deal with desperate. It keeps me solvent. But if you come to me without considering the consequences of nonpayment, you are a fool, an idiot."

Suzy ran at Luke, but Eddie stepped in her way. "Don't get close to him! He's too wily."

Suzy was clearly struggling for control, but she stepped back. "I found him, Henley. I walked into my house, and there he was,

hanging from the crossbeam in the great room. I knew I would somehow make you pay. Then the cops told us that he hadn't died right
away. His neck hadn't broken. He slowly strangled. That's when I
knew that not only would you pay, but so would someone you loved."

Eddie, Bud, and the driver were as mesmerized by Suzy and
Luke as I was, though Eddie was aware enough to keep his gun
pointed at Luke. When Drew moved behind me and whispered in
my ear, they didn't notice.

"Step slowly to the side and then behind me," he instructed. "I'll
block you as you get your hands free."

"Are you…?"

"I am."

Hope bloomed once again, fragile and alluring.

"So," Luke said, "you plan to what? Kill us?" He indicated Drew,
me, and himself. "And that will make it all better?"

"It will make it even!" Suzy screamed.

"Killing me and two totally uninvolved strangers will make it
even? Huh." He frowned like he had to think about that one.

"We didn't know they'd be uninvolved strangers." Suzy looked
at Drew and me, resentment clear on her face. "It was supposed to
be Tori."

When everyone shifted their gazes our way, I froze. I was one step
behind Drew but at least two steps from that piece of metal. I probably looked scared to death, but hopefully they'd assume the fear was
over my impending demise, not over getting caught before I was free.

Drew stood with his hands behind him as if still bound. I was
the only one who could see the blood flowing from the gashes he'd
gotten as he worked to slice the tape, the crimson liquid dripping
from his fingertips.

"So killing Tori was supposed to make me get all upset?" Luke drew the attention back to himself, and I wondered if he realized what Drew and I were about.

"You love her," Suzy said.

"I do?"

"I've seen you two together. I've seen the way you look at her."

Luke's eyes hardened. "You've been spying on me? On us?"

"You've got to know your enemy to know his weakness," Eddie said.

Yikes, Eddie. Keep your mouth shut. Using the word *enemy* in reference to Luke didn't seem like a wise thing to me.

"And Tori's your weakness," Suzy said smugly.

"Then I guess I'm glad you got the wrong woman." He smiled.

Thanks a lot, I thought as I began rubbing my wrists over the piece of metal on the fender. I flinched as I caught the side of my hand on a ragged edge. The metal sliced into my flesh, and I felt the gush of warm blood.

"But the right woman's here," came a voice as the front door flew open. Tori stormed in, looking glorious in her anger. "Nobody hurts Libby without dealing with me."

Chloe looked up just in time to see Aunt Tori disappear into the gray building.

"Aunt Tori, no! Wait!"

She ran toward the door, an automatic response because she wasn't certain what she could do.

"Stop her, Carl," Mr. Mowery called, and Carl grabbed Chloe's arm, pulling her to a halt.

Chloe felt desperate as she tried to free herself. "My mom and my aunt are in there!"

"Yes, dear," Mrs. Mowery said. "So sad. But that doesn't mean we'll let the kidnappers harm any of them." She smiled sweetly, all her wrinkles dancing on her face.

She reported the latest news to the dispatcher, then listened. "ETA five to ten minutes," she told the circle in the parking lot, and Chloe's heart sank. That was forever!

Mrs. Mowery looked at her husband, who nodded decisively.

"We're going in," Mrs. Mowery told 911 and flipped her phone shut. She dropped it in her purse, then pulled out her handgun and handed it to Mr. Mowery. Chloe watched in horrified fascination as he fiddled with it.

"Putting a bullet in the chamber," he explained. "Now I want you girls to stay out here and wait for the cops. We'll go in and see what we can do for Drew, Libby, and Tori."

Mrs. Mowery reached inside her bag again and pulled out a cylinder that she handed to Jenna. "Pepper spray. If someone runs out, push down here and aim for the eyes."

She reached back in the bag and pulled out something about the size of a big old cell phone. She slapped it in Chloe's hand. "It's a stun gun. Turn it on, and if any of them comes near you, just touch him with it for a few seconds. He'll collapse."

Chloe glanced at the device in her hand, then at Jenna who seemed as bemused and scared as Chloe felt.

Back in the purse Mrs. Mowery went. This time she pulled out a wicked-looking knife.

"Where's the sheath?" Mr. Mowery asked. "I told you to keep it in the sheath."

"It's in the purse. I don't want it at the moment, James." She set her purse on the ground. "Don't let me forget that when we leave."

Chloe blinked as Carl and Mr. Melchior suddenly began swinging baseball bats.

"I always carry a couple," Carl explained when he saw her staring. "I drive some very wealthy people, and I want to be able to protect them. I can't carry a gun, though, because of my record. So I carry these."

"Stack up behind me," Mr. Mowery ordered. "Carl, Andrew, Tinksie. Remember, if you don't get closer than twenty feet to those men, they can't hit you with the Taser."

Chloe's stomach was jumping all over the place, and her palms were so wet she could barely hold on to her pink stun gun. "You can't just go barging in there! They might be dangerous!"

"So are we," Mr. Mowery said, and Mrs. Mowery, Mr. Melchior, and Carl all nodded.

"What you don't know, Chloe, is that James was career Army," Mrs. Mowery said. "He was in Korea, fresh out of West Point, and then he served two tours in Vietnam. He retired as a lieutenant colonel." She smiled at him with pride. "He knows what he's doing. And so do I. I've had every self-defense course known to man, and I'm a better shot than James."

"Besides," Mr. Melchior said, "they can't kill all of us before we get them."

Chloe frowned, not sure whether that was logic or wishful thinking.

□ □ □

All eyes turned to my sister as Tori strode into the garage. Her gaze went straight to Luke, who shook his head in gentle rebuke.

"Tori, Tori, Tori. What am I going to do with you?" he asked. "I'd just been feeling pretty good because you were safe."

"And I'd been feeling terrible because you and my sister weren't."

I glanced at a thunderstruck Suzy. How did Tori's presence complicate things? Another person to kill? Another body to dispose of? I felt the tape give a bit at my wrists and did my best to ignore the lactic acid gathering in my arm muscles from the quick, repetitious sawing motion. One thing I was determined about: if Eddie Mancini was going to try and kill me, I would make it as difficult and as look-me-in-the-eye-Eddie-you're-killing-your-kid's-mother as I could.

"Go stand by your sister," Suzy directed Tori.

Tori smiled at her and walked to Luke. She slid an arm around his waist and turned defiantly to Suzy. Luke put an arm about Tori's shoulders and gave her a little squeeze.

Suzy glared at them, furious and frustrated. Prisoners were supposed to cower, to do as you wanted, not defy you. Her team might have the guns, but Luke's team had the upper hand.

"So, four people to kill and dispose of," Luke said, still as cool as if we were at tea with the Queen. "I figure with two, it was to have been a lovers' quarrel. Three would have made a nice lovers' triangle. But four gets complicated, doesn't it?"

"I probably should tell you that the police are due momentarily," Tori said.

It *was* her in the limo that followed us! "Where's Carl?" I called.

Everyone ignored me, and Drew looked pained as he eyed me over his shoulder.

"The idea," he growled to me out of the corner of his mouth, "is not to call attention to ourselves. Remember?"

"Nobody paid any attention anyway," I muttered back. "Not *vivid* enough."

He gave a totally inappropriate bark of laughter that he tried to turn into a cough. Now everyone did turn to us, and it wasn't the least bit difficult to appear scared.

Suzy snorted at us in disgust and turned back to Tori. "How did you get here?" She turned to the van driver. "How did she get here, Jay?"

Jay, Taser still in hand, looked most unsettled.

"Know that limo behind you?" Tori smiled sweetly at Jay.

Jay flushed, as did Bud, turning a strange color in the yellowish overhead light. "But there were kids in it," he whined. "I saw them."

Kids? Not my kid! Not Jenna! *Oh, God, that terrifies me!*

"Not only were there several of us inside, but we talked to the cops the whole way here. We gave them the address of this place. They're on their way."

"I'm out of here." Eddie turned on his heel and made for the door.

The sound of the gun firing in the close confines of the garage was ear shattering.

23

□□□

WHEN THE GUNSHOT RANG OUT, Chloe thought she'd puke right there in the parking lot. A wave of cold washed over her, immediately followed by a flash of heat.

"Mom!" She raced toward the door, Jenna on her heels screaming for her dad, but the Old Guys Rescue Team beat them to it.

Oh, God, please, please let Mom be okay! Please! I'll be a missionary! I'll go to hot places without water and cold places without summer! I'll do whatever You want!

□□□

I dropped to my knees, my ears ringing. Drew grabbed me and wrapped his arms around me, pulling me under him to protect me as glass from a light fixture rained down.

"You will stay where you are, Suzy. You too, Mancini." The voice was strong and as cold as an alpine winter. "Next time I won't shoot a light."

I glanced up and saw Luke with a gun in his fist.

"You were supposed to search him!" Suzy yelled at Eddie.

I shook my head at her foolish recrimination and at a strange new noise. I thought I could hear babies wailing.

"I did!" Eddie protested weakly, staring in disbelief at a cut on his arm where a piece of the ceiling light had sliced him. Blood bubbled up, and he turned as white as Princess after a bath.

"He can't stand blood," I yelled. "Remember?"

Drew leaped to his feet and rushed Eddie, grabbing the gun hanging limply in his hand.

The outside door flew open, and in rushed James, Carl, Tinksie, and Andrew, armed to the teeth and blinking in the dimness. James leveled his gun at Luke.

"Not him," I called as I climbed to my feet. "Her." I pointed to Suzy.

James changed targets. "On your knees!"

Suzy dropped.

The babies continued to wail.

Chloe and Jenna rushed in, yelling, "Mom!" and "Dad!" at the top of their lungs. They looked terrified.

"Over here, Chlo." I held out my arms, and my daughter flew into them.

Jenna skidded to a stop when she saw her father holding a gun on Eddie. "Daddy?"

"Hey, baby." He smiled sweetly at her and held out an arm, but didn't lower his weapon. She slid up to him for a quick embrace.

"Come over here with us, Jenna," I called to her. "Your dad's a bit preoccupied."

She made her way toward me, glancing back at Drew as if she

couldn't believe her eyes. Her dad, the tough guy. I put an arm around her and the other around Chloe. Duct tape hung from my wrists, and I was getting blood from my many nicks and cuts on both of the girls. I did not care.

I noticed a movement out of the corner of my eye, turned, and saw Jay, clearly intent on escape, sidling unobtrusively back into the shadows at the front end of the big truck by which we stood. Chloe followed my gaze. She pressed something into my hand, and I saw a stun gun in metallic pink.

"Push here." She pointed.

I took the weapon and slipped around the rear of the big truck. Not intent on stealth but speed, I reached the shadowy front fender just as Jay back-stepped to the same spot. He started to turn to run when I placed the gun against his side.

"Oh no, you don't," I said. "Get back there. And no funny business. I owe you."

Jay glanced back, spun, and swung his Taser at me, ready to fire again.

I shoved my pink stun gun into his side and pushed the button.

Jay screamed and collapsed.

"Libby!" It was Drew, sounding frantic.

"I'm fine." I decided I very much liked having him worried about me.

"She's behind the truck," Chloe explained. "One of the guys was trying to escape."

Tori raced over, and together she and I dragged the limp Jay back to the open area, dropping him in front of Bud.

I held my stun gun out for him to see. "More than one shot here."

He tried to look brazen. "You wouldn't have the nerve."

I flicked my eyes at Jay. Bud's followed, and wisely he didn't move.

Tori disappeared for a second, then reappeared with Jay's Taser in hand. "I think she does have the nerve," she told Bud. "And if she doesn't, I certainly do."

Bud's head turned from one of us to the other. His shoulders drooped.

"Chloe and Jenna," I said. "There's duct tape in the back of the white van."

"Got it," Chloe said, and the two raced outside.

Babies continued to cry, and I finally placed the noise as coming from the office. "Are there babies in there? Little babies?" The cries were the high-pitched, wavery cries of newborns or nearly newborns with lungs adjusting to air.

"Suzy!" Tori was clearly shocked, not an expression I saw on her face often. "You have your babies here? What? You wanted to introduce them early to their mother, the killer?"

Suzy ignored her and stared at Luke, who was clearly the one in charge. She should have looked subdued, kneeling on the floor with her hands behind her head, but she didn't. Her spine was straight and the light of hatred still flashed in her eyes. "Let me go. Let me get Vickie and Joey and go."

"We should let you go because you have kids?" Luke almost laughed at the idea. "We're probably doing them a favor keeping them from being raised by you."

"Let me go or I tell the cops Tori's a thief." Spite spilled from her mouth like venom.

My shoebox! But how did Suzy know?

Tori flinched and frowned.

"My earrings." Suzy glared at Tori.

Her earrings? What was she talking about?

"You think I didn't know?" Suzy railed. "I might be sloppy, but I'm not dumb."

That last is debatable, I thought as I looked at the remnants of her foolish and criminal caper.

"Remember that ruby and diamond ring you wore one night in the spring? It was my first time back at the casino since Joe died. Ron thought it would help me forget because I do love gambling. Stupid of him to think anything would make me forget Joe."

"Where is Ron, by the way?" Tori asked, probably to distract Suzy from her accusations.

Suzy shrugged. "Probably at the poker table. There's a high-stakes game going."

"So he didn't plan to help you kill us?"

"Do you see him?"

So if I had things correct, Suzy wanted to murder Luke and Tori in revenge for her brother's suicide, and she'd brought along Eddie, Bud, and Jay to help her out. Her husband wisely opted out, whether from scruples or ignorance, I didn't know. And she'd brought her newborns along for the great event.

"As I was saying, that night we met up with the Udells, and Mrs. Udell kept crying because she'd lost a family heirloom, a ruby and diamond ring, amazingly like the one you'd been wearing. And there's the rope of pearls with the diamond clasp you wore a month or two ago, just like the one Bette Warrington had worn two nights earlier when they had dinner with us. And how about that diamond brooch you were wearing the other night? I don't know who you took it from yet, but I'll find out."

Tori flushed and wouldn't look my way. All I could think was the verse that said, "You may be sure that your sin will find you out."

"Oh, Suzy." Luke gave a slow, sad shake of his head. "Didn't you know that Mrs. Udell's ring was returned to her? Someone found it and turned it in to the casino. Bette Warrington was wearing her necklace when I saw her at the SeaSide a week or so ago at a charity dinner. She was telling the story of how honest the chambermaid was who found it behind the bed and turned it in. I think the woman got a reward of a couple of hundred dollars."

I wondered how much she had gotten from Luke to be the conduit to recovery.

Suzy looked frazzled at the edges. The hate was turning to panic. "My earrings! Eddie saw her wearing them Tuesday night!"

"He must be mistaken." Luke shot a glance at the still-sweating Eddie, who was leaning against a support pillar to hold himself and his bleeding arm erect. "I have it on the best authority that they will be found under the sofa cushion in the suite where you and Ron are staying."

Tori stared at Luke, her heart swelling with love for this impossible man. Had he truly returned all the things she'd taken? She still couldn't bring herself to say *stolen*. It was too nasty a word, too low an action. Except she had stolen from Libby. There was no getting around that one. Or Eddie had at her request.

And she had trusted Eddie! The thought made her furious. People didn't put one over on her. *She* flimflammed *them!*

She glared at Eddie, but he was so pathetic it wasn't worth the energy. She glowered at Suzy instead. "Did you send me all those puzzles?"

"What puzzles?" Tinksie demanded.

"Ah, puzzles," Luke said. "Yes, tell me about the puzzles."

"They gave you quite a scare, didn't they?" Suzy asked. In spite of being cornered by a mob of old guys, teenagers, a professor, and a garbage picker, Suzy was remarkably snide. Tori had to admire her brazenness.

"ARE YOU NEXT. YOU ARE OVERDUE. PAY UP OR ELSE. LAST WARNING. Yeah, they scared me, especially when Mick turned up dead with the ARE YOU NEXT one on his chest."

"And you thought Luke sent them, didn't you?" Suzy sneered.

Tori looked at Luke with his slick Hollywood appearance, not one hair out of place in spite of all that had happened. "For a bit, though I couldn't understand," she admitted softly. "But I chose to give him the benefit of the doubt."

And it had paid off big-time. Luke might have his own weird set of standards and skate awfully close to the edge of the law, but he was a man of principle. Granted, he set the principles, but he stuck to them. It was okay to take money at a ridiculous rate of interest because the people who borrowed from him were foolish to get entangled in the first place. But if they were going to borrow anyway, it might as well be from him. If he could make good money in the repayments, his good luck, their bad. But it was now quite clear that he didn't take from those who didn't deserve it. That was where she had failed.

I think Dad will really like him, Tori thought, vaguely aware of the screech of tires outside. Apparently the cavalry had finally arrived.

24

□ □ □

IT WAS HOURS BEFORE THE POLICE released us. They were very gracious, treating all of us with courtesy, especially the girls, who kept having weepy spells and clingy moments now that the trauma was over. Somewhere the officers found Chloe and Jenna a couple of handheld electronic games that hypnotized them between bouts of tears and what-ifs. They also sent out for Chinese for us as they talked to us and took our statements. When we all piled back into the limo, we were too weary to talk during the short trip back to our lane.

I sat next to Drew, pressed tight to his side. He held my bandaged hand in his. Chloe leaned on me, her head on my shoulder. She held my other hand. On Drew's other side, Jenna leaned into him, her arms wrapped around his like a vine around a porch support.

Cozy. Strengthening. Wonderful. The stuff of dreams. So close to my fantasy of family that I was torn with the fear that the closeness would vanish like a smoke ring when we opened the doors and real life blew in.

Tinksie, James, and Andrew sat with their heads resting on the back of the seat, their mouths slightly open as they napped. I was filled with affection for them and their undaunted zest for life. From the Kimmel Center to bearding bad guys, they lived fully.

I want to do the same, Lord. Since we made it through today and I may see old age after all, I want to do the same.

The police had taken Suzy away as the babies cried and she screamed that they couldn't separate her and her children.

"Should have thought of that sooner," an unsympathetic cop muttered.

The door hadn't even shut behind her when it flew open again to two women from child protective services. They gathered up the crying babies and took them off. Poor little kids. I imagined that after everything got sorted out, they'd be returned to their father, but what did it do to you growing up with your mom in jail?

"At least they're too young to remember the agony of the arrest and trial," I muttered to my sister.

She nodded. "All they'll have to deal with is a parent in prison. But, hey, look at how well we coped."

I studied my sister and was amazed anew at her. I had found Madge, who introduced me to Jesus, and I'd had the Lord's help over the past thirteen years. Tori had faced it all on her own. I found myself wondering how much longer her own bootstraps would continue to support her. *Let me be there for her when they break, Lord.*

Tori wasn't with us as we drove home. While I struggled to put one foot in front of the other as I walked to the limo, Tori in her rich green pantsuit that made her hazel eyes deep green, her makeup still flawless in spite of her brush with death, almost danced as she followed Luke to the car he had rented.

"See you Friday sometime," she called with a careless wave. She looked lit from within. Incandescent. In love. Vivid.

Oh well.

I studied Luke as he watched her and saw what Suzy had seen: a man thoroughly smitten with a woman.

"I used to worry that he couldn't love me," Tori had confessed to me when we found ourselves alone in the ladies' room at police headquarters. "He's so confident and secure, why would he need me?"

Then she grinned and kept grinning as she washed her hands and floated out of the room, because this evening she had learned with the rest of us in the garage something she hadn't understood before. Luke saw her flaws and still loved her. And it appeared my selfish, willful sister loved him enough to put her life at risk for him. And maybe a little bit for me. Unbelievable.

Not that that gave her the automatic right to take the big bedroom and to attempt to woo my child from me, but it was a step in my coming to terms with who she was and accepting her that way. Much as I disliked admitting it to myself, I could see that I was as critical and judgmental of her as Mom and Nan were of me. After the grace God had shed on me, the least I could do was share some of it with Tori—in attitude until she allowed me to share in words.

I had decided I liked Luke back in the garage when he confessed to saving Tori's bacon by returning the jewelry she had stolen. I understood that she hadn't filched the pieces out of malice or greed but for the thrill of getting away with something. So did Luke. He was going to make an interesting brother-in-law.

I had to admit that I didn't like his profession, especially the loan shark part. Maybe the people who came to him were foolish and desperate, but that didn't mean he should take advantage of their situations and addictions. But only Jesus could redirect him, just as only Jesus could change Tori.

"Well, my father will like him," I said as we pulled up to the curb by our lane.

Drew knew exactly what I was talking about with this comment out of the blue. "He's vivid."

I laughed and Chloe sat up, looking at both of us strangely. "What's so funny about that?"

Knowing I could never explain, I shooed her out of the car and climbed out after her. I turned to give Tinksie a hand as Ruthie descended on us.

"Where have you been?" she demanded of Drew. She stood with her hands on her hips, her eyebrows slammed together.

He didn't sigh or roll his eyes or mumble things under his breath—he was such a *nice* man—so I did it for him, at least the sighing part. The other two parts I did mentally.

"It's a long story," Drew said. "I'll tell you in a few minutes."

Ruthie opened her mouth to protest, but Jenna spoke faster.

"Hello, Mom. How are you?" Her voice was almost steady.

Ruthie blinked in surprise, then broke into a great smile, giving me a slight picture of the young girl she had once been. "Hey, Jenn. How's my girl?" She opened her arms and hugged Jenna.

"Ruthie? Ruthie Canfield? Is that you?"

We all turned to see Carl standing beside the limo with a huge smile on his face. "I've been wondering what happened to you."

"Carl!" Ruthie released Jenna and focused on him. "You have?"

"Yeah, after Mick died. I was afraid something had happened to you too."

Ruthie spread her arms and actually did a little twirl. "As you can see, I'm fine."

She did look relatively good. She must have showered sometime today, and though she was still wearing my clothes, her hair was clean and her skin had a bit of color.

"You going back to AC tonight?" Ruthie asked.

Carl nodded. "Want a ride?"

And just like that Ruthie was gone.

"Well, at least you got a hug out of her before she took off." Chloe patted Jenna's back kindly.

"Yeah. I guess that's something anyway."

"But it's not the best something," Drew said. "*You* were the best thing."

"Me?" Jenna's voice squeaked with surprise.

I smiled at him. He really was a wonderful man.

"You." Drew gathered her close for a hug. "In spite of the fact that she hurt you repeatedly over the past few days, you approached her."

"Graciously," I added.

Jenna's shoulders straightened as she stepped from her father's embrace. "I did good?"

"You did more than well," Drew said. "I'm very proud of you."

Jenna glowed.

"It's that boundary thing," Chloe said. "You've got to decide what your boundaries are and then let everyone know. She's your mom, and you'll be polite to her, but you're not riding off with her on the back of some motorcycle."

"Or in some mile-long limo," Jenna added.

"And I'm not going to jail to visit my father," Chloe said. "Maybe someday I'll write to him, but that's it. He was going to kill my mother and my aunt!"

I didn't want her entangled with Eddie at all, but I also didn't want her building up a layer of hatred toward him. It was too destructive an emotion. Boundaries allowed for forgiveness. God modeled that truth for us when He gave us principles for living but offered forgiveness when we failed to meet His standards.

But that was a talk for another day. Chloe was thirteen, a mature thirteen in many ways, but still thirteen. She'd been scared and threatened today. Lectures on the virtues of letting go of offenses could wait. There were plenty of years for those talks. In the meantime, I'd ask God to give her a heart to pray for Eddie's salvation. I should pray daily for the same thing myself, and I actually might.

"Libby?" Andrew Melchior put a hand on my arm. "I've been doing some serious thinking over the last few hours. I'm not certain that Stella was wise when she wanted you and Tori to live together in her house, especially since it's clear you are bearing the bulk of the responsibility."

"She most certainly is," Tinksie said, outspoken as always.

I smiled at his concern. He had proven a good man to have around in a crisis, and I appreciated his being part of the team that helped Chloe, especially since he barely knew us. "It may not have been the wisest thing Aunt Stella ever did."

"Well, I wouldn't have been good legal counsel for her if I hadn't worked out an escape clause." His hazel eyes danced behind his lenses.

"There's a way out?" I felt hope spring to life. I could go home!

Drew sighed. "I definitely will have to buy E-ZPass."

"Do you want a way out?" Andrew asked.

Did I? "Not if it will cost Tori her inheritance." That much I knew.

"It won't. Nor you."

"Chloe?" I raised my eyebrows in question. She shrugged, clearly uncertain.

"We need to think about this, to pray about it."

Andrew blinked a bit at the mention of prayer, but his eyes were warm with understanding. He patted my hand. "Of course, my dear. Take your time. I'll be at your service when you decide. It has been a joy to assist you today."

"Andrew." It was Tinksie, and she looked belligerent for some reason. "Tell her."

"Not now, Tinksie." He spoke to her with what sounded like a warning.

"Tell her," Tinksie repeated.

"James, it's time to take your wife home," Andrew said, his voice tinged with anger.

I felt embarrassed by this sudden show of contention between these people who had seemed to care deeply for each other. What in the world could Andrew have to tell me that would raise such ire in Tinksie? What secret? What information? Had Aunt Stella left some other instructions?

James studied me for a minute, then turned to Andrew. "I agree with Tinksie, Andrew."

Andrew looked as if his pet cocker spaniel had taken a chunk out of his leg.

James gave a slight smile and his voice was gentle. "It's time. Way past time. Tell her." Then he took Tinksie's arm. "Come on, kid. I need a drink."

I watched them walk down the lane, two old people with tigers' hearts thumping in their chests.

"I'd never have met them without Aunt Stella," I told Andrew. "For that I must be grateful to her."

"How about us?" Jenna asked. "You wouldn't have met us either."

I put my palm against her cheek. "That would have been a great loss." I looked over her head at her father. "A great loss."

He grinned, and pinwheels of color and hope twirled through me.

"But what are you supposed to tell Mom, Mr. Melchior?" Chloe asked. "I'll never sleep until you tell."

Tinksie suddenly turned and shouted, "April twenty-third."

I frowned at her. April twenty-third? Certainly a significant date, at least to me, but what did it have to do with anything?

Then the pieces clicked into place and I nodded. Suddenly a lot of things made sense, a lot of questions were answered.

"April twenty-third's your birthday, Mom." Chloe looked confused. "What's that got to do with Mr. Melchior?"

I searched his face, wondering how different Tori's and my lives might have been. I didn't know what I felt, what I was supposed to feel at the enormity of what might have been.

"I was forty-eight," he said, his hands spread beseechingly. This suave, confident man seemed—what? *Fearful* was the best I could come up with. Afraid of my reaction and my response. His uncertainty seemed only fitting given my own.

"I was married with three children. Stella was forty-five. We thought about the situation from every angle possible. The only thing we never considered was an abortion. We didn't believe it was right."

I nodded. Abortion wasn't right, but an adulterous relationship of many years' standing was?

"Stella was the one who thought of Jack and Mimi."

"I imagine they wangled a good price?" I asked with unexpected bitterness. I wondered how much money had exchanged hands.

His smile wasn't pleasant. "Oh, we were happy to contribute regularly to your care. It was the other issues that were problematic, like getting to see you. You'd have thought that with all my years before the bar, I'd have been able to do better, but…" He shrugged. "It took everything I had to get Stella the once-a-year visits."

Had she done Tori and me any favor by putting us in Jack and Mimi's care? I stared at the man before me, a distinguished and accomplished professional who upheld the law instead of breaking it. I thought of Aunt Stella, who had doted on me, in contrast to Mimi, whom I never could please. But I'd met Madge because I was raised by Jack and Mimi, and because of Madge, I knew Jesus and had an anchor in my life.

God's hand at work, making bad situations turn into good ones, redeeming hurt and wrong with salvation and—I glanced at Drew—love?

Andrew continued, "She couldn't handle the idea of you girls going to some stranger where she'd never see you again. Those visits were her lifeline. She'd come home full of stories about you, about how beautiful and smart you were. She would have the photos she'd taken framed and keep them out in the bedroom where she could see them. 'See how much they look like us?' she'd say. And she'd cry."

His eyes filled with tears, and in reaction, mine did too. I tried to put myself in Stella's place. What would my life be without Chloe?

"And then Jack and Mike ended up in jail. Stella was so concerned for you two. She asked Mimi if you could come live here with her, with us, but Mimi said no. She was facing enough bad opinion without being known as the mother who wouldn't keep her kids." He sighed and shrugged. "Life is compromise."

I stared at this man, my father, and wanted to yell that no one had asked my opinion about these compromises. Instead I clamped my lips tightly. Bruised as I felt, I knew Andrew and Stella had done what they thought best. I also knew I was too emotionally exhausted to do or say anything for fear it'd be the wrong thing. But we did need to talk.

"Andrew, will you come to dinner tomorrow evening? Just you and me?"

He glanced toward the house with its shiny black door. "I haven't been in there since Stella died." He looked old and alone, his charming veneer stripped by fatigue and sorrow. Vulnerable.

"Tomorrow night," I repeated. "Seven o'clock. Learn to know me a bit. Then you can take on Tori."

With a nod, he turned and walked toward the Avenue of the Arts, his hand raised to flag a cab.

Chloe was staring at me wide-eyed. "Is he—?"

I nodded. "My father. Your grandfather."

Chloe looked after him and watched him climb into a cab. "At least he's nice."

"At least he's nice," I agreed. Such a little thing to say about one's parent. Such a big thing when you couldn't say it.

Drew spread his arms to shepherd us all into the house.

"Girls, bowls of ice cream," he ordered as he walked me through the living room, dining room, and kitchen and out into the garden. "Four of them."

He slid the door shut, leaving them behind. I saw their faces as they watched his hand slide down and take mine. Their eyes were huge, and they had their hands over their mouths to keep from laughing—or screaming. A parent being romantic with someone not the other parent must be somewhat traumatizing, though it didn't worry me enough to keep from threading my fingers through Drew's.

He led me across the patio to the back of the yard by the weeping cherry. He stopped and looked back at the house. I followed his gaze and saw only a waterfall of graceful, leafy branches.

"No one can see us," he murmured as he pulled me close.

"Mmm." I leaned into him. "Good man." After the day's terrors and revelations, he felt solid and true. "Bet they can see our feet." They were intertwined as our fingers had been. "They'll be scarred for life."

He grinned. "They'd better get used to it."

My heart somersaulted against my ribs, and I rested my head on his shoulder.

"You okay?" He rubbed his hands up and down my spine.

I nodded as I felt the day's stress seep away. "Seems to me you've had to ask me that question way too many times in the short time we've known each other."

"When it bothers me, I'll complain. In the meantime, before our chaperons arrive…"

He kissed me.

Epilogue

□□□

Six months later

WE STOOD ON THE CURB on the first evening of the new year, listening to the sound of "Oh, Dem Golden Slippers" once again as
another string band marched by. It was my first Mummers Parade in
spite of having lived within an hour of Philadelphia all my life. I was
pretty sure it was going to be my last if I ever defrosted enough to go
home.

Tonight was our last night in Aunt Stella's house. Mark and
Tim across the lane had introduced us to a professional couple who
worked with Tim, and they were delighted with the chance to buy
the house.

Both Tori and I had decided not to invoke Andrew's escape
clause, which amounted to him, as executor of the estate, having the
authority to declare the co-tenant restriction invalid. Instead we
thought we should abide by Stella's will since it spelled out her final

wishes for her daughters. It was the one thing we could do for her. But now my sister and I were equally glad to be going our separate ways. The six months had been difficult for both of us. We were so dissimilar, and proximity hadn't healed the many rifts of thought and principle. Rather it had spotlighted our diverse opinions on almost everything.

"Sleep with the man, girl," she kept telling me, one of our biggest areas of disagreement. "You're going to drive him away with this little virgin business."

"He's a Christian too, Tori. His position on sex is the same as mine. After marriage, like the Bible says."

She snorted. "Ben didn't say so, you know. He had an illegitimate son."

"Ben is someone Drew studies, not someone he emulates, especially when what Ben says or does is contrary to Scripture."

She'd roll her eyes and rush out to meet Carl and Ruthie at the limo.

When Ruthie first started riding back and forth on Tori's Atlantic City runs, Tori had tried to be nice. At least that's what she said. Since she and I define *nice* differently, I wasn't quite sure what she meant. Whatever, the niceness didn't last long.

"The woman is certifiable," Tori declared. "She should be medicated."

"You should ask her if she's taking her pills."

Tori seemed horrified. "Not me. Do I look like a nurse? I just put up the privacy window and make believe she's not there."

We also disagreed on how to react to Andrew. I had spent time with him, had him to dinner frequently. In fact, the four of us—Drew, Chloe, Jenna, and I—were to meet him for dinner at his favorite restaurant tonight at eight.

"I don't want to know him," Tori insisted. "He abandoned me for thirty years. Why should I forgive that?"

"Why shouldn't you? He's a nice man. Lonely. He needs us." I didn't add that he needed Jesus, because I knew she'd have a fit. But he did, and he let both Drew and me talk about issues of faith. He'd even stopped being embarrassed that we were so naive as to buy into faith. In fact, he was beginning to ask intelligent questions, and I had high hopes for him.

I couldn't say the same for my twin.

"It's so much more than 'You say *to-may-to* and I say *to-mah-to,*'" I told Drew as I huddled close in an effort to keep warm in the frigid January chill.

"Well, it's almost over." He slid his arm across my shoulders.

"The one thing I'm really going to miss is having you across the street." I meant it. Not seeing him every day would be hard with me at home and him up in northern Pennsylvania.

"I've got my E-ZPass all mounted on the front window, ready to cross into the wilds of New Jersey as often as I can manage it." He kissed the tip of my nose. "I'm just glad it's only for seven months."

The first Saturday in July was to be our wedding day. I felt the unfamiliar bulk of my engagement ring under my glove. I'd been wearing it exactly—I glanced at my watch—eighteen hours and fifteen minutes, having received it at midnight as the New Year broke. Drew and Sam Pierce, the jeweler, with help from the girls, had put the small, beautifully wrapped ring box inside a shoebox stuffed with lots of little beautifully wrapped empty jewelry boxes, then wrapped them all with the *Inquirer*'s Sunday comics.

When Drew handed me the gift, I knew the shape immediately. "They never found the jewelry," I said sadly. "Whatever Eddie did with it, it's gone. And he's not talking."

"Well," Drew said, "at least I can guarantee that the contents of this box are not stolen."

The right box was the tenth one I opened, and by that time I was laughing and crying so hard I could barely see his face when he said, "I love you, Lib. I came to Philadelphia to learn about Ben, but I found something much better. I found my second chance provided by the gracious hand of the Lord. I'd like to be your second chance. Will you marry me and let God make all things new?"

I don't know how long it took him to come up with that speech, but it was all I'd ever longed for and more.

"Finally!" A voice floated from the second-floor landing. "Now we can come down and get something to eat?"

"Did she say yes?"

"What do you think?"

Giggling and almost as excited as Drew and me, our daughters came streaking down the stairs.

They were the main reason we were waiting the full year to marry. We wanted them to see that time is needed to test a relationship even between committed believers, because marriage is a covenant that should be entered into with great care and not be broken. We also wanted to give God time to confirm ever more strongly that our commitment was wise and right. On this latter point I had no doubts.

I watched my breath plume and dissipate as "Oh, Dem Golden Slippers" filled the air once again. I leaned against my golden future and smiled.

DEAR READER,

Have you had the faith-building experience of having God care for you and provide for you even though you didn't realize at the time that He was working? It's fascinating to see the end result of situations that seemed hard or bad at the time but which ended up leading to rich and wonderful outcomes.

Libby sees this phenomenon in her life when she realizes that being raised by Jack and Mimi might have been hard, but it allowed her to meet Madge and, through her, the Lord.

One of my personal situations that seemed like the end of the world as I expected it to be occurred when I was twenty-six and had to have a total hysterectomy. As a result I would never be able to have any children. Yowzah! What was God doing?

Into this hard situation came Chip and Jeff, our adopted sons. God was providing for them as well as for Chuck and me, though at the time of the surgery, it didn't look like it.

God is ever faithful, having plans to prosper us and give us hope and a future (Jeremiah 29:11).

Our responsibility is trusting God even when things seem hopeless. One of the blessings of getting older, whether a year or a decade, is that we can look back and see how God has been there for us in the past. His previous faithfulness in things both large and small is a great assurance that He will be there for us in our current situations. "Never will I leave you; never will I forsake you" becomes even more real (Hebrews 13:5). Once again we can place our fragile faith, our lives, our hopes in His loving hands.

May you rest in Him today.

Gayle Roper

Readers Guide

1. One of the hardest persons to deal with in Libby's life is her twin. Why is it so often family that causes some of our deepest conflicts?

2. For a moment, Libby considers abortion for her unwanted teen pregnancy. Why do you think this procedure is so often the automatic response? Do you consider it a viable solution? Why or why not? What should be our response to those who have gone ahead with the termination of their pregnancies?

3. What do you think are three things that enabled Libby to rise above what could have been crippling circumstances when she became pregnant at such a young age?

4. What are some of the things Madge did that made her such a pivotal person in Libby's life? Has there been anyone like that in your life? How can you be that person to another?

5. What are some of the things besides twin sisters that try to lure our children from us and from the Lord? How do we protect our kids?

6. Do you have close contact with someone who is bipolar? What are some of the difficulties you have experienced as a result? Have you found any solutions to making life easier for everyone?

7. When Drew reacts strongly to the streak of color in Jenna's hair, Libby cautions about picking your wars. What does this mean? What are wars worth picking?

8. What is your reaction to the life choices Tori made? What do you think about her getting away with theft?

9. Have you or someone you know had experience with the short-term paycheck loan shops like the ones Luke owns? Is it ever appropriate to use one? How does using one fit in with the concept of good stewardship?

10. Both Chloe and Jenna live with hurts inflicted by the choices of others. Has this ever been your experience? Or have you ever caused hurt to others by your choices? Does the application of 1 John 1:9 ("If we confess our sins, he is faithful and just and will forgive us our sins and purify us from all unrighteousness.") fix all these hurts?

Solution to Are You Next

Solution to You Are Overdue

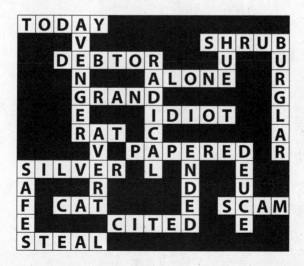

Solution to Pay Up or Else

Solution to Last Warning

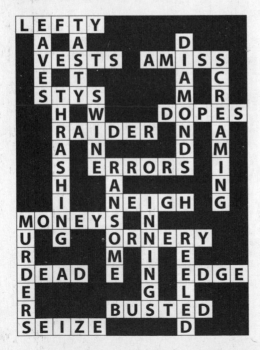

BE SWEPT AWAY INTO THE
Seaside Seasons series
BY GAYLE ROPER!

Spring Rain, book one
Book one of this series underlines the issue of God's forgiveness in the hearts—and lives—of a modern-day family.

Summer Shadows, book two
Together Abby and Marsh discover that God is in the business of putting broken lives back together so that they are more beautiful than ever.

Autumn Dreams, book three
Two Baby Boomers dedicate themselves to untangling life's puzzles—and a local mystery.

Winter Winds, book four
The Seaside Seasons series concludes with a tale of romance, crime, startling mix-ups, and a few hard hearts that just might get a much-needed midwinter thaw.